The Garden on Holly Street

Megan Attley is the pseudonym of a bestselling and prolific women's fiction writer. She lives in South Wales with her husband, two children and three crazy (but beautiful) dogs.

The Garden on Holly Street

MEGAN ATTLEY

ORION

First published in Great Britain in 2019 by Orion Books,
an imprint of The Orion Publishing Group Ltd
Carmelite House, 50 Victoria Embankment,
London EC4Y 0DZ

An Hachette UK company

1 3 5 7 9 10 8 6 4 2

A CIP catalogue record for this book
is available from the British Library.

ISBN 978 1 4091 8306 8

Typeset by Deltatype Ltd, Birkenhead, Merseyside

Printed in Great Britain by Clays Ltd, Elcograf S.p.A.

www.orionbooks.co.uk

For my family, with love always. X

PART ONE

Spring Seedlings

CHAPTER I

'Pardon?' Abby Hamilton shifted in the chair – her armpits prickling with sweat in shock – then she adjusted her green tabard. 'I don't understand.'

'I'm terribly sorry, Abby, but it's down to cutbacks.' Georgia Dawson, manager of Greenfields Care Home smiled, her grey eyes calm as she gazed at Abby. She didn't look terribly sorry. In fact, she didn't look sorry at all as she sat there, back ramrod straight, in her navy Marks & Spencer trouser suit, with her sleek grey bob that it was rumoured she had styled at John Frieda's ultra-chic London salon. Travelling from Manchester to London for an expensive haircut showed that Georgia certainly wasn't suffering from the cutbacks. 'We're having to let some staff go. We just can't afford to continue employing so many here when we've recently lost some of our residents.'

'But ... you'll have more residents coming in. This place has a fabulous reputation and of course you'll never run out of residents because everyone's got to grow old, right?'

Or most people do ...

'Indeed, we do have a fabulous reputation, and yes, we are highly likely to have more residents in future ...'

3

Georgia pursed her bright red lips then nodded, as if agreeing with herself. 'And I promise you, Abby, that if circumstances change, we won't hesitate to contact you.'

Abby took a deep breath and scanned the room, desperate for inspiration, something to tell Georgia that would allow her to keep her job. It was all she had left. But the desk piled with paperwork and the Manchester city skyline through the first-floor window offered her no reprieve.

'We're giving you notice, as is written in your contract.' Georgia's voice had risen, as if her throat was tightening as she delivered the news. 'But should you wish to leave sooner to find alternative employment, then I'm sure something can be arranged.'

'Please don't do this. Please. I need this job!' The room swayed and Abby gripped the sides of the chair to steady herself.

'These are difficult times ... For everyone.' The care home manager peered over her silver-rimmed half-moon glasses, and her eyes hardened, their grey now flinty. 'So ... if you don't mind, I have other staff to speak to. Let me know if you decide to work out your notice period.'

Abby got unsteadily to her feet. She'd lost her boy-friend, her home and now her job in the space of six weeks. It was almost as if the universe was trying to tell her something. Or it would be if she believed in that kind of nonsense.

She took the envelope that Georgia proffered then trudged out of the air-conditioned office and into the corridor. Four of her colleagues were lined up there like naughty children waiting to see the head teacher. They stared at her, desperately reading her face for clues, so she dropped her eyes to the floor. She couldn't speak, couldn't even wish them luck as she made her way to the poky staffroom with its scale-encrusted kettle and five green-cushioned chairs.

Sinking into one of them, Abby absent-mindedly fingered the slit where the orange foam was displayed like the innards of a body. She thought of the times she'd stuffed the foam back in during her coffee breaks, only to return to the staffroom to find that someone else had widened the split by picking at the seams or had carelessly dropped biscuit crumbs into it. Abby took care of things – it was in her nature – but not everybody was like her. She knew that now for sure.

But that was life.

Abby released a sigh before pushing herself to her feet. No point dwelling now, it wouldn't change anything. In fact, perhaps it would finally give her something to write about in her blog. It had been a while since she'd fired up her old laptop and logged into her WordPress account, since she'd felt up to letting the world know what was going on in her life, since she'd found the text on Gavin's phone and her world had crumbled to dust … She squeezed her eyes shut tight against the pain and forced his handsome and familiar features from her mind. Thinking about what she'd lost would not help right now. She needed to be strong because no one else was going to hold her together.

Abby opened her locker and pulled out her bag. Her shift was over and with it, her time at Greenfields Care Home. She stuffed the letter into her bag, pulled her tabard over her head, then placed it on the back of a chair as she shrugged into her coat.

She knew that she wouldn't come back to work out her notice – it would be much too painful saying goodbye to the residents and her colleagues.

And Abby Hamilton really didn't like goodbyes.

Abby closed the front door behind her and sagged against it. Her muscles ached, her head was tight and she was covered in dust. But at least she'd finished moving her boxed belongings into the two-bed rental flat on Holly Street in Didsbury. Considering how quickly Abby had needed to move, she'd been lucky to find such a lovely flat. Not that she'd wanted to up sticks, but after what had happened, she hadn't really had a choice.

She wandered through the flat, admiring the hardwood floors, the plain magnolia walls and the lovely bay window in the spacious lounge. Everything in the flat was fresh, new and clean which was a very good thing as far as Abby was concerned. She needed a fresh start and hoped that this move would help her get it.

All she had to do now was to unpack the many boxes and two large suitcases that were scattered around the spare bedroom and kitchen. She grimaced. Once she took everything out, she'd have to find places for it all, and right now that seemed insurmountable. Perhaps if she just had half an hour's rest, she'd feel up to it.

She'd make a coffee and light a cigarette and—

Wait! Light a cigarette?

She hadn't smoked in over ten years, but when she'd found the text on Gavin's phone, her first reaction had been to march out of their pretty three-bed semi in Wythenshawe straight to the Tesco Extra where she purchased two bottles of Pinot Grigio and a packet of

Marlboro Lights. She'd drunk the wine but managed to avoid smoking any of the cigarettes, preferring to feel the comfort of having the box in her bag should she desperately need the crutch of nicotine. And, this afternoon, with the early spring sunlight fading outside and the impact of her day's labour settling into her thirty-six-year-old bones, she really, really fancied a smoke. And why shouldn't she have one?

Abby found her battered brown handbag – the one that Gavin had given her three Christmases ago – rooted for the packet of Marlboros and the disposable lighter, then headed down to the car park to light up.

On her descent to the ground floor, she passed the doors of the people who lived below her and wondered who was inside and if they were curious about her too. Abby had used the small lift to get her belongings up to the flat but had vowed to use the steps most days, unless she had something too heavy to carry. Now she was thirty-six, she needed to stay active to help keep her toned, and it would hopefully mean that she'd get to meet her neighbours too, possibly even make some friends.

When she reached the small entranceway, she pressed the release button to open the door and stepped out into the cool air. The car park was quite full now, but then it was Saturday afternoon and most of the residents of the flats would no doubt be preparing for an evening of Saturday TV with a takeaway or perhaps were getting ready to head off into Didsbury village for a meal or to hit the bars. A shadow fell over her as she thought of all the couples and families, of all the people who had someone.

Abby pulled a cigarette from the pack and stuck it in her mouth like some kind of talisman against loneliness. She was about to light up when she realised that if any of her new neighbours came down to their cars, they would see her smoking, and that wasn't exactly the first impression she wanted to create. So she walked around the side of the building and kept going until she reached the rear where it seemed more private. But it was also a right mess. The estate agent had mentioned something about a garden but Abby had been so impressed by the flat and so desperate to find somewhere quickly, that she'd declined to look around outside. She could see the area from her bedroom but she'd barely even looked out of the windows, so keen had she been to sign on the dotted line and secure the lease. As long as it was furnished and had plenty of inside space where she could hide away from the world, that was all she'd wanted. But now she could see the garden that stretched out before her, it was evident that it was nothing more than a dumping ground for unwanted furniture; it looked like an unkempt mess of overgrown shrubs, grass and litter.

She walked up and down, eyeing the tangled flower-beds and unpruned bushes, the litter and cigarette butts that choked up what could have been a lovely space, and something inside her shifted. It was a sense of loss so strong it caused a physical pain, and she stifled the moan that threatened to escape from her.

'Such a waste,' she murmured, the unlit cigarette bobbing between her lips as she spoke. When the flats had been built, the garden must have been drawn into the plans, the designer keen to give the small community an outside space that would possibly bring them together.

Instead, it had been ignored as the inhabitants of Willow Court got on with their lives inside.

It struck Abby that Gavin had been exactly the same; when they'd bought their semi-detached house – some years back when they'd both been in their twenties – Gavin had been keen to fully renovate the inside, but had shown no interest when Abby had suggested doing something to the small paved back garden. Gavin had frowned, coughed and muttered something about not having time to mow grass or plant flowers and, as with most things in their relationship, Abby had bitten her lip and kept quiet, not wanting to start a row that made their growing differences glaringly apparent. It was easier to keep quiet, pretend everything was all right and that they wanted the same things from life. She had become good at biting her tongue during their time together. The Abby she had once been would have given her a good shake and told her to speak up for herself, to make sure that she got what she wanted and needed from her relationship. But time, and Gavin, had worn her down. Even if Abby had a small patch of grass to mow in the summer, Gavin would have dashed off to his evening session at the gym anyway, rather than staying at home, with Abby, to enjoy it.

'Bloody weight-lifting bastard!' She shook her head. She had called him all the awful names she could think of, but the words didn't change the fact that they'd had a relationship born of long-term togetherness. They knew each other well and there was affection there, possibly still even love. Then he'd turned their lives upside down. 'Bloody cheating pig!'

'I beg your pardon?'

Abby froze.

Someone was behind her.

Someone had caught her talking to herself.

She whipped the cigarette from her mouth then turned and met the pale, watery-blue eyes of an elderly man. He frowned at her from behind thick-rimmed black glasses then ran a hand over the mottled dome of his bald head.

'Oh! Uh, sorry ... I wasn't speaking to you. I was just talking to myself. You know, as you do.' She gave an embarrassed laugh, hoping he might at least smile, but he glared at her in a way that made goosebumps pop out on her arms.

'You were talking to yourself?' He straightened up for a moment, and she realised that he was taller than he'd first seemed – certainly taller than she was – then he hunched over again, and a flicker of pain passed over his features, as if the effort had been too much.

'Yes.'

He shook his head then eyed her scruffy jogging bottoms and dusty T-shirt.

Abby plucked at her top. 'I was moving in ... To one of the flats ... 3A actually. I'm Abby Hamilton. We might be neighbours.'

'Neighbours?' His frown deepened, drawing his bushy white eyebrows together so they sat like fat white caterpillars above his glasses. 'None of you youngsters know the meaning of the word.'

Abby was about to argue then thought better of it. He was right, really. Even after living in their house for more than ten years, she and Gavin had barely known the families residing either side of them. Enough to say good morning and to share the odd comment on the weather, but certainly not enough to go out for drinks or to pop in to one another's houses for coffee. And Abby had often wished that she could pop around to have coffee and cake with a neighbour, to invite them for a barbecue in the summer or to just get to know them better. With the hours that Gavin worked and the time he spent at the gym, Abby had often been lonely, and hearing the laughter and music from the other side of the adjoining wall had stirred longings in her that she hadn't known she'd had.

So when she'd heard Gavin's phone buzz on the bed-side table that terrible evening six weeks ago, and she had read the words – the descriptions of bedroom acts – which she'd never used herself and never would ... Well, she could have done with a neighbour to run to then. Instead, she'd run to a shop for alcohol and tobacco. She had to admit that this man, whoever he was, had a point.

Abby noticed that his gaze had dropped to her hand and his eyes widened behind his glasses as his cheeks flushed.

'Are you OK, sir?' She called him that because he certainly didn't seem keen to volunteer his name.

'You were smoking!' He snarled at her, making her flinch.

'No ... I uh—'

'Yes, you were! I see the cancer-stick in your hand.' He wobbled in his leather slippers as he waved his walking stick at her.

'I didn't even light it.'

'But you were going to light it. Is it you then, making all this mess? Disgusting! Absolutely diabolical! Filthy, dirty ...' His voice cracked and he turned away from her.

Abby watched him, wondering what was wrong. Was he having a heart attack? A stroke? Oh God, was one of her neighbours about to die on her right after she'd moved in? She could just imagine the headline in the local tabloid: *Spurned Spinster Kills Elderly Neighbour with Unlit Cigarette, Murderer Abby* or *The Community Garden Killer*.

She stepped closer to him and raised her hand, wondering whether to touch his shoulder just to check if he was all right, but she was also afraid to make contact. After all, the way he'd brandished his heavy-looking stick, she suspected he could cause some serious damage with it.

'Sir? Are you OK?' she asked, her voice small, not sounding like her at all.

He coughed then, his whole body shaking with the effort, before turning to face her.

'Smoking is so bad for you. It causes awful diseases and you should stop. Immediately. Before it's too late. It sets a bad example to the children around here and just *look* at this mess.' He gestured at the state of the garden and Abby nodded.

'It is quite bad.'

'People just don't care anymore. No one cares.' His voice was quieter than before, tinged with sadness.

'I wouldn't have thrown this down, you know? I'd have binned it. I don't litter.' She wasn't sure why she felt the need to explain herself, but she did.

He met her eyes again then shook his head. 'Just make sure you do put it in the bin, although what difference one will make, I don't know ...'

He turned and shuffled away, seeming smaller now,

hunched over his walking stick as if the encounter with her had reduced him physically. Abby suppressed the urge to shout after him. Who did he think he was bossing her around and making assumptions? There was no way she could have made all this mess and she certainly wouldn't have made it any worse. He was right that one more cigarette butt wouldn't make a difference but even so, she'd have put it in the bin.

Why was she worrying anyway? In his slippers, with that heavy walking stick and thick white stubble on his face, he could've just wandered out of Greenfields. She'd dealt with men and women like that over the years and knew that, most of the time, they didn't mean to offend anyone.

She looked at the cigarette in her hand and frowned. Suddenly it didn't seem so appealing, so she pulled the packet from her joggers and stuffed it back in. For the time being, she'd just keep the packet as a safety net for when things got really bad.

Abby cast her eyes over the garden again. It really was a fabulous space and had so much potential. If someone had the inclination, they could make it lovely, somewhere to be proud of, somewhere to come and sit and relax. If they had the inclination …

Twenty minutes later, Abby was sitting cross-legged on the wooden floor of her lounge, dressed in her pyjamas with her freshly washed damp hair pinned up with a butterfly clip. She had a box in front of her that she'd draped with a tea towel and on it sat a plate of beans on toast. There was a table in the kitchen, but it felt too formal to eat there alone, so she'd come into the lounge and turned on the TV, wanting the company of Saturday night television to drown out the voices swirling tornado-like in her head.

As she sipped the lukewarm wine she'd forgotten to put in the fridge earlier, she tried to push the old man from her mind, but she kept seeing the scorn in his eyes. Yet when he'd spoken, and his voice had cracked, she'd sensed that there was more to his distress than he'd been prepared to share.

And being alone, tonight of all nights ...

It was Gavin's birthday, a fact she'd tried to ignore all day, even as she'd tramped up and down the stairs of their home, taking her belongings out to her ancient red Fiesta. Gavin hadn't been around, of course, he'd agreed by text to not be there when she went back for her things. She'd stayed at her friend Lisa's apartment after she'd walked out on him, only going back when she knew he'd be at the gym or work, knowing that seeing him would be too painful, that it was too raw and she was – even though she hated to admit it – still too angry to face him. Yet today, he turned thirty-six. Gavin was a few months younger than Abby and it had been their in-joke that he was her toyboy. Now he had someone younger – a lot younger – so the joke was on Abby.

Gavin was probably out somewhere with his new floozy, partying the night away in a too-tight top that showed his bulging biceps to perfection. He'd doubtless be flexing for photos, his eyes too bright, his smile too wide. If Abby dared to look tomorrow, he'd be all over Facebook, his flushed cheeks and inane grin evidence of a great night out. A night that Abby wasn't there to share. A night that would probably end in all of those lewd sexual acts that Abby had read about on his phone; all the things that she'd always been far too embarrassed to talk about, let alone try. Did people really do those things? Abby had always thought they were like sex scenes in movies: over-the-top, too much like hard work, and physically impossible unless you had a neck as long as a giraffe and a body as flexible as a gold-medal-winning gymnast.

For a moment she thought about trying to locate her laptop and putting her current thoughts onto the page, but she realised it would be buried at the bottom of a box somewhere and moving seemed like too much effort.

So she drained her glass, refilled it from the bottle on the floor next to her and turned up the TV, then ate her lonely supper for one, trying to ignore the salty tears that trickled down her cheeks and mingled with her wine.

CHAPTER 2

Arthur shuffled into his kitchen and went automatically to the kettle. He checked the water level then reached out to switch it on and realised that his hand was shaking. What on earth? He'd exchanged a few stern words with a woman claiming to be a new neighbour and now he was so disturbed that he was shaking?

He left the kettle to boil and went through to his lounge. The room was filled with shadows, the last rays of the evening spring sunshine too weak to light up the space. Everything was exactly as he had left it less than an hour ago. The TV screen was blank and grey, the book he had been reading lay open on the small coffee table next to his armchair, and his mug sat beside it on an old coaster that showed a hotel in Spain he'd once stayed in with Julia.

'Julia . . .' He whispered her name, the familiar cadence passing over his tongue and stirring his heart. The name of the woman he had loved and cherished for half a century. It was more than a year since she'd passed but he still expected her to enter the room, carrying a tray with two mugs and a plate of biscuits that they would enjoy in front of a Saturday night game show. If he closed his eyes, he could almost smell her floral perfume, hear the swish of her skirt against her petticoat as she moved, and feel the cool weight of her hand as she touched his shoulder.

'I'm not sure about that woman at all,' he said to the room, breaking the spell that had settled over him like a net of grief. 'Do you know, Julia, she claimed that she's moved into one of the flats.'

He paused and listened as if waiting for his wife to reply.

The silence stretched out in the room.

Of course, no reply came. He sighed, then went to his chair and sat down, propping his walking stick against the coffee table, the boiling kettle now forgotten as his thoughts were filled with his wife.

'You'd probably think she's a nice young woman ... see the good in her.' He chuckled. 'You always saw the good in everyone, my darling. *See* ... the good in everyone, I mean.' He couldn't talk about her in the past tense. It felt wrong – so terribly wrong. 'But she was about to smoke, you see. That filthy habit that causes such awful diseases, and if only she knew how it feels to have ... to suffer as you did, then I'm sure she wouldn't ...' He closed his eyes again, trying to imagine how it felt to have Julia's hand settling on his right shoulder. He placed his hand there, searching for hers, wishing he could find it and keep her with him for ever. 'I told her, darling. I told her to stop smoking. Whether she'll listen or not, who knows? And I also warned her not to litter. I hate what's happened out there in your garden. If only you could see it. But no, much better that you can't.' He shook his head. 'I couldn't bear for you to see it. If I was fitter, I'd go out and make it beautiful again just how you like it. But I'm an old man ... just a useless old man. This damned hip makes me so slow. I can't even stand up straight anymore ...'

He lapsed into silence as bleakness settled over him like a clammy, suffocating blanket. His hand slipped from his shoulder and he let it rest on the arm of the chair. He couldn't believe they were his hands, these wrinkled, liver-spotted things with their swollen joints and grey hairs sprouting from his knuckles. When did he get so old? When did Julia get old enough to ...?

He turned to the chair on the other side of the coffee table. It was just close enough to reach, close enough to take her hand as they laughed at something together or to pass her a mug of tea as they read the morning papers.

But it was empty.

As empty as his flat. As empty as his bed. And as empty as his life.

A solitary tear escaped his right eye and trickled down his cheek before getting trapped in the stubble he hadn't bothered to shave for over a week. He wiped at it absently with the back of his hand then stared at the streak of water on his skin.

What was the point in any of it anymore?

A sudden bang from above jolted him to his feet and he winced as pain seared through his hip. Feet raced across the floor above quickly followed by another bang and Arthur's grief was replaced by red-hot anger.

That bloody child!

Arthur grabbed his stick, headed for the front door, then slammed it behind him. It bounced off the latch, but he didn't care; he was too furious to fuss about locking his flat and he wanted to catch the little bugger upstairs in the act.

He took hold of the banister and started to climb, using his stick to support him, rage giving him an unwonted burst of energy. He knew that the lift would have alerted the little rascal to his ascent, so he pushed himself up each step, muttering about badly behaved children and irresponsible parents, until he reached the landing and the door of the flat directly above his own. He panted, trying to catch his breath before he knocked on the door. From inside, he heard squeals of laughter. Someone was evidently having a great time – and at his expense, no less. The expense of his peace! Peace that he was entitled to, for crying out loud!

He realised that the door was ajar, so he rapped his knuckles on the wood and waited. It fell silent inside. He knocked again, harder, causing the door to swing open wide enough for him to see inside. And there, soaking wet and covered in soapsuds, stood that wild teenage girl who often babysat for the little boy, Ernie.

Arthur stared at her, then around the hallway of the flat at the complete and utter chaos, before his eyes landed on Ernie as he came skidding around the corner. He tutted. 'How very irresponsible of you both. Not only have you made a dreadful mess of your father's flat, Ernie Jones, but you've disturbed my Saturday evening. I should phone the police and get them to come and take you away!' Even as he spoke, he was conscious of how hard his heart was pounding and of the searing pain in his hip.

The girl folded her arms across her chest and scowled at him. 'What, for having a water fight? In his own home?'

She gestured at the seven-year-old boy who wasn't looking half as confident as she was.

'For disturbing the peace!' Arthur shouted. 'For noise pollution. I can't even relax in my own home.' He thumped his walking stick on the floor.

'Look, Mr Mayer' – the girl's expression changed – 'we didn't mean any harm. It's just I'm looking after my cousin – *again* – and we were having a laugh. We didn't mean to disturb you, did we, Ernie?'

'No! No, we didn't.' The little boy hung his head and stared at his wet feet. Water dripped from his hair onto the laminate flooring and Arthur watched as it pooled there.

'That could come through, you know?' He pointed at the water. 'You could bring down my ceiling … Ruin all my possessions … Destroy my home. You lot ought to be bloody evicted. And where's your father?'

The children glanced at each other and something flickered over Ernie's face. Arthur couldn't tell if it was fear or sadness, although why it would be either, he had no idea.

'I'm sorry.' Ernie raised his bright blue eyes and Arthur nodded. Ernie was just a little boy; it was the responsibility of his elders to teach him how to behave properly, and that meant this cousin of his as well as his father, who rarely seemed to be around.

'Well, make sure you mop all this water up so it doesn't destroy my ceiling. Last thing I want is to look up and see you pair staring down at me.'

He turned and walked towards the lift doors, suddenly exhausted and longing to reach the comfort of his armchair, but aware that he wasn't up to walking down the stairs. Back in his flat, he would sit with a mug of tea as he watched the sky change from twilight to darkness, while the celebrities and presenters on the TV chattered inanely in the corner, his only company through the long Saturday night.

Ernie closed the door as soon as Mr Mayer had gone and turned to face his cousin. He expected to find her looking worried but instead she was grinning.

'Do you think he'll tell on us, Jax?'

She chewed her bottom lip and her eyes widened. 'You know ... he might do. He's certainly angry enough.'

'Really?'

'Yeah ... In fact, he's probably gone downstairs to phone the police right now.'

Ernie's tummy rolled, the way it did when he was nervous about a spelling test in school. He wasn't very good at spelling, even when he tried really hard to learn the words his teacher sent home with him.

'What should we do?'

'I think we should ... hide under the bed.'

'But won't the police break the door if we don't answer it?' He thought about the show Jax had let him watch about a police crew from London. They'd shouted a lot and broken some doors to get in.

'We'll need to be very quiet.' Jax put a finger to her lips then tiptoed across the hallway with the exaggerated movements of a cartoon character.

'Are you teasing me, Jax?'

She turned away from him but he could see her shoulders shaking and the big bun on top of her head was wobbling.

'Jax?'

'No. Of course not. I never tease you ...'

'Look at me.'

When she did, her face was red and her smile was so wide he could see the tiny elastic bands on her braces. The icy feeling that had formed in his belly faded at her expression.

'You are joking!' He pointed at her then started to laugh. 'You're teasing me.'

She nodded.

'So, he's not telling on us?'

'Nah! Don't be daft. He's just a grumpy old fart.'

'A fart?' When he'd said fart in school he'd had a big row and lost his playtime for two days. 'My teacher said that's rude.'

'It's just a word, Ernie. Old people say stuff like that to try to control us. Don't you take any notice.' She approached him and put her hands on his shoulders. 'Ernie? Are you listening?'

He nodded.

'No, I mean *really* listening. You don't have to do what older people say all the time. And don't worry; he won't get you in trouble. He barely ever leaves his flat from what I can tell.'

'Is that because he has a walking stick?' Ernie asked, thinking about how Arthur had gripped the handle of the stick as he'd thumped it on the floor. Arthur's fingers had looked all funny and bumpy like knotted rope and Ernie had wondered if they were sore.

Jax shrugged. 'Maybe. Perhaps he can't get out. Or perhaps he's just one of those people who pretend they can't walk far so they get extra benefits.'

'What are benefits?'

Jax opened her mouth then closed it and sighed. 'Don't worry about it. Just something they were on about on *Loose Women* this week.'

'What's *Loose Women*?'

Jax started to giggle. 'It sounds so funny when you say it. Come on, Ernie, let's clean up and I'll put a pizza in for tea.'

'Cheese and ham?'

'If you like.'

'Jax ... Why is Mr Mayer so grumpy? Does that happen to all old people?'

Jax reached out and smoothed Ernie's damp hair back from his forehead.

'I don't know, Ernie. I don't think so. Just to some.'

Ernie nodded.

'I don't want to become grumpy when I get older.'

'Well don't! It's not compulsory.'

'What's compulsory?'

'Oh God, Ernie, you're getting a dictionary for Christmas. Come on, let's find the mop.'

As Ernie followed his cousin through to the kitchen, he vowed never to become grumpy. Even when he got really, really old, he'd always be kind. Just like he remembered his mummy being, and she had always said, 'Kindness doesn't cost a thing.'

So Ernie would be kind for free, just like Mummy said. He wished she could see him now and that he could know for certain if she was proud of him. But if she was proud of him, then she'd be here, wouldn't she? He bit the inside of his cheek – as he'd learnt to do when the sad feeling started in his chest – and made himself think about climbing trees and building dens and how it had felt when that wasp had stung his knee last summer. He was getting good at being brave and he was very proud of himself for that.

CHAPTER 3

Abby rolled over in bed and blinked. It took a few moments for her to register her surroundings, to realise that she was in the bedroom of her new flat. She pulled the duvet up to her chin and closed her eyes again; if she could just drop back off to sleep then she could escape reality for a bit. But a growl from her stomach told her that wasn't going to happen. She never could sleep on an empty stomach, especially not the morning after she'd drunk a whole bottle of wine. Hunger and hungover did not mix well.

She pushed the covers back and swung her legs over the edge of the bed, yelping as her cold toes hit a box she'd left in front of the bedside cabinet. Why had she tried to get out of bed on that side anyway? It was like she was conditioned to sleep on the left, as if, even though she now slept alone, she couldn't allow her body to take up the whole bed, to venture over to the side where Gavin's warm body should have been. Even on mornings when she woke up after they'd had a row, she'd be able to slide closer to his reassuring warmth, to thaw her toes – that were always cold – on his legs and to find comfort in another human being, in knowing she wasn't completely alone.

She leant forwards and squeezed her toes, waiting for the throbbing to subside. At least she didn't have to put up with Gavin's morning routine anymore. She'd tried to tell herself for years that it didn't bother her but it really had, especially when she'd longed for him to turn and take her in his arms, to cuddle her while they both slowly woke up. Instead, as soon as he came round, he'd jump out of bed, drop to the rug and do fifty press-ups. All before he'd had so much as a cup of tea. Not that he drank tea, preferring to make himself fresh juice in his top-of-the-range juicer swiftly followed by a sludgy-grey protein shake. Abby had tried to tell him that those protein shakes were the cause of his dreadful wind and what he thought was IBS, but he just wouldn't listen, dismissing her suggestions as Google-doctor madness. Abby suspected that even if he went for a medical and had a dietician tell him that his protein shakes were the cause of his chronic flatulence and heartburn, he'd still refuse to give them up. Gavin was terrified of losing an ounce of muscle and would rather fart constantly than fail to appear totally ripped.

Once the throbbing in her toes had subsided, she got up, pulled on her dressing gown and padded along the hallway to the bathroom. It was warm with early morning sunshine and she could hear birdsong from just outside the patterned glass. As she washed her face, she started to feel her spirits lifting. Perhaps it wouldn't be so bad having her own place. After all, it was refreshing to be able to use a bathroom that smelt fresh and clean and wasn't tainted with Gavin's early morning odours. It was nice to be able to wash her face without being shoved out the way as he hogged the mirror before leaving a rim of shaving scum around the sink. And she certainly didn't miss having to snap photos as he flexed his biceps and paraded his naked torso around, telling her exactly what angle to capture, that he then posted on Instagram with hashtags like *#bodybuilder*, *#hunk* and *#shredded*.

Oh Gavin . . .

It hadn't been all bad or she wouldn't have stayed with him – it was just easier now to focus on the negatives about their relationship because it hurt less than dwelling on what she'd lost.

In the kitchen, Abby switched the kettle on and looked around. She still hadn't unpacked everything she needed but as long as she could locate the teabags, a spoon and a plate, she'd manage for now. Once she'd made tea and toast, she set them down on the kitchen table then turned on the digital radio that she'd treated herself to for her birthday. The radio could be a great comfort; it made her feel as though there were still people out there, carrying on with their lives, even if she felt as though her own had stalled.

She'd done her calculations, and with rent and groceries, as long as she was careful, she could manage for some time on her savings, and the inheritance her mum had left her. She'd spoken to Gavin about the idea of him buying her out of their shared property, but they hadn't made any definite arrangements yet, although Abby knew it was something she'd need to deal with soon. She didn't really want to dip into the money that she'd tucked safely away in an ISA but it was there if things got tight. After she and Gavin had got together at fifteen, they'd mapped out their whole future, from the house they'd buy to the holidays they'd have and how many children they wanted. She shivered. Sometimes, life just didn't work out the way you thought it would, but at fifteen, they'd been confident with the arrogance of youth, about themselves and where they were heading. Gavin had already been working with his father's building company during school holidays and at weekends, and when they finished year eleven, he began working full time.

Abby had thought she knew what she wanted to do, too. She would go to college to study English Literature, Media and History at A level, but Gavin had persuaded her not to go. He'd told her he didn't like the thought of her going off to college and being surrounded by new people who might change how she saw him, and she'd been so in love with him by then that she'd been afraid to upset him. Instead, she'd managed to get some hours at the local corner shop and soon that had morphed into more hours and before she knew it, she was in her mid-twenties and they were putting down a deposit on their first mortgage. Once that had happened, there was no quitting the job to go back to studying, they just couldn't manage without her wage. In fact, Gavin had suggested that she try to find a few more hours' work somewhere else to bump up her incomings, so she'd found casual work at a care home that soon became her full-time job. A few years later, she moved from there to Greenfields. By that point, Gavin had been earning more money and when they were both twenty-nine, they'd decided the time was right to start trying for a family. Gavin had told her to quit work and let him take care of her. But something had stopped her, a warning voice that told her that giving up her independence was risky, and she was glad now that she'd listened to that voice and kept squirrelling money away. Because look at what had happened. And although she no longer had the job, losing it hadn't been her choice – it had been foisted upon her.

Her mobile buzzed on the kitchen counter, dragging her from her thoughts, and she went to check it, wondering for a moment if perhaps it was Gavin. She swallowed her disappointment, first at the fact that it wasn't him and secondly at the fact that she'd hoped it might be. The text was from her friend Lisa.

Abby sighed. Lisa, in her usual no nonsense manner, had invited her out for brunch in Didsbury village. Or rather told her that she would be meeting her for brunch:

In an hour. So you'd better go and get ready.

Sixty-five minutes later, Abby opened the door to the Italian café that Lisa had chosen for their brunch and looked around. Seeing that Lisa was already seated in a booth, Abby went over and sat opposite her friend. She looked gorgeous, as usual. Her sleek dark red bob framed her heart-shaped face, her emerald-green eyes sparkled, and her alabaster skin glowed luminescent, as if she'd spent the weekend at a spa.

'Hello, darling!' Lisa got up and came around to Abby then leant over and hugged her. Abby's face was squashed against Lisa's stomach and her friend's silver bangles dug into her cheek. But it wasn't the pain of metal digging into her face or the fact that she could barely breathe that brought tears to her eyes; it was so nice to feel her friend's loving hug.

Lisa was wearing an off-the-shoulder pale green jumper

that brought out the colour of her eyes and she'd paired it with skinny jeans and a pair of brown ankle boots. With her height and strong curves, everything she wore looked stylish and Abby wished, not for the first time, that she had just an ounce of Lisa's panache.

When Lisa finally released her, all Abby could smell was vanilla and rose. Lisa's favourite perfume hadn't changed in all the years she'd known her. She had moved to Manchester from South Wales when they were in year eleven at school, and Abby had taken the quiet redhead under her wing. Back then, Abby had been the more confident one, but these days their roles were reversed. Lisa had studied art and design at college and university, and now worked as a plus-sized fashion designer.

Lisa was also in love, and had been engaged to her partner, Fiona, for the past six months. Fiona owned her own floristry shop in Didsbury and it was there that they'd met. Lisa had gone in to order flowers for her mother's birthday, their eyes had locked over pink roses and gypsophila and that had been that. Their wedding was planned for next Christmas and Lisa had already asked Abby to be a bridesmaid. Abby hadn't yet fully committed to the role, hoping she'd be able to make her excuses before dress fittings became a reality, but she'd nodded and smiled enough to keep Lisa from nagging her ... for now. The thought of being centre stage at an event, even her best friend's wedding, made Abby's stomach clench.

'You look amazing as always.'

Lisa smiled. 'The love of a good woman, Abby. You should try it.'

Heat filled Abby's cheeks. She'd once shared a drunken

kiss with Lisa when she'd visited her university digs in London, but as good a kisser as Lisa had been, Abby just hadn't felt that spark of attraction that she had with Gavin. When she'd gone home after the weekend, she'd felt a bit guilty about kissing someone else, but then Gavin had confessed to snogging a barmaid that same weekend – sworn on his mother's life that it hadn't gone any further than that – and Abby had felt absolved. But she was also unable to blame him for cheating on her. She'd vowed to put it behind her, blamed alcohol and high spirits, and classed it as a small hiccup in their long-term relationship.

'I love you, Lisa, but it's not really my thing.'

Lisa shrugged. 'The thought of bumping uglies with a guy turns my stomach, so I completely get you.' Even though she'd left Wales at fifteen, Lisa's accent was still musical – her soft Welsh lilt always made Abby more aware of her own Mancunian twang.

'Have you ordered yet?' Abby was keen to divert the conversation away from sex. It had been so long since she'd had any and the last time had been rather a disappointment, as it soon became evident that Gavin had not been in the mood. Then again, he'd rarely been in the mood over their last year together, citing tiredness and stomach cramps as reasons for his waning libido.

'Not yet, no.' Lisa shook her head. 'I was waiting for you and it's my treat.' She held up her hand. 'No arguments! Seeing as how you're now unemployed, you need to watch your pennies.'

'Thank you. But as soon as I'm settled in, I'm cooking you and Fiona dinner.'

'Deal!'

They sat in silence for a few minutes as they read the menu, and Abby tried to push all thoughts of Gavin's failure to perform – and how it must have been because he hadn't fancied her anymore, possibly because her neck was too short and she couldn't put her feet behind her head – from her mind. Of course, there had been the old waxing debate that Gavin had liked to bring up from time to time, and although Abby knew he preferred her lady-garden smooth, she just couldn't stand the agony of having it completely waxed. So perhaps that had been the straw that had broken the camel toe ... *camel's back*! She shook her head and took a deep cleansing breath. Sometimes her thoughts exhausted her, and she was glad no one could see inside her head because they'd probably get her sectioned immediately.

'I've been thinking you should have a housewarming party so we can help you christen the flat. That would be fun,' Lisa said casually.

Abby smiled but the idea made her shoulders tighten. She had always wanted to entertain and hadn't because of Gavin. But doing it now, when she and Gavin had so recently split up, when she would be solely responsible for hosting the party, made her toes curl. Which was exactly why she knew she should seriously consider it; she needed to make some changes in her life and moving out of her comfort zone was an important one.

'OK, good idea.'

A smiley waitress came and took their orders then sashayed away, sticking her pencil into her blonde bun. The café was Sunday-morning busy, with people of all ages enjoying their brunch as they read the papers, typed on lightweight laptops, or simply caught up. The sounds of cutlery clinking, coffee machine frothing, and Radio 2 playing filled the air, along with the scents of toasted teacakes, bacon and hash browns. Even though she'd had toast not long ago, Abby was very hungry so she'd ordered pancakes with maple syrup and crispy bacon and a grande latte.

'How's the flat coming along?'

'Well I've moved everything in, but I haven't unpacked properly yet.'

'I would've helped you but with Mum being taken ill ...'

'Don't worry about it. I was fine, and besides, all that carrying boxes was a fabulous workout for my bingo wings. How is your mum?'

'Oh, she's all right, I think. She's back at home and on the sofa resting now but it gave her a scare. I'd be there now but she told me to stop fussing around her.' Lisa sniffed. 'Anyway, she's got Dad.'

'Yes, it's good she's not alone. Did they find out what caused the chest pains?'

'A minor heart attack apparently, so she's rattling with medication and has been told to take it easy. I'm not sure she'll listen though ... you know my mum.'

Abby nodded. Lisa's mother was nothing if not stubborn. She was only just speaking to Lisa again after about four years of intermittent radio silence. Lisa hadn't told her parents she was gay throughout her twenties because she'd known how her staunch Roman Catholic mother would react. She'd confided in her father first; he was more liberal and understanding than his wife, and he'd helped her to tell her mother, but the news hadn't been taken well and Gill had refused to speak to Lisa for over a year, and then been frosty for another three. It was deeply sad that a parent could react like that, and to her only child, but Lisa had borne it well. She had carried on with her life, and eventually, Gill had started to come round – although she still pretended that Fiona was just Lisa's 'flatmate', so how the wedding was going to work, Abby had no idea.

'Anyway, I don't want to dwell on Gill and her pig-headedness. We're already missing you at our place. Fiona said she's especially missing the cups of tea you brought us in the morning. The best she'd ever tasted apparently.'

Abby laughed. 'I do make a good cup of tea. You have to let the teabags steep properly.'

She'd enjoyed those mornings, too, when she'd taken her friends tea and biscuits and they'd sat and talked before the day properly began. She'd sat at the bottom of their bed opposite the striking couple – Lisa with her dark red hair and pale skin and Fiona who was, in Abby's opinion, a doppelgänger for the incredibly beautiful Alesha Dixon – and it had made her feel less alone. It had also lit a spark of hope inside her, that she could find a flatmate or even, one day, fall in love again. Living with Gavin long since ceased to be about cosy cups of tea in bed and long conversations where they'd bared their souls to each other. But it seemed that it was possible if you found the right person for you.

'Apparently, I just don't make tea as good as you. So … how are you, love?'

'I'm OK,' Abby said. 'Just getting on with it, I guess.'

'Gav wasn't there when you collected the rest of your things?'

'Oh no. He wouldn't want to see me. He might feel compelled to apologise and he hates apologising.'

The waitress arrived with their orders and they waited for her to set the plates and mugs down before speaking again.

'I don't think I've ever seen Gavin contrite,' Lisa said as they tucked in.

'No. It doesn't happen often.'

Abby sipped her latte and winced. Too hot to drink yet.

'Have you met any of your neighbours at the flats? Any hotties there you could hang out with?'

'Well, your idea of hot is certainly different from mine, but not that I've seen. The only person I've bumped into so far is an old man and he ... didn't seem too happy to meet me.' The guy's angry face came back into Abby's head and she shuddered.

'That bad, eh?'

'I went outside ... around the back of the flats where there's some kind of community garden. It's all over-grown and messy with fag butts and litter everywhere. I had ...' She bit her lip. Lisa was dead against smoking and she didn't want to admit what she'd been about to do but she also didn't want to lie to her friend. 'I bought some cigarettes ... just after I saw the message on Gav's phone. It was instinctive—'

'You're not smoking again?' Lisa frowned.

'No, I'm not.' Abby's cheeks burned at her friend's disapproval and at the memory of the anger she'd faced yesterday. 'I just bought them on impulse and after I'd moved everything into the flat, the old craving reared its head. So, I went outside for a smoke, but I didn't actually light it. Anyway, this guy caught me with the fag in my mouth and had a right go at me.'

'Good for him.'

'No!' Abby inhaled slowly. This wasn't right – Lisa should be on her side. 'It wasn't good at all. He was vile. Accused me of littering and gave me a right dressing-down.'

'What did you say?'

'I felt a bit like a naughty schoolgirl to be honest.'

'Well if it's as messy as you said it is, perhaps he's fed up.'

'Perhaps ... but there was still no need for him to be so rude.'

Abby raised a forkful of pancake to her mouth and chewed. She hoped there wouldn't be an encore of yesterday. She was far too raw to endure that kind of hostility, especially from one of her neighbours.

'So, enough about me ... tell me about your week.'

An hour later, Abby was holding her sides. Lisa had re-galed her with details of how she'd dealt with a particularly snooty model she'd used for one of her plus-sized autumn ranges, then launched into a blow-by-blow account of visiting her mother at the hospital and witnessing how Gill had treated the poor NHS staff. Lisa had made what could have been a tragic tale seem funny; she was able to see the humour in even the bleakest of situations and that was one of the things Abby most loved about her.

'Anyway, Abs, have you thought at all about moving on now? You know ... seizing the day and all that? Perhaps by looking for a new job or retraining.'

Abby picked up her mug, saw it was empty, then put it back on the table. How many refills had she drunk over brunch? That was the thing about being with Lisa; she completely forgot about time and had been enjoying Lisa's stories so much that she'd been lulled into a false sense of security, hoping that her own situation had been forgotten.

'Oh ...'

Lisa reached over the table and squeezed Abby's hand. 'Tell me.'

'I'm OK. I'm not exactly seizing the day, but I am trying to focus on my future. What else can I do?'

Lisa gazed at her for a moment then tapped her hand on the table, hard enough to make the cutlery on their empty plates clatter.

'I'll tell you what you can do, Abby. You can do better than that. You're not going to just exist now, wondering what Gavin is up to, wondering what might have been. You're going to start living again, and by living, I mean thinking about what you want to do with your life then putting yourself out there and having some fun. We're not getting any younger.'

'What and I'd better get a move on before my biological clock starts screaming?'

'No. That wasn't what I meant.' Lisa licked her lips. 'Look, not everyone has to reproduce. You can be happy and fulfilled without having children. Sometimes, it's just not in your future.'

Abby watched Lisa's face carefully. She knew that Lisa and Fiona had discussed their own options and whether having children was something they planned to pursue, and they'd decided that they would focus instead on travel and their careers. There were options available to them as a same-sex couple, but they'd made their decision and so far, both of them seemed OK with it. Abby wished she didn't have a yearning to be a mum but she'd had it for as long as she could remember, especially when she had come so close … Only now, the prospect of motherhood seemed further away than ever.

'I'm not being insensitive, love. I know what you went through after … things didn't work out.'

'It's up there with the worst times of my life,' Abby muttered. 'I think about what could have been … about my baby every day.'

Lisa reached out and squeezed her hand. 'I know you do, sweetheart. I know. Your little one would be what … about six or seven now?'

Abby nodded. She'd be a mum. She and Gavin would be parents. Would it all have turned out differently if she'd carried her baby to full-term?

'It wasn't meant to be,' Abby said, repeating the words that had acted as a mantra whenever she'd felt the old pain resurfacing.

'However,' Lisa continued, 'not wanting to seem dismissive here. Not at all. But what I think is that you could consider getting back into dating.'

'Back into dating? When was I ever *in* dating?'

'Good point. I suppose you and Gavin got together when you were very young and never had a chance to see what else was out there. I mean, *who* else was out there.'

'I'm not interested, Lisa. It's too soon.'

Lisa nodded. 'I'll let you have that for today and a little while longer but only if you promise to allow me to set you up at some point soon.'

'With who?' Abby's stomach churned at the thought of dating; she knew she'd do everything in her power to avoid it. She had zero confidence left and as Gavin was the only man she'd ever been with, she wouldn't know where to start with someone else. It would just feel wrong. Weird. How could she ever be naked with somebody else?

'I don't know yet but there are lots of great dating apps now, so we'll come up with a plan.'

'Right.'

'I know you hate the thought of it and there's no guarantee you'll find someone you like, but you need to be proactive about this at some point. Say you'll consider it and we can leave it there … For now at least.'

Abby took a deep breath then released it slowly. 'All right. I'll consider it. But it better not be like those adverts where they match you with someone just because you both like peanut butter and you end up dating a budgie.'

'A budgie?'

'Oh, I don't know, it was some sort of animal.' She scratched her head. 'Actually, it might have been an owl.'

'Okaaay. Fab–u–lous! That's settled then.'

Abby smiled at Lisa but under the table she pressed her nails into her palms. Lisa might think it was a fabulous idea but Abby wasn't sure about it. In fact, she didn't feel *fab–u–lous* about it at all.

Back at her flat, with Sunday afternoon stretching out before her, Abby decided to try to be proactive, as Lisa had suggested. She found her laptop, turned it on, then curled up on the sofa with it open on her lap. She considered reading about different career options but it seemed too exhausting to wade through right now, so instead, she tentatively typed 'Dating Apps' into the search engine. A few names appeared and she stared at them, wondering how on earth she'd know which one to pick if she did decide to try one.

As she scrolled down, some images appeared under Top Stories and her heart beat faster. Stories like: *When Dating Apps Go Bad* and *I Met My Husband on a Dating App and He Was Already Married.* They made her cringe. Yes, there were some happy endings but some sorry tales too. Besides, she felt a bit guilty even looking at these sites, almost as if she was cheating. Even after everything Gavin had done, Abby had to admit to herself that the idea of looking for another man made her uncomfortable. Did that mean that she was conditioned into being his doormat for ever then? Would she never be able to escape his shadow?

She sighed. It was early days and she needed some time to adapt. Lisa meant well but she was so used to dashing around at 100 miles per hour and she wanted Abby to do the same. But Abby wasn't ready; she knew it deep down and vowed that when she next saw Lisa, she'd be completely upfront about it.

Abby clicked onto the favourites tab and her blog site popped up. She followed the link and ran her eyes over the familiar header with its pinks and purples and the black and white image of an anonymous woman nursing a large coffee in front of a laptop. It wasn't Abby, of course, it was an image she'd bought from stock photos, but she thought of it as her blog-self, as if this faceless nameless woman was her alter ego.

Abby had found comfort in her blog, in being able to pour out her thoughts and feelings, her doubts and concerns, and over time, the responses she'd received to her posts had grown and comforted her. She wasn't completely alone; other people went through similar experiences too. Losing her beloved mum two years earlier had altered something in Abby and she knew she'd never be the same person that she had been before that defining moment. But when she'd posted about it openly, others had confessed to sharing those feelings too. Gavin had never completely understood it, the deep dark grief for her mother that sent her heart racing and jolted her from sleep in the early hours of the morning. When she'd broken down and sobbed, he'd told her not to cry, patted her back and told her that everything would be all right. But it hadn't been, had it? Gavin couldn't comprehend the rawness Abby felt at losing the woman she had loved with all her heart. Abby's mother had been friend, mum and cheerleader, and while she'd been alive, Abby had still believed that anything was possible. After she'd gone … Abby's world had shifted and had never felt quite right since. It made the loss of her little one even harder to bear because her mum was no longer there to comfort her about it.

She closed the laptop down as tiredness crept in, bringing with it that ache in her bones that made her want to sleep. Brunch with Lisa had been fun but the idea of trying to write about her complicated emotions was too enormous a task, so she wouldn't bother right now. Her thoughts were too jumbled, too painful and she wasn't sure what hurt the most; her longing for her mum or her hurt over Gavin and what might have been had their baby survived.

CHAPTER 4

The following Friday, Abby let herself into the communal entrance then allowed the door to close behind her. It shut against her bottom with a *click* and bumped her forwards, causing her to lose her tenuous hold on one of her shopping bags. As the handle slipped from her grasp, she lurched forwards but she was too late. The sound of glass shattering and the scent of wine immediately filled the air.

'Bang goes my Prosecco!' she muttered. It was basically the end of a week she'd prefer to forget what with her car failing its MOT on Tuesday so she'd had to fork out several hundred pounds to put it right, then on Wednesday she'd washed a red bra with her whites, turning them all pink. On Thursday, she'd kept a low profile, hoping nothing else would go wrong, then today she'd ventured out in her repaired car, complete with four new tyres and new brake pads, to get some shopping. And look what had happened now ...

She placed the other three heavy shopping bags carefully on the tiled floor then opened the bag she'd dropped to inspect the damage. The bottle she'd bought as a treat to cheer herself up had indeed smashed and the bag was filled with a sweet apple and peach aroma.

Bubbles popped in the pool of Prosecco, taunting her with how delicious it would have tasted. She pulled a handful of tissues from her bag and tried to absorb some of the liquid, but it was clearly going to require more than a few Kleenex.

She stood upright and looked around for something she could use then gasped as she realised she was being watched. The old man from the communal garden glared at her from a doorway.

'I ... uh ... dropped my shopping and a bottle broke,' she gabbled.

He stepped out into the communal entrance, his walking stick gripped in his right hand. He was leaning heavily on it, his knuckles white.

'So now you're stinking up the entranceway too. Smells like a pub in here now.' He shook his head, the nasal tones of his thick Mancunian accent hanging in the air between them.

'Sorry ... but it was an accident. I went shopping and I bought some wine and ... now it's broken.' She gestured at the bag on the floor.

When she met the old man's eyes again, he was staring at her blankly, as if she was some alien creature he couldn't quite place.

'Look ... I'll clean this mess up right now. I have some disinfectant in the flat, I'll fetch it down with my mop and—'

'Just you make sure that you do. Don't want other people thinking it's me boozing on a Friday afternoon.'

'I wasn't boozing in the afternoon, I ...' She stopped because he was already turning away. Irritation crawled under her skin. 'You know it's quite rude to turn your

43

back on someone when they're still speaking to you.'

He turned to face her.

'Rude? You're calling *me* rude! Listen, young woman, it's you who's rude ... moving in here with your stinking cigarettes and your afternoon boozing and your stomping up and down those stairs, mithering your neighbours. How's a man supposed to rest around here? Can't hear myself thinking most days what with you and that disrespectful child right above me. It's become so noisy around here since you moved in – and that's not for the better!' Spittle flew from his mouth with the final word and Abby flinched.

As he disappeared into his flat and slammed the door behind him, Abby stared at her shopping, blinking with shock. The bag holding the broken bottle had somehow fallen to the side and wine now ran across the tiles, heading towards the staircase. Abby was consumed by a need to abandon the bags, race up to her flat and bury her face in her duvet. But she knew she couldn't do that. Someone could come down the stairs, possibly the child that the old man had mentioned, and slip on the wine.

Abby arranged her shopping bags around the spill, then jogged up the stairs to fetch some cleaning products. She couldn't help wondering why the man had such a problem with her. All the things he'd accused her of seemed exaggerated. How had she managed to upset and offend him so greatly when she hadn't done anything at all? It felt very unfair.

Abby had been prepared to give him a chance to redeem himself following their first meeting but it seemed that he had no intention of affording her the same courtesy. Yet as much as she wanted to be angry with him, Abby knew that people had reasons for their behaviour that weren't obvious to an onlooker. Perhaps he really was a vile old man, but perhaps there was more to him than she'd seen. Abby certainly hoped so because she didn't want to have to move again, but the thought of living so close to someone who seemed to hate her so much was not conducive to healing. And she knew that she had to take care of herself now.

After all, there was no one else to do it, was there?

The shopping had been put away in the cupboards that Abby had finally settled on as being *the right ones*. She'd forgotten how much of a nuisance it could be if the teabags and mugs were at the other end of the kitchen from the kettle and how irritating it was to try to get the cheese grater out from under all the Tupperware. When the plastic pots had fallen onto the kitchen floor for the third time that week, and Abby had bumped her head – again – leaning into the cupboard to try to put them right, she'd cracked and spent an afternoon reorganising.

The late afternoon sunshine was creating a warm haze in her lounge and it made her feel as if there was hope in the air. Spring had always made her feel that way in the past, but this year, the lifting of the spirits had thus far been absent. But suddenly, being in her clean flat with a well-stocked fridge and cupboards, as well as two new paperbacks she'd picked up at the supermarket, the weekend alone didn't seem like a terribly unpleasant prospect. In fact, she was actually looking forward to the idea of stretching out on the sofa with a curry for one and a nice glass of wine. Luckily, she already had a bottle of rosé in the fridge.

Actually, she'd pour a glass right now. Why not? She didn't need to go anywhere this evening and she could even take it outside and have a better look at the communal garden.

Wine and one of her new paperback books in hand, she descended the stairs carefully, ensuring that her white lace-up pumps made the minimum noise on the stairs. The last thing she wanted was to disturb the old man again and have him accusing her of 'clomping around'.

She let herself out of the front door then made her way around the side of the building to the garden. It wasn't cold, but it wasn't particularly warm either, so she pulled her cardigan tighter around her then looked for somewhere to sit. She spotted a bench to the far right of the garden by a rather sorry-looking shed, so she went over to it. The seat looked clean enough, although it would benefit from a sanding down and a lick of varnish, just like the shed. She settled down on the slatted seat and took a sip of her wine.

Willow Court was a large red-brick building made up of twenty-four two- and three-bedroom flats. There were different communal entrances located around the building with each section of six having its own entrance. Abby knew that the old man had the ground floor flat to the left of the front door but had no idea who else lived in her block. From this side, the rear window of her flat could be seen on the second floor above those of her downstairs neighbours then off to the left were other flats that had separate entrances. The windows of the flats were like blank mirrors, their dark glass screening the inhabitants from curious eyes. A bird flew behind her, its flight reflected in the windows as if it were actually making its way through the building. For all Abby knew, there could be birds within the flats, dogs, cats, reptiles … There could be all manner of things inside. She wondered if anyone was looking out right now, watching her watching them.

She turned on the bench to look instead at the large patch of garden and the brick borders surrounding it. The grass was overgrown and patchy, dogs evidently used it as a toilet spot and small mounds of earth suggested that there might be cats using it for a similar purpose. The borders were a jumble of choked plants, litter and weeds; it was hard to tell what should be growing there and what had made its way uninvited. But as she leant forwards and looked more closely at the nearest red-brick border, she could see tiny green shoots poking through the surface of the soil, straining against everything that surrounded them. What chance did they have, those tiny plants, trying to grow in among the debris of modern life? It seemed so sad that their future was hopeless, that they'd struggle to reach the rays of sunshine and likely be crushed under Coke cans or dug up by cats using the area as a litter tray.

Life was tough, whether you were a human being or a tiny shoot, and everyone needed some TLC now and then. She wondered … then shook her head. It was a silly idea. She was far too busy to try to change the fate of some tiny shoots that could, for all she knew, actually just be weeds.

A rustling at the far edge of the garden caught her attention and she peered over at what she'd assumed was a pile of rubbish. She'd thought someone had dumped bin bags there under a ratty old tarpaulin, and not even registered that it could be something else, so when a small head popped out from behind the tarpaulin, she gasped.

It belonged to a young boy with a mop of dark blond hair, and she watched as he emerged and began rooting around in the shrubbery, picking up twigs and leaves and scattering them over what she'd mistaken for a junk pile. Then she realised what he was doing; he was making a den.

He seemed completely oblivious to her presence, and she was worried about startling him, so she gently cleared her throat. He turned and spotted her. His eyes widened and his mouth formed an O.

'Hello!' Abby waved.

The boy seemed to weigh up the situation, his eyes darting around the garden as he debated whether or not to run.

'I've just moved in here.' Abby pointed at the flats. 'On the second floor ... above an elderly gentleman.'

The boy frowned. 'You can't be above Mr Mayer because that's where I live.'

'No ... what I meant was two up from him. Mr Mayer is it?'

'Ah ...' He nodded. 'You're the lady above my flat.'

Abby stood up. 'Nice to meet you. I'm Abby.'

He approached her slowly but didn't get within reach, staying just far enough away like a nervous cat would do. 'I'm Ernie. I live in the flat with my dad. Sometimes my cousin, Jax, looks after me.'

'Are you building a den?'

Ernie's cheeks flushed and he pushed his fringe out of his eyes. 'I'm not supposed to be out here, really.'

'Why not?'

Ernie looked around as if checking for someone. 'It's Mr Mayer. He doesn't like people hanging around in the garden.'

'Has he told you that?'

'When we moved in. He told my dad that it wasn't for playing in and my dad said best not upset the old geezer.'

'I see. Well I'm sure he won't mind really ...' Abby thought about Mr Mayer's face when he'd thought she was smoking out here. 'But I won't tell if you don't.'

His face broke into a smile, exposing the gap where his two lower front teeth should have been, and it lifted Abby's heart. He'd seemed so serious since he'd spotted her, as if he had the weight of the world on his young shoulders.

'Deal.'

Ernie glanced back at his den and Abby could see that he was keen to carry on building. She didn't want him to feel uncomfortable, so she picked up her paperback from the bench and showed it to him. 'I wouldn't mind having a read out here as long as I'm not disturbing you. Would that be OK?'

Ernie looked at the book then at the wine in her hand. 'Yes. That's fine.'

'Thank you.'

Abby smiled then sat down, sipped her wine and opened her book. But even though she pretended to read, the words swam, meaningless, before her eyes as she focused more on Ernie over on the other side of the garden. He was busily gathering foliage for his den, chatting away to himself as he worked, and she was sure she heard the words 'apocalypse', 'zombies' and 'fortress'. It made her smile. The garden might be a dreadful mess, it

49

might be a mass of weeds and overgrown rose bushes, but a little boy had managed to transform it into his play-ground. His young imagination was seeing things that she couldn't, he had turned the space into so much more, and that knowledge tugged at Abby's heart. If a little boy could see the potential of the space, then so could others, those who could actually do something about it. How nice would it be for Ernie and other children in the flats on Holly Street to have a garden out here where they could play without fear of stepping in dog mess or cutting themselves on a broken bottle?

She closed her book and leant against the back of the bench, allowing her own imagination to wander. Once upon a time, she'd seen the world as being full of poten-tial. There had been possibilities, hopes and dreams. She'd cradled one of those dreams inside her, keeping quiet about it until she knew for certain, not even telling Gavin until she'd seen the twin blue lines on the thin white plastic stick. That had been over seven years ago, and she'd learnt that sometimes, dreams don't come true, even when you're tricked into thinking they will.

For a long time, Abby had been going through the motions of her life, acting as if she were content but knowing, in her heart, that something was missing. She wanted to learn to see the world as a child did again, to be able to imagine whole new worlds in the garden the way Ernie did. Of course, she'd prefer for there not to be an apocalypse, but just to have the ability to live in the moment and to have hope once more. If a little boy could do it, then so could she. And with that, Abby made a decision – to begin her new life, here and now.

She raised her glass to Willow Court then whispered,

'To the future. To poking my head above the weeds of my past.'

And she hoped with all her heart that this was the new beginning she needed.

Ernie ducked under the tarpaulin and entered the stuffy warmth of his den where it smelt like soil and grass. He was pleased with how it was coming along, especially now he'd put the covering of foliage over the roof like he'd watched Bear Grylls do on TV. He loved the survival shows and watched them over and over again. It was where he'd learnt the words 'foliage' and 'survival'. It would be great to have Bear Grylls as a dad. Ernie bet Bear took his kids everywhere with him and taught them all his survival techniques.

Not that Ernie wanted to change his dad. He loved him very much, he just wished he was around more. Some of his friends at school (and there weren't many but he had a few) talked about the time they spent with their dads, how they took them to football and rugby and the cinema. Ernie would love to go to the cinema to see one of the new *Star Wars* or *Marvel* films and had asked his dad if he would take him for his birthday, but even though his dad had smiled and nodded, Ernie didn't know when it was going to happen. When Dad was home at the weekends, he was often too tired to do much more than sit in front of the TV and watch the sport. Ernie had asked Jax if she would take him, but she'd said Neil didn't leave her enough money to take Ernie to the cinema and it was a case of eating or going to see *Star Wars*. Ernie had decided that he'd prefer to see a film but Jax had laughed and told him not to be silly.

He hated it when she laughed at him like that. He bet his mummy wouldn't have laughed at him.

The horrible sad feelings fluttered in his tummy again. But at times like this, when he knew his dad wouldn't be home until late at night, if at all – because sometimes his dad didn't even come home on Fridays like he said he would – and Jax had told him she couldn't come over because she had plans, Ernie missed his mum more than ever. If she were here, he'd be in the flat with her now, helping her to make dinner or watching TV with her and laughing as she laughed. It wasn't often that Ernie remembered her laughing but when she had, she'd looked so pretty. He had a photo of her smiling that he'd hidden inside his *Where's Wally* annual from last year. Ernie had felt that he had to hide it because his dad always frowned when he saw pictures of his mum, so it was better to keep it out of sight. Ernie kissed it every night before he went to sleep but he always put it back safe so his dad wouldn't throw it out as he'd done with the rest of his mum's things.

And now there was a new lady living here – Abby. She'd just spoken to him and she was outside reading her book and drinking pink wine. His mum had liked pink wine but whenever she'd drunk it, she'd become sad and cried even more than she did most days, so Ernie had always been afraid when he'd seen it in the fridge. When his mummy got sad, his dad got cross and there had been rows ... a lot of them.

But at least there had been noise then. Now it was always so quiet, and the flat seemed so big when he was there alone.

Ernie peered out of the opening of his den at the lady.

He liked her long brown hair and her brown eyes like chocolate. She was pretty and she'd been nice to him. Ernie knew he had to be careful around strangers though, as his teacher had told him all about stranger danger and how someone could seem nice, but they might take you away and hurt you. He wasn't worried because he had his zombie stick with him in the den, so he'd be able to fight back if anyone tried to attack him. Ernie knew how to scare away a bear – he'd learnt it from TV – so someone so small wasn't going to be able to hurt him. Anyway, Abby seemed nice and even a bit sad, kind of like his mummy, so she probably needed someone to be nice to her. And all she wanted was to read quietly in the garden, so that was fine with Ernie. It was kind of nice to have company and he wondered if she might even invite him for tea. Jax had left him a peanut butter sandwich in the fridge and two cans of Coke but Ernie would really like a warm dinner. Perhaps chips and beans or a nice gravy dinner like Dad sometimes made when he was home. Dad always bought the best steak pies and made delicious buttery mash that Ernie would eat every day if he could.

His tummy growled and he pressed his hand to it. He'd go in and eat his sandwich in a bit, but he needed to secure his roof first. He doubted Abby would offer him dinner and he knew it wasn't polite to ask. But perhaps she would be his friend now.

Ernie didn't have many friends and that was why he was going to be the best at survival techniques. Because when the zombie apocalypse came, he'd be ready. He'd help everyone, and be a hero with lots of new friends. Starting with kind and pretty Abby.

CHAPTER 5

Abby had toyed with the idea of a flat-warming party, as Lisa had suggested over brunch, and finally decided to host one. It would be way of marking a turning point in her life, of celebrating her independence and newfound – if not necessarily coveted – freedom. It had been over a week since her last encounter with Mr Mayer from downstairs and this week had been better than last with a few trips to the library and a good sort-out of her clothes followed by a trip to the local greyhound charity shop. However, she was still nervous every time she descended to the ground floor in case she bumped into her elderly neighbour again and had found herself holding her breath to listen out for him whenever she went downstairs to the communal entranceway. It was no way to live, for sure, but Abby hadn't a clue what to do about it. She'd almost cancelled the party twice when she'd thought about how Mr Mayer might react to her having guests, then her stubborn side had spoken up and told her to pull herself together. She could not let a grumpy old man rule her life; she'd already let one man do that for long enough and now she was taking back control.

Abby had fired off some text messages at the start of the

week, not wanting to ring people because it was always more awkward to decline an invitation if the person inviting you was at the other end of the line. Sending a text gave them the chance to come up with an excuse. In the end, she'd had two 'thanks but I have plans' and three acceptances. Through the week, whenever she'd thought about the party, her stomach had flipped over. She hated being the centre of attention and hoped that enough people came so that she'd be able to let them all chat away as she played the quiet host. It would be an achievement if she could pull it off, a step in the right direction.

The timer on the oven pinged, so she went and checked on the mini quiches. They weren't quite ready so she put them back in and reset the timer. She checked the fridge for the tenth time, and yes, the beers and wine she'd bought for the party were still in there chilling nicely. As were the two tubs of olives, the sundried tomatoes and the fresh cream and mixed berry pavlova she'd been unable to resist.

Everything was under control.

Except for Abby's nerves.

She went to her bag that hung from the back of the chair, opened it and pulled out the cigarette packet. She raised it, flipped open the lid then sniffed the familiar aroma. Just one of these would calm her, bring back that old relaxed buzz she so often craved. She placed a cigarette in her mouth and imagined lighting it, pulling the blue-grey smoke down into her lungs then letting it escape slowly from between her lips. It would be so familiar, so relaxing, so … Addictive!

If she started again, if she allowed herself just one, she knew she'd be unable to stop.

She eyed the cigarette again, ran it under her nose for one more sniff, then tucked it back in the packet and dropped it into her bag.

Not today. She would refrain for today. All she could do was take it one day at a time.

The timer pinged again so she removed the quiches from the oven then put the tray of mini salmon en croutes in. It made her smile that most of the food she'd bought had 'mini' in the name – mini quiches, mini salmon en croute, mini profiteroles, mini apricot brie bites – the irony being that if she ate enough of these mini delights, there'd be nothing mini about her!

Which reminded her, she needed to get changed. Not into a mini skirt – heaven forbid – but into jeans and a clean T-shirt at least. And she really should brush her hair and powder her face.

Twenty-five minutes later, she walked back into the kitchen and gasped at the smoke-filled room. She'd forgotten about the damned en croutes, had clearly forgotten to set the timer too, and now there was a rather unpleasant smell filling the kitchen. She opened the oven door and jumped back as more smoke flooded the kitchen. When it had cleared enough for her to peer into the oven, she saw that the mini salmon en croutes were now teeny-weeny black rocks; they would taste revolting now, so she pulled the tray out and dumped them into the sink. Her heart sank as she realised that it was 7.20 p.m. and her guests would be arriving soon, entering her flat that now stank of burning fish.

As if the smell wasn't enough, the alarm in the hallway started screaming, evidently alerted to the smoke from the kitchen. She hurried around, opening all the windows, then stood below the white plastic circle attached to the hallway ceiling and fanned the air beneath it as vigorously as she could. When the bleeping finally stopped, her ears were ringing and she had broken a sweat. Great! This did not bode well for her party at all.

Back in the kitchen, she located her mobile and checked the screen for messages, hoping that her friends might have cancelled at the last minute so she could forget the whole sorry thing, get into her pyjamas and spend the evening in front of the TV.

Then the intercom sounded, alerting her to an arrival downstairs. She buzzed Lisa and Fiona up, relieved that they'd arrived first, then opened the door and waited for them to reach her floor. 'Lisa! Fiona! Great to see you. How are you both?' Abby hugged them then led them through to the kitchen.

'Good thanks, love.' Lisa handed her two bottles of red wine. 'Something smells good.'

'Does it? I just burnt some of it.'

'I can't smell burning just pastry and …' Lisa sniffed. 'Cheese. Yum!'

'Thank goodness for that. It's that swanky party food. Thought I'd treat us seeing as how it's not every day I have a flat-warming. Right, what can I get you to drink?'

Ten minutes later, after a quick tour of the flat and once drinks had been poured, they went through to the lounge and sat down.

'How're you settling in?' Fiona asked as she crossed her long denim-clad legs.

'Pretty well, thanks. For the first week, I felt as if I was on a strange kind of holiday, but now it's starting to feel more like home.'

Fiona nodded, her long dark hair shining with health.

'That's good. Lisa worries about you all the time – so do I.'

'Thanks, but there's no need. Really. I'm getting along all right. The rain we've had for the past week has been miserable, but I've been to the gym a few times – shock horror, right? – and I've caught up on some reading, too, and had a good sort-out of my old clothes. It's been nice to have more time … to myself.'

The thought hung in the air. More time. She had more time because she was alone now, because she wasn't running around pandering to Gavin, giving him lifts and making him protein-rich meals and waiting for him to come home. She was surprised by how accepting she sounded about it all, as if this was actually a positive thing for her. If she could make her friends believe it, then she might believe it herself. It was a good thing to be in charge of her own time, to eat what she wanted, when she wanted, to go to bed early and get up late if she felt like it. Going to the gym had been strange and, of course, she hadn't gone anywhere near the one Gavin frequented, but she'd felt the need to try to better herself, and her fitness was as good a place to start as any. It had been tough, and she'd ached for days after each session, but at least even the pain felt constructive.

'I don't read enough anymore.' Lisa shook her head. 'What with work and wedding planning and dashing around to see Mum, there's just not enough time.'

'She passes out as soon as her head hits the pillow at night.' Fiona nodded.

'It's hard when you're working and juggling everything else.' Abby sipped her wine.

'Talking of that ...' Lisa licked her lips. 'Have you had any thoughts on what we discussed over brunch?'

Abby raised her eyebrows. 'We discussed quite a few things.'

'You know what I mean.'

'Do I?'

'Yes, you know, about dating again.' Lisa smiled. 'But only if you're ready. You don't even need to actually start dating just yet, but we could sign you up to a few dating websites and you could have a look ... check out the talent.'

Abby tried to think of something to change the topic without being too obvious about it but her mind had gone blank. She opened and closed her mouth, feeling like a landed fish, then jumped as the intercom rang again. She wasn't used to having visitors – Gavin never wanted to entertain any of her friends – 'But I love it when it's just *us*, Abby' – and this would take some getting used to.

'Help yourself to crisps.' She gestured at the coffee table as she walked past, secretly grateful that she had been saved from answering Lisa.

She pressed the buzzer and a few moments later, she opened the door to Jane and Mark, a married couple she'd known since her first job at the corner shop. They'd both gone to work there straight from school about the same time as Abby and had stayed in touch ever since. Abby wasn't very close to them, and sometimes found Mark a bit overbearing with his macho confidence, but they met up a few times a year on special occasions like birthdays, Christmas and house-warmings. She'd also been to both of their children's christenings and their wedding reception, which had come after baby number two.

'Hi, Abby.' Jane opened her arms to hug Abby, but it was awkward with Jane's huge pregnant belly in the way. 'It's so good to see you. We don't see you often enough, do we, Mark?'

'No, we don't. Good to see you, Abby.'

'Don't you look well?' Jane said as she stood back and smiled at Abby.

'So do you.' Abby smiled. 'How long left?'

'Three weeks and counting. I'll be glad to get this one out, let me tell you.'

'I'll be glad to get it out too.' Mark laughed. 'This has been a tough pregnancy.'

'Oh, yes, it's been *such* a tough one for you, Mark, hasn't it? I don't know *how* you've coped.' Jane nudged her husband's arm and he laughed.

'Go on through to the lounge and I'll get you some drinks. What'll you have?'

'Juice for me and a Coke for Mark, please,' Jane said as they stepped into the flat. 'Mark's not drinking in case I go into labour early and he needs to drive.'

'I'd secretly love a beer but Jane is right. She can hardly drive herself to the hospital if she's in labour, can she?' He shrugged. 'So Coke would be lovely, thank you, Abby.'

Abby nodded as she smiled at them both. Even after all these years together, they were still basically joined at the hip. She couldn't help being reminded of how Gavin had made all their decisions for them both. She'd never put herself in that type of relationship again.

'You're eating though, right?'

'Try and stop me.' Jane rubbed her belly which looked as though it was stretching her navy dress to maximum capacity.

Abby poured a glass of orange juice and one of Coke and took them through to the lounge. It was strange seeing her living room filled with people, but it also made her realise how she'd missed out on entertaining in the past. Growing up, she'd wanted to play host and imagined the delicious meals she'd cook for her friends and family, and how much fun it would be having company and all spending time together. Of course, it hadn't worked out that way at all.

Her friends were already chatting, so she took a seat and tuned in to their conversation, pushing away the wave of sadness that came from thinking of her mum. Mark was telling them about the chain of stores he was managing now, having worked his way up from shelf-stacking to regional manager. He spoke about his job enthusiastically and told several anecdotes about his colleagues that he laughed about while those around him smiled politely, or stared into their drinks, as if they'd missed the funny part but were trying to show willing or to avoid his eyes. She wondered how it must feel to know exactly what you wanted from life. Jane hadn't gone out to work after their first baby was born; she'd said it wouldn't be worth it as all her wage would have gone on childcare, and she loved being a stay-at-home mum, while Mark clearly loved his retail career. They had a nice home, two cars, a golden Labrador called Benji and went on holiday to Tenby once a year. It was a settled life and seemingly a happy one.

Whereas Abby had no idea where she was going or what

she wanted. She was drifting, uncertain and directionless. Abby started to feel very hot.

'Must get the party food!' she blurted, causing her guests to look at her curiously. She got up and left the room quickly, her cheeks burning.

Just as she entered the kitchen, the door went again. She answered it to find Helen and Josh standing there.

Abby had known them since high school. They hadn't been a couple then but had got together at a school reunion ten years ago. At six foot two, Helen was almost a foot taller than Josh and she was stick-thin, while Josh was quite stocky.

'I love your hair!' Abby said, admiring Helen's fresh blonde crop.

'Oh, thanks! I got tired of tying it back all the time and decided to go for the chop.' Helen ran a hand through her blonde pixie cut.

'Yeah, I have the same problem.' Josh rubbed his smooth bald head.

'So you do.' Abby grinned at him. He'd always been a joker, ever since school. Although he wore contacts now, she could recall a time when he'd just had new glasses and, wanting to lighten the mood during a maths test, he'd drawn eyes on them with permanent marker then pretended to fall asleep. He'd been grounded for a month afterwards because the ink had to be professionally removed. His parents were furious. It hadn't deterred him, though, and over the years he'd got up to a variety of similar antics that often ended up with his parents being called in to speak to the head teacher. Abby realised how much she'd missed seeing them both. The years had flown past and it was strange seeing them older, yet still the same. She must look like that to them too.

She poured wine for them both then directed them towards the living room while she sorted out the nibbles. She set the fancy array of food on large oval serving plates, along with some dips and vegetable crudités. It looked good and she was proud of herself.

Abby carried the plates through to the lounge and set them out on the coffee table then did a quick drinks check. When glasses had been replenished, she perched on the arm of the sofa next to Fiona.

The evening wore on with conversations, laughter, the clearing of plates and the refilling of glasses, and Abby found that she was having a really good time. As she got up to go and fetch the desserts, Helen followed her.

'I'll give you a hand shall I?'

In the kitchen, they stacked the dishwasher then Abby got the pavlova out of the fridge along with the mini profiteroles.

'God I'm like a bloody tap.' Jane entered the kitchen, her cheeks flushed with the exertion of getting up and down to pee so many times. 'Baby's doing a tap dance on my bladder, I swear.'

'But you're so lucky.' Helen blurted out then blushed. 'Gosh I'm sorry. It's just that I'd love to be in your position, even if I had to pee a thousand times a day.'

Abby winced inwardly. It was often difficult bringing friends together, especially when some had successfully created a family and others hadn't. Jane and Mark had experienced no problems getting pregnant, but Helen and Josh had been trying for six years and had been through two unsuccessful rounds of IVF. Abby knew how badly

Helen longed for a baby and understood the emptiness that came from having hopes raised then dashed and the darkness that came afterwards, when all hope seemed lost.

'I know.' Jane nodded. 'I'm sorry it hasn't happened for you. Yet.'

Helen sighed. 'I don't know if it ever will. After two rounds of IVF and all that came with it, I'm starting to give up hope.'

'IVF does work for a lot of people, though.' Jane eased herself down onto a chair at the kitchen table. 'It happened for my sister's friend. So never give up,' she said knowingly.

'It's hard when you've been through so much and ended up with nothing at the end of it.' Helen leant against the counter and sipped her wine. 'It was draining, both emotionally and physically. It almost drove a wedge between Josh and me because of the pressure. Plus, of course, my hormones were all over the place with the treatments and I wasn't myself at all.'

'I bet it was.' Jane nodded sympathetically. 'I do feel for you both.'

'Thank you.'

Josh had wandered into the kitchen and seemed to sense that something sensitive was being discussed. 'Everything OK?'

'We were just talking about IVF and how difficult it's been.' Helen chewed her bottom lip.

Josh met his wife's eyes, and something passed between them. It was a look of understanding, of mutual endurance, of hardship and of love. Whatever else happened, it was clear that Helen and Josh loved each other very much.

'It has.' Josh went over to Helen and slid his arm around her shoulders. 'We're not sure at this point if we'll go through it again. I mean … it's difficult because neither of us is getting any younger, but also, we'll have to fund the treatment ourselves and it will mean some big life choices if we do.' Josh rubbed his head.

'We'd have to downsize the house and cars, forget about holidays …' Helen drained her wine glass and stared off into space, as if she'd run through these ideas a hundred times and still couldn't make it all fit.

'But it would be worth it, wouldn't it?' Jane drained her glass. 'Imagine how you'll feel when you see that second blue line on the test.'

Abby held her breath. The comment seemed a bit insensitive of Jane when there was a chance that IVF could fail again and when Helen and Josh had such big decisions to make.

'It would be worth it, yes, if that was the definite result, but if not … if it doesn't work then where do we go from there?' Helen's voice wavered on the final word and she shrugged as if wishing she had the answers to this difficult problem then she raised her eyes and stared straight at Jane's bump. 'If only we knew.'

The temperature in the kitchen had dropped and Abby was on edge. She had a feeling that a conversation that had begun as one woman's longing for a baby had moved on to a rather sensitive debate and she hated confrontation.

'Exactly.' Josh nodded then flashed Abby a glance that said *Don't worry, I've got this.* 'We're going to see how this summer goes and make a decision one way or the other in the autumn. There are, of course, other options that we could consider ... like adoption, but we need some time together first without the pressure and the hormones and the ups and downs of the whole experience. What we really need is space to think.'

'Of course. You have to do what's best for you.' Jane pushed herself upright. 'Talking of which ... what's best for me right now is to use the toilet.'

'More drinks?' Abby opened the fridge and peered inside it, hoping that the conversation would magically change to a lighter topic by the time she picked another bottle of wine. Just moments ago, she'd been so proud of bringing her friends together and now she was feeling distinctly uncomfortable. Her own loss had been so long ago and yet whenever people spoke about babies and pregnancy, it always resurfaced. It was no longer as painful but seeing her friends suffering made her remember her own pain and the tough decisions she'd had to make at the time.

When Abby placed the fresh bottle of wine on the table, Josh opened it and filled their glasses. 'Do you want us to take the desserts through?'

'That would be great, thank you. I'll bring the bowls and spoons in a minute.'

Alone in the kitchen, Abby took a few deep breaths. It wasn't Jane's fault that she'd had babies so easily and she never meant any harm, but she could be a bit insensitive at times.

'There you are, Abby!' It was Mark, and Abby suppressed a groan. Getting stuck alone with him could be taxing, especially if he'd had a drink. He could be quite boring if he got onto certain topics and he did seem to love the sound of his own voice. But tonight, thankfully, he was sober.

'So how are you, Abby?' Mark filled his glass with Coke from the bottle on the table.

'I'm fine, thanks.'

'Anyone on the horizon?'

'What?'

'You know ... Got a new fella yet?' he said as he waggled his eyebrows.

Abby stared at the spoons in her hand.

'Mark!' Jane shook her head as she waddled back into the kitchen.

'Yes, dear?'

'I told you not to ask that! Sorry, Abby, he lacks tact sometimes.'

Pot, kettle ...

'It's fine. I'm fine but no ... no one on the horizon.' Abby gave a hollow laugh then took the spoons and serviettes through to the lounge where she placed them on the table next to the desserts then sat next to Lisa.

'What's up?' Lisa asked quietly.

'Guess.'

'Someone asked if you're dating?'

Abby nodded. Why did everyone seem so obsessed with her love life?

'Well that was a bit bloody insensitive, wasn't it? I haven't even managed to get you on Tinder yet, have I?' Lisa nudged her to show she was joking.

'It's fine.' Abby waved a hand. 'Mark didn't mean anything by it. He was just asking.'

'Ah ... Mark.' Lisa peered around Abby, but Mark and Jane were still in the kitchen. 'Just asking was he? Innocently? He's always been a bit of a tw ... twit!' She squeezed Abby's hand. 'He should know better at his age.

be looking for someone.'

'No, it doesn't.' Abby nodded, deciding not to comment on the fact that Lisa had only earlier asked her again about setting her up. They all meant well but they didn't know how it felt to be her.

'As I said to you, when you feel up to it, I'll help you find someone suitable to date, but there's no rush. To be honest, I don't think Mark would have meant any harm but he's like all of us ... We never thought Gavin was good enough for you and we would love to see you move on and find happiness. Does that make sense?'

'It does.' Abby looked up as Jane and Mark entered, the latter looking rather sheepish, so she suspected Jane had probably had words with him. 'Oh! I forgot to bring more wine through. Back in a minute.'

She went back to the kitchen and got two more bottles out of the fridge then opened them. She was about to take them to the lounge when something stopped her. She could suddenly feel her mobile burning a hole in her pocket so she pulled it out and swiped the screen. The Facebook app was there, taunting her. All this talk of finding someone new had reminded her of Gavin – not that he was ever really far from her thoughts. She shouldn't look, she knew she shouldn't, but she couldn't help herself. Just a peek ...

App opened, she located the search bar and typed in Gavin's name. She'd unfriended him a few weeks ago but his profile wasn't private, so she knew she could see everything he'd been up to without needing to be his friend. Gavin liked to be seen, even though Abby had tried to warn him about how risky it was having his life exposed for all to see. He'd just laughed at her and she'd known it was his vanity that made him keen to plaster his life everywhere. He liked the attention and Abby suspected that he also liked the idea that he might attract more female admirers that way.

Gavin's profile picture showed at the top of the list. She hadn't looked at it for a while but being here like this, with other couples, made her want to see what he was doing. She'd just take a look and hopefully feel vindicated. Wouldn't she? It would just confirm to her that she'd done the right thing walking out on him ...

But as his full profile flashed up in front of her eyes, her mouth fell open.

Bloody hell ...

She flicked through his photos, one after the other, all twenty of the most recent ones, taken in the past two weeks. There he was, grinning away with that other woman draped all over him. In Abby's house. The house they'd bought together, the house she had loved for so long.

'I can't believe you've done that.' She exhaled shakily. 'You shithead! That's my bloody home and my crockery! How dare she eat off the plates I chose for us?'

She slammed her mobile down on the worktop then grabbed a glass from the cupboard and filled it from a fresh bottle of rosé. She gulped it down, then filled it again, trying to ignore her trembling hands.

Voices and music from the lounge carried through – she knew she didn't want anyone seeing her like this. She needed to digest what Gavin had done first, so she padded out of the front door and crept down the first flight of stairs to the landing where she sat on the top step, nursing her wine. Her stomach churned as the images played like a movie reel in her head as she took some deep calming breaths to try and keep the wine down.

How could Gavin have done that already? Posted it so blatantly for all to see? Had their relationship been so insignificant to him? Had it meant nothing? Nothing at all? Had *she* meant so little to him that he'd set another woman up in their home within weeks of her moving out? Gavin had clearly moved on, been more than keen to do so it seemed, and that thought pierced her heart like an arrow. If there had been a shred of doubt in her mind up to now, it had just turned to dust and been blown away on the breeze.

It was truly over.

There was no going back.

She wiped angrily at the tears trickling down her cheeks. The last thing she wanted to do now was to cry over Gavin. It was such a waste of energy that she could be using more positively …

'Hello, Abby.'

The little boy in his too small grey T-shirt and jeans startled her.

'Oh … hi, Ernie.'

'… Are you sad?'

'Sorry?' She sniffed, then realised that her nose was running, so she dug in her pocket for a tissue, but found it empty.

'Do you need a tissue?'

She nodded.

'I'll get you one.' He disappeared back into his flat then reappeared within seconds, carrying a whole toilet roll.

'We don't have proper tissues, but this is what I use.'

He handed it to her and she placed her wine glass on the step next to her, so she could pull some paper from the roll.

'Thank you.' She handed it back to him then wiped her eyes and blew her nose, aware that Ernie was watching her.

'Is it your birthday?' Ernie asked, pushing his tongue through the gap where his teeth had fallen out.

'No, why?'

He pointed at the ceiling. 'I heard people going up to your flat and one of them said it was a party, so I thought it might be your birthday.'

'Ah … No, I was having … *am* having … a housewarming.'

He frowned at her.

'It's a party to celebrate moving into a new place.'

'Oh, right. Wasn't it any good then?'

'Why do you ask that?'

'Because you're sad.'

She picked up her wine and took a gulp. 'No … no, the party was fine but I was just …'

'Is it the pink wine?'

'The pink wine?'

'Making you sad. My mummy used to drink it and she always got sad when she did.'

Abby watched him, weighing up what he'd said about his mum. He spoke about her in the past tense. Had she died or left?

'No, it's not the wine.' She offered a smile. 'Although it probably doesn't help when I'm feeling a bit … sad already.' She put her glass back on the step. 'I just … uh

'… I found out that someone I used to care about has moved on.'

Ernie jumped onto the bottom step then back off it.

'Moved on how?'

'Uh … Well, he's moved another lady into my old home.'

Ernie's blue eyes widened. 'Was it your husband? Is that why you moved here?'

'Kind of. I moved here before he moved the bit— the other lady into my old house but …' Abby sighed. How could she explain the complicated behaviour of adults to a child? 'It still made me feel kind of sad, I guess.'

'Well, my daddy lives with me but my mummy moved away. When I was five I woke up and she was gone, and … and …' He kicked the step twice then said quietly, 'She didn't come back.'

'I'm sorry.' Abby thought of her own father who'd walked out when she was a baby. At least she'd been too young to know him. Poor Ernie. 'You must miss her.'

Ernie nodded. 'I do sometimes. But my dad is home today and we're having chip shop chips and gravy!' His eyes lit up. 'I love chip shop chips.'

'Mmmm. Me too!'

'Oh …' His face fell.

'What is it?'

'I don't know if there'll be enough for you, too. But you can share mine if you want.'

Abby laughed. 'Of course not! I do like to have chips sometimes but I've had party food so I'm really full. But thank you.'

He nodded, relief showing on his face, and Abby was warmed right through. This little boy, who was clearly very excited about his dinner, would have shared it with her. Goodness knows what his father would have said about that, though.

The door on the ground floor swished closed and she realised that someone had just entered the building. The scent of salt and vinegar rose into the air and Ernie flashed her a grin. 'Dad's back with dinner. Will you be OK now?'

'Yes, I'll be fine. And thank you, Ernie.'

'OK. See you later, Abby!' As he skipped off around the corner, Abby got to her feet, picked up her glass and crept back up to her flat. Even though she was curious about the single father who'd raised such a cute little boy, the last thing she wanted was to be introduced to him now, just after she'd been having a cry over her ex and his new housemate. *Playmate* more like …

Outside her door, she wiped her eyes again, then pulled her shoulders back and gave herself a little shake. She had guests and a whole new life ahead of her, so she was going to enjoy the evening and put all thoughts of her cheating ex from her mind.

CHAPTER 6

Ernie perched on the sofa with his plate of steaming chips and gravy on his lap. Dad usually insisted that they eat at the kitchen table but tonight was a treat so they got to eat in front of the TV. His dad had taken the recliner chair closest to the telly that had a small table next to it where his can of economy lager stood along with the remote.

'Thanks, Dad,' Ernie said then popped a chip into his mouth. As he chewed, the familiar flavour filled his mouth and he smiled. Times like these made him happy. They made him wish that his dad would stay for longer this time. Seeing him at weekends made Ernie look forward to Friday nights but he couldn't help but wish he worked closer to home and was around every evening.

Neil pointed the remote at the television. 'Just in time for kick-off, Ernie!' He flashed his son a smile which Ernie returned. He liked watching football with his dad, but mainly when their team won because when they lost, his dad got cross at the TV.

Ernie chewed another chip, and although he tried to focus on the football, his eyes kept returning to the recliner chair. His dad's hair was quite long now. He used to keep it really short when Ernie was younger; he would

74

take him to the barber with him every other Saturday morning to have his done, too. Ernie had liked those times when they went out together then came home to Mum's shouts of delight at her handsome boys. But now his dad's hair was messy, curling over his collar, and he never shaved his face like he used to. Mum used to shriek with laughter if Dad needed a shave and she'd tell him he'd get no kisses from her while he was all bristly. Even though Ernie had been only five, he still remembered some things like that. He made himself remember the good times because they helped when he was sad.

'What're you grinning about?' his dad asked, shaking his can. 'Dammit! Empty already.'

'I'll get you another! Stay there, Dad.' Ernie put his plate on the sofa next to him then got up and went to the fridge. He pulled a can from the box then closed the door.

Back in the living room, he handed the can to his dad then returned to his chips.

'Dad?'

'Huh?'

'There's a new lady living upstairs.'

'Huh.'

'She's really nice.'

'Is she now?' His dad turned to him. 'Did you make her a new home card?

'No.' Ernie's cheeks warmed but his dad was smiling, so he knew he was teasing. 'I saw her outside in the gard— I mean in the car park, then on the stairs. Her name's Abby.'

'Cool. Well, be nice and polite to her and make sure you don't annoy her. I get enough complaints from that grumpy git downstairs.' His dad tutted.

Ernie nodded solemnly.

'Dad?'

'Yes, son?' This time Neil kept watching the TV and didn't turn to look at him. Ernie pushed a chip through the slick brown gravy on his plate then held it up and took a bite.

'Uh ... In school, my teacher said there's a trip at the end of term.'

'Right.'

'Yeah ...' He finished the chip then paused. His teacher said it would cost fifteen pounds and that they would go to a big playcentre with swings and slides and trampolines, and Ernie really wanted to go, but he felt nervous about asking. Right now, Dad was happy and enjoying his tea and watching football. If Ernie asked him for money, he might get sad like he sometimes did.

'That's nice.' Dad drained his can then scrunched it with one hand and tossed it at the small bin in the corner. It hit the rim then bounced off and droplets of beer splattered over the carpet and the wall. He grunted then jumped up and put the can in the bin before returning to his chips.

'Dad ... Do you think I could go?'

'How much is it?'

'Fifteen pounds.'

His dad sighed then turned to him. 'I'm sorry, Ernie. I wish I could say yes, I really do, but I don't think we can stretch to that this month. Maybe next time?'

Ernie nodded. 'OK. Thanks, Dad.' He swallowed his disappointment, not wanting to make his dad feel bad about being short of cash.

When they'd cleared their plates, Ernie got up and

carried them out to the kitchen then got another beer out of the fridge. He took it back into the living room and gave it to his dad then sat down again. He stared at the screen, watching the men running around on the pitch, their bright shorts and T-shirts making him think of something his friend, Jack, had said about footballers earning lots of money.

'When I grow up I want to be a footballer – then I'll buy us a big house with a garden and a dog and a big fridge full of food.'

His dad laughed at him. 'Last month you wanted to be a vet. Now it's a footballer?' He smiled but his eyes seemed sad and Ernie wondered if he'd made him worry about the trip they couldn't afford. 'Well, see how it goes. Make sure you try out for the school team and get lots of practice.'

'Good idea, Dad.'

'Bloody hell, ref! Are you blind?' His dad jumped out of the recliner and shook his hands at the screen. 'Stupid … idiotic … half-wit!'

As he sat back down, Ernie shuffled on the sofa then shouted, 'Yeah, should've been a red card, you bloody … you prick!'

'Ernie! What did you just say?' His dad's eyes were wide and his mouth had fallen open.

'But that ref … he's a prick.'

'You can't use words like that!'

'Why not?' Ernie stared at his dad, wondering why his face had gone bright red. Was he angry?

'It's … it's rude.' His dad clapped a hand over his mouth but not before Ernie saw his smile. 'Where did you hear that word?'

'In the playground.'

'Well, don't repeat it, lad. OK?'

'OK.' Ernie nodded. 'Why is it a rude word?'

'It just is.' His dad swigged from his can then shook his head while laughing softly. 'Tell you what, Ernie, let's have some ice cream, shall we?'

'Oh yeah! Shall I get it?'

'No, lad, you stay there and I'll fetch it this time.'

'Thanks, Dad!'

When the match finished, Ernie went to his room to get ready for bed. He closed the door behind him then opened his school rucksack and pulled out the letter about the trip. He placed it on his bed and smoothed it out, then ran his finger over the words. He couldn't read them all because they started to dance in front of his eyes, and he had that queasy feeling in his tummy that trying to read always gave him, but he knew what they said because he'd memorised it when the new teacher had read it out in class. It was no good keeping the letter because he knew he wouldn't be able to go, so he folded it over then ripped it into pieces and tucked them into a crisp packet on his chest of drawers.

He'd just tell them that he didn't want to go and it might be a different teacher in next week anyway – they had changed a lot since Mrs Parry had been off – so he'd keep quiet and hope no one asked about it. Like how he kept quiet about the fact that he struggled with reading and spelling. He couldn't bear to say that he couldn't afford the trip. That one time, when one of the teachers had asked if everything was OK at home, he'd been terrified she'd find out Dad was away working, and Ernie would be taken away by the police. Jax had warned him to be careful about what he said to his teacher and he didn't want to be taken away. He loved his dad and just wanted him to be happy. He lay down on his bed and curled his legs up in front of him, hugging them tight.

When he opened his eyes, it was dark in his bedroom – the curtains with the zoo animal print that he'd had since he was a baby were still open. He got up and turned his light on then closed the curtains. He only vaguely remembered lying down and hadn't realised he was tired.

He opened his door and listened. The TV was still on so he went back to the living room. Dad was snoring on the chair, his neck at a funny angle and his mouth open.

Ernie got the crocheted blanket that his mum had made years ago off the sofa and draped it over his dad. Then he turned off the TV, picked up the empty beer can from the floor by the chair and put it in the bin.

He went to the bathroom, brushed his teeth and washed his face, then went back to his room and put his pyjamas on. They were a bit tight now but at least they smelt nice because Jax had washed them with that fabric softener he'd seen on TV. He'd asked her to get some because he liked the advert where the mum washed her baby's clothes then kept sniffing them. He liked the smell too.

Once he'd switched off the light, he climbed into bed and lay there for a bit, listening to his dad's snoring, which was so loud, it even reached his room. He hoped Abby and Mr Mayer couldn't hear it too because his dad would be embarrassed.

But Ernie didn't mind the snoring, because it meant that his dad was nearby, and it made him happy knowing that he'd see him in the morning.

CHAPTER 7

The local library, which had been open for over a hundred years, was such a pretty, old building set within its own peaceful grounds. Abby entered through the large oak doors, and looked around. She loved the peace and quiet of libraries, the shelves full of books with whole worlds waiting to be discovered within the many pages.

Behind the desk to her right, two librarians stood in front of a computer, one of them typing something on a keyboard. In the far corner, the screens of the computers available for the public glowed brightly. Only one was currently in use and that was by a young man wearing a baseball cap and hoodie.

She walked towards the back of the ground floor, savouring the familiar smells of paper and photocopier ink, and trying to step quietly to avoid fracturing the perfect silence. At the end of the floor was a staircase which she climbed, making her way up to the non-fiction section. She didn't know exactly what she was looking for, but she'd woken that morning with a desire to pursue self-improvement and what better way than to develop her knowledge here? Also, ever since she was a child she'd found libraries comforting places to be and after seeing those photos of Gavin on Facebook, she needed some comfort. There was something about the peace and quiet, the books on the shelves and the atmosphere, that offered a sense of security; nothing changed dramatically in a library and it always felt like nothing ever would. Abby knew she could come to the library and sit there with a book, or a notebook and pen, and no one would find that odd. She could fill her brain or empty it, depending upon her mood. Her mother had started taking her to the library when she was little more than a toddler and a lifelong love for the calm book-filled havens had begun. That was another reason why she loved libraries; they made her feel closer to her mother.

When Abby reached the top of the staircase, she turned left and stopped. There, in front of historical non-fiction, was Mr Mayer. It was as if someone had just zapped her with a taser and her whole body stiffened. She released a shaky breath then filled her lungs, trying to get her body back under control.

His head was lowered as he looked at the shelves, his profile clear for Abby to see. She watched as he ran a finger over the books then settled on one and pulled it from the shelf. Abby glanced behind her, but two teenage girls were making their way up the stairs now, so she'd have to squeeze past them if she wanted to retreat. If she went forwards, she would have to pass her unfriendly neighbour, so she stayed where she was. In a form of limbo.

Mr Mayer carried the book unsteadily over to the non-fiction reading corner and sat down at one of the tables. Abby didn't want to just stand there watching him, so she decided to pretend she hadn't seen him and hope that he wouldn't see her in turn. Besides, up to this point in their acquaintance, he'd been nothing but hostile towards her, so it was highly likely that even if he did recognise her, he wouldn't bother to make conversation.

Abby tried to walk casually over to Home and Garden and turned so that her back was to him. She browsed the titles on the shelves, trying to act natural (whatever natural looked like). She ran her eyes over books about self-help, dealing with stress and anxiety, yoga, mindfulness and parenting. Then she reached the shelves with books and magazines about how to decorate, basic DIY and how to create the perfect home. Further along, there were books about gardening and growing your own fruit and vegetables. She had to make a concerted effort to keep her eyes on the books and not to turn round to see if the old man had noticed her.

Abby closed her eyes, deciding to let fate choose her next read, holding out her hand and running it up and down before settling on a hard spine. She pulled it from the shelf and stroked the dust cover, allowing her fingers to feel her next book before she found out what it would be.

'Are you all right?' A familiar voice made her open her eyes and her heart sank. She turned to find Mr Mayer staring at her from behind his thick-rimmed black glasses, his bushy white eyebrows meeting above his nose. Did this man ever do anything other than frown?

'Yes. Why wouldn't I be?'

'You were standing there with your eyes closed. I wondered if you felt unwell or ... something.'

'Oh ... I was just trying to decide what to read.' She attempted a breezy tone but it came out strangled.

'Well I don't know why you're looking at gardening books. You don't have a garden.'

'No, I don't, but that doesn't mean I can't read books about it.'

He pushed his glasses up his nose. 'Seems a bit silly to me. Kind of a waste of time.'

Abby glanced at the book tucked under his arm, counting to ten in her head to avoid snapping at him.

'Well you're reading about Henry VIII's foreign policy. Are you about to wage war against France? Or Spain? Or ...' She took a deep breath. 'The emperor?'

His nostrils flared and his lips twitched, but they soon resumed their usual downward turn.

'I find history fascinating, actually. In fact, last night I watched a documentary on Tudor England and I wanted to find out more.'

'Well, I watched a gardening programme and I wanted to find out more.'

They stared at each other, him in his dark green wax jacket with his flat cap sticking out of the pocket and his stay-pressed grey trousers. Abby tried not to focus on what appeared to be a toothpaste stain on the left side of his jacket. He really didn't look as though he took care of himself and even though he wasn't that close, the smell of cooking clung to him, as though he'd worn the clothes for a long time without washing them.

'What programme was it?' Mr Mayer challenged her.

Abby sighed. 'I can't recall the name now.'

'What channel was it on?'

'Oh, for crying out loud! What are we ... children? Anyone would swear you're actually enjoying this.' She hugged the book she'd pulled off the shelf to her, then turned back to the bookshelf and tugged at another one, causing the books either side to fly off and onto her trainer-clad feet.

'Ow!' She instinctively folded over and squeezed her injured toes.

'That'll teach you.'

She flashed him a glare, but he'd already started walking away, leaving her feeling like she'd somehow lost some kind of battle. Reading about historical foreign policy had clearly given Mr Mayer the edge.

Abby picked up the books to set them back on the shelf, then thought better of it. She'd show him! If she wanted to read books on gardening, then she bloody well would.

But she'd wait for a bit first before going down to the desk and checking them out. Just to avoid having to see Mr Mayer again. He was such a grumpy old fool and he was really starting to get to her. She'd done nothing wrong and yet, he seemed to feel the need to challenge her at every meeting, as if she annoyed him just by existing. Of course, the thought that she was hiding up here – a thirty-six-year-old woman – just to avoid bumping into him again did make her feel a bit ridiculous.

A voice at the back of her mind told her that he was old and probably lonely, but she flicked it away as she would an annoying wasp. Abby had no time in her diary for hostile old men, especially ones who laughed when she dropped three hardback books onto her poor toes.

She'd read some of these books and show him! Abby would become a master gardener, she'd grow herbs and roses and apples and learn how to landscape. But she'd start with the books in her arms, and first she'd read ... she scanned the titles and snorted in spite of her irritation – the very first book she'd pulled out was titled *Constipation: common garden plants with laxative properties.* This might be one for Mr Mayer.

'And did it work?' Lisa nudged Abby as they strolled around the ground floor of Harvey Nichols. The lights were bright, and they bounced off mirrors and surfaces, making Abby wonder how the employees didn't have permanent migraines.

'Did what work?' Abby picked up a lipstick tester and dabbed it onto the back of her hand.

'The natural laxatives ...' Lisa giggled, flashing her slightly wonky front teeth that Abby had always found endearing, and Abby shook her head.

'I have no idea. I took the books home out of sheer stubbornness I guess, but what do I need natural laxatives for?' Abby smiled. 'Although in retrospect, it was quite funny.'

Lisa tucked a stray hair behind her ear with the rest of her dark red bob. As she smoothed it back, the princess-cut diamond set in a white-gold band flashed on her left hand, catching the department store lights.

'Sounds like you should offer that old man some. Perhaps it's constipation making him grumpy.'

'I thought the same.' Abby laughed as she put the tester back and picked up another. 'To be honest, I'm really disappointed that he's so mean. It would've been nice to have friendly neighbours.'

'Well there's the little boy isn't there? What about him and his dad?'

'I haven't even met his dad yet, but yes ... Ernie's

a sweet boy. Although he seems to spend a lot of time alone in the garden.'

'Better than being cooped up on an Xbox or PS3 or whatever it is that the youth of today favour.'

'Ooh look at you sounding all grown-up. Just because you're getting married!'

'I am, aren't I?' Lisa pulled a face. 'Scary!'

'Not at all. It's perfect. You're right though about Ernie and the garden. It is better than being inside all the time. It's just that ...'

'That?' Lisa tilted her head.

'Well the garden's such a mess and after seeing Ernie out there, I wish it was better for him, you know?'

'Don't tell me that you're thinking about tidying up the community garden?'

Abby chewed her bottom lip.

'You are, aren't you?'

'Well, it's a good open space and it could be really nice if someone did something with it. Of course, I wouldn't have a clue where to start but I have wondered what it would be like if it was tidied up and had some flowers and a proper space for Ernie and the other children in the flats to play.'

'I guess it would be a project for you if you decided to tackle it. Just don't take too much on, all right?'

'I won't.'

'Abby ... I haven't had a chance to ask how you're feeling about Gav and his new roomie.' Lisa grimaced. 'Sorry, roomie sounded so much better in my head.'

'It's fine. I guess that's what she is.' Abby pushed her shoulders back then met Lisa's eyes. 'I'm not exactly delighted, I'll be honest.'

'It's a bit bloody quick isn't it?'

Abby nodded. 'When I first saw the photos last weekend, I felt sick – I just wanted to punch things.'

'I would have.'

'No you wouldn't. I have to admit that the thought of smashing my fist into his nose – hers too – did cross my mind but I'm not sure how much better I'd feel afterwards. Probably worse because I'd look like I cared. And I don't want to care … not anymore.'

Lisa stepped closer, hugging her, and Abby closed her eyes.

'I've got you, chick.'

'Thank you.'

When Lisa finally released her, Abby forced her lips into a smile. 'Now come on, let's treat ourselves to something, shall we? I could do with a new lipstick.'

'That's a really good idea.'

Abby held up her hand to show Lisa the tester colours. 'Either one of these suit me?'

Lisa tilted her head. 'I'm not sure. Aren't you supposed to put it on the inside of your arm? Or is it your stomach?' She patted her pale pink blouse where it was tucked into the navy skinny jeans that showed off her rounded thighs and bottom. She towered over Abby today in her pink heels, and Abby couldn't help admiring how beautiful Lisa really was. Her kindness and her warmth, combined with her quiet confidence, made her so magnetic.

'Really?' Abby frowned.

'I read somewhere that the back of your hand doesn't give you a good colour match. It's the wrong skin tone or something like that.'

'Right. Well I'm not putting the tester straight onto my mouth. I don't know who else has tried it.'

'Can I help you with something?'

Abby and Lisa eyed the woman who'd just interrupted them. She looked like she'd walked straight out of a magazine with her poker-straight blonde hair, enormous blue eyes with thick black lashes that extended about five inches from her face and her perfect fuchsia trout pout. Her black outfit complete with white sash told them that she was from the make-up counter.

'Ahhhh …' Abby lowered her hand and slipped it behind her back but Lisa grabbed it and held it out.

'You can indeed.' Lisa waved Abby's hand in front of the woman's face. 'She needs some lipstick and doesn't know what colour suits her best.'

The woman's face changed ever so slightly then, reminding Abby of gentle ripples crossing the surface of a pond. For a moment, she wondered if the woman was, in fact, passing wind, but then she realised she was trying to smile.

'Botox!' she muttered.

The woman's pupils widened but her eyebrows and forehead didn't move at all. 'Excuse me?'

Heat rushed to Abby's cheeks as she realised she'd said it aloud. 'I … uh … I'm considering getting Botox for my friend's wedding.'

The woman tried to smile. 'I would recommend it one hundred per cent. It's magical stuff. Just look at me. You'd never believe I was almost thirty, would you?'

Abby bit the inside of her cheek and glanced at Lisa but her friend was staring at the make-up counter woman in horror.

'Why on earth would you have Botox at your age?'

The woman pouted. 'I absolutely have to look my best in this job or no one will ever buy the products. Besides, I was getting wrinkles here and here ...' She pointed at the corners of her eyes and at the sides of her full lips.

'Of course.' Lisa nodded but the way her nostrils kept flaring told Abby that she was holding back. In the world of design, Lisa had seen her fair share of models afflicted by the drive to find perfection, and she had very strong feelings about it all. 'Anyway ... I'm thinking that my newly single friend here needs a makeover. Not anything too drastic ... but some new make-up would be a nice start for her.'

'What?' Abby stepped backwards, shocked. 'I do not need a makeover.' She had visions of leaving the store looking like the woman in front of them, and as beautiful as she was, she was more waxwork than woman. Abby was quite attached to her crow's feet and the fine lines that had etched themselves either side of her mouth. They might show her age, but they also showed that she had experience of life and in a strange way, she felt that she'd earned them.

Lisa met her eyes. 'It'll be nice for you to have ... uh ... what's your name?'

'Tiffany.'

'OK, it'll be nice if the lovely Tiffany here shows you what make-up suits you.'

Abby eyed Tiffany's orange face and neck – that she suspected had taken at least four coats of creosote – and her perfectly drawn-on eyebrows. 'Really?' she asked Lisa, while signalling with her eyes that it was time to leave.

'Really.' Lisa leant closer to Abby and whispered, 'At

least let her help you choose a lipstick. A treat like a new lipstick, a massage or a choc chip muffin can really help lift your spirits. I know this is only make-up, and it won't change what's happened or make everything magically disappear, but little things like this can build your confidence again.' Then she smiled at the store assistant. 'Come on, Tiffany, show us what you've got.'

Tiffany nodded then hooked her arm through Abby's. 'You're going to look wonderful! Now take a seat and we'll get you a brand-new face.'

'That's what I'm afraid of,' Abby muttered under her breath.

CHAPTER 8

Later, Abby perched on the edge of the leather sofa in the bridal shop as she waited for Lisa to emerge. There were mirrors everywhere, and today, of all days, that was her worst nightmare come true.

The makeover that Tiffany had bestowed upon her meant Abby could barely move her face for fear of it cracking. Her lips were so thickly painted with plumping gloss that she could feel them expanding by the minute and her eyebrows – perfectly decent brown brows, she had thought – were stiff with gel. By the time Tiffany had finished with her, Abby felt certain she could have given some of the teenagers of Manchester a serious run for their money in the eyebrow stakes. Gone were her natural brows and in their place sat two arched slugs that made her forehead ache with their weight.

Of course, Tiffany had gone the whole hog and even styled her hair, *All the better to show off your gorgeous new look!*

So Abby's brown hair had been scraped into a chignon at the back of her head and welded there with hairspray and clips. Any laughter lines she'd had when she'd entered the store were gone, pulled back with the force of her hairstyle and filled in with concealer.

She didn't recognise herself, and had it not been for the fact that she'd been with Lisa, she wouldn't have believed it was her when she entered the bridal shop to be greeted by her reflection.

Prunella, the bridal shop owner, emerged from the changing rooms with a smile on her lovely, normal face. It was the first time Abby had met her, but Lisa knew her well, having designed a plus-sized bridal range exclusively for her. With her voluptuous curves and impressive height, Lisa knew what it was like to be plus-sized and wanted other women to feel good in their clothing, especially in their wedding gowns. Abby loved how Lisa was so confident and comfortable in her own skin, from her shiny red hair to her pale creamy complexion, and she knew Lisa would never succumb to fad diets or exercise regimes to change herself.

Prunella reached Abby then clapped her hands together.

'Oh, you just wait until you see her! She is absolutely stunning. I swear if it was my own daughter getting married, I wouldn't be more emotional than I am right now.' She gave a sniff then pulled a tissue from her sleeve and dabbed at her eyes.

Abby nodded. Although Lisa wasn't getting married until next December, she'd told Abby she wanted to get the dress sorted in plenty of time. Abby knew that some brides had their dresses ready years before the big day and found this curious herself; she wondered what would happen if they changed their minds. Or put on weight. Or lost some. Surely that would cause problems in the whole process.

'Ready?' Lisa's voice came from around the corner that led to the changing rooms.

'Ready and waiting.' Abby sat up straight, wishing she could open both eyes properly but the right one seemed glued shut at the outer edge with mascara. Her belly flipped suddenly, as the reality of the situation dawned on her; Lisa was getting married. She was going to be a bride and Abby was about to see her in her wedding dress. It was surreal, yet wonderful.

'Here I come!'

As Lisa stepped into view, Abby instantly filled up. Her friend looked absolutely stunning, just as Prunella had said. The strapless ivory satin gown clung to her generous curves then fell from her waist like a waterfall. As she moved, the skirt shimmered, revealing layers of petticoats in silver and ivory chiffon. Her hair was lifted from her face with a silver and pearl headband and fresh-water pearls sat in her small ears.

'Lisa ...' Abby squeaked. 'It's gorgeous. You're gorgeous. You look like a Disney princess.'

A designer friend of Lisa's had made the dress for her and Abby knew it had taken several previous fittings to get it to this stage. Lisa had had it delivered to the shop because she didn't want it at home where Fiona might accidentally see it. Prunella was providing the brides-maids' dresses and accessories, so she was happy to keep hold of the wedding dresses too. Fiona was coming for a separate fitting later that month.

'Do you think so?' Lisa smiled, her eyes bright with joy.

'Fiona will fall in love with you all over again.'

Lisa sashayed over to her and hugged her.

'Hey, be careful! You don't want an imprint of my slug brows on your dress, do you?' Abby laughed.

'Dear me, no!' Lisa leant back and met Abby's eyes.

'I knew you'd look amazing but even so, I'm overwhelmed. You're so beautiful, Lisa, and Fiona is very lucky indeed.'

Lisa pulled Abby back into her arms and squeezed her so tight that Abby gasped. 'My eyebrows, remember ...'

'It's fine.' Lisa said against Abby's shoulder. 'I do love you, you know?'

'I know and I love you too.'

They held each other for a few moments longer and Abby's heart soared for her dear friend.

When Lisa released her, she gently cupped her cheeks. 'Thank you so much for coming today. I know ... it must be hard for you but—'

'Why would it be hard for me?'

'Well ... with what you've been through recently. I was afraid to ask, and I've been putting it off but I had to know what you thought. You're my oldest friend and you know me better than anyone and I needed to know if you thought the dress suited me.'

'Oh, it does. It's perfect. And of course, I'd come. I love you and my own ... rather rocky love life would never make me resent yours.'

Lisa's eyes welled with tears and she shook her head.

'Lisa, I'm so happy for you. You know that, right? I'd never want you to think I wasn't or that I in any way resented your happiness.'

'I know.' Lisa sniffed

'But ... I do need you to promise me something.'

'OK.' Lisa looked wary.

'You're not going to want me to have a makeover like this for your wedding, are you?'

'Do you mean ...' Lisa grabbed Abby's shoulders.

'Yes, I guess I do. I'd be honoured to be your maid-of-honour. I'll even make a speech.' Her heart pounded at the thought of getting up in front of a wedding party, but she'd do it for Lisa. Although she'd need a glass or two of champagne to help calm her nerves on the big day.

'Oh, thank you! Thank you! Thank you!' Lisa turned to Prunella. 'Abby's going to be my maid-of-honour!'

'Congratulations!'

'And no ... you don't have to wear a scrap of make up if you don't want to.' Lisa kissed Abby's cheek. 'I promise you that. You're beautiful just the way you are.'

'Thank you. But I will wear some – I don't want to be a frocky horror or anything – just not this much. I can't even feel my lips now.'

Lisa looked directly at Abby's mouth, concerned. 'I think you'd better wipe that stuff off, actually. Looks like you're having some sort of a reaction to it.'

Abby rushed over to the mirror and gasped at her reflection. Her lips looked like they'd been pumped full of air, making her resemble a cartoon character. She opened her bag and got a tissue out then wiped off as much of the lip gloss as she could.

'What am I going to do if it doesn't go down? I'll never be able to go out again! I'll ruin your wedding photos. I'll be one of those women who appears in the gosspip magazines ...' She grimaced; her mouth didn't seem to be doing what she wanted it to and was adding extra letters to some of her words. 'Gosspip. I mean ... gossip magazinesh ... to tell my horror shtory about how I succumbed to vanity and ruined my mouth. God, Lispa,

LOOK at my mouf!' The tingling in her lips was intensifying and she saw panic in the eyes of her reflection.

'It'll go down, don't worry. And the wedding's a long time away yet.' Lisa squeezed her shoulder. 'But ... if the worst should happen ...' A smile played on her perfectly normal lips. 'Then we'll just give you a plate of spaghetti.'

'A plate of shpaghetti?'

'Yes ... because it looks as though you're eating spaghetti with those lips.'

Lisa winked at her in the mirror then flashed her a smile to show she was teasing, and Abby smiled back. At least she thought she was smiling but she couldn't be sure.

Abby waved at Lisa as she drove away then trudged towards Willow Court. She'd had a fabulous day out – bar the makeover – and now she was exhausted. They must have walked for miles around Manchester and her feet were aching, even in her flat brogues. She'd just placed her hand on the communal door when she realised someone was watching her. She turned and found Ernie peering at her from around the side of the building.

'Hello!'

'Hello, Ernie. How are you?' Abby smiled back, relieved that her lips were working again, even if they weren't completely back to normal. She walked back down the steps and approached him.

'I'm OK. I've been working on my den.'

'Have you now? That's nice.'

He walked towards her. 'What have you been doing?'

'I went shopping with my friend. She's getting married in the winter.'

'Who's her husband?'

'Well she's not married yet, so she doesn't have a husband … and she won't have a husband anyway, she'll have a wife.'

Ernie frowned, then nodded. 'Like Josie Greenway in my class. She has two mummies.'

'Some people do.'

He dropped his gaze to his scruffy trainers. 'She's lucky.'

'Pardon?'

'I said she's lucky to have two mummies.'

'She is? And why's that?' Abby smiled.

'Oh … Nothing.' Ernie shook his head then tucked his hands into his jeans pockets.

Abby noticed that his jeans seemed to be about an inch too short on his thin legs and that his arms were covered in goosebumps.

'Shouldn't you have a jumper or a coat on? It's quite cold now with that breeze.'

He shrugged. 'I left it upstairs and couldn't be bothered to go back for it.' He looked at the tote bag on her arm. 'Did you buy anything nice?'

Abby nodded. 'A few small things … Some food and some treats from M&S.'

'Treats?' His eyes lit up.

'Yes.' She opened the M&S bag and peered inside. 'Let's see what we have … Do you like wraps, Ernie?'

'What's a wrap?'

'It's kind of like a sandwich but the bread is thin, and it's wrapped around the filling. Look.' She held out the packet of chicken, sweetcorn and mayo wraps.

Ernie looked at the packet. 'It sounds nice.'

'Would you like them?'

'I shouldn't, they're yours.'

'Do you know what? I already ate two in the car, so if you don't have these, they'll probably go to waste.'

He met her eyes and smiled, poking his tongue through the gap where his teeth should be. 'Thank you, Abby. You're kind.'

She handed him the packet, resisting the urge to give him a hug. 'Well friends should be kind to each other, shouldn't they?'

He nodded. 'Shall we share them then?'

She was about to decline but something told her to stay a bit longer, so she smiled. 'Go on then.'

They walked back to the steps and sat down then Ernie opened the packet and offered it to Abby. She took a wrap out then handed it back to him. She was about to take a bite when something occurred to her, so she slid her warm scarf from her neck and gently wrapped it around Ernie's shoulders.

'You're making me feel cold with those goosebumps on your arms.'

He smiled shyly and pulled the scarf tighter around him.

They ate in companionable silence, gazing out across the concrete slabs that made up the paved area in front of the flats and that led to the car park. When they'd finished, Abby pulled some tissues from her bag and passed one to Ernie. He wiped his hands on it then rubbed it over his mouth.

'Thank you, Abby, that was nice.'

'You're very welcome.'

Abby shivered as the breeze picked up and lifted her

hair. A Coke can rattled across the car park then bumped against the tyre of a red van before rattling away again.

'Right, I'd best get inside and sort something out, but before I go, will you promise me something, Ernie?'

'Yes.' He nodded, his eyes serious as he waited.

'That you'll go and get a jumper or a hoodie.'

'Oh … OK.'

'It's making me feel cold just looking at you shivering and I don't think my scarf is sufficient to keep you warm if you're out here much longer.'

They walked towards the building together and when they reached it, Ernie keyed in the code then braced himself and pulled the heavy door open. When he held it open for her, Abby's throat tightened.

'Thank you, Ernie. That's very sweet of you.'

'S'OK.' His cheeks coloured and he lowered his eyes bashfully then held out her scarf.

They climbed the first flight of stairs together then Abby walked towards the next flight. 'I'll see you soon, Ernie.'

'Abby?'

'Yes?' She turned to face him.

'Did you … did you get stung by a bee?' He peered at her from beneath his brown lashes.

'Stung by a bee?'

'When you were eating ice cream?'

She shook her head. 'No. Why?'

'I did once when I was a baby and my mouth swelled up big like that.'

'Ah.' She nodded. 'I know what you mean now. No, I wasn't stung, I had a reaction to some lipstick and it made my lips swell. I've taken some tablets, so hopefully it'll go down soon.' She touched her lips and winced at how puffy they still felt.

'They said on telly you should go to the doctor if it doesn't go down.' His blue eyes clouded with concern. 'Will you be OK, Abby?'

'Yes, of course I will.'

'Good. Bye, then!' He gave her a wave then ran towards his front door.

Abby chuckled as she watched him go inside. He was a sweet boy and so polite. She liked being around him.

Suddenly realising that she hadn't checked for post, she went back down to the entranceway and dug in her brown leather handbag for her keys.

'Dear me … I think I've seen it all now.'

Abby started at the voice and bit back her retort of *What have I done now?*

Instead, she raised her eyes from her keys.

'Mr Mayer.'

He shook his head.

'Burn your mouth, did you?' He was wearing the same outfit she'd seen him in five days ago at the library and he still had the toothpaste stain on his jumper, but his feet were clad in tartan slippers instead of his shoes.

'Burn my mouth?'

'On a cigarette.' He had his stick in one hand and the other was toying with the hem of his jumper where a thread had come loose.

Abby exhaled slowly as she opened her postbox. Finding it empty, she slammed it shut again before locking it.

'Well, did you?'

She started to count to ten, intending on staying calm,

but a retort sprang from her lips before she could stop it. 'Do you wait for me to come home or something?'

'Pardon?' His eyes widened.

She dug the nails of her empty hand into her palm. 'You weren't out here when I got home so I'm assuming you heard me speaking to Ernie then came out to have a go.'

'Have a go?' He looked shocked. 'I'll have you know I came out here to take my recycling to the bins and when I came back in, you were standing there.'

'Oh.'

'Looking like a clown.'

'A clown?' She shook her head then realised he was referring to her makeover.

He chuckled but it sounded forced. 'Well yes, look at you with those swollen lips. You should see a doctor you know, it could be something nasty.'

'Something nasty!' Abby's rage rose in her throat like bile. He was right, of course, she knew she looked ridiculous but it hadn't even been her decision to get the stupid makeover done in the first place. But he didn't know that and he was being extremely rude. 'I actually had a ... a makeover today in a department store because my friend thought it would cheer me up. I've been so ... down recently after my relationship ended and I found out that my bloody boyfriend was cheating on me! You can stand there and judge me all you like but I've had enough! This is meant to be a fresh start for me ... I needed a new home so I moved in here. It seemed like a nice block of flats and I was hoping ... I was hoping to find some nice neighbours. And I have!' She pointed at the ceiling. 'I found a lovely little boy who has been nothing but nice to me! But I also found *you* and I have tried to be nice to you but all you do is hurl abuse and insults at me as if I've gone out of my way to offend you. And I haven't! I've done my best to be polite and friendly, but you seem to delight in making me sad. Why do you do that? Why?' She exhaled shakily, her heart pounding in her chest. She knew she was in danger of losing control but she couldn't stop herself. 'You seem determined to push me out of this place and do you know what? You win! How's that? I'll look for somewhere else because I can't stand the thought of coming down here every day to find you smirking and grumbling and being such a horrible old man.'

She glared at him as tears stung her eyes and she wiped them away with the back of her hand. My Mayer's lips were opening and closing and his hand holding the stick seemed to wobble.

'I have tried to be pleasant, Mr Mayer. I really have and I'm sorry that my very presence here offends you. I'll start looking for somewhere else to go. I'll need to wait for my lease to run out, but rest assured that I'll be gone as soon as I can. Then you'll be free to go back to living whatever kind of peaceful existence you had before I moved in here with my smoking and my stomping and my big fat lips!' Abby's voice had risen to a shout, making her breathless as she uttered the final words.

Mr Mayer seemed to shrink in front of her, then he nodded and turned away, disappearing into his flat. She heard the key turn in the door and a deadbolt slide across.

Abby gasped as she tried to pull air into her lungs. Her entire body was trembling and queasiness hovered in her gut even though her mouth was bone dry.

Then, as if someone had thrown a bucket of icy water over her, guilt seared through her. How had she lost her temper like that with a poor old man? She'd worked with the elderly for years; she was renowned at Greenfields for her patience with even the grumpiest of residents. Now, she seemed to have changed so much that she barely recognised herself anymore, and it wasn't just because of her recent makeover.

Abby turned and climbed the stairs, her heart heavy and her bones aching as if they'd been pierced with hundreds of rusty nails. She thought she was in control of her life and her behaviour, thought she was at least making some progress and that she was heading in the right direction, but what had just happened suggested otherwise. Abby wasn't winning here; she was losing. Big time. And she couldn't deny that it had something to do with Mr Mayer but a lot more to do with Gavin and his new bloody roomie.

It was time to take stock and think about what was going wrong here. She'd been drifting since she'd moved out of her home and walked away from Gavin, and it clearly wasn't working. It was as if she'd anchored herself to him over the years and their relationship had defined her. She'd altered so much from who she'd been growing up and was nothing at all like the woman she'd thought she'd be.

Abby needed a focus, something to pour her energies into that would have a positive impact on her. She'd always been a kind person, she prided herself on that and on her ability to see the best in a bad situation, even when she'd lived in Gavin's bulky shadow. Something had changed, and Abby knew it wasn't for the better, but she didn't know how she was going to make it right again. Where did she go from here?

CHAPTER 9

Abby rubbed her hair with a towel as she walked through the flat. She'd used cleanser on her skin then scrubbed her face to get rid of all the foundation from the makeover, but even after all that, she still had shadows around her eyebrows from the black gel and her lips were fuller than usual, although at least the pain had subsided. She felt clean on the outside, if not cleansed emotionally. That was going to take more than a hot shower.

She was still smarting after her run-in with Mr Mayer and her rant kept replaying in her head like a scene from a horror movie. How could she have lost control like that in front of someone she barely knew? Yes, he had been rude and mocked her but she'd completely lost her temper and said a load of things to him that should, really, have been directed at Gavin. After all, he was the one who'd cheated on her and destroyed her life as she knew it.

She could go down and try to apologise to him but she suspected that he probably wouldn't be interested. He'd locked his door with the deadbolt and she doubted he'd open it again if he knew it was her. No, that ship had sailed, and she'd be best looking for a new flat and moving on as soon as she could. Although, she was sad at the thought of saying goodbye to Ernie.

In fact, there was no time like the present to start searching for somewhere to live. At least by moving out, she'd do something the old man would approve of. Her final act of kindness or something like that . . .

She hung the towel over the back of a chair, walked through to the lounge then sank onto the sofa with her laptop, her feet tucked underneath her. She turned the computer on and as she waited for it to come to life, she tried to summon some hope. She was taking control now and doing something positive. She had to give herself a pat on the back for that, even if she had embarrassed herself by letting rip on Mr Mayer.

When her frequently visited websites showed on the screen, her finger automatically hovered over the Facebook symbol. It would be so easy to log in then contact Gavin, to ask the questions that burned inside her and find out why he had moved a new woman into their home so quickly. But she had a feeling that knowing the answers wouldn't make her feel any better, so she moved her finger away and clicked on the search engine instead.

However, after an hour of searching for flats, she was left feeling even more disheartened. There was nothing suitable out there and everything she could afford looked dreadful. She did know, though, that new properties came up all the time, and she'd signed up to several property websites for email alerts that matched her search criteria.

She closed her eyes, took a few deep breaths then opened them and looked around her lounge. It felt homely now with her belongings in just the right places for her. She'd created a space where she felt safe, where she could relax, and leaving it would be a real shame.

Her eyes fell on the library books she'd borrowed – she read the titles again, smiling at the constipation one, then something pinged in her brain like a microwave timer. She typed *gardening* into the search engine.

She scanned the results and clicked on a few before landing on a gardening blog. The front page had lots of pretty and colourful images that made something inside her lift, like her spirits always did as she walked through a park on a summer's day.

She clicked on the most recent post and started to read.

Abby shifted on the sofa, realising how thirsty she was. As she looked at the clock on her laptop, she discovered that almost three hours had passed since she'd started reading the blog. It was fascinating. She'd been particularly drawn to the blog's ideas about taking a small plot of land – any land, anywhere – and turning it into a place where things could grow. There were sections on how to improve the quality of the soil, how to create the right environments for different kinds of crops and how to turn the fruits of your labour into jams, pickles and more. There were also posts about the health benefits associated with gardening and how it could not only make you fitter physically but also emotionally, mentally. The physical exercise of gardening could help you avoid, or at least manage, certain medical conditions and working around green things and watching them grow was apparently good for your mental health. It sounded too good to be true.

The blogger, Jason Armstrong, had written a bit about himself in the 'About Me' section of the blog. He said that he'd suffered a family bereavement and found gardening and reconnecting with nature therapeutic. He hadn't said who he'd lost though and Abby wondered who it was. Had it been his mother or father, one of his siblings perhaps? Possibly even a partner. He was also Manchester based, although he didn't give specifics about his location – which was very sensible, of course. There was a small photo below the text of a group of people in dark green T-shirts with their arms around one another's shoulders. They were grinning at the camera and from their faces, it was clear that their smiles were not just superficial. What wasn't clear was which one of them was Jason; Abby wondered how old he was as the men on the photo looked like they ranged from late teens to seventies.

There was no denying that Abby felt lighter somehow, as if stumbling across this blog had offered her a reprieve from worrying about moving and about Mr Mayer, from the pain over Gavin's betrayal and the huge dent it had placed in her already fragile self-confidence. She bookmarked the blog then placed her laptop on the sofa next to her and closed the lid.

She needed a drink before she turned into a dried-out husk, so she went through to the kitchen and filled a glass with tap water and glugged it down.

According to Jason Armstrong, there was potential in any patch of earth if the will to turn it into something better existed. Plants needed water and they certainly had plenty of that with the grey English skies. She also knew where there was a plot of land badly in need of developing. It would mean a complete overhaul and a dramatic transformation – but for the first time in a long while, Abby felt a flutter of excitement.

She had time and energy to burn and she needed a

project, something to focus on. Of course, she'd decided she'd move out but that couldn't happen for at least five months, so in the meantime, she could work on the garden out back. She didn't think anyone would mind; it didn't exactly look as though anyone cared what happened to the garden. She'd be doing her neighbours a favour if she turned it into something better, wouldn't she? And, as a resident herself, she had just as much right as everyone else to use it. She could imagine the garden with neat beds full of flowers and Ernie running about down there without having to worry about stepping on dog poo or broken glass. Other children from the flats would go out there to play too and it could become a place for the residents of Willow Court to gather and relax.

She went to the fridge and got out the half-bottle of wine that she had left over, grabbed a glass from the cupboard then went through to the lounge. Back on the sofa, she filled her glass and sipped the cold fruity rosé. There'd be no crying over pink wine this evening; Abby had an idea germinating and she finally felt hopeful. She had the seedlings of a plan and something to build upon. At last.

Just to make sure that she didn't change her mind in the morning, she decided that she'd email Jason and ask to meet him, seeing as how he was from Manchester, just to find out a bit more about what he did and how, and to check if it really was doable. The thought of emailing a complete stranger and asking to meet him filled her with nervous excitement because it wasn't something she'd normally do and it was certainly something Gavin would have disapproved of, but that also made her feel empowered. She was rebelling against the Abby she'd become, the Abby that Gavin had wanted her to be, and was acting more like the Abby her mother had raised. Her mother had been such a feminist, often letting Abby know that she disapproved of how Abby had changed to accommodate Gavin's wants and needs. It had made Abby smart – her mother's blunt expressions of concern at how Abby seemed diminished by her relationship – but she'd swallowed her arguments to the contrary as her mother's health declined, not wanting to upset her. Instead, she'd gently tried to reassure her by telling her that Gavin was a good partner and that she loved him, which she'd believed – or wanted to believe at any rate – was true at the time.

Email sent, she sat back and enjoyed the rest of her glass of wine. Warmth filled her as she pictured how the garden on Holly Street could be transformed. Little Ernie could help and she could find out more about him. What he'd said about his mum made her worry for him and he'd seemed so sad when he'd mentioned his friend who had two mums and how lucky he thought they were. Ernie looked like he'd benefit from having some fresh homegrown fruit and veg and she already knew that he liked being out in the garden.

She picked up the bottle of wine and was about to refill her glass when someone knocked on her door. She checked her mobile. It was almost ten thirty on a Friday night. Who would visit her at this time? She hoped it wasn't Ernie's dad come to complain because she'd given him that chicken wrap.

She put the bottle and glass on the coffee table then headed for the front door.

'Hello?' She stood to the side of the door and listened. 'Who's there?'

'It's me.'

Her stomach dropped to the floor. It couldn't be. Why would it be?

'Who?' she asked, trying to buy some time and needing to hear the voice again just to be sure. She ran her hands through her hair and blew into her palm, wondering if she had time to brush her teeth.

'Me.' Throat clearing. 'Let me in, Abby. Please.'

'Why should I?'

A pause. 'I need to talk to you.'

She placed her hand on the lock but didn't turn it. The resolve she'd felt just moments ago to turn her life around now teetered like a house of cards that could collapse around her if she opened the door. But if she didn't open it, she would never know what this was about. Sometimes not knowing was far, far worse.

'OK. But I'm warning you ... I'm not in the mood for any of your nonsense.'

She turned the latch then pulled the door open.

And what she saw there, made her jaw drop.

'Gavin ... What's happened?'

She stared at his dishevelled appearance, so different from the grinning Lothario he'd seemed to be on the Facebook photos. Concern for him, which she couldn't control, filled her at the sight of him, even after all that he'd done to hurt her.

She stiffened as he stepped forwards and took hold of her shoulders.

'Abby ... Abby, it's all gone terribly wrong.' His voice was so quiet it sounded as if it was coming from far away.

'What do you mean?' She struggled to swallow because her mouth was so dry.

' ... I have some news, and I have no idea what I'm going to do about it.'

'What news?'

'It's Belinda.'

'Who's Belinda?'

'My girl— I mean ...'

'The woman you've moved into our home?'

'Yes. You see ... Belinda ... She's ... She's pregnant.'

PART TWO

Budding Begins

CHAPTER 10

A bby stared at Gavin, wondering how it had come about that he was standing at her front door at gone ten thirty on a Friday night.

'Belinda is what?'

'I said ... she's pregnant.'

'I thought you did.'

'Abby, I need to come in. Please?'

'Abby glanced behind her as if searching for inspiration, but this was really up to her. Part of her didn't want to let him in; this was her space, her Gavin-free sanctuary and she was worried that allowing him to enter would taint her new home. But another quick assessment of his haggard – yet familiar – face and the desperation in his eyes pushed the worries aside. 'I guess so. Come in.'

She stepped back, then watched as he walked into the hallway, his head turning from side to side as he looked around. Gavin's tall, muscular frame in her new flat was something she'd never thought she'd see; something she hadn't wanted to see if she was honest, and he was as incongruous there in that moment as a snowman would have been. But at least a snowman would have melted, then she could have cleaned it up with a mop and bucket and carried on. She had a feeling that Gavin's presence would not be so easy to eradicate.

'Do you want a drink?'

He turned and nodded. 'Please.'

'I have wine, or there might be a beer in the fridge left over from ...' She bit her lip. It seemed wrong to tell him about the flat-warming party. But why? 'From when I had some people round.' She raised her chin. She wouldn't apologise for having a new life now, a life where she had parties and entertained without Gavin. Not that Gavin had ever wanted to entertain anyway.

'Beer would be great.' His lips turned up slightly at the corners then quickly returned to a thin line.

'OK ... uh ... Go on through to the lounge and I'll be there in a moment.'

Abby hurried along the hallway to her bedroom, shut the door behind her and leant against it. She was wearing her pyjamas – Gavin clearly wanted a serious conversation and it wasn't exactly attire she'd be comfortable having one in – so she changed into a pair of jeans and a black V-neck top. She stood in front of the mirror, ran a brush through her hair. Casual but not scruffy. She hoped it said: *Yes, I'm dressed and look good but I'm not making an effort for you.* She placed her brush back on the dressing table then applied a slick of pink lip gloss to her slightly fuller than usual lips – a result of the lip plumper incident from earlier that day.

Well, it would have to do and it wasn't as if she wanted Gavin to fancy her, was it? She just wanted to look good so he'd realise what he'd given up.

No! She didn't care what he thought.

Well ... just a bit. It wouldn't hurt her confidence if

he thought she looked good. Especially in light of the fact that he'd moved on so quickly with *big boobs Belinda*.

Now she was being petty.

But a baby! He was having a baby with that woman ...

She shook her head at her reflection, took a deep breath then opened the bedroom door.

OK. She could do this. She really could.

Couldn't she?

In the lounge, Abby was surprised to see Gavin settled on her sofa – one arm over the back – with his long denim-clad legs spread out in a fashion that suggested he'd made himself at home. His light grey T-shirt was stretched over his broad shoulders, showing off his toned abs and slim hips, emphasised by his low-slung jeans. Even though he didn't look his usual polished self, he still looked good. With that physique, it would be hard not to. Irritation bubbled in the pit of Abby's stomach and she bit the inside of her cheek for a moment to steady herself.

'Here.' She held out the beer she'd grabbed from the fridge.

'Thanks.'

She eyed the spot next to Gavin on the sofa but decided to take the chair instead. Before she sat down, she picked up her wine glass, clutching it in front of her as if it could protect her.

'So ...' She gave him the floor.

'Oh, Abby.' He released a long sigh. 'How did we get here?'

As he sipped his beer, Abby dug the nails of her free hand into her palm. How could he even ask that? She was assuming the question was rhetorical, because if it wasn't, what did he want? A rendition of 'Cry Me a River' by Justin Timberlake? She could do that ... Ah, Justin. Hot, caring, devoted husband and father. So unlike Gavin.

'Abby?'

'Yes?'

'You were staring into space.'

'Was I? Sorry.'

Not sorry. Not at all.

'I asked how we got here.'

'I thought it was rhetorical.'

'It was what?'

She sighed inwardly. 'Never mind, Gav. I don't mean to be rude but ... what are you doing here?'

'I needed to see you. To talk to you.' He lowered his eyes to his beer bottle and ran his long fingers over the condensation, moving them up and down. The motion was hypnotic, transporting Abby back to happier times when they'd sat like this, times when they'd fallen into bed, laughing and kissing, surrendering to their feelings for each other. Times before their relationship turned sour, before she saw Gavin for who he really was and before he hurt her. A long time ago. She had moved on and that was a good thing, so why didn't it feel good right now?

'I miss you, Abby.' The last words were barely audible, so quiet that Abby wondered if she'd imagined them, heard what her subconscious wanted to hear.

'No. This can't happen. Tell me what you said when you first arrived.'

He shuffled forwards on the sofa, as if trying to bridge the gap between them. Abby moved further back into her chair and crossed her legs.

'I don't ... I don't know how to explain. I want to be honest but I also want to just enjoy being here with you.'

'Gav, don't be ridiculous. You told me your girl— your ... *whatever*, Belinda is ... that she's pregnant. Is it yours?'

He met her gaze and his eyes widened a fraction. She saw him seize on the opportunity for freedom and his tone changed when he replied, suggesting a sense of relief. 'You know ... It might not be. I'm not entirely sure it is, to be honest. It could well be someone else's.'

'Gavin, if it's your baby you have to accept responsibility for it. Did you get Belinda pregnant?' She delivered the question curtly.

He shrugged, causing the irritation that had started in her belly to rise to her chest.

'I don't know. I might have.'

'Did you have sex without using protection?'

He nodded.

'You knobhead.'

And he was! A complete and utter knobhead. Why the bloody hell had he come here? It wasn't what she needed and it was so unfair. Her eyes stung with tears, brought on by anger and sadness, but she refused to allow them to fall.

'I know, Abby. I've made such a mess of things.'

Abby took a large slug of wine and braced herself. It was going to be a long night.

Drinks refreshed and the urge to go outside for a smoke suppressed – just – Abby returned to the lounge. Gavin looked up from his mobile and smiled pleasantly at her, as if he was here for a social visit and not to ruin the world she had built for herself. He tucked his mobile into his pocket then patted the sofa next to him.

'Come sit here, Abs.'

She looked at the space he'd patted, then at the chair. One was safe and sensible, the other an emotional and physical time bomb.

'I don't think I—'

'Please, Abby. You're so far away on the chair and this is so difficult. We're friends, aren't we?'

'We were. At least I thought we'd be able to be civil, until you moved Belinda into our house before I'd even closed the garden gate behind me.'

He shook his head. 'You'll always be my friend. I can't bear to think of you not being in my life anymore.'

'You ... can't ...' She ground her teeth together. It had always been about him, and still was by the sound of it. And yet ... She had missed him in some ways. Not many, granted, because he had been a total idiot, but she'd been with him for such a long time and it had been strange not seeing him every day, not hearing him around the house, knowing that she wouldn't hear his key in the lock as the evening wore on. Was it normal to miss someone like this? Was it wrong?

She passed him a fresh bottle of beer then lowered herself onto the sofa, taking care not to spill her wine. The alcohol probably wasn't a good idea – it was likely to lower her inhibitions – but then Gav only wanted to talk, didn't he? It's not like he'd want anything else from her, not when he had Belinda.

She slid backwards on the seat then tucked her legs up under her.

'What are you going to do about it then?'

'About the baby?'

'Of course about the baby. Unless there's another issue you haven't told me about?'

He swigged from his beer bottle and she gazed at the familiar contours of his face – at the way his right eye twitched slightly while he weighed something up, at how his Adam's apple bobbed as he swallowed. He was so familiar, as familiar to her as her own reflection. And this close, she could smell his cologne – the one she'd bought him last Christmas if she was correct – a heady, woody, floral scent that improved as it warmed on his skin.

'I have no idea. I'm … terrified … quite frankly. This was never part of the plan.'

'The plan? You mean cheating on me was planned?'

'No! No, of course not, Abs. I never meant to hurt you.'

'But you did, Gav. Badly.'

He stared down at his hands where they picked at the label on the beer bottle. She noticed that he'd bitten his nails down to the quick, a bad habit he'd had when he was younger but had managed to break. Clearly, if he was biting them again, to the point where they bled, he was going through turmoil. In spite of her resolve to stay strong, a wave of pity and compassion washed over her.

'If I could turn back time, Abs, I would.'

He looked up and the blue of his eyes was like a Caribbean lagoon. This close she could see the flecks of gold that made them appear to glow from within. His black hair was short around the sides and longer on top, reminding her of the Shelby brothers in *Peaky Blinders*. His beard was short, just longer than stubble, and she knew that if she ran her hands over it, it would tickle her palms.

'No one can turn back time, Gav. Even if we could, something obviously wasn't right or you'd never have cheated.'

'I so badly wish I hadn't. You finding that text message like you did ... It was dead awful. I'm so sorry.'

She inclined her head to acknowledge his apology, although she didn't know if she could ever fully accept it. 'Where's Belinda now?'

'She went to her mother's tonight in a bit of a strop. Said she'd give me some space to digest the news, because I wasn't exactly jumping for joy, but I couldn't sit there alone. I thought about the gym but I'd already been today and it didn't burn off enough steam. I knew seeing you would help.' He smiled hopefully at her.

Abby sipped her wine and battled with the emotions swirling around inside her. This was more difficult than she'd imagined it could be. She was angry with him, of course she was, but she also wished everything could just go back to how it was. Not at the end, because she knew they weren't happy then, but back to when everything seemed rosy and she had believed he loved her.

'I don't want a baby now, I'm not ready for it. Thing is, Abs, that after the m— the miscarriage ... I decided I didn't want to go through that again. It was just too painful.'

His words tugged at Abby's heart but this was about the here and now and not about what might have been. Gavin had to accept responsibility for this, however sad he felt about the child they'd lost. 'Well you'd better get ready quickly because you've got what – nine months, or less?'

'About seven.'

'Seven?' That meant that Belinda was already about two months along. She'd had two months of a little baby growing in her womb, safely tucked away, warm and secure. Gavin's baby. Abby's stomach rolled.

'I know. I don't think I can do it.'

'I don't think you have a choice.'

He leant his head back on the sofa cushion and somehow moved closer to her at the same time, then he lifted his hand and gently stroked her cheek before resting his hand along the sofa behind her.

'What should I do, cuddle muffin?' His voice softened as he said the final two words.

Abby started at his old pet name for her. She hadn't heard it in what felt like an age and his goofy smile made her cringe.

'Don't call me that, for starters.'

He slid his hand down from the back of the sofa to her shoulder and its heat seared through her top, its strength and weight solid as he rested it there.

'But you *were* my cuddle muffin. My Abby-muffin-top,' he said, still smiling.

She winced. He'd often teased her about her muffin top – she'd tried to laugh it off but she didn't have to take it now.

'Don't call me that either, Gav. You don't have the right,' she snapped.

She shrugged off his hand and sat up straight.

'Sorry. I just want to be close to you.'

He reached out again and ran his hand up and down her spine – the caress instantly relaxed her, weakened her. He sensed it and increased the pressure of his touch. Abby turned and found him right beside her, his face so close she could feel his breath on her cheek. It would be so easy to surrender to habit, to give in to her rising desire to be held and comforted, to just be with Gavin, the man she knew so well.

He moved even closer, the hypnotic rubbing on her back making her whole body tingle, and suddenly his lips found hers, his strong arm pulled her towards him, his tongue found its way into her mouth and ...*What was she doing?* She squealed and jumped up.

'My wine!' She looked down at the damp patch that was spreading on her legs like some kind of Rorschach inkblot.

'Ooops!' Gav stood up too. 'Better get those off you immediately.'

'No, Gavin! Get off me! This is wrong. All wrong. What we had can't ever be saved now. You shouldn't have done that. I'm glad I spilled my wine.' Hot shame crawled over her. She was ashamed that she'd kissed him, ashamed that she'd let him touch her and ashamed that she hadn't been stronger. It had just been such a long time since she'd had human contact, since someone had kissed her and touched her like that, and in the moment she'd wanted it. But she knew that she'd have regretted it wholeheartedly if she'd gone ahead with it. Sex with Gavin would do nothing other than confuse matters. Besides which, he hadn't come here for that, had he? He'd come because he needed to talk, because he was confused. Being together after so much time apart had made them crave temporary relief from the sadness and sense of loss caused by their break-up. But it would have been a huge mistake. Not only had Gavin hurt and betrayed her, but their relationship hadn't been working;

Abby hadn't been happy for a long time. And now Gavin was going to be a father. To a child he'd conceived with another woman. There was no going back.

'I'm so sorry.'

He slumped on the sofa, buried his face in his hands and started to cry.

CHAPTER II

E rnie was bored. It was Saturday morning and his dad should be home but he'd rung last night to say that he had to work late and into the next morning. Jax had stayed overnight but she had work at the supermarket today, so she'd left Ernie with the usual sandwich in the fridge and two cans of fizzy drink. She'd told him to stay indoors and watch TV because of the rain, but since Sky had been cut off, they only had a few channels and Ernie didn't feel like watching Saturday morning cookery shows or news updates. He'd tried playing zombies but it wasn't the same inside, and he would've played bin basketball but he couldn't find the ball.

He turned the TV off and wandered into the kitchen. Rain blurred the window that looked out towards the road. It really was awful outside but Ernie hated being stuck indoors.

His dad had said he'd be back after lunch. Ernie peered up at the clock above the fridge but the lines and crosses on it made no sense to him at all, and even if he'd known what they meant, they all just seemed to move around the more he looked at them.

He thought about what his mum used to do when his dad was expected home, or when they were having visitors. She used to clean. She'd turn the radio on, grab the feather duster from the cupboard in the hallway then dance around the flat, usually with Ernie right behind her. Sometimes, his mum would pretend he was all dusty and tickle him with the feather duster until he sneezed and cracked up laughing. Then they'd have a break for biscuits and hot chocolate, and his mum would cuddle him on the sofa. His chest tightened suddenly and the small kitchen seemed to shrink, so he shook his head and pushed all thoughts of his mum from his mind.

Ernie knew what he could do. He was quite grown-up now so he would make the flat nice and clean for when Dad came home. Dad would be so proud of him and so happy, too.

He went to the cupboard in the hallway and opened the door. Instantly he was hit by a waft of smelly trainers and the stale vanilla car air freshener that his dad had hung in there last summer to try to mask the unpleasant odours. He reached for the light switch and flicked it on but nothing happened. Ernie peered into the gloom and spotted the feather duster. It was hanging from a hook above the vacuum cleaner that had sat there, gathering dust, since they'd had the carpets replaced with pretend wood floors. Dad had said it would be easier to keep clean.

Ernie stood up onto his tiptoes and flicked the feather duster off the hook, then stepped back into the hallway and took a deep gulp of clean air. The cupboard needed a good sort-out but he couldn't do it if he couldn't see inside it. He'd do the dusting instead.

As he walked into the lounge, he absent-mindedly ran the feather duster over his cheeks and forehead, remembering happier times. Times that had stopped, and he had no idea why. He wondered how Mum was keeping her new place clean without her feather duster.

In the lounge, he dusted the TV, the cabinet, Dad's recliner chair and the back of the sofa. He went to the window and dusted the sill, the pile of envelopes with their red stamps, and the coffee table. He was a lot faster than he'd thought he would be and he still had hours left before lunch. Looking up, he saw that the bare bulb had a long cobweb hanging from it that stretched across to the corner above the door. It reminded him of the long chain that Jax wore from her belt to her pocket with her keys at the end. That had to go – he hated spiders.

But he couldn't reach it from the floor.

He'd get a chair from the kitchen and stand on that.

Ernie dragged the kitchen chair into the lounge then set it under the light bulb. He climbed onto it and raised the feather duster, but he still couldn't quite reach, so he pushed up onto his toes and flicked the feather duster at the cobweb.

Almost ...

He leant forwards and did it again, catching the end of the cobweb and sending it sailing through the air to the doorway, but as it went, the chair wobbled under him and he lost his balance. Ernie found himself soaring through the air, his arms flailing as the feather duster slid from his grasp.

Three things then happened all at once: the feather duster landed on the sofa, the chair clattered onto its side on the fake wooden floor and Ernie landed with a thud next to it.

As salty blood filled his mouth, and pain seared

through him, he released a quiet moan. Ernie started to cry, wishing terribly that his dad would come home.

Arthur glared at the ceiling. *What the blazes was that?* It was just gone nine on a Saturday morning and already that little lad was up to no good.

He had no intention of putting up with a Saturday filled with disruptions – he had to go upstairs and have a word with the girl who babysat. Or Neil, if he was home. But Arthur usually heard his upstairs neighbour arriving home on Friday evenings and couldn't recall hearing him last night. Not that he listened out for Neil, of course, he wasn't an eavesdropper.

Still, whether Neil was there or not, Arthur needed to have a word about the noise.

He grabbed his walking stick and ambled towards the door. White-hot pain seared through his hip as he climbed the stairs, and with each step he gritted his teeth together before taking the next one. He could do this; pain wouldn't stop him having a peaceful weekend.

When he finally reached the floor above, he paused to catch his breath. Old age was no fun at all and he hated how reliant he'd become on his stick and how his body was preventing him from doing the things he used to be able to do. When he was a young man, he'd been strong and fit; Julia had loved his muscular arms and toned stomach. He hadn't been big like some of those vulgar lads he saw around Manchester now with their skimpy vest tops and bulging biceps, but he had been toned and strong. He'd been able to scoop Julia into his arms as if she was made of feathers, and many times he'd do it just to make her giggle in that adorable way she had, before begging him to put her down. As a gentleman, he'd done as she'd asked, of course, but not before giving her a big kiss and telling her he loved her. Arthur had declared his feelings to his wife every day of their marriage, and he was glad of that now; Julia had always known that she was his number one. His one and only.

He suddenly remembered that he was standing in front of Neil's front door for a reason, so he shook himself and Julia drifted from his thoughts like smoke on the breeze. He regathered the anger he'd felt downstairs and knocked hard on the door.

No one came to answer it, so he knocked again, this time with his stick. Three hard raps.

Nothing.

So he tried again.

He paused as he heard a noise coming from inside. It reminded him of a wounded animal, an unmistakable cry of pain. Something in Arthur shifted and he looked around him. He needed to get into the flat – something was very wrong.

There was a pot to the side of the door with a plastic plant in it. Arthur suspected it was meant to look like a bay tree, but it was a cheap replica, the type of thing Julia loathed. He nudged the pot with his stick and it moved easily, revealing a silver key.

'How utterly irresponsible.' He shook his head then used his stick to pull the key towards him. He bent over very slowly, using his stick to support himself, and managed to grab the key.

When he was upright again, puffing from the exertion, he looked at the key in his palm. Arthur was nervous this would look like breaking and entering but he wasn't sure he had a choice. Another cry from inside made the decision for him and he slid the key into the lock, turned it then pushed the door open.

'Hello?' he called into the hallway that smelt of chips and damp, with a hint of fake vanilla lacing the air. 'Are you all right?'

He listened carefully and sure enough, he could hear sniffing coming from the lounge. He made his way to the room and gasped when he saw the little boy lying on the floor.

Arthur gasped in horror. 'Ernie?'

The small boy raised his head and Arthur winced. There was a bruise on Ernie's cheek, his nose was bleeding and his eyes were red and puffy. Next to him, there was a chair on its side with a broken leg.

'What happened? Where's your father? Do you need an ambulance?'

As he asked the questions, not waiting for answers, Arthur hobbled over to Ernie and held out a hand.

'Can you stand?'

Ernie nodded, then took Arthur's hand and stood up on shaky legs. He was quivering all over and Arthur was filled with concern.

'Sit on the sofa, lad.'

He helped Ernie to sit, then he lowered himself next to him.

'Ernie, I need to know right now if you need to go to the hospital. Do you think you've broken anything?'

Ernie raised a shaky hand. 'The ...' He sniffed. 'The chair. I broke the chair.'

'I can see that, lad, but it's not the chair I'm concerned about. Have you hurt yourself?'

Arthur peered at Ernie. The bruise on his cheek was darkening but his nose didn't appear to be bleeding now.

'My ... my cheek and my tongue hurt.' Ernie poked out his tongue and Arthur could see that the end was bloody, but it didn't look too bad.

'What about the rest of you? Did you bang your head?'

'I don't think so. My elbow is sore too but I can still move it.'

Ernie demonstrated how he could swing his arm back and forth, and Arthur nodded.

'And I can do this.' Ernie stood up then bent over and touched his toes.

'Good, good. Watch you don't hurt yourself again. Come on now, sit back down, lad. And how sore is that cheek?'

'Pardon?' Ernie sat back on the sofa with a bounce that made Arthur wince with the pain in his hip. He pulled in a breath through gritted teeth.

'On a scale of one to ten, with ten being very bad pain and one being no pain at all, how much does your cheek hurt?'

Ernie raised his hand and touched the bruise then winced. 'It's a ... a six. No, a seven.'

'OK. Well we'll need to see how it goes over the next half-hour and if it doesn't stop aching you will need to go to the hospital.'

Ernie's eyes filled with fresh tears. 'I can't! My dad is coming home and I'll miss him. I can't leave the flat.'

'Where is your dad, Ernie?'

Ernie's mouth fell open. 'Jax is looking after me.'

'Really?' Arthur made an elaborate show of looking around the room. 'I can't see her anywhere.'

'She … she's gone out for a bit.'

'Where?'

'I can't say.'

'OK …' Arthur sighed. The boy was clearly in no state to be cross-examined and Arthur didn't want to add to his distress. He just wanted to make sure that he was all right and then get on with his Saturday.

'Ernie … I need to go back down to my flat but I can't leave you here alone.'

Ernie made to protest so Arthur raised a hand.

'No arguments, I'm afraid. You either come with me or I'm phoning for an ambulance. I can't leave you here injured, and with my dodgy hip I can't keep walking up and down the stairs to check on you. I've some bacon open on the counter and I need to go and grill some for breakfast. I don't suppose you like bacon do you?'

Ernie nodded. 'And I like sausages.'

'Sausages, eh? And eggs?'

Ernie nodded.

'Knock, knock!'

'Sorry?' Ernie's mouth fell open.

'It's a joke. I say "knock, knock" and you ask who's there.'

'OK.' Ernie's eye narrowed in concentration.

'Knock, knock!'

'Who's there?'

'Egg roll and sausage.'

'Egg roll and sausage who?'

'Egg rolled off the table and I never sausage a mess.'

Ernie pursed his lips and frowned, evidently not getting the joke.

'I never *saw such* ... saus-age ... a mess.' Arthur waited, then smiled as understanding broke out on Ernie's face.

'Sausage a mess!' He giggled. 'You're funny, Mr Mayer.'

'You can have great fun with words, lad.'

Ernie's cheeks darkened as if he was embarrassed but then, Arthur thought, it could be the shock of his fall.

'Have you had breakfast?'

'Jax made me cornflakes.'

'That's not enough for a growing lad like you. Come and help me make a fry-up.'

The boy's eyes widened.

'Sound like a good plan? We can listen out for your dad and let him know where you are when he gets back.'

Ernie nodded then licked his lips. As he stood up, Arthur noticed that he stumbled slightly then poked out his tongue and tried to look at the tip. It was very red and it had to be sore too.

'You'll be all right, lad. We'll get some ice on your tongue and your cheek and it'll soothe the pain. Now ...' Arthur pushed himself upwards and steadied himself with his stick, breathing deeply to keep his discomfort off his face. He hated to show his frailty to anyone, even a child. 'Come along then. Grab anything you want and let's go and eat. I don't know about you but my stomach thinks my throat's been cut.'

Ernie gasped. 'How's that?'

'Just a saying, lad, that's all. It means I need my breakfast.'

Arthur made his way to the door, and when he turned back to check that Ernie was following him, his heart gave a squeeze. The little boy was trying to right the now three-legged chair.

'I don't think that's going to work somehow, Ernie. Your dad will have to fix it when he gets home.'

Ernie nodded but his face crumpled, and Arthur suspected it was to do with more than the physical pain of his fall.

'Don't worry, Ernie, it wasn't your fault the chair broke and I'll tell your dad that.'

'Thank you.'

Ernie smiled at him, so Arthur gently ruffled the boy's hair then they made their way downstairs together, each of them taking their time, one weary and stiff with age and arthritis, one weary and stiff with aches and pains from his fall.

CHAPTER 12

'I'm not sure about this,' Abby said as Lisa pulled into the industrial estate car park.

Lisa met her eyes in the rear-view mirror.

'It'll be fun and it will also be good exercise. After what you went through last night, you need to get your heart beating naturally again.' There were certain words that really brought out Lisa's Welsh lilt, 'naturally' being one of them – it sounded so sing-song and lyrical.

Fiona turned in her seat and smiled at Abby. 'It will be fun, honey. And if it's not, we can cross it off the list.'

Abby still felt shell-shocked after the events of the previous evening. Seeing Gav like that had been surreal and when he'd kissed her and touched her … She shivered remembering it. It had felt familiar and yet wrong, but for a moment she'd wanted to hold him and for him to hold her. She'd weakened for just a fraction of a second and it had nearly sent her back to stage one, to the point where she'd just discovered that he was a cheat and that their relationship was over.

Gavin had sobbed for about ten minutes on and off, apologised about twenty times more and repeatedly asked where things had gone wrong. Abby had tried to be kind and patient but her tolerance had worn thin as it became clear that Gavin was trying to find a way out of the mess he found himself in. It was as if he expected Abby to fix it all for him. She'd encouraged him to finish his drink then told him she needed to get some sleep as she had an early start the next day. It had been clear that he hadn't wanted to go, but she'd given him no choice.

After Gavin had left, she'd sent Lisa a text and Lisa had immediately phoned back, listened to her cry, then told her to be up bright and early for a trip to a possible hen night venue. Abby had agreed, although she'd have agreed to anything last night just to get out of the flat, but when Lisa and Fiona had turned up and told her where they were going, doubts crept in.

They got out of the car and walked towards the large grey building. The morning was dark and wet and their trainers squelched across the tarmac. Her friends were clad in matching black Lycra tops and cropped leggings. Fiona's wavy black hair was pulled into a bun at the nape of her neck and Lisa's hair was pulled back from her face with a wide polka-dot headband. Neither of them had put any make-up on and they both looked relaxed and fresh-faced. Abby hadn't put any make-up on either, to a different effect – she knew she looked far from fresh-faced, with her puffy bloodshot eyes and her pasty skin. She'd dressed in a pair of grey leggings and a baggy black T-shirt, but hadn't been able to find her sports bra, so she'd pulled on an elastic crop top instead. She didn't possess proper Lycra workout gear, and she wore leggings and a T-shirt when she went to the gym. She wasn't comfortable in anything so tight and revealing. She thought her friends looked great in theirs but didn't have the confidence to expose her own curves in such a way, so a baggy T-shirt covered her bumpy bits.

When they reached the entrance, Abby paused, her legs refusing to carry her any further. She was tired and sad and she just wanted to go home. Lisa turned to her and gestured for her to follow but Abby shook her head.

'Abs?' Lisa gave her a quick hug. 'It'll be fine, you know? It doesn't feel like it right now, but it will. And, of course, we're here for you.'

Fiona nodded, her smile as bright and pretty as Alesha Dixon's. 'We're here for you, Abby, and we always will be. Now come on, let's get sweaty.'

'OK then.' Abby's voice sounded as unconvinced as she felt inside, but she didn't want to let her friends down, so she forced herself to follow them.

The trampoline centre smelt of sweat, deodorant, cleaning products and – strangely – chips. The ceiling was high with exposed rafters and long strip lighting, the walls were protected with six-foot-high-trampolines set at a forty-five-degree angle, and above these sat posters showing people enjoying themselves as they bounced, socialised and ate in the cafeteria – which explained the smell of chips.

'Now, don't forget that we're looking for a good venue to have some pre-wedding fun.' Lisa nudged her as they paid at the counter then headed into the trampoline section.

'But why trampolining?' Abby asked.

'Why not?' Lisa grinned. 'We don't want the traditional night out on the town getting drunk, or the weekend away in Blackpool or Ibiza. It's just not our style. We'd prefer something a bit more active and unusual. This seemed like a good option.'

'I'll take your word for it.' Abby knew she sounded like a grump but hoped Lisa would forgive her and blame Gavin's unexpected arrival the previous evening.

Thankfully, it was early Saturday-morning quiet, with just a few young children and tired-looking parents dotted around the place. Abby had been fearful of arriving to find the place packed with exuberant teens and people in their early twenties – those who were full of energy and, as yet, unmarked by life's excesses – but luckily there wasn't a nubile twenty-something who could've starred on *Love Island* in sight. She tugged the hem of her T-shirt down, her self-consciousness deepening by the minute as she thought of what she was about to do.

Once they'd tucked their belongings into lockers, Lisa led the way to the trampolines. There were about twenty of them leading to the far wall. It looked like some sort of giant pavement where people weren't supposed to step on the cracks.

'Come on then!' Lisa jumped onto the first trampoline, turning around and around, as her hair flicked up and down behind her yoga headband.

'*Woohoo!*' Fiona flung herself onto a different square and bounced up and down, moving her body into a variety of poses that suggested she'd done this before.

'Hurry up, Abby!' Lisa shouted.

Abby glanced around to check no one was watching, then padded over to the black square next to Fiona and took a few gentle bounces. The trampoline moved in time with her, sending her up, bringing her back down – it wasn't too bad, actually. There was something quite fun about it, so she started to push harder and harder until she too was sent higher and higher.

She turned to see Lisa moving across the room, bouncing in long strides that carried her from one trampoline to the next, her legs and arms flailing around as the momentum propelled her. Fiona followed her girlfriend, so Abby started to do the same, screeching with laughter at the loss of control.

When they'd done two circuits of the room, with Abby and Fiona in hot pursuit of Lisa, so that Lisa was gasping as she tried to stay one trampoline ahead of them, they ended up back where they'd started, all three of them giggling at their silly game. But it was so enjoyable to just play, to act like this without worrying about how they looked or what would happen when they'd finished. It was purely living in the moment and the most fun Abby had had in a long time.

Lisa's face was bright red and her forehead and chest were coated with a sheen of sweat. She slowed her bouncing and held up her hands in mock surrender. 'I give up!'

'We win!' Fiona winked at Abby.

'That was so much fun. Did you enjoy it?' Lisa asked them both.

'Brilliant!' Fiona was panting, her chest moving up and down as she took deep breaths. Her eyes were bright and full of excitement.

Abby gave a thumbs up because she could barely catch her breath.

'I think we just burnt off a load of calories and that's as good an excuse as any for some brunch.' Lisa gestured at the cafeteria sign at the far end of the centre.

'One more circuit, first?' Fiona asked, wiping her arm across her forehead.

'Oh go on then.' Lisa nodded. 'But I'm going to need the loo soon, even though I went right before we came out. Shouldn't have had that extra coffee.'

Once they'd caught their breath, they each selected a square and began to bounce, then Fiona took the lead as they sprang from one square to the next, the three of them squealing with breathless laughter. But halfway around, Lisa suddenly stopped bouncing and turned to Abby. Her eyes were wide with horror and she was holding her legs together tightly. She waved her hands up and down to tell Fiona and Abby to stop bouncing.

'What is it?' Abby carefully made her way across the trampolines to Lisa, worried that she had hurt herself by twisting an ankle or pulling a muscle.

'You know I said I thought I needed the loo?'

'Yes?'

'Don't laugh ... but it happened anyway.' Lisa looked down at her legs.

'What?' Fiona had joined them. 'Lisa you haven't ...?'

'I have. That last bounce ... when I went up, some wee came out.'

Abby met Fiona's eyes and they started to smile. Their smiles broadened and turned into hysterical laughter. Abby laughed so hard she worried she might have an accident too.

'It's not funny you two. I do my pelvic floor exercises all the time! I guess gravity or something just took away my self-control.' A smile spread across Lisa's face and Abby and Fiona giggled even harder. 'Now stop it or I'll wee even more. Come on, I need to get to a toilet fast.'

Fiona and Abby bounced their way back to the front while Lisa shuffled gingerly along, keeping her thighs squashed together as if she was wearing an invisible band around her knees.

When they reached the lockers, Fiona handed Lisa their rucksack containing a change of clothes and she headed off to the ladies'.

'You going with her?' Abby asked.

'I better had. I think I need to get changed too if we're going to eat. You coming?'

'I'll follow you,' Abby said.

Fiona nodded before jogging after Lisa.

Abby looked around her. The centre was still quiet, apart from a few families scattered around. It had been so liberating letting go, reminding her of how it felt to be a child again. All she had thought about as she'd bounced was her body and the way it was moving, about how good it felt to have her heart work harder, her limbs stretching in all directions.

She wanted to feel that again, so she ran at the closest black square and gave a whoop as she jumped onto it. There would be plenty of time to think and worry later. But right now, she was going to have some more fun.

'You don't need that much sauce on your chips, Lisa.' Fiona shook her head. 'You've drowned them.'

Lisa poked her tongue out. 'I like ketchup with my chips.'

'Don't you mean that you like chips with your ketchup?'

Fiona smiled at her own joke then sprinkled her own chips with vinegar.

'That was great fun.' Abby took a sip of her water. 'Thanks for bringing me.'

'I wouldn't have had you miss me peeing my pants for the world, Abby.' Lisa frowned. 'I can't believe that happened.' She was smiling but blushing too, and Abby could tell that for all that she was laughing about it, Lisa was a bit embarrassed.

'I doubt you're the first and you won't be the last.' Abby placed her glass back on the table. 'It's probably quite common.' She snorted and Fiona joined her, the two of them covering their mouths but not doing a very good job of disguising how funny they found Lisa's accident.

'Well next time we come here, I'm wearing one of those pee pads.'

'Pee pads?' Fiona's eyes widened.

'Yes, you know ... Tennis ladies, isn't it?'

Abby snorted. 'Tena ladies, not tennis. Although you could wear them for playing tennis too, I guess.'

'Seems like I need them. I'm so embarrassed, having bladder weakness in my thirties.' Lisa dipped a chip into tomato sauce before popping it into her mouth. 'What will it be like by the time I turn seventy?'

'I'm sure it's not a permanent issue,' Abby said. 'It was just the upwards motion and your bladder was fighting gravity or something like that. You know ... something scientific would explain it I'm sure.'

'Well I'm going to do more Pilates from now on.' Lisa nodded. 'I'm not risking becoming incontinent.'

Fiona coughed and Abby turned away, knowing that if she looked at Fiona again she'd start laughing and be unable to stop. They ate in silence for a while then Fiona asked, 'How are you feeling now, Abby?'

'That was certainly good for me, but now that my heart rate has slowed … bloody Gavin has popped back into my head once or twice.'

'That's bound to happen.' Fiona squeezed her hand. 'Him turning up at your flat and invading your space … it's going to knock you sideways.'

'I'd have knocked him sideways if I'd been there.' Lisa shook her head.

Abby smiled. Lisa probably would be able to take Gav with her height and frame, even if he did spend hours in the gym. She could be quite intimidating, both physically and verbally, if she was crossed.

'I'm angry with myself because I …' Abby took a deep breath. 'I let him kiss me.'

'You did what?' Lisa lowered her fork. 'You kissed him? You didn't tell me that last night.'

'I was still processing it myself. I didn't want it to happen, didn't expect it to happen. It just did.'

'Not the old *I fell onto his lips*, excuse?' Lisa sniffed with disapproval.

'No … I got him a drink then he asked me to sit by him and I felt sorry for him and a bit confused because … you know … through it all, part of me' – she met their eyes in turn – 'a very tiny part of me, kind of misses him. I get lonely sometimes.'

Lisa nodded. 'I get that, hun, I really do.'

'He rubbed my back and that always relaxes me, then he got closer and he smelt so familiar and it was like my body and my heart responded to him before I could think straight. I did stop him though.'

'And what did he say when he removed his tongue

from your mouth?' Lisa had stopped eating and was toying with her napkin.

'That he missed me and that he's scared because ... well because Belinda is pregnant and ...' She sighed. She'd told Lisa about the pregnancy last night but not about the kissing – that wasn't a conversation she wanted to have over the phone. 'I told him to grow up. I said I get that he misses me because it is difficult but he made the choice to cheat on me and he made the decision to move her into our home so quickly. I think he has regrets but he has to deal with this. After all, there's a baby on the way.'

'Poor baby.' Fiona shook her head. 'I just hope he takes responsibility for his actions before that child arrives.'

'That's not Abby's problem though.' A tiny line had appeared between Lisa's brows. 'You're not responsible for his happiness. Not at all. He has no right to come looking for comfort from you. He's a grown man.'

'I know that. I told him before he left that we can't cling to the past as a way of avoiding the future. We have to accept that life has changed and move on, and that there was a reason all of this happened. It was difficult because I do still care about him and that won't disappear overnight, whatever he did.'

'Of course it won't.' Lisa leant closer, peering into Abby's face.

'I feel vulnerable and angry and confused but I'm glad I didn't rant and rail at him. I'd have regretted that. I think I kind of helped him to see what he needs to do now. He has to put what we had behind him and look to his new life.'

'He never deserved you,' Lisa said, shaking her head. 'He's not good enough for my girl.'

Abby smiled. 'You always say that. And thank you for being here for me ... both of you. Especially for making me laugh this morning.'

Lisa flicked a hand in the air. 'Glad my early onset incontinence amused you.' She winked, letting Abby know that she was teasing, and Abby knew then that whatever Gavin had done, Lisa would always be there for her.

'So what are our thoughts about this place as a venue for our hen night?' Fiona asked.

'I'm really not sure after that fiasco.' Lisa shook her head.

'It would be great but you'd need to pop some pantyliners into the party bags.'

The three of them giggled at that, then Lisa went to order them more coffees. As the trampoline centre filled up around them, Abby tried to think about anything other than Gavin, because she had to do the same as she had told him to do; she had to let him go.

CHAPTER 13

'Have a seat there, lad.' Arthur pointed at the sofa. He and Julia had always used the chairs, and the sofa had been for guests.

Ernie sat down and peered around him. He'd stopped crying, at least, but occasionally he sniffed, as if the shock was still hanging over him and would take some time to fade.

'What would you like to drink?' Arthur asked.

'I ... don't mind.' Ernie peered up at him, his eyes filled with unease that Arthur put down to being in a strange flat. He flicked his head to move the dark blond hair from his forehead, and Arthur imagined Julia saying, *'That boy needs a haircut.'*

'I have tea ... or coffee, and I might have some cherry juice in the fridge if you want something cold.'

'Cherry juice?' Ernie frowned.

'It's good for my arthritis ... apparently.' Arthur gave a low chuckle.

'What's arthritis?'

'It's inflammation ... swelling in my joints.' He held out his hands and Ernie stared at his swollen knuckles.

'They look sore.'

'They are sometimes, but more than anything, they're

a nuisance because my hands don't work as well as they used to.'

Ernie nodded solemnly. 'I broke my finger once and the doctor taped it to my other finger and I couldn't write properly for weeks in school.'

'Yes, it's probably a bit like that.' Arthur couldn't help smiling at Ernie's innocence. 'Would you like cherry juice then?'

Ernie held out his own hands and wiggled his fingers. 'Yes please. Especially if it stops me getting bumpy knuckles.'

Arthur went to the kitchen and opened the fridge. Luckily, there was half a bottle of cherry juice in there, so he poured some into a glass. He glanced at the kettle, but decided it would take too long to make tea, and he wanted to speak to Ernie, so he poured himself a glass of juice too. The bacon was still sitting on the counter, so he got the frying pan from the cupboard and set it on top of the hob ready to make them some breakfast after they'd had a chat.

Back in the lounge, Ernie was still sitting on the sofa but he was peering around him, his mouth slightly open, as if he found Arthur's home fascinating.

Arthur handed him the glass then hobbled over to his chair. He'd had to leave his stick in the kitchen as he carried both glasses through, and as he sank into his seat, he did wonder how he'd manage to get up again.

'Do you like it?' he asked.

Ernie nodded as he lowered his glass and Arthur noticed the red mark the juice had left above the boy's top lip like a drawn-on moustache.

'It's good. Thank you, Mr Mayer.'

'You're welcome.' Arthur sipped his own juice then placed the glass on the side table. 'Ernie ... can I ask you some questions?'

Ernie sat up straighter. 'Yes, Mr Mayer.'

'First of all ... please call me Arthur. Mr Mayer is so formal and makes me feel even older.'

'OK, Mr Mayer.'

'Arthur.'

'Arthur.' Ernie pressed his lips together, as if using Arthur's first name felt wrong.

'Right, lad. You said that Jax was looking after you but she'd gone out for a bit. Where has she gone?'

Ernie blinked quickly and his eyes flickered around the room, as if hoping he'd find the right answer.

'You don't need to be afraid, lad. I just want to find out what's going on.'

'But will the police come?'

'No, lad. Why would they?' Had someone told him something like that would happen then? He gasped inwardly, remembering that he'd threatened to call the police on Ernie and his babysitter before when they were making lots of noise. Had he frightened the poor child that much? Shame filled him and made his stomach churn.

'If you ring them and they ... they take me away.'

'No, Ernie, please don't worry. I'm not calling the police. I promise you that. I just want to help if I can.'

'Jax ... she's gone to work.'

'To work?'

'Yes.'

'How old are you, now, Ernie?'

'I'm seven. Nearly eight. But I'm a big boy, Mr Mayer.'

'Arthur.'

'Yes.'

'I know you're quite a big lad for seven,' Arthur said, crossing his fingers behind his back, because Ernie was actually quite small, 'but you're still a bit young to be left alone.'

'My dad is meant to be home soon.'

Arthur nodded. 'He usually comes back on Fridays doesn't he?'

'Yes. But he had some work to finish in Sheffield this morning so he'll be home by lunchtime.'

'I see.' Arthur digested the information. 'Do you have a number to ring in case you need to reach Jax or your dad?'

'Yes. It's stuck on the fridge.'

'Right.' Arthur thought about that. If only he'd thought to ask before they'd come down to his flat, but his main concern had been making sure that Ernie was safe. The throbbing in his hip was getting worse, and he knew that another trip up the stairs would leave him in agony for days, so he couldn't go back up for the number, and he didn't want to send little Ernie up again because he might not return. Besides which, Ernie had said his father would be home around lunchtime, so the boy could stay with him. 'Well, seeing as how your dad will be home in a few hours, I think you'll be OK to stay here.'

'Thank you.' Ernie sounded so relieved that it tugged at Arthur's heart.

The lad really was very polite – someone had clearly taught him some manners. Arthur realised he had been very wrong about Ernie and his family and it made him feel ashamed. Living alone and having little human contact had changed him from the man he used to be and he wondered what Julia would think about that. He'd have hated for her to be disappointed in him.

'Doesn't your mum live with you, then?' he asked gently. He knew that there had been a woman in the flat with Neil and Ernie at one point, but that had been some time ago, and Arthur had been so caught up in his own life and then his loss of Julia, that the world around him had carried on without him paying it much regard.

'No. She went away.' Ernie stared down at his feet, swinging his legs because they didn't quite reach the floor.

'Sorry to hear that.'

'It was a long time ago. When I was five.'

'So you don't see her at all?'

Ernie shook his head but didn't say any more, and Arthur could see that it hurt him.

'Where's your family?' Ernie asked, taking another sip of his juice. 'I thought you had a wife here. I used to see her from the window sometimes when she was in the garden but I was too small to play outside on my own then. Mummy knew her and I remember she gave me sweets once but Mummy was sad and she … she didn't like to go out much so I used to stay in with her. Did your wife leave like my mummy?'

Arthur tried to think of how to explain death to a seven-year-old boy.

'My wife is … gone, lad.'

'Gone where?'

'I lost her … Julia, just over a year ago.' Arthur's throat tightened, giving his voice a choked sound.

'Where did she go?'

'She passed away.'

'Passed away where?'

'She died, Ernie.'

'Oh … I'm sorry.'

Arthur nodded. He rarely said the words out loud, not having anyone to talk to about it anyway, but telling a child was actually easier somehow. With a child, it was more a matter of fact. A seven-year-old would not expect further explanation, whereas an adult would expect details or at least a show of grief so they could offer a platitude.

'Not your fault, lad.'

'Don't you have any children?'

Arthur realised why Ernie had asked the question. He'd spotted the black and white photo on the sideboard of Julia holding George as a baby.

'I don't, no.'

'Whose baby is that then? Is that your wife?'

'Yes that's Julia and George. He was our son.'

'Where is he now?'

'George …' Arthur swallowed hard. He rarely spoke about Julia, let alone George. Time and age had conspired to tuck George safely away in his mind, as if that would mean his son would never suffer again.

'Did he pass away too?' Ernie's question made Arthur go cold. Admitting that he'd lost a child was something he loathed doing, as if it was a reflection of his own failure as a parent.

'He did. When he was ten.'

'That's younger than Jax but still older than me.'

'He was ill for a while. He had a condition called cystic fibrosis, and although these days more is known about it … back then, not so much.'

'When did he pass away?'

Arthur realised that he'd tried not to think about this much at all, that he deliberately didn't count the years or note the dates. His loss of Julia dominated his thoughts and it was almost as if George had been a dream he'd once had. A wonderful dream, when he'd had not just a beautiful wife but an intelligent and loving son.

'In 1975.'

Ernie's mouth moved and he frowned. 'That's ... a very long time ago.'

'It is.' Arthur nodded. 'But time is relative.'

'What does that mean?'

Arthur laughed in spite of the sadness of their conversation. He'd forgotten how many questions children had and how difficult it could be to answer them. But strangely, he didn't mind. It was so rare that he had company, and it made him remember how nice having a conversation could be.

'It means that forty-odd years sounds like a long time, but to me, it has flown past. It could have been yesterday.'

'Are you still sad?'

'Yes, lad. Sometimes, it makes me very sad.'

'You know what might make you feel better?' Ernie licked his top lip, as if sensing that he had a cherry juice moustache.

'What?'

'Some food. Dad says that sometimes it helps to comfort eat.'

'Is that right?' Arthur laughed long and hard. This boy was a good 'un, indeed.

'Dad says that if he's feeling low, a chip butty gives

him a spring in his step again, and Jax says that chocolate always makes her feel better.'

'Chocolate and chips?'

Ernie nodded.

'How about bacon butties?'

Ernie's eyes lit up. 'Yes, Mr Mayer ... Arthur ... they help.'

'Two comforting bacon butties coming right up.' Arthur shifted forwards on his chair and tried to push himself up using the arms. No luck. He tried again but he was stuck.

'Are you OK, Mr May— Arthur?'

'I need my stick, lad.'

'Where is it?'

'In the kitchen.'

'I'll get it.'

Ernie disappeared then quickly returned with the stick, which he handed to Arthur before taking hold of his free hand.

'What're you doing, lad?'

'Helping you up.'

'No, no, I'll be fine with my stick.'

But as Arthur planted the stick firmly on the floor then used it to lever himself up, Ernie kept hold of his other hand until he was standing. It was a small gesture, and one that made little physical difference at all, but nonetheless, it made something inside Arthur flutter. It was a faint sensation, but one he knew he'd felt a long time ago, back when he had a life that was worth living. When he'd had loved ones and knew that he mattered, that he was important to his family, even if not to the wider world.

'Can I help you to cook the bacon?' Ernie asked as he gazed up at Arthur.

Arthur had to clear his throat twice before he could speak, so moved was he by Ernie's gesture and his innocence. 'Of course you can, Ernie. Of course.'

The happiness on the little boy's face made the fluttering inside Arthur expand, and he knew in that moment, that although Ernie might be almost seventy years younger than him, they had something in common: they had both known loneliness. They had both suffered loss. They both responded to kindness.

As Arthur cooked the bacon, Ernie watched closely, his tongue sticking out the side of his mouth as he listened carefully to everything Arthur said to him. And when they carried the food to the table, Arthur's heart rose to see it laid for two. For today, at least, he wasn't alone, and neither was Ernie.

And Arthur knew that he would do whatever he could to ensure that Ernie's life was a little bit better from this point on.

CHAPTER 14

Abby headed up the stairs to her flat feeling more buoyant than she had in a long time. Perhaps it was the endorphins from the trampolining, perhaps it was from all the laughing or perhaps it was just because she'd been out with two good friends and had an enjoyable morning. What she did know for certain was that it had been an absolute tonic and even though she was sweaty, full of breakfast and coffee, and needed to shower and wash her hair, she still felt pretty damned good.

Lisa and Fiona were so much fun to be with and Lisa's little accident and how well she had handled it, only served to remind Abby how amazing Lisa was.

She opened the door then closed it behind her and kicked off her trainers in the hallway. What would she do with the rest of the day? What would she eat and drink? What would she watch on TV?

'Whatever I want!' she said to her hallway, experiencing a sense of euphoria at the reality of her situation. She didn't have to answer to anyone and could spend her day however she liked. In fact, she might even pop out and purchase some gardening tools so she could make a start outside.

*

Ernie swallowed the last of his bacon sandwich then wiped his mouth with the napkin Arthur had given him. After they'd cooked the bacon, Arthur had made a strange noise when he'd sat down, as if he was in pain, and Ernie had been worried. He knew Arthur was old and that his lumpy fingers hurt him sometimes, and that Arthur had trouble with his hip and that was why he needed the walking stick. Arthur was his new friend and he really didn't want him to be unwell.

'That was delicious, thank you.' He carried his plate to the sink then went back for Arthur's.

'You're welcome, lad. It's been a while since I've had company for breakfast.'

'Could I have another drink, please?'

Arthur nodded. 'There's more cherry juice at the back of the fridge. I normally have an emergency bottle there.'

Ernie went to the fridge and peered inside. It was very clean and everything was lined up neatly. It didn't smell like his fridge at home with the shelf that was sticky with banana milkshake that Jax had spilled, and the salad drawer that held a wrinkly green thing that might have been a cucumber or a spring onion. Dad bought those bags of salad, and apples and bananas, but he never put them in the salad drawer. Jax had told Ernie to leave the green thing in the fridge to see if it evolved into a snake or a lizard at some point, and although Ernie doubted it would, he didn't like to throw it out just in case.

He spotted the bottle of cherry juice and reached for it then something caught his eye. There were small pots of trifle on the top shelf. Ernie loved trifle but had only ever had it at birthday parties and Christmas. He really fancied one but he knew it would be rude to ask.

'What've you seen?' Arthur asked from the table.

'Nothing.' Ernie closed the fridge and took the cherry juice to the table.

'If there's something in there that you'd like, tell me.'

'I'm OK.' Ernie felt his cheeks getting hot and he rubbed at them.

'I think I know what you've seen … the trifles.' He waggled his eyebrows. 'Want one?'

'For breakfast?' Ernie asked.

'If you like!' Arthur smiled. 'This once anyway.'

'Really?' Ernie's belly fizzed with excitement.

'Absolutely. Let's be devils, shall we? Go get us one each.'

Ernie nodded and hurried back to the fridge.

As they ate their trifles, scooping jelly, custard and cream from the plastic pots, Ernie watched Arthur carefully. He had always seemed quite scary when they'd passed him outside or in the hallway, with his big bald head and thick black glasses that made his eyes seem bigger than other people's. He also had fat white eyebrows that frowned a lot and hair growing out of his ears. But Ernie didn't mind how Arthur looked anymore because he had been kind, and his teachers always said that kindness was what mattered most, not what someone looked like. And he made the best bacon sandwiches. Ernie hoped they would stay friends now. It would be nice to have some friends in the building.

After they'd washed and dried up and Arthur had put the plates away, they went back through to the lounge. Ernie liked the room because it was the same size and shape as his lounge but it had different furniture and it smelt different, like old newspapers and peppermints. It was how Ernie thought grandparents would smell.

'Shall we have a game of something?' Arthur asked.

'A game?' Ernie's stomach somersaulted and he looked around the room, wondering where Arthur's Xbox 360 or PS3 was kept. He pictured them playing on one of those shooting games like some of the boys at school had, or one where they had to be different cartoon characters and race around in cars. This morning was getting better and better.

'Yes, lad. Open that cupboard there and get the small black box out.'

Ernie opened the cupboard door and coughed as dust motes drifted out into the air. He found the black box and when he tried to close the door again, it got stuck.

'It's the lace cloth on the top. Just lift it up then close the door.'

Ernie did as Arthur told him then took the black box over to him. It was quite small and Ernie couldn't see how it would have an Xbox inside. Perhaps it was a controller for the Xbox or a fold-up headset so they could play games online.

'Ever played dominoes?' Arthur asked as he lifted the lid off the box then emptied the contents onto the table next to his chair.

'What are donimoes?'

'Dom-in-oes,' Arthur said the word slowly, as he set the small white rectangles on the table top, and Ernie copied him, but each time it came out wrong, until they were both laughing.

'Ah, lad! You've made me smile this morning.' Arthur pointed at the chair close to his. 'Sit here.'

Ernie took the chair and turned to his left so he

could face Arthur properly. The white rectangles clearly had nothing to do with Xbox or PS3, and it looked as if Arthur was trying to tile a floor, like Ernie's dad had done in the bathroom.

'Right, lad, these are domino tiles and each one has a value based on the number of spots or pips. We're going to start with a basic blocking game and as we go, I'll explain the rules and how the weight or rank of the tiles works. Does that sound OK?'

'Don't you have an Xbox then?' Ernie asked.

Arthur snorted then pulled a handkerchief from his cardigan pocket and wiped his nose. 'No, lad, I don't even have a basic computer. I can't be doing with those noisy flashing things. This is a good old-fashioned game and once you get the hang of it, you might enjoy it.'

'OK.' Ernie smiled. He didn't really mind that it was a different game because he loved games, as long as they didn't involve lots of reading, and he liked learning how to do new things. He also liked the cool smooth feel of the shiny white tiles and how they clinked when they touched, as if they were made of coloured glass.

So Arthur explained the rules and Ernie listened, and soon he forgot that his cheek ached and that he'd broken the chair in his flat; he forgot that he was sad that Dad hadn't come home last night and he forgot that he'd been lonely after Jax had left for work that morning.

He also forgot that he'd once thought Mr Mayer was a grumpy old man.

CHAPTER 15

Abby carried her flask of coffee and the gardening tools she'd purchased the previous afternoon down the stairs and out into the garden. She smiled as the Sunday morning sun warmed her face, reassuring her that summer wasn't too far away. She'd woken early, determined to get outside and make a start on tidying up the garden. It was such a mess that she'd be unable to plant a thing until she'd cleared what was there first. Her sudden productivity was probably helped by the fact that she'd checked her emails that morning and found a reply from the blogger, Jason Armstrong. For some reason, seeing his name in her inbox had made her stomach flip and she'd opened it with a sense of anticipation about what he'd have to say. Of course, he could have told her that he couldn't possibly meet with a strange woman to discuss gardening, but instead his reply had been friendly and enthusiastic, and he'd suggested they meet on Wednesday afternoon at a local café. That was only three days away and the thought made her heart flutter. She wasn't really sure why, but she put it down to the fact that it was out of character for her to email a stranger and to agree to meet up with them.

Abby had almost texted Lisa to tell her she was meeting

him, but she'd decided to leave it for now in case Lisa got carried away and saw it as some kind of date. Which it wasn't. Abby didn't know what Jason looked like or even how old he was; he could be the complete opposite to her type and either too young or too old for her. Although what her type was these days, she had no idea. Besides, she was meeting him to talk about gardening – nothing more.

She set her flask down on the bench then her tools on the ground and looked around. Where to start? She'd bought some regular black bin bags, but also some gardening refuse sacks from the supermarket – shocked at their price – but had thought it best to be environmentally friendly, rather than putting the green waste in the black bins. But it wasn't just garden waste that she could see. The abandoned furniture, including a three-legged table and what appeared to be an old-fashioned stereo cabinet, would need to go, as would the litter – drinks cans and cigarette packets – as well as the torn and yellowed newspaper pages fluttering around in the breeze like giant autumn leaves. She'd start with the litter for now then contact the building management company about the larger items. Surely it was actually their responsibility to make sure that the garden wasn't seen as a dumping ground for unwanted furniture? She pulled her mobile from her back pocket and fired off a quick email to them, not knowing how long they would take to sort the mess – seeing as how they'd apparently ignored it up to this point – then she snapped some photos. It would be nice to keep a record of before and after, even if she may not be here for much longer if Mr Mayer had his way.

Then she rolled up her sleeves, tied back her hair and got to work.

Three hours later, Abby sat on the bench and removed her gardening gloves. She'd worked up a sweat but had filled eight bin bags full of rubbish and, so far, three full of garden waste like twigs and weeds. Her back and shoulders were aching and her knees were sore from where she'd knelt on the brick borders to better get at the jumble of plants. The activity had given her a true sense of satisfaction because she could actually see the results. In fact, she'd celebrate now with a coffee.

She took some more photos then removed the cup from the flask and filled it with hot milky coffee, sitting back to admire her efforts.

Arthur drained his tea then swilled the mug under the kitchen tap. He wasn't looking forward to confronting Neil this morning but it had to be done. He'd enjoyed the time he'd spent with Ernie yesterday, in spite of how it had come about. It had been good to have company, to be able to make Ernie smile and to teach him something, like how to cook bacon and play dominoes. Arthur had forgotten how pleasant it could be to have company, or perhaps he had made himself forget. It was all too easy to dwell on what one didn't have, to lose oneself in self-pity, and Arthur tried not to do that. But one little boy had reminded him of how enjoyable the company of another human being could be. What scared Arthur now was the fact that it might not happen again and he'd go back to being alone.

He shrugged then straightened his shoulders. What would be would be, and at his age, he'd take whatever happy times came his way. What mattered right now was that Ernie was all right and that he would continue to be safe and secure. Neil had finally arrived back at the flats in the late afternoon, his noisy car engine instantly recognisable, and Ernie's little face had lit up. It had sparked a memory in Arthur of how his own son had always been delighted to see him at the end of each day, and he had been almost breathless with emotion. He'd pulled himself together to go out and greet Neil and to explain what had happened to Ernie, fully intending on telling Neil what he thought about his irresponsible parenting – but the younger man had looked so tired and so worried at the news that Ernie had been hurt, that Arthur had held back, believing it could wait. Ernie had wrapped his arms around his dad's waist and it had been evident in the way that Neil held his son that, even if he was a bit lacking in sorting out appropriate childcare, he clearly loved Ernie.

Now, however, Arthur was going to speak to Neil: man to man. He couldn't leave it after seeing how Ernie had been hurt yesterday; it would be on his mind all the time. He didn't feel it was interfering so much as offering some kindly advice, although he did know that it might not be welcome. However, he was willing to take any abuse that might come his way, as long as it meant that Neil would put something better in place for Ernie. He only wished he'd noticed that something was amiss sooner, that he hadn't been so harsh on the child about noise and unruly behaviour.

Ten minutes later, once he'd caught his breath outside Neil's door, he knocked with his stick and waited. Neil opened the door and his eyes widened when he saw Arthur standing there. Ernie appeared too, his hair wet from a recent shower or bath and wearing a T-shirt featuring a character from a TV show that Arthur had seen on telly recently, though he couldn't recall the name of the damned thing.

'Mr Mayer!' Ernie rushed at him and stood so close he was almost on Arthur's toes. 'I was just telling Dad how you showed me how to play donimoes.'

Arthur smiled, momentarily forgetting why he was there. 'It's Arthur, remember? And what's the game called, lad?'

'Oh ...' Ernie screwed up his face, 'Donim ... domim ... dom-in-oes!'

'That's right!'

'Uh ... yeah ... thanks again for that, Mr Mayer.' Neil met Arthur's gaze then swiftly looked away. 'I'm really grateful to you for looking out for Ernie yesterday.'

'Neil ...' Arthur cleared his throat and pulled himself up to his full height. 'Could I have a moment of your time?'

Neil nodded. 'Would you like to come in?'

'Thank you.'

Neil stepped back and Arthur walked into the flat, feeling at once justified and also sad; he wanted to ensure Ernie's future safety and wellbeing, but he didn't want to make Neil feel bad. However, Ernie had taken priority in his mind.

Abby, showered and changed, was walking the short distance to the local carvery to meet Lisa for lunch. Fiona had gone to meet a friend, and Lisa had sent Abby a text to say that, seeing as how it was a beautiful sunny day, and they'd burned off so many calories on the trampolines yesterday, they deserved to enjoy a good Sunday lunch.

She'd added that they could put the world to rights over a bottle of wine, which sounded like a pretty good plan.

After a morning spent clearing the garden at Willow Court, Abby felt she deserved a good meal, and the idea of spending a few hours with Lisa was definitely preferable to sitting alone at the flat with beans on toast.

She spotted Lisa as soon as she entered the pub and she weaved her way through families and couples to the table next to the window. They hugged then Abby sat down and Lisa poured her a glass of white from the open bottle.

Lisa's hair was swept back with a bright pink headscarf that matched her pink and white polka-dot dress, and her face was bare of make-up except for a slick of lip gloss. Her green eyes were bright and clear, and her ready smile made Abby smile too.

'Cheers!' Lisa held up her wine glass.

'Cheers!' Abby clinked her glass against her friend's.

'So what's all this about gardening?' Lisa asked after she'd taken a sip of her wine. 'I was a bit surprised when I heard what you'd been up to this morning.'

'Well I did tell you I was thinking about sorting the garden out, didn't I?'

'But I didn't think you were serious.' Lisa chuckled.

'Why not?' Abby bridled.

'Well … it's a community garden for a start and it shouldn't all be down to one person. I don't want to see you do a load of hard work then someone else come along and ruin it. Or take the credit.'

'Oh I don't care about that. I mean … I do care about it not being ruined but I don't care about someone taking the credit. I just want to make it better there. And you know what?'

'What?'

'My neck is stiff, my shoulders ache and my hands are blistered …' She wrapped them around her wine glass, enjoying the soothing cold against her palms. 'But I feel good.'

'I'll take your word for it.'

'It was good exercise, Lisa, and I really felt as though I achieved something.' Abby got her mobile out of her bag, opened her photos and passed her mobile to Lisa. 'Here, look.'

Lisa scanned through the photos, using her thumb and forefinger to enlarge some of them while Abby sipped her wine and gazed around. The smell of roast dinners filled the air and her stomach grumbled. At the next table, a woman tried to get her toddler to eat a carrot but he kept shaking his head and turning away. She looked up and shook her head at Abby then and rolled her eyes. Abby smiled in return. It must be hard in some ways having little ones and at least she got to eat her meals in peace – a luxury Gavin wouldn't have soon.

'You did a lot of work, hun.' Lisa handed Abby's mobile back. 'What's next?'

'Well, I'm going to meet with a blogger I found online and I'm hoping he'll give me some advice.'

Lisa's eyes widened. 'You're meeting a man?'

'Yes,' Abby said flatly, dropping her mobile back into her handbag then tucking it under the table.

'Like a date?'

'No, it's not a date! I knew you'd think that.'

Lisa pouted. 'A young man?'

'I'm not really sure.'

'What do you mean you're not sure?' Now Lisa was frowning.

'I don't actually know how old he is, but he seems nice.'

'How do you know?'

'I read his blog.'

'His blog? Bloody hell, Abs, you read a guy's blog and now you're meeting him? When?'

'Wednesday afternoon.'

'Where?'

'At the café.'

'You are so not going there alone.'

'He seems fine.'

'Were you born yesterday? Have you not seen what happens to young women who meet men they don't know? They disappear and have their hands chopped off, their teeth pulled out and get found years later in ... abandoned warehouses.'

'That was a movie, Lisa.' Abby laughed.

'Whatever! You are not going alone.'

'So I'm going to meet this perfectly nice blogger and say what? I hope you don't mind but I brought my friend along because she still thinks we're eleven?'

'Why not?'

'It's a bit ... paranoid, isn't it?'

'I'll come along but sit at a different table and we can have a sign in case something goes wrong.'

'A sign?'

'Yes. Like ... you can pretend to get a text or ...' Lisa looked around her then picked up the bowl of sugar sachets. 'You can drop one of these on the floor and I'll know to come over.'

'Then what will you do?'

Lisa sniffed. 'I'll make a citizen's arrest.'

'You'll what?'

'I'll arrest him and stop his creepy antics right there.'

Abby sighed and shook her head. 'Lisa, for all I know this guy could be eighty if he's a day, and if I feel at all uncomfortable with him then I'll leave immediately.' She sighed. 'But if you do want to come, then fine, but please don't make any arrests. In fact, I don't even want you to look directly at him. You can be there but be seen and not heard. OK?'

Lisa nodded. 'All right then. Unless I feel it's necessary. Anyway, what's his name?'

'Jason Armstrong.'

Lisa snorted, causing the woman with the toddler to glance in her direction.

'What's wrong with that?'

'Arm-strong?'

'Uh huh.'

'Well let's hope he's not creepy and that he lives up to his name. Then he can come and use his *strong arms* to help you out in your garden. Plus ... if he's really nice, you never know ...'

'Never know what?'

'You might fall in love over the compost or he might invite you into his potting shed. Hey ... I bet he only cuts the grass when he gets *mow*-tivated.'

Abby shook her head.

'And ... it might be the right *thyme* for love.' Lisa laughed at her own joke. 'Or ... he'll say ... I love you from my head ... *tomatoes*.'

'Enough!' Abby giggled. 'If I didn't love you, I'd have

to abandon you right now for making such bad jokes, you know that, right?'

'But you do love me and you know I love you.'

They clinked glasses again then Abby told Lisa all about Jason's blog and what she knew about him so far – which wasn't very much at all – but even so, it was nice to speak to Lisa about a man who wasn't Gavin. Even though she wouldn't be going on a date.

No, definitely not a date.

'Thank you.' Arthur accepted a mug of tea from Neil then set it on the coffee table. He noticed that there were rings where coasters hadn't been used and that one corner of the thin wooden table was chipped. Either Neil was struggling for money or he wasn't particularly house proud.

When Neil had sat in the chair opposite, Arthur cleared his throat. He'd rehearsed what he wanted to say all morning, but it wasn't going to be easy, however many times he tried to word it gently.

Then, Ernie entered the room and sat next to Arthur.

'What are we going to play today, then, Arthur?' Ernie said.

'Uh, Ernie, do you think yer dad and I could have a chat in private?'

Ernie looked up at Arthur, his face etched with worry, his eyes cloudy. 'Have I done something wrong? If I have, I'm very sorry. I … I try to be good. I do, honestly.'

'No, Ernie, you've done nothing wrong and you are a good lad. It's just some … grown-up stuff.'

Ernie opened and closed his mouth then hung his head.

'Go on, Ernie.' Neil nodded at his son. 'I'll take you out for some food when Mr Mayer's gone.'

'OK, Dad.'

When Ernie had closed the door behind him, Arthur cleared his throat again.

'Right ... uh ... Neil, there's no easy way to say this and I'm really sorry if you think I'm interfering but I'm concerned about Ernie.'

He looked up but Neil was nodding gently.

'I've noticed that the lad spends quite a bit of time here with that girl ... Jax, is it? And then sometimes, like yesterday, when she's not here and you're in work, he's all alone.'

Two pink spots had appeared on Neil's cheeks and he was staring into his mug.

'Now, I'm not here to criticise you, but I am worried about him. See, yesterday, like I told you, I heard an almighty bang and I found Ernie hurt. He's so young, Neil ... Too young to be left alone for long periods of time. I know he's quite a responsible lad and fairly sensible but anything could happen to him.'

Arthur picked up his mug and sipped at the tea. He winced; it was too weak for his taste but he wouldn't let on. He waited for Neil to reply, expecting anger or excuses but none came. So when he did look over at Neil again, he was surprised to see that Ernie's father was visibly upset.

'Hey now, lad, what is it?'

Neil released a shaky breath. 'I'm so sorry. I was worried something like this might happen and now it has – I'm just so thankful that Ernie didn't come to serious harm.'

'No he didn't ... and I'm glad I was around. I'm glad I could help.'

'Thank you so much.'

'Is everything all right, though?' Arthur prompted. 'Ernie's mum isn't around is she?'

Neil shook his head. 'She left us. It's ... it's hard. We both miss her but there's nothing I can do. I tried to change her mind but she wasn't well ...'

'Physically?'

'Depression. She declined rapidly after having Ernie. She had that ... postnatal depression. See ... she was a beautiful woman, meant for better things.'

'Better things?' Arthur frowned.

'She wanted more. A big house of her own ... money to buy clothes. To travel.'

'And she couldn't do all that because?'

'She got pregnant with Ernie by mistake. I don't think she wanted to marry me, to be honest, but she did it because she was pregnant. She had dreams of being on TV or going to Hollywood and being famous.'

'Doesn't everyone these days?' Arthur tutted his disapproval.

'She could have done it, though. I shouldn't have been careless but I hoped, see, that if she got pregnant and we got married ... I hoped she'd be happy. I was wrong.' Neil frowned. 'I was an idiot and I made her unhappy. I guess I trapped her. She wasn't meant for this ...' He gestured at the flat.

Arthur sipped his tea and thought about what Neil had said. When he'd married Julia, they'd only had a small ground floor flat in a different part of Manchester, but it had been like a palace to them. Julia had kept

172

it clean and tidy – not finding herself a job until after they'd lost George and she'd needed something to keep her mind busy – while Arthur had gone out to work and they had been happy, simply being together. They hadn't wanted more than they'd had, hadn't expected more, and that sense of acceptance seemed to be missing for a lot of people these days. Everyone wanted more, and in Arthur's opinion, it was probably why so many people ended up unhappy. Wanting what you couldn't have was different to aspirations, especially in the sense that a lot of people now didn't seem to want to work for anything; they wanted it all handed to them on a plate.

'I'm so sorry, Neil. You've had a rough time of it. And working away must be tough too.'

'I'm trying to get a transfer but my sales job involves driving, so even if I get based locally, I can't avoid having to travel. Jax used to be around more but she's growing up and has her own life and I've just been trying to ignore the fact that Ernie's been ... neglected.'

Arthur shook his head. 'That's a strong word, lad. He's fed and watered and it's clear how much he loves you. But I do think he needs an adult around more of the time. Look ... we've known each other for a good few years. Not well, I grant you that, but you know enough about me to know I usually keep myself to myself. Ernie mentioned that Julia used to say hello to your wife of a morning when she'd be heading outside to the garden.'

'Your wife was a lovely lady.' Neil smiled. 'I'd see her on occasions too and I do remember Lauren mentioning her.'

'She is ... was.' Arthur pushed his glasses up his nose. 'Look ... why not let me help you out a bit?'

'How could you do that?'

'I could watch the lad when you're not around.' He paused, surprised at his own offer. He'd considered how he could help them out but until this point, hadn't been sure that this was the right way. Only now ... he'd said it. 'I ... had a boy of my own once. A long time ago but he ... passed away before he became a man.'

'I'm sorry to hear that.'

Arthur nodded. 'It was very difficult. However, I know a bit about parenting ... well, I might even be a grandfather now if my George was still here. What I'm saying is ... that I'd be happy to watch Ernie for you when you're away. If you'd be happy with that too.'

'Please, Dad?' Ernie had appeared in the doorway, opening the door without Arthur even noticing. 'We can play more don ... dom-in-oes and stuff and Mr Mayer has some really cool model planes and things downstairs.'

'I don't know ...' Neil chewed his lip. 'It's one hell of an ask.'

'Look ... you have to make your own mind up about this but it would be a solution for you ... even a temporary one. He's in school through the week so he could come to me for his tea and I'll see him up to the flat afterwards or he could even stay at mine. There's a spare room with a bed and he can make it his own. I never use it anyway. You can phone him anytime you like and check that he's OK. Then if you're going to be late at weekends, he can stay on until you're back. Plus he can come up here whenever he wants to get his things or to spend time up here in his room.'

'Why would you want to help us like this?' Neil asked.

'You know, I don't think people help one another

enough these days. I think we're all so busy dashing around and none of us have enough time to even have a proper conversation anymore. People have forgotten what it means to be neighbourly. If my Julia was around, she'd love to have Ernie stay. She longed for a grandchild.'

Neil rubbed his eyes then ran his hands through his hair.

'This is a lot for you to consider, Neil, so why don't I head back down to my flat and you can think on it. It's a big decision for you to make.' Arthur pushed himself up and straightened his cardigan. 'I'll let myself out.'

'Wait!' Neil stood up. 'I have an idea. I was planning on taking Ernie out for lunch to that carvery down the road. They have a Sunday special. How'd you … how'd you fancy joining us?'

Arthur opened his mouth to decline but no words came out.

Dinner? With company?

Not a long Sunday afternoon alone with cold chicken, frozen vegetables and instant gravy?

Company. Food. Conversation. He felt nervous but excited at the same time.

'I'd love to join you.'

'Yay!' Ernie jumped up and down.

'On one condition.' Arthur sharpened his tone, and Ernie stopped bouncing and stared at him. Arthur felt his lips curl into a smile. 'It's my treat.'

Ernie started bouncing again.

CHAPTER 16

O n Wednesday afternoon, Abby felt ridiculously nervous as she paced outside the café where she'd arranged to meet Jason. Her nervousness was down to two things: one, he could be, as Lisa had suggested, a dangerous creep who preyed on vulnerable women with a penchant for gardeners; and two, he might actually be really nice and Abby would mess the meeting up and act like an idiot.

She repeated the words: *It's not a date* over and over in her head, but still her palms remained clammy and her heart fluttered like a ribbon tied to an electric fan.

'Whoever you're meeting might appreciate it if you actually go inside.' A voice broke into her thoughts.

'Pardon?' Abby looked up and met brown eyes so dark they were almost black. They were set in a face so perfectly sculpted that their owner could have been a model, and as she appraised him, she noticed his lightly tanned skin and strong jaw covered with what looked like two days' worth of stubble. His wavy blonde hair was highlighted by time spent in the sun and it looked as though it needed cutting, but it suited him. As her eyes made their way from his face and over his broad shoulders encased in a black V-neck T-shirt, he spoke again.

'You kept saying, *It's not a date ...*' He smiled, revealing small square teeth. 'So I suggested that you go inside and meet him or her. They might be getting worried about where you are.'

Abby's cheeks burned as she realised that she'd been speaking out loud.

'Oh God! How embarrassing!' She shook her head. 'I'm ... a bit nervous.'

'So you *are* on a date? A blind date?' His eyes stayed on her face, his gaze so intense she felt as though the sun was shining just for her.

'No! Not at all. I'm meeting someone ... he's just ... a blogger. No one special. Just ... someone I want to get some gardening advice from.' She gave a small laugh then waved her hand dismissively, immediately cursing herself for being such an awkward idiot.

'I see.' He nodded. 'Those boring gardening bloggers, eh?'

'Ha!' Abby laughed a bit too enthusiastically. She was now at a loss for words. She felt like an idiot for mumbling to herself, and for being rude about the kind blogger who'd agreed to meet her.

'Well ... I'd better get a move on. I'm meeting someone too.'

'Oh! Of course. Uh ... bye.'

He gave a wave as he opened the door and went inside and Abby watched him go. He was certainly delicious but she was sworn off men and had more pressing matters to deal with right now. She checked her mobile and saw that she was ten minutes late. Better get inside ...

*

As she entered the café, she scanned the tables, and there, at a table near the window, pretending to read a bridal magazine, was Lisa. As Abby passed her to get to the counter, Lisa gave her a wink and Abby nodded in response. At least she had backup should the blogger turn out to be a creep, even if it did feel a bit over the top, a bit like a game or a cheesy TV show. Although she had to admit that it was also quite a lot of fun and might give her a tale to tell if she had to make a speech at Lisa and Fiona's wedding.

At the counter, she told the waitress Jason's name, and the woman pointed at a table in the far corner. The blogger had already arrived apparently, but seeing as how the table was currently empty, he must've gone to the toilet.

Abby took a deep breath and made her way over to the table then pulled out a chair. She checked that Lisa could see her, should she need to get her attention, then she sat down.

'Hello!'

The man who took a seat opposite her made her breath catch in her throat.

'Everything all right?' he asked, his dark blond brows meeting above his sparkling eyes.

'Uh ... yes. Oh gosh ... I'm so sorry.' She shifted in her seat. 'I didn't realise it was you! I must've sounded horribly ungrateful.'

He shook his head. 'It's fine. I understand completely.'

'You do?'

Her eyes started to wander over his broad shoulders, so she forced them back to his face.

'Of course. I get anxious about meeting new people too.'

'You do?' *Stop repeating yourself!*

'To be honest, I think most people do.' His smile warmed her right through and she was glad she'd opted for the white linen trousers and a red and white polka-dot blouse. Jeans and a long-sleeved shirt would have been too warm on this sunny day, especially in light of her faux pas. She willed the heat to leave her cheeks and throat; she knew she'd be all blotchy and red right now.

'Shall we start again?' she asked.

'Yes, let's. Jason Armstrong.'

'Abby Hamilton. Nice to meet you.'

They shook hands and she hoped that her palm wasn't as clammy as she suspected it was against his warm dry hand. When he released her, she discreetly wiped it on her trouser leg.

They ordered coffees and slices of carrot cake that looked too good to ignore, then Abby started to apologise again but Jason reassured her that he wasn't offended, and he was so kind and gently spoken that Abby felt even worse.

'Tell me why you contacted me, Abby.'

She explained about the garden on Holly Street and about how she wanted to improve it and Jason listened carefully, nodding and making all the right noises. It encouraged her to keep talking and she found herself telling him about her neighbours and the sense of isolation and neglect that permeated the flats, how she hoped that a communal garden might help alleviate some of that. She told him about Ernie, feeling herself brighten as she pictured his cute face, then about Mr Mayer and how he also seemed so negative about the outside space. She left out the bit about going out for a smoke, feeling a bit self-conscious in front of this lovely man, and she didn't say anything about Gavin, either.

'Have you recently moved to the area then?' he asked.

'Yes. I've always lived in Manchester but after a painful … break-up, I needed to find somewhere to live.'

'Ah … the painful break-up. We've all been there, haven't we?'

Abby nodded but she couldn't understand why anyone would let go of Jason. Not only was he gorgeous and intelligent but he also seemed like a great listener. He probably had a partner waiting for him at home.

'I'm fine now.' She sipped her cappuccino, appreciating the silky foam on the surface and the bittersweet drink underneath. 'Well … I'm getting there.'

'It will ease with time, no doubt.'

'On your blog it said that you find gardening therapeutic.'

'I do.' He nodded. 'It's good for the mind and the body.'

'Because of the greenery?'

'Yes!' He laughed. 'And the exercise and seeing things grow. It's all about the cycle of life and it makes you feel connected to the earth … to the planet.'

'I did feel good at the weekend after I started clearing out the garden. Would you like to see it?'

He nodded, so she swiped her phone screen, found the photos then handed her mobile to him. He flicked through them, enlarging some, then he paused as her mobile buzzed and his face broke into a grin.

'Who's Lisa?'

'What? Why?'

He turned around and gave a wave. 'It that her with the dark red hair?'

'Yes.'

'Why did she ask if you think I'm going to taste as good as the carrot cake?' His grin spread from ear to ear and a mischievous twinkle had appeared in his eyes.

Abby hung her head and feigned interest in said carrot cake. It was particularly delicious but she'd been trying to take her time, not wanting to gobble it down in front of Jason. But now something far worse had happened ... Lisa had blown her cover!

'Oh no!' She willed the ground to swallow her up. 'She didn't?'

He handed her mobile back and there was the text from Lisa in all its glory, the words followed by an emoji of two hearts pierced by an arrow.

'She came just to ... to keep an eye out for me.'

'Because you were meeting a strange man?'

'Well ...Yes.'

'That's very wise and what I always tell my sister to do.'

'You do?'

'Always. Do you think Lisa wants to join us?'

Ten minutes later, after Lisa and Jason had been properly introduced and they'd ordered more coffees, Abby was laughing so hard she thought she might split the seams of her linen trousers. Jason was not just handsome and bright, he was also very funny. He'd regaled them with stories of his time working at a garden centre. It was where his love of gardening had originated, as he'd got to know the names of the plants and the environments they needed to thrive. He'd hinted at losing someone close to him, something Abby already knew from reading his blog, but not gone into any detail, and Abby hadn't wanted to pry, but he seemed so positive and happy. He taught biology part-time at a further education college and spent the rest of his time working on council-funded community gardening projects.

'I can't believe that a woman asked for a plant that was green with leaves.'

'Oh yeah we get them all at garden centres. Not as bad as the DIY stores where they ask for stripy paint, but getting there.' He drained his coffee then set the mug back on the table. 'One of the best was when a little boy who must have been about five or six came in with his grandfather. They were looking for a child's gardening set, so I pointed them in the right direction. I heard the grandfather say, "Let's get home and dig up those potatoes then, shall we?" The little boy replied, "OK, Grandad, but I think it was really silly of you to bury them in the first place."'

Abby and Lisa laughed.

'It was a good job. Got me through some tough times, although I do enjoy teaching now. Wow, is that the time?' He gestured at the clock on the wall. 'I'd better get going.'

Abby was surprised to feel disappointment hit her like a bucket of icy water.

'It was really good to meet you both. I'll have a think about your garden now that I've seen the photos and get back to you with some suggestions.'

'That would be great, thank you so much.' Abby stood up to shake his hand but he leaned forwards and kissed her on one cheek then the other. She breathed in his scent, a combination of sandalwood and fresh air, then sat back down as he kissed Lisa goodbye too.

'I'll be in touch soon.' He pulled out his wallet and dropped a few notes onto the table.

'No, it's fine! I'll get this,' Abby said.

'You can get the next one.'

Abby watched as he left the café, attracting plenty of admiring female glances as he went, then she sighed long and hard.

'Did you hear what he said?' Lisa nudged her.

'He'll be in touch?'

'He said you can get the next one. That means he wants to see you again.' Lisa's eyes were wide and shining and Abby didn't think it was down to the two slices of cake and the three coffees she'd consumed.

'He was just being kind. It's something people say.' Abby waved a hand dismissively.

'Abby ... he likes you.'

'I like him ... but in a friendly way.'

'Yeah, all right.' Lisa giggled. 'I thought he seemed really decent. You could do a lot worse.'

'Look ... he's nice but he's probably married or engaged or something else. Besides which, I'm not looking for love, remember?'

Lisa hugged her with one arm. 'I remember. But at least he's going to help you out with your garden.'

'I'm really excited about that now. It's going to be beautiful – and it will be something positive to focus on and I'll hopefully get fit in the meantime.'

'You'll have strong arms for certain.' Lisa winked. 'Like Jason Armstrong.'

'Stop it, already!'

In spite of her belief that Jason did just see her as a fellow gardener, Abby couldn't get his image out of her mind. It didn't help that his scent still lingered on her skin where he'd kissed her cheeks. This was silly ... the garden really was her focus now and Jason was just a by-product of that. But what a by-product ...

'Another coffee, Abs?'

'Go on then but just one more.'

As Lisa gestured for the waitress, Abby gazed out of the window in the direction that Jason had taken. It occurred to her that she hadn't thought about Gav, Belinda, and their baby for over an hour and that had to be a record for her. Spending time with Jason and planning for the community garden on Holly Street had kept her mind off her past. She'd never forget her child, knew that there would always be a corner of her heart devoted to the dream that had almost been, but to let go of Gav and the pain would be a good thing indeed.

Whether Jason was involved with someone or not wasn't important. What mattered right now was that she was taking positive steps, doing things she wouldn't have done before, and she was enjoying herself. Knowing that she would hear from Jason again did give her a bit of a glow inside, and she imagined it sitting there in her belly like a tiny seed, waiting to be tended. If it was nurtured, then who knew what could grow from this one meeting?

CHAPTER 17

Two weeks passed before Abby heard from Jason and she'd just about given up hope when an email arrived in her inbox. It came with an apology for the delay: apparently he'd been very busy with work and a few projects he was involved with, as well as having to return to Kent for a family emergency. He'd attached some plans that he said might work for the garden on Holly Street and said Abby should take her time looking at them, then give him a call when she was ready.

Over the past two weeks, she'd done some job hunting online but not found anything that particularly interested her, or that was a good match for her experience and rather limited qualifications. It did seem as though she might need to retrain or study for more qualifications, but she'd take things one step at a time. And for now, she knew what she wanted to do. So she'd focused her energies on the garden – clearing, weeding, sweeping, and she'd even hired a pressure washer to get the worst of the moss and staining off the patio slabs and the brickwork. The garden did look a whole lot better, although now that the buildings manager had arranged to have the old furniture taken away and the whole place had been cleared, it looked quite bare. Hopefully, Jason's suggestions would put that right.

An hour later, she'd printed out his plans and made some notes about what she would need. Jason had suggested she visit the local garden centre where he used to work, and tell them that he'd sent her so that she'd receive a generous discount on whatever she bought. It was all very proactive and positive and she felt as though she really was taking control of her life and making things happen rather than just going with the flow. In fact, Gavin had barely crossed her mind at all, except for during a few quieter moments when she'd wondered how he was dealing with his situation and if he'd taken to the idea of being a father now.

She'd also started up her blog again. She'd uploaded the before and after photographs of the garden as a work in progress and her blog had received quite a few views and comments, most of them offering advice about how to prepare the soil for different seeds and shoots and about what to plant and when. Granted, spring was giving way to summer but it wasn't too late, especially if she bought some 'garden ready' bedding plants to give the things a head start. She'd also become fascinated by the idea of how the garden could make money, becoming an investment that could work for the people of Willow Court and the community.

Her previous belief that she'd have to move out because of Mr Mayer had also been pushed to the back of her mind and she refused to consider it at the moment. She hadn't bumped into Mr Mayer since their altercation several weeks ago, but she had noticed a few times when she'd passed his front door that the TV hadn't been blaring, and that had made her think that perhaps he was out. Perhaps Mr Mayer had found something to take his mind off his troubles and she hoped so; because nobody deserved to be alone and unhappy. Not even grumpy old men.

Ernie hurried into the spare room at Arthur's flat to get changed out of his school uniform. He couldn't believe it was Thursday already; the days flew past now and before he knew it, Friday night came and, with it, Dad was home.

He'd been having a great time since he'd decided to clean the flat and had fallen off that chair. Arthur had come to his rescue like one of those superheroes in the movies, but wearing a cardigan not a cape, and now Ernie was no longer spending so much time alone in the flat when his dad was away. Jax still did the school run, unless his dad was about, which he had been for two days last week when he'd taken some holiday leave, and even though she usually had to rush off to work once she'd walked Ernie back to the flat, he was then able to go to Arthur's where they had loads of fun.

Arthur was very kind and wise, like old men in movies always were, and Ernie was learning a lot from him. He'd never had grandparents but now he felt as though he did and he was very proud of that fact. In school, when the other children spoke about their grandparents, now he spoke about Mr Mayer, but he called him Grandpa Arthur, because he knew if he called him Mr Mayer, or just Arthur, that the other children would think it was strange.

This evening, Arthur was making spaghetti Bolognese

for tea and Ernie couldn't wait. It was one of his new favourites and Arthur always bought garlic bread to go with it. They sat at the table in the kitchen though, as Arthur said it was good to have a conversation over dinner and not to stare at the TV screen, and Ernie liked that too. Arthur always asked about his day and was interested in his stories. He even told him about what it was like when he was a lad, which Ernie found fascinating. After tea, they'd have ice cream and sometimes jelly, or apple crumble and custard, then they would spend some time on their model planes. Arthur had found several kits in the spare room when he'd tidied it up so that Ernie could stay in there. He'd seemed surprised that the kits were there and had been about to throw them away when Ernie asked him if they could build them. So they had. The current one was a plane that was used in World War II, which was a very long time ago, but Ernie still found it interesting to hear about it. But he'd needed to make an excuse to go to the toilet when Arthur had asked him to read the instructions. He'd also tried to leave his reading book and spelling log in his tray at school, because Arthur always wanted to know how he was getting on.

It made his tummy ache when he thought that Arthur might not like him if he realised that Ernie was stupid like some of the boys in his class said he was. But Arthur always said nice things to him like how good he was at building things and how well he knew his times tables. So perhaps Arthur didn't think he was stupid at all. He really hoped not because he liked having a grandfather, even if he couldn't call him that out loud – he didn't know how Arthur would react, after all.

Ernie thought that he might even love Arthur, but he

was too shy to tell him in case it made him sound soppy and silly, so he tried to show him by being a good boy instead. Ernie also hadn't visited his den much over the past two weeks because he'd been so busy, but yesterday afternoon, he'd gone out to check on it and he'd been amazed at how different it was out there. Someone had cleaned the place up, there were no cans or sweet wrappers blowing around and all the flowerbeds were clear of weeds and cat poo. It was like the garden at school at the start of the year when they came back after February half term: ready for planting things. Luckily, Ernie's den had still been standing, although why it hadn't been moved was a surprise to him, but perhaps whoever had cleaned up liked it; it *was* a good den. He'd rushed back to Arthur's, keen to tell him about the garden but something had stopped him. Whenever he'd mentioned the garden before, Arthur had seemed to go into what his teacher called a daydream, and it made him seem far away. Ernie didn't like that so he decided to keep it a secret for now. He didn't want to do anything to make Arthur sad.

Arthur put the tray with the garlic bread on it into the oven then stood up again. He waited for a few moments to catch his breath before going to the fridge and getting out a bottle of cherry juice. It was Ernie's favourite drink, apart from hot chocolate topped with marshmallows, and Arthur liked buying things that made the boy happy. Neil had insisted on giving Arthur some money to help with feeding Ernie through the week, but Arthur had put it to one side, believing that he could give the money back one day, or spend it on something for Ernie. Besides which, it wasn't as though Arthur needed the money with his pension and savings. What did he have to spend his money on at his age and without any family of his own to spoil? The summer holidays would be upon them in a few months and Ernic would hopefully be spending more time with him then while Neil was away working, so the money Neil had given him could go on Ernie then, if the lad needed anything.

Arthur had thought he was managing his existence quite well, but now that he'd spent some time with Ernie and Neil – including a few occasions when they'd eaten out, as well as last Saturday when Neil had invited him up to his flat to watch the football – it made him painfully aware of exactly how lonely he had been. It wasn't good spending so much time alone and, looking back, he was actually afraid that he'd become a bit depressed; something that he'd never have wanted to admit to anyone. He'd always been so wrapped up in Julia, particularly when she'd been ill and he'd known their days together were numbered, and when he'd lost her, he hadn't known how he'd manage to go on. If he'd had George still, that would have been a comfort, but his son had been gone long before Julia, and Arthur was left completely alone. Now, having energetic young Ernie around brightened his day and gave him a routine that he enjoyed. He got up and gave the lad a good breakfast then, most days, he'd get the bus to the supermarket and buy them something nice for dinner, pop into the newsagent's to pick up another model plane kit or another board game before heading home for lunch and a nap before Ernie returned. It was always a joyful time of day for Arthur, because he'd hear stories about Ernie's day and the lad's youthful enthusiasm and curiosity about life was so positive; it made Arthur feel as though he had a reason to be around again and that was something he hadn't felt since Julia passed on. He knew that Ernie had been a tonic for him and he also hoped that he might be the same for Ernie and his father.

He had to admit that he was more tired than when he'd only had himself to care for. He was doing more, which meant that he was bound to be, but he liked that he was needed now, that he had to get out of his chair to open the door to Ernie and he had to get dinner ready or the boy would be hungry.

A few times, though, Arthur had been struck dumb by nostalgia when Ernie had said and done certain things. The emotion had intensified when he'd been clearing out the spare room and found some of George's model planes that he'd never had the chance to make. It had taken the breath from his lungs and left him reeling. His son, his precious boy, was no longer around and that was so difficult to believe when Arthur looked at Ernie. How could a child be taken from the world, have their life stolen away by illness? Even after all these years, he still couldn't come to terms with the fact that George would never have a family of his own, never see old age himself. And then there was Julia; how she had grieved for their only child and yet ... she had been so strong, putting Arthur first and holding him together. Her grief had been boundless but she had got up each day and made them tea and toast; she had organised them, insisted they take holidays and that they keep living, even though her heart was broken. Time had eased the sharp ache of their loss but not a day had gone by when they didn't talk about George and the love he had brought with him. He had been a bright and sensitive lad and he would have been a good man.

The timer on the oven pinged, so Arthur turned the heat off then used the oven glove to get the tray with the garlic bread out. He gave the Bolognese sauce a good stir then drained the spaghetti. Simple actions but ones that offered comfort.

Arthur heaped the food onto two plates, poured cherry juice into two glasses then called, 'Ernie, dinner's ready, lad!'

The sound of Ernie's small feet hurrying towards the kitchen was the best sound in the world, and one he would never tire of hearing. He chuckled to himself at the irony.

CHAPTER 18

Abby wiped the back of her hand over her brow and stood up. She'd spent the morning planting seedlings for a variety of vegetables including carrots, sprouting broccoli, green beans and kale. She had a section of the garden where she'd planted herbs like basil, coriander, dill and parsley, and with the recent sunshine and showers, they appeared to be thriving. In the fruit patch were strawberry plants, blueberry bushes and rhubarb, all of which could be used for fresh fruit or for jams and chutneys if there was a surplus. She'd also invested in two portable four-tier greenhouses that she had set up near the old garden shed and where she would grow tomatoes and peppers.

Jason's plans had suggested using one section of the garden for vegetables, one for herbs, one for fruit and one for flowers. She'd used his name at the garden centre and had received a very pleasing discount, as well as being given some seedlings for free. They had looked a bit worse for wear but she hoped she could save them with some TLC. She certainly had plenty of time and energy to devote to the garden and just had to hope that no one from the flats decided that they'd help themselves without asking. She hoped that people would want to get involved, to work together. So far, she'd had a few of her neighbours come out and ask what she was doing and some of the younger children had offered her a hand with planting the seedlings, including Ernie. The little boy had been delighted that she'd left his den standing but had also told her that he thought it made the garden look a bit untidy, so he'd said he'd take it down if she wanted him to. Abby had told him that it was his decision, but if he did decide to take it down, then she thought they could find some room in the old shed for his things if he wanted.

She picked up her bottle of water and took a long drink. Ernie had looked so much better than when she'd first met him. It wasn't just that his clothes fit better, it was more that he had a healthy glow and his ready smile was bigger than ever. As they'd sat side by side on the bench the previous evening, Ernie had told her that he'd been spending some time with Mr Mayer, something that had surprised Abby, but she hadn't let Ernie see that. Apparently, Ernie had fallen and the old man had come to his rescue then offered to help Ernie's father out with childcare. Ernie had dashed off then, after hearing his father's car pull up out the front of the flats, and Abby had mulled over his words; surely a man who made such a generous offer couldn't be that bad a person? And whenever Ernie spoke about Mr Mayer, his face lit up; he was clearly very fond of him. Could that little boy have broken through the old man's cold veneer and warmed his heart?

'Hello?' A voice broke into her thoughts, pulling her back to the present.

She looked in the direction of the path that led around

from the front of the flats. The voice sounded familiar, but it wasn't Gavin's and she didn't have many male visitors. Make that *any* male visitors.

'Abby?'

Jason appeared; tall, tanned and breathtakingly handsome in a pair of khaki combat trousers and a matching T-shirt. His name was embroidered on the top left of the shirt with the yellow community gardeners' logo of three stick people holding hands around a tree. He must have come straight from work, even though it was Saturday.

'Jason!' She touched her hair self-consciously, aware that she was a sweaty mess, and that her black shorts and old burgundy T-shirt, with a hole under the right armpit, weren't exactly the clothes she'd have chosen to wear if she'd known he was coming.

'Sorry to arrive unannounced. I tried to phone you but your mobile kept going to voicemail, so I thought I'd take a chance and turn up. A little boy around the front told me you were out here.' He placed his hands on his hips and looked around, nodding and smiling. 'Impressive, work, Abby. Did you do this all yourself?'

She tucked a strand of hair behind her ear then shook her head, wondering if she looked as exhausted as she felt. 'I did the initial clearing then the buildings manager removed the furniture that had been dumped here and since then I've had some help.'

He raised an eyebrow. 'From?'

'Some of the children.'

He shook his head. 'You'll need more help than that. What about asking your neighbours?'

She shrugged. 'I could do but I don't want to seem pushy.'

'Abby, you're not just doing this for yourself are you? This is, and should be, a community project.'

She smiled shyly up at him, hoping he'd think the glow in her cheeks was from time in the sun and not the blush that it actually was.

'Anyway, seeing as I'm here, how about I give you a hand?'

'But you've been at work all morning.'

'I'll let you into a secret, shall I? I don't have anyone waiting for me at home, I have plans to meet a few friends for a drink tonight – but that's not until seven – and I'm hoping that if I help you now, you might offer me some lunch.'

He smiled at her and she almost melted. His eyes were so dark and so intense that it made her feel light-headed. It was wrong for a man to be this good-looking, surely, especially seeing as how he was also so nice. It was a dangerous combination.

'You've got yourself a deal.'

She gave him a high five then handed him a trowel.

In the flat, while Jason washed up in the bathroom, Abby made some sandwiches. She only had some cold chicken and salad in the fridge but the bread was a delicious wholegrain cob she'd picked up the previous day, so it made the sandwiches look good at any rate. She piled them on a tray then tipped two bags of crisps on the side – one ready salted and one salt and vinegar.

She got two large bottles of water out of the fridge then two blonde beers. She'd discovered a taste for the Belgian beer after trying one at Lisa's, and after a long morning's work, she felt that she deserved a treat, as did Jason.

Her stomach did a loop the loop. She couldn't quite believe that the handsome and burly gardener had turned up to help her, let alone that he was currently in her bathroom. She'd noticed that he'd had a haircut since she'd last seen him and as they'd worked in the garden, side by side, she'd found her eyes drawn to the nape of his neck where the hair was shortest, and she'd wondered how it would feel to run a hand over his head, if her palm would tickle as it ran over the graduated cut of his blond hair. And those forearms, exposed by the short sleeves of his T-shirt! Strong, muscular and with fine white-blond hairs that glinted in the sunlight. Abby suspected she'd had too much sun, because she couldn't deny that she was feeling a bit ... flirtatious around the handsome gardener; that parts of her that she'd thought long ago buried – like the parts that had felt desire or allowed herself to feel desirable – seemed to be awakening in Jason's presence as the plants did under the warm glow of the sun.

She laughed to herself. What on earth was she thinking? Jason was just a good bloke who'd come to help; he probably did this with everyone who emailed him, and she was no different. Just because she found him a bit ... OK, *very* attractive, did not mean that the feelings were reciprocated.

So, they could have lunch then Jason would return to his life and to his evening with friends, while Abby soaked in the tub then watched TV with a pizza for one. And that was fine, because since she'd started overhauling the garden, she had been sleeping better than she had done in years. All the hard physical work and fresh air was doing wonders for her sleep, as well as making her pleasingly toned and tanned. She looked better than ever, and felt pretty damn good too.

'That looks great.' Jason was leaning on the doorjamb smiling at her, and in spite of her thoughts about him not being interested, her heart sped up.

'It's just sandwiches.' She held out the tray. 'Can you carry this into the lounge?'

'Why not take it outside?'

'Great idea. Are these OK?' She held up the beers.

'One of my all-time favourites.' He wiggled his eyebrows, making her laugh again.

As they made their way down the stairs then back out into the sunshine, Abby had a feeling that Jason could easily become one of her all-time favourites too.

In the garden, they sat on the bench as they ate the sandwiches and drank the cold beers. The sun was warm on Abby's face and the beer went straight to her head, making her feel relaxed and happy. They discussed everything and nothing; organic gardening, what to expect in terms of yield from the plants and how to deal with common pests like greenfly. Jason was knowledgeable but in a helpful way; Abby never felt that he was lecturing her or patronising her, and that was so different to how things had been with Gavin.

Somehow, the conversation had drifted on to other things like books and music and Jason had admitted that although he did like a lot of rock bands, he also enjoyed the odd Ed Sheeran song. He'd even sung her a few lines from 'Perfect' and Abby was impressed by his lovely voice. She could have sat there and listened to him sing all afternoon, but she'd probably have ended up flinging herself at him groupie style. Drinking in the afternoon sunshine and a handsome man were a perilous combination …

'Thanks for lunch, Abby. It was lovely.' Jason drained his beer then set the bottle on the tray.

'It was just sandwiches.'

He smiled. 'You're not good with compliments, are you? They were very nice sandwiches. See, a lot of people don't realise that sandwiches can be dull and routine, or tasty and satisfying. It's all to do with the butter to filling ratio: too much butter or spread and it ruins the sandwich; too little and the sandwich can seem dry.'

'I had no idea that sandwiches were such complicated things.' Abby tilted her head as she gazed at him, wondering if he was teasing her or if he really took his sandwiches that seriously.

'I've given sandwiches a lot of thought over the years and tried a lot of different ones. Yours are very good indeed.'

'Well … thank you.'

'Unfortunately, now … I'd better be going.' He sighed. 'I've a few things to do before I go out this evening.'

The beer and sandwiches turned heavy in Abby's stomach. Of course this lovely man had plans on a Saturday night. He probably had a special someone, or more likely a queue of them around the block.

'Going anywhere nice?' Abby didn't want to ask but the words tripped off her tongue anyway.

'Just the Lamb and Flag.' He shrugged. 'With a few mates.'

'Lovely.' Abby stood then picked up the tray.

'I don't suppose …' Jason chewed his bottom lip then

tucked his hands into his pockets. 'Would you like to come? If you're not busy that is.'

'Me?'

He looked around them. 'No one else here.'

He was asking her to the pub on a Saturday evening. It was far more than meeting for coffee or working on the community garden together. It was a big step. Was she ready to take it, even if it didn't lead anywhere? Would she be disappointed if she took this step then found that Jason only wanted to be friends?

As she weighed the situation up, her heart answered for her: if she didn't go, she'd regret it and spend the evening wondering why she'd declined.

'Oh … uh … Yes! I'd love to come. If you're sure that's all right?'

'Of course it is. The pub is nothing special but they serve a great draught IPA plus it'd be great to introduce you to my mates.' His cheeks turned pink and he peered at her from beneath his dark lashes.

'Shall I meet you there?' Abby said.

'I can come and pick you up if you'd like?'

'No, you'd be going out of your way then and I doubt you want to take the car. I'll meet you at the pub.'

'About seven?'

'Fabulous.' Abby was glad she was holding the tray because it stopped her from punching the air.

They walked back around to the front of the building then Jason headed towards a white van. He turned and gave a wave before getting in and starting the engine. As he drove out of the car park, Abby used her fob to let herself into the building while balancing the tray on one hip, then she entered the cool air of the communal entrance. Her heart was fluttering and she knew she had a goofy grin on her face. For the first time in her adult life, she was going out on Saturday evening with a handsome man who wasn't Gavin. It was exciting, thrilling and she felt rather daring. She liked the new Abby very much indeed.

As her eyes adjusted from the brightness outside, she realised that Mr Mayer's door was ajar. Her stomach lurched; what if he was waiting for her like he'd done before? She was feeling so happy after a lovely morning and the last thing she wanted now was a confrontation. She held her breath and walked towards the stairs, hoping to ascend without being noticed, but the door creaked open behind her and she froze.

'Abby?'

She turned to find Ernie smiling at her from Mr Mayer's doorway.

'I heard the door and thought you might be my dad.'

'Ernie? What're you doing in there?'

'I came down to see Arthur while Dad picks up some chips.'

'Oh … right. That's nice.'

'We're going to have a game of donim … dom–in–oes.'

'With Mr Mayer?'

He nodded then poked his tongue through the gap where his bottom teeth were just starting to show. 'Arthur says I'm getting good.'

'Dominoes, eh? I haven't played that in years.'

'You should come in and have a game.'

'I … don't think Mr Mayer would like that.'

'Why not?' Ernie swung his leg back and forth then

turned on the spot like a tiny ballerina. 'He's helping me with my tables and my spelling. He could teach you dom–in–oes too, if you want.'

'Maybe another time.' Abby smiled. 'Enjoy your chips and I'll see you later.'

'Ernie, lad, what're you doing out here.' Mr Mayer appeared in the doorway and gently ruffled Ernie's hair.

'Talking to Abby. I thought she was my dad, back with our chips but it wasn't him yet.'

Abby gripped the tray tighter, wondering if the elderly man would criticise the fact that she was carrying a tray with two empty beer bottles on it.

'Hello there.'

Abby met Mr Mayer's eyes. Was he actually addressing her with that kindly tone?

'Hello.'

'How are things with you?' He pushed his glasses up his nose and his lips turned into a smile. Not a grin, but a polite and rather warm smile. Ernie was smiling up at Mr Mayer as if he was full of admiration for him.

'Very well, thank you.'

She paused for a moment, not sure what to do next. She didn't want to be rude and walk away when this was the most civil Mr Mayer had ever been, but neither did she feel she could stand there in silence indefinitely. Besides which, she needed to decide what to wear. What did one wear to go to the pub to meet a man and his friends when it wasn't a date but you very much wanted to sleep with said man? How casually should she dress?

'That's good to hear.' Mr Mayer nodded

Ernie suddenly tilted his head to one side. 'I think that's Dad's car! Never fear, Mr M, our chips are here!'

Arthur chuckled then ruffled Ernie's hair again. 'I'd better get those plates in the oven to warm. Goodbye, Abby.'

'Bye …' She watched as he disappeared into his flat, then Ernie opened the main door and stared out into the car park. 'See you soon, Ernie.'

'Bye, Abby!'

As Abby climbed the stairs to her flat, she had to admit to being pleasantly surprised. Mr Mayer had been polite to her! And she could see how very fond of little Ernie he was. Something had clearly happened to provoke a change in the elderly man, because he was so much softer than on the previous occasions when she'd encountered him. Perhaps now would be a good time to start telling her neighbours about her plans for the garden – and Mr Mayer could be a good place to start.

CHAPTER 19

Abby had changed four times, done her make-up, washed it all off, then started again. It was already six o'clock and she didn't have that long before she'd need to leave. It was her own fault she was running late, though, after deciding to Google Jason's name along with 'Kent'. What was that old saying about curiosity and the cat? Dammit! Why had she done it? She felt as though she was snooping on a perfectly nice man and now she knew things that she couldn't un-know ...

She pulled on her next outfit, black jeans with a charcoal-grey smock top and a black cardigan. That would have to do. She slid her feet into flat black pumps and returned to the mirror where she dusted her face with some mineral powder followed by some blusher on her cheekbones, then finished with a slick of lip gloss. She'd left her hair down but washed and blow-dried it so it shone. The time outdoors had lightened some of her mousy-brown strands to a light golden brown and she had to admit that she liked it. She was even considering having some highlights done after seeing how much she liked the sun-kissed ones.

She had five minutes to spare, so she sank onto the end of her bed and took some deep breaths. Her heart was racing because of a combination of nerves and excitement about seeing Jason again.

She really, really liked him. Yes, he was physically attractive, but there was so much more to him. He had a smile that brightened his whole face and he was genuinely *nice*; he did so much to help in the community, like today, offering her a hand, even though he'd already been at work all morning.

So she would go tonight and smile and keep what she'd discovered to herself. If, at some point, Jason wanted to tell her about it, then that was up to him.

'Another round?' Jim asked as he stood up.

'I'll give you a hand, love.' Jim's wife, Emma, went to the bar with him.

'I'm not sure I should have any more.' Abby looked at Jason. 'I don't normally drink much beer and that IPA is quite strong.'

'I promise I'll make sure you get home safe.' Jason smiled. 'We'll make this the last one.'

'I've had a great evening.' Abby looked around the cosy pub at the happy faces of people enjoying a Saturday evening in good company. Jason's friends had been warm and welcoming and made her feel completely at ease. Like him, they were involved in the community gardening arena. Luke was one of the accountants, Jim was an architect who worked pro-bono whenever he could help, Emma was a GP but she got involved with projects on her days off and Tom, the youngest member of the group at twenty-eight, was part of the gardening workforce like Jason.

'I love a good pub quiz, especially with this lot.' Jason

patted Luke on the arm. 'Luke's got a good brain on him all right.'

Luke laughed, his cheeks glowing from the effects of beer. 'I'm brighter than you, that's for sure.'

Jason shook his head. 'He's modest too.'

'Quiz champion, I am!' Luke patted his ample belly. 'Shame about this though, but when I'm cramming for quiz night, I tend to cram food into my mouth at the same time.'

'Why don't you get a bit more involved in the physical side of gardening too?' Jason asked. 'You'd soon see the weight come off.'

'We can't all be as hunky as you, Jason. It wouldn't be fair on the ladies of Manchester. How would they get anything done?'

'Yeah, yeah.' Jason laughed then rolled his eyes at Abby. 'Oh the banter, right?'

Jim and Emma appeared with a tray of fresh drinks and Jason turned to Abby.

'You were pretty good in the quiz too.'

'I answered two questions.' Abby laughed.

'That none of us knew the answers to.'

'A childhood spent reading.'

'You were interested in the Tudors then?'

'I was fascinated by them, I used to devour paperbacks about Anne Boleyn and Henry VIII. I had no idea that knowledge would serve me well in a pub quiz.'

'Got us some bonus points.'

Abby nodded, pleased. When the questions had come up about the Tudors, she'd known the answers straight away. The human brain never ceased to amaze her with its capacity to store information away for years then pluck it out as if from thin air.

'Thanks for coming.' Jason's eyes were bright and his smile was wide. He was, quite possibly, the most handsome man she had ever seen. Her stomach lurched as she recalled what she'd read about him. 'What is it?'

'What's what?'

'Your whole face just dropped. Did you remember something bad?'

'Oh … no, I was just thinking about … how awful it must have been for Anne Boleyn when Henry turned his back on her.' She sucked in a breath, hating having to lie to Jason but she couldn't tell him what had really been on her mind. 'She lost him, her world and her life.' Abby knew she sounded ridiculous.

Jason's eyes widened but he inclined his head. 'True. Lots of sad stories throughout history.'

'Indeed.'

She reached out and gently touched his hand, before pulling away again. She just wanted to let him know that she was there for him, should he ever feel the need to tell her more.

When she raised her eyes to meet his, she was startled again by how deep and dark they were, as if she could tumble into them and lose herself for ever. And that would never do. Abby had been lost once before; she knew that she could never allow that to happen again. However nice Jason was, and whatever he'd been through in the past.

Human beings were fragile and so was Abby's heart. So she had to keep it under lock and key.

*

'I was thinking about that old shed in the garden.' Jason was walking her home. Abby had tried to tell him that she'd be fine but he'd told her that he'd never rest unless he knew she'd got back to Willow Court safely.

'What about it?'

'We could give it a lick of paint, spruce it up a bit. What do you think?'

'I think that's a great idea. It would be a shame to leave it looking scruffy when the rest of the garden looks so much better.'

'I'll have a check at home to see if I have any spare paint. I'm sure there's some there but I have no idea what colour.'

'Thank you. That's very kind.'

'It wouldn't take us long to paint it.'

We. Us. Jason was intending on coming round again then. In spite of her decision in the pub, it seemed as though Jason liked her. This was so difficult because she really liked him too. Was it that they were drawn to each other then? That a seed of something had been planted between them and that it could grow into something bigger? It certainly felt that way.

All too soon they arrived at the entrance to Willow Court.

'Do you ... want to come in?'

'For coffee?' He raised an eyebrow.

'Yes, if you want. I do have tea and coffee in the flat.'

Jason laughed. 'I probably shouldn't. I'm working tomorrow and have an early start, but thank you. Perhaps another time?'

'Sure.' Abby opened her bag and rooted around inside

for her keys, keen to have somewhere to look other than at Jason.

'Abby?'

'Mmmm.'

'Please look at me.'

She closed her bag and met his eyes.

'I had a great time tonight and I ... I don't do this very often ... Well, not ever to be honest, so if I'm a bit ... rusty, then please forgive me.'

'There's nothing to forgive, Jason. I had a great time too.'

'Thanks.'

'I did. And I'm so grateful for your help with the garden and for all your advice.'

'That's been my pleasure.'

He took a step towards her and was so close that if Abby had raised her hand, it would have brushed against his. So when he lifted his hand and gently brushed her hair from her cheek, her breath caught in her throat. He stroked her skin, his touch as light as a feather, and warmth curled through her chest, wrapping itself around her pounding heart.

'I'm a complicated person, Abby. I want ... I wish ... that I wasn't and that my slate was clean, so to speak, but there are things in my past that can't be erased. I want to just exist in this moment, but my baggage is heavy, and even though I wish I could kiss you right now, I don't think it's fair to bring you into my world.' He gave a wry laugh. 'Of course, I could be totally misreading the signs here and perhaps you don't fancy me at all. As I said, I am rusty at this.'

Abby covered his hand with hers, pressing it against her cheek.

'You're not misreading anything but I have baggage too. I'm not … ready for anything new at the moment, even if I want to be.'

He nodded then leant forwards and brushed his lips against hers. It was over so quickly that she wondered if she'd imagined it but her whole body tingled, confirming that it had happened.

'Can we be friends though?' He held her gaze.

'Most definitely.'

He tucked his hands into his jeans pockets and stepped backwards.

'Goodnight, Abby. Text you in the week?'

'Please do. Night, Jason.'

Then she turned and walked towards Willow Court. When she reached the entrance, she surrendered to her curiosity and looked behind her, and there he was, waiting for her to go inside. She gave a wave that he returned, then let herself into the building.

It would have been so easy to kiss Jason back, to encourage him to come home with her. Part of her wished she had done, that she had surrendered to her feelings of desire and the need to fall asleep in a man's arms, to wake up and not be alone. But another part of her knew that they'd done the right thing; Jason might be nice but he'd been through a lot and until they knew each other better, they needed to take things slowly. Perhaps nothing would come of their friendship, perhaps they were destined to spend a brief time in each other's lives then pass each other by. Whatever happened, Abby was glad of one thing; Jason had stirred feelings inside her that had been buried for a long, long time.

And now she really felt alive.

CHAPTER 20

Arthur opened the wardrobe door for the first time in a long time, and as Julia's floral perfume drifted out, pain bloomed in his chest. Unable to get rid of her belongings, he had kept them safely in her wardrobe, just as they had been when she was alive. Her dresses, trousers, skirts and blouses hung from the rail and in the chest of drawers under the window, the rest of her clothes were neatly folded. He couldn't let them go; he couldn't even bear to look at them most of the time, because it brought her back with such startling clarity that his grief threatened to overwhelm him completely and he feared it would swallow him whole.

But he'd remembered something earlier that morning and he wanted to see if he could find it.

He steeled himself then reached up for the box that sat on the shelf above the rail of clothes. He wobbled slightly, unsteady as he brought the box out, then set it on the bed and sat next to it. His heart was racing with the effort of retrieving the box and because of the intensity of emotion swirling through him. Day to day, he could just about manage his grief but at times like this, it was difficult. However, Ernie had been such a tonic for his pain and he was thankful every day for the lad's company.

He placed a hand on the lid of the box and gently wiped away the dust that had settled there, then he pulled a hanky from his cardigan pocket and wiped his hand.

'Let's see if what I want is in here, shall we?' His voice seemed lost in the early morning light of their bedroom.

Lifting the lid, Arthur set it on the bed, then peered inside. He had been right; the books he'd recalled were inside, where he had put them after Julia had passed. He couldn't bear to leave them on the coffee table where they'd sat ready for her to peruse of an evening after dinner. But after noticing over recent weeks that someone had cleared the community garden and started working on it, he had thought of the books again. He suspected that it was the buildings manager who had cleared away the furniture and debris from the garden. When he had taken a look outside a few days ago, he noticed that someone had raked over the beds and planted some seedlings, and it had been difficult to see. Then, after watching a gardening documentary on TV last night, something had made it imperative that he find the books, as if he feared that in the fog of grieving, he might have accidentally thrown them out.

Julia's gardening books. Three of them with dog-eared dustcovers and yellow Post-it notes sticking out of the pages. Pages she had bookmarked because she wanted to plant those particular flowers or because she wanted advice about how to treat common garden pests. He opened one of the books and his stomach lurched when he saw Julia's handwriting on one of the Post-it notes, her script long and looped, beautiful as he had always thought it was. Arthur had never written cards to people; he had always let Julia do it, knowing it would be far nicer for them to read her elegant hand than his stilted spiky writing – writing that was far worse now that his hands had become so gnarled. He traced the blue ink from her fountain pen:

Rose aphids – check shoot tips and underside of leaves. Increase in spring and early summer. Can squash with finger when possible. Avoid pesticides.

A chuckle escaped him then, a balm to his pain. Julia could talk for hours about roses and tulips and a whole host of other flowers. She was so enthusiastic about the garden and had made it her space. She had created a true oasis and they had loved nothing more than to take a cup of tea outside on a summer's evening and enjoy the garden she had planted. She'd point out the various species of butterfly, dragonflies, ladybirds and bumblebees, as well as the birds that came to feast on the treats she left out for them. She'd even had a few squirrel visitors from the nearby park that had come to try their luck on the birdfeeders. Rather than have them steal from the birds, Julia had left them small piles of nuts and seeds. She had loved nature in all its forms and her enthusiasm for it had been one of the things Arthur had adored about her. Julia had had such a good heart, such a happy disposition and she really had been the sunshine of his life. Even after they'd lost their only son, Julia had kept on going, holding Arthur together too.

A knock at the door startled him, dragging him from his reverie. He got up with the aid of his stick then made his way to the door.

'Morning!' Ernie sang as he smiled up at Arthur.

'Good morning, lad. You're up early, aren't you?'

'It's seven forty-five.'

'Is it now?' Arthur must have been thinking about his wife for a longer than he'd realised.

'I just came to ask what we're having for tea tonight.' Ernie grinned and Arthur's sadness dispersed as if the lad had waved a magic wand.

'Hmmm.' Arthur leant on his stick with both hands. 'Let me think.'

'How about … pie?'

'Pie?' Arthur laughed. 'I do like a nice steak and kidney pie.'

'Ewww! Not kidney.' Ernie shook his head.

'Not kidney. Righty-o. How about … chicken and vegetable?'

'Yes please! With gravy and mash?'

'Great idea.'

'Jax taking you to school?'

'Yes, she's just packing my lunch while Dad's getting dressed for work. He said he deserved a later start today and he might do the same every Monday.'

'Good for him. Now, hold on!' Arthur held up a hand then shuffled back into his kitchen and plucked a bright red apple from the bowl. He returned to the door and handed it to Ernie. 'Take this for your break time.'

'Thank you.' Ernie gazed at the apple that appeared huge in his small hand, then he flung his arms around Arthur's waist and hugged him. 'See you later.'

As Ernie skipped back up the stairs, Arthur leant against the door. Along with Neil, who had turned out to be a decent man just trying to make his way through life – Ernie's presence in his world was a gift Arthur would never take for granted.

*

Later that day, Ernie raced up the stairs to the flat. He couldn't wait to change out of his uniform then get down to see Arthur. Jax still collected him from school and some days she came in for a while too, but he liked the days when he went straight to Arthur's best.

'Slow down, Ernie!' Jax panted behind him, still scrolling through her mobile.

'If you stopped checking on your boyfriend all the time, you'd move quicker!' Ernie called to her.

'You cheeky beggar! I'm not checking on him.'

'Yeah, yeah.' Ernie giggled as he reached his front door. 'Jax and Callum, sitting in a tree, K-I-S-S ... K-I-S-S-S ... I-N-G!'

Jax arrived at the top of the stairs and scowled at him. 'Don't you dare say that to anyone else, Ernie.'

'Whatever!'

'You're getting too big for your boots, you know that?' Jax smiled at him then she unlocked the door. The spare key was now downstairs with Mr Mayer.

Inside the flat, Ernie went and changed then opened his rucksack and pulled out his lunch box and water bottle. His spelling book fell out onto the bed so he picked it up and stuffed it back in his bag under the rest of his books. He didn't want to have to explain why he'd got such a bad mark again. The other boys in his class had laughed at him for getting two out of twenty, but he just couldn't help it. Some words were OK but longer ones always made him panic, and even though he'd tried to copy from the boys next to him on his table, he didn't always manage to write the words down correctly. Sometimes, he was able to copy and get up to fifteen out of twenty but this morning, the boys around him had been covering their work with their pencil cases because Billy James had whispered to them that Ernie always cheated. Ernie had denied it but then he'd got that sore lump in his throat and Billy had said that Ernie was a cry baby. Ernie didn't want to be a cry baby so he'd dug his nails into his legs to stop himself from being one.

He tucked his rucksack under his bed where he could forget about it. Dad was ringing soon then he'd go and have tea with Arthur and hopefully build some more of their plane. Arthur said he was clever at building things and it made Ernie feel good, not stupid like Billy and the other boys said. If only he could leave school now and never go back.

'Ernie, your mobile's ringing.' Jax called from the kitchen. Arthur had suggested that Dad get him a cheap mobile so they could stay in touch. Ernie didn't take it to school because it was an older phone and not a new touchscreen one like the other children had. But he was secretly delighted with the mobile as it meant he could message Dad when he was working away, then Dad always rang him after school to see how his day went. It made him feel more secure, knowing that he could get hold of Dad whenever he needed to.

'Ernie?' Dad's voice echoed in the mobile.

'Hiya, Dad!'

'How was school?'

'Good, thanks.'

'Did you have reading today?'

Ernie chewed his lip. 'Yeah ... we read ... a Roald Dahl book. Miss read it to us and it was really funny.'

'I used to like Roald Dahl when I was a kid too. What about spelling?'

'Nah. It's ... later in the week.' Ernie held his breath; lying to Dad made him feel bad but he couldn't face telling him about the test. Dad never said he had any problems with spelling, so Ernie thought that perhaps he was just the stupid one, although Kerry Baker in his class said that her mum couldn't do maths and that was why she couldn't either, so perhaps it came from his mum.

'Dad?'

'Yes, Ernie.'

'Did ... does Mum have ... is she a good speller and reader?'

The line went silent and Ernie peered at the screen to see if he'd lost his signal.

'Dad?'

At the other end of the line, his dad sighed softly before replying. 'Your mum did have some trouble with spelling, yes. She never liked writing letters unless I'd checked them for her first.'

'She did?' Something in Ernie loosened, a bit like when he woke up stiff from building his den and had a good stretch. Perhaps, if Mum couldn't spell very well either, Ernie wasn't stupid.

'Yeah ... I'll tell you more about it when I come home.'

Ernie held his breath. Dad was going to tell him about Mum?

'On Friday?'

'Actually ... I was going to surprise you but I've got tomorrow off, so I'm on my way home now.'

Ernie's belly flipped. '*Yaaaay*! What time will you be back?'

'Not until later but I'll come to Arthur's to get you, shall I?'

'Sounds good, Dad! We're having pie for tea. Shall I ask him to keep you some?'

'No, lad, it's fine. I'll eat when I get home or pick something up on the way. You enjoy your tea and be good for Arthur.'

'I will. See you later!'

Ernie put his mobile on the kitchen counter then smiled at Jax. 'Dad's coming home tonight.'

'Cool! So you going to wait here?'

He shook his head. 'I'm having tea with Arthur first and Dad will come there for me.'

Jax nodded then peered at her mobile screen. 'Damn it! I didn't realise that was the time. I've got to get to work. You'll be OK to go down yourself?'

Ernie nodded. He'd just wash his lunch box and water bottle out first then go for his tea. If Dad was home, he wouldn't sleep at Arthur's tonight, but at least they would have some time together first.

Ernie couldn't wait to speak to his dad more about his mum – it was making Ernie's belly fizz like a bottle of Coke. Ernie had so many questions about Mum, so he'd have to pick the most important ones. He didn't want to ask Dad everything in one go, he wanted to save some things for later, but at least he could find more things out about her.

He ran back to his bedroom and grabbed his water bottle and lunch box off the bed then took them to the kitchen. It felt like, since Mr Mayer had become his friend, everything was getting better.

*

Abby had been thinking about Ernie and Mr Mayer and how much she wanted to stay at Willow Court. If the elderly man had given Ernie a chance, then perhaps he would give her one too. If she had more time, and didn't have to leave, she could do so much with the garden!

She'd take him something as a peace offering; see if they could find some common ground. It was possible that he might even appreciate what she'd done.

She went down to the garden with a small pot from the pile that she'd been storing in her kitchen, then out into the garden. She scooped some of the fertilised earth from the flowerbed then gently lifted one of the parsley plants. With the recent sunshine, it was growing well, and didn't most people like fresh parsley to go with things like fish? She patted the earth around the plant down then carried it back to the entrance and let herself in.

Outside Mr Mayer's door, she took a deep breath then knocked firmly.

From inside, she heard shuffling footsteps then the door swung inwards and Mr Mayer stood there, looking rather surprised.

'Oh! I thought you would be Ernie.'

'Sorry.' Her hand went to her chest. 'I … uh … I wanted to bring you this.' She smiled at him and held out the small plant – Mr Mayer stared at it.

'Thank you.' He took it from her and squinted at it, removed his glasses and brought it closer to his face, then put his glasses back on.

'Parsley eh?'

'Yes. Fresh herbs can brighten any dish!' Abby grimaced; she'd meant to sound light-hearted, but instead sounded slightly manic.

'Indeed they do.'

'My Mayer … could I … could I come in for five minutes, please? I'd like to talk to you about something.'

He frowned and she braced herself for a refusal, then he shrugged and stood back, so she walked into his hallway. A delicious savoury smell met her nostrils and her mouth watered instantly.

'Go on through to the lounge.'

She did so then took a seat on the sofa. Mr Mayer set the parsley down on a small table between two armchairs then sat down on one of the chairs, balancing his walking stick against the arm.

'What can I do for you?' he asked, his head tilted to one side as if he was assessing her.

'I know that we haven't exactly seen eye to eye since I moved in, and I did fully intend on looking for somewhere else to live … but see …' She wrung her hands together in her lap. 'Mr Mayer, I really like my flat and I really like Willow Court. It's a good place to be and I'd like … I've decided to stay. I've been doing some work in the garden … trying to improve it and—'

'That was you?'

'You've seen what I've done?' She imagined him looking around outside and admiring how hard she'd worked.

He sniffed. 'I went around the back of the flats for some fresh air and I thought that the buildings manager must have arranged a tidy-up.'

'It's a bit more than a tidy-up … I've been planting flowers and herbs and some fruit and veg and I was thinking that we could even make the garden profitable by selling some of the produce on. It could raise money for a local charity, or for some equipment for the children who live here, or for the older residents.' She smiled, pleased with how far she'd come and hoping that Mr Mayer would be too. 'I want to create a beautiful space that everyone can enjoy.'

Silence fell in the room and Abby shifted in her seat. Wasn't he going to say something? She stared uncomfortably at the blank television screen where their reflections were distorted and dull.

'What makes you think that you can make decisions for everyone else who lives here?'

'I'm sorry?'

'You've been here for what ... five minutes and now you're taking over the garden. Who said you could do that?'

'I ... I thought it was for the best. I had some time on my hands and I came across a gardening blog and wanted to make a difference here. It seemed such a shame to see that lovely outdoor space wasted, turned into a dumping ground for furniture and a toilet for cats and dogs. I only meant to do good.' She scanned his face but his expression was confusing. His bushy eyebrows had settled above his glasses and his mouth was set in a thin line. The grooves at the sides of his mouth seemed deep enough to hold pens and he had closed his eyes, as if needing to shut Abby out. 'Mr Mayer?'

'Miss Hamilton,' he said finally, opening his eyes, his voice tight so that the lines at the sides of his mouth appeared deeper. 'You had no right to take control of the garden. No right at all.'

'But no one else was taking care of it and I wanted to improve it for everyone to enjoy. I don't see what the problem is.'

The smell of cooking seemed stronger now, almost choking, and she could hear something bubbling on the stove, presumably potatoes or vegetables that had come to the boil.

'Someone ...' His voice broke and he cleared his throat. 'Someone *was* taking care of it. The garden was beautiful once. My Julia made it into a wonderful space but when she got ... when she was unwell ... she couldn't do it anymore.' He lifted his glasses and flicked the back of his hand over his eyes in turn.

'I'm so sorry, Mr Mayer. I didn't realise. The last thing I wanted to do was to cause you any pain. It really was. But wouldn't you like to see it in all its glory again? Do you not think that Julia would have wanted that ... for the children of Willow Court at least? Children like Ernie.'

'Please leave.' His voice had risen. 'Now! And don't ... don't ever say her name again. You know nothing about my wife and what she wanted.' He pushed himself upwards, still not meeting her eyes, and gestured at the door.

'But, Mr Mayer ...'

He held up a hand and shook his head. 'No! No more. Just go.' His hand was shaking and his face had reddened.

Abby sighed, her legs felt unsteady and the happiness she'd hoped to share was slipping through her fingers like sand. As she left the flat, her heart was heavy. It seemed that nothing she ever did would please her elderly neighbour. She had every right to feel angry with him right now, for being so selfish, for not trying to see it from anyone else's point of view, but all she felt was sadness. He must be very unhappy indeed if he couldn't see outside of himself, to the potential for their neighbours.

There was clearly nothing she could do to change his mind – but she would carry on with her plans regardless. There was no stopping her now.

Arthur heard the door close and he settled back into his chair. His stomach was churning and he was trembling all over.

What had just happened? He had a feeling that Ms Hamilton was trying to do something positive, but the fact that she'd wanted to make the garden beautiful ... it was what Julia had done and it cut him to the core. Something in him had snapped.

A loud ringing in his ears made him shake his head. What was that? It grew louder and behind it the thudding of his heart was like a drum increasing in tempo. Jagged white lines marred his vision and he gasped as he tried to catch his breath.

Then an agonising pain seared through his skull and he dropped his stick, clutching at his head. The force of it was blinding. He held his hands in front of his face but he couldn't make them out; they were blurry formless shapes. He dropped from the chair to his knees as his limbs turned to jelly, suddenly too weak to support him, and the floor came up to meet him.

He tried to shout for help but nothing came out.

Then everything went black.

CHAPTER 21

Ernie pulled the door to the flat closed behind him then trotted down the stairs. He couldn't wait for his pie and mash, he really liked how Mr Mayer mixed real butter with the potatoes; it tasted so much nicer than with margarine. Mr Mayer had told him that butter was his secret to making great mashed potatoes.

'Hello, Ernie!' Abby smiled up at him but her eyes looked tired.

'Hi, Abby.'

'Where are you hurrying off to?' She stopped on the first landing between Ernie and Arthur's flats.

'Arthur's ... He's cooking my dinner.'

Abby frowned. 'Is that right?'

'Yes he's doing us pie and mash.'

'Sounds lovely. How's school been?'

'OK ... same as usual.'

'Good. Glad to hear it.'

'My dad's coming home today instead of Friday but I'm having dinner with Mr Mayer first.'

'That's lovely, Ernie.'

He grinned at her. 'I know!'

'Well ... enjoy your dinner!' Abby nodded at him then he hurried down to the ground floor and knocked on Mr

Mayer's door. There was no answer, so he knocked again. What if Mr Mayer had gone out? Perhaps he'd forgotten something he needed for dinner. He tried the handle and it opened easily so he went inside.

'I'm here!' Ernie closed the door behind him then entered the kitchen. The pie smelt delicious. The potatoes were bubbling away but they were up too high and water kept spitting over the side of the saucepan then hissing as it hit the heat. Ernie turned the heat down, wrinkling his nose at the way the water had turned the top of the stove a grimy yellow.

'Arthur?' he called as he left the kitchen and headed for the living room. It was strange to arrive and not be greeted straight away.

That's when Ernie saw him.

'*Arthur*!' Ernie shouted as he ran to his friend who was lying on the floor. He crouched next to him, gently touching his face. Arthur's glasses had slipped up and were sitting above his eyebrows and his mouth was open, a silvery trickle of drool running onto the floor.

'Mr Mayer?' Ernie tapped him on his arm. 'Arthur! Are you OK? Are you sleeping?' His chest hurt and tears burned at the corners of his eyes. This wasn't right. Arthur didn't sleep on the floor and he wasn't waking up. He felt his face and it was cold. He had to help him but he didn't know how …

He pulled his mobile from his pocket and rang his dad's number but it went straight to voicemail. He thought about ringing Jax but she'd be in work and her mobile was usually turned off.

What was he going to do?

He had another idea.

'Don't worry, Arthur,' he said, removing his hoodie and laying it gently over the old man's body. 'I'll get some help.' He paused for a moment, not wanting to leave Mr Mayer but knowing that if he didn't, he couldn't get help. He took a deep breath then he ran from the room and out of the door, his heart pounding so hard in his chest that he felt as if he'd just run the school cross-country.

Abby reached her landing, feeling weary from her conversation with Mr Mayer, and pulled her keys from her pocket. She gasped when she spotted the tall figure standing in front of her door, thinking for a moment that Jason had come to surprise her, but as he turned around, her heart sank.

'Bloody hell, Gav! You scared the life out of me. What the hell are you doing here again?'

He held out his hands. 'I'm sorry, Abby. I just ... I, uh ...'

'*How* do you keep getting past the security door downstairs?! I mean ... who keeps letting you in? Never mind, actually! Do you know what? I'm not in the mood for this right now. You can't keep just showing up here. This isn't *Groundhog Day*, I'm not going to keep going through this just because you need a shoulder to cry on. You're a grown man and you need to sort yourself out.'

She pushed past him and unlocked her door then stood there, making it clear that he wasn't invited in.

'Abby ... I'm sorry ...' He held up his hands as if in surrender. 'I just came to thank you for your advice when I was last here and to tell you that we've decided to keep the baby. What you said about accepting responsibility for my actions was so right. You're always right.' He gave a small laugh. 'I just wish I'd realised it sooner.' He stepped closer to her.

'Well that's great, Gav, but … you could have texted me to tell me that.'

Abby took a step back, not liking how close Gav was getting to her.

'I just wanted to find out what you thought about—'

'*Abby*!' The desperation in Ernie's tone as he appeared at the top of the stairs sent Abby's heart into a panic.

'Ernie, what's wrong?' She rushed over to him, full of concern at his pale face and the terror in his eyes.

'It's …' he gasped. 'It's Arthur!' Tears ran down his cheeks and he grabbed her hand and pulled her towards the stairs. 'Please come! I don't know what's wrong with him. He's … he's on the floor and he's cold and his face has gone grey and he won't wake up. Please come!'

'It's OK, Ernie. I'm coming.' What on earth was wrong? Poor Ernie seemed terrified.

She held his hand tight as they hurried down the stairs, her own throat aching with concern, both for the little boy clinging to her, and for the elderly man she'd left alone not long ago.

If anything had happened to Arthur because of what she'd said to him, she'd never be able to forgive herself.

As she entered Arthur's flat and went through to his lounge, her mouth fell open.

'Ernie. I want you to go upstairs and tell the man who was outside my flat to come here. He might already be on his way down … so just go and get him.'

Ernie was crying as he stared at Arthur.

'Ernie!' Her tone was sharper now and it made the little boy meet her eyes. 'Go, quickly!'

He nodded then ran out of the room.

'Mr Mayer?' She knelt next to the old man on the floor. His skin was grey and his mouth was hanging open. 'Can you hear me?'

She gently pushed his sleeve up his arm and felt his wrist. Nothing. Nothing at all.

She took a deep breath then tried again.

And there it was. Faint, but there nonetheless.

He had a pulse. He was still alive.

'Hang on in there, Mr Mayer. I'm going to call an ambulance now.'

She pulled her mobile from her bag and dialled 999.

PART THREE

Summer Shoots

CHAPTER 22

Abby stared at the mug on the table in front of her. It was still full. How long had it been there? Gav had made her a coffee before he'd left, and she'd been so lost in her thoughts that she'd forgotten to drink it. She kept picturing poor Mr Mayer over and over again; lying there on the floor, so helpless, cold and grey ... His mouth gaping open.

Had it been Abby's fault? Had she made him so angry that he'd suffered a stroke?

When she'd phoned for an ambulance, she'd been in shock and had struggled to answer the most basic questions about Mr Mayer's condition, and by the time she found the words, he'd regained consciousness. Abby had been instructed to check Mr Mayer for facial weakness, arm weakness and speech problems. He'd been unable to smile; only able to lift his arms briefly and not very high, and he hadn't been able to reply to her questions. A tear had trickled down his cheek as they ran through the assessment and Abby had wished in that moment that she could change how she had acted in the last few hours.

The ambulance had come quickly and after the paramedics had assessed Mr Mayer, they'd taken him straight to the hospital. They'd asked about next of kin, but Abby hadn't known of anyone to call. When she'd asked Ernie if he knew whether Mr Mayer had any children, Ernie had mumbled something about a boy called George, but it hadn't made any sense to Abby and she'd put it down to Ernie's distress. Poor Ernie had wanted to go in the ambulance, but he was far too young for that, and Abby had felt torn between needing to stay and keep an eye on him until his dad came home, and wanting to make sure that Mr Mayer was all right. Gav had still been there, hanging around like a bad smell, doing nothing to help.

She'd watched as they'd wheeled Mr Mayer out of his flat, out of Willow Court and into the ambulance, then whisked him away, siren blaring in the early evening air. Once she'd taken Ernie back inside, she told Gav to take him up to her flat and to make him a drink while she checked that everything was off in Mr Mayer's flat.

When she went back inside, a funny metallic smell made her rush to the kitchen where she found a pan of potatoes on the stove that had boiled dry. She turned the heat off and carried the pan to the sink then ran the tap over it. As the burnt pan hissed, and steam floated up into the air, it hit Abby that she was in her neighbour's flat, alone, and that he'd just been rushed to hospital. What if he never came home again? She shook her head, hating the morbid direction of her thoughts, and tried to focus instead on the practicalities. She inspected the damage to the pan and saw that it was ruined, so there was no point trying to wash it. She left it in the sink then went to the oven and turned that off too. There was a pie inside, which she got out and left on the side to cool down.

It seemed that everything had happened so quickly – Mr Mayer had been snatched from his life in minutes. He'd been cooking dinner for him and Ernie, blissfully unaware that he would suffer what seemed to be a stroke, unaware that his life was about to change for ever. The pie sitting there on the side had made Abby's stomach churn. One minute, Mr Mayer had been going about his life, the next, the pie that he was going to eat was abandoned. Forgotten. Life was so fragile, so precious, so … fleeting.

She'd taken a few deep breaths; the thought that life could end in an instant was too upsetting and too horrendous to entertain. It was clear that Ernie adored Mr Mayer and from what she'd seen, the feelings were mutual. She didn't know much about her downstairs neighbour, but what she did know made her feel terribly sad. Life was difficult enough at her age, but he was elderly, he lived alone, had lost his wife and didn't have any friends or relatives that she knew of. He must get dreadfully lonely at times.

After she'd checked the rest of the flat to ensure that everything was turned off, she was ready to leave when a thought struck her. Mr Mayer didn't have a key with him, so perhaps she should take one now, or else he'd be unable to get back inside his own flat.

She looked in the bowl on a small dresser near the front door and found a key on a Manchester United key ring. The key ring was dated, the surface tarnished, and she suspected that the old man had had it for a very long time.

She tried the key in the lock to check it was for the front door, looked around the flat one last time then let herself out and climbed the stairs, slowly, giving herself time to prepare before she had to face Ernie again. The little boy would need a lot of support and reassurance, and Abby had to be in the right mindset to offer those things.

Gav and Ernie had been sitting at the kitchen table, as Gav prattled on about football and Ernie stared into space. It was clear that Gav felt extremely awkward. He'd asked to speak to Abby alone but she'd scowled at him and told him it would have to be later, so he left as soon as he could. That was the thing with Gav; he needed to be the centre of attention or he lost interest.

Abby had spouted some clichés to Ernie, hoping to soothe his angst, and he'd offered her a smile but it hadn't reached his eyes. The young boy knew about loss – he'd lost his mother after all, when she left, and Abby could tell that he was worrying about losing Mr Mayer too. Running out of things to say, Abby took Ernie's hand and they sat in silence for a while. Not long after, Ernie's mobile had rung to let them know that his dad was almost home.

When Neil had walked through the door, the way Ernie ran to him and hugged him had brought tears to Abby's eyes. Ernie needed his dad, and Abby had been a poor substitute, even though she had tried. A thought had flashed through her mind then; whether she'd have been able to comfort her own child, whether her little one would have looked at her the way that Ernie looked at his dad, and she'd hoped that would have been the case. If she'd been a mum ...

Abby had given Neil a quick summary of events and he'd listened carefully then asked her to let him know of any developments as soon as she knew. He promised to return the favour if he heard first. They'd swapped numbers to ensure that they could be in contact when necessary. There were other things Abby would've liked to ask Neil; things about him and Ernie and the potential for the garden, but it didn't feel like the right time to talk about these things with her neighbour who she barely knew. She'd also been afraid that she'd crumple if she stayed too long, that her own fears and distress would bubble over, and that was the last thing Ernie needed to see.

And now, Abby realised that her right hand was throbbing from clenching it around something. She opened it to reveal Mr Mayer's key. She must have held on to it after she returned to her flat, not noticing that she'd been squeezing it tightly.

Dusk had fallen around her making the lounge shadowy. She got up and turned the lamp on then carried her mug to the kitchen and poured the cold coffee away. She placed Mr Mayer's key in her bag.

Seeing this happen to Mr Mayer made her think about other elderly people in the area and the wider Manchester community. How did they cope if they fell? If they had no one visiting them, no one who cared? Mr Mayer was lucky in that he'd become friendly with Ernie and Neil, but if he hadn't then Ernie wouldn't have found him and he could have lain on the floor indefinitely. It was horrid to think that this was a reality for many people. It could happen to her too, of course. She might be younger than Arthur, but if anything happened to her, who would know? Her mum had passed away and she'd never known her dad; Gav had a whole new life and Lisa was often so busy. She knew Lisa would try to get hold of her regularly and that she'd become worried if Abby didn't respond, but that could take days. Abby could be here, alone, stranded and the world would carry on oblivious. Life could be very lonely and frightening if you didn't have anyone – and that would be so much harder when you were older.

Abby needed to do something for him. Tomorrow morning, she'd go down to Mr Mayer's flat and check if he had an address book or something so she could let his friends and relatives know that he was in hospital. There was bound to be someone she could contact. Besides which, she wanted to get rid of the burnt saucepan and the pie, before they stank the flat out, and she'd empty his bins while she was there. At least then she'd feel as though she was doing something to help. Sitting here thinking about how lonely Mr Mayer must have been and how lonely she was wouldn't help anyone. Being proactive was the best course of action to stop her dwelling on things and to ensure that Mr Mayer had someone around who cared. It might also help to assuage some of the terrible guilt she'd been feeling because of how she'd treated Mr Mayer in recent weeks. He'd seemed so angry and hostile, but there had evidently been more to it than that, and she, as a grown woman who had worked with the elderly, should have noticed it sooner.

The next morning, Abby woke early, her mind buzzing with the events of the previous day. At first, she was fairly certain she'd dreamt about Mr Mayer, and as she gained full consciousness, she became sure that she had. She'd been walking along a beach as the tide went out. The sky had been grey, with storm clouds on the horizon, and there had been a brisk wind, laced with brine, that had whipped at her pyjamas and her hair. Her bare feet had sunk into the wet sand and it had sucked at her toes as she'd taken each step, until the sand had become stronger, covering her feet and clinging to her legs, and she'd had to work harder to move.

Then she'd seen him: Mr Mayer, up ahead, almost at the cliffs. She'd called to him but the wind had carried her voice away and the tide had turned; now it was coming in, the foam fizzing as it crashed against the shore.

Her voice had risen and she'd waved her arms, but each movement had only helped the sand to claim her, and soon she was buried up to her waist. Her unconscious mind had registered that if she struggled, she'd end up completely buried, so she'd stopped moving and willed Mr Mayer to turn around and see her.

And he had.

Just like that.

But when he'd turned and she'd seen his face …

She hugged the duvet to her chest.

'It was just a bad dream.' She shook her head. 'Just a dream. He's going to be fine. He's probably having his porridge and annoying the nurses.'

She hoped with all her heart that she was right.

After she'd showered and dressed, she rang the hospital to ask about how Mr Mayer was, but they wouldn't give out any information over the phone because she admitted that she wasn't a relative. She considered ringing again and pretending to be related to Mr Mayer, but worried that the same person might answer and recognise her voice, so she'd leave it until later.

She decided to head down to his flat. She'd heard Neil and Ernie earlier on, leaving for school, so she assumed that Neil must be taking the day off. At least he'd be there if Ernie needed him today. She wasn't sure whether it was wise to send Ernie to school after the upset of the previous day, but then if he stayed at home, he might just keep going over it. School could prove to be a good distraction.

Downstairs, she let herself into Mr Mayer's flat and closed the door behind her. It felt wrong, like a home invasion, and she stood by the door for a few moments, wondering whether to leave, but the aroma that lingered in the air from yesterday's burnt dinner firmed up her resolve to help. If Mr Mayer was in hospital for days or weeks, he'd need some things from home. Besides which, there was the burnt food to deal with.

Abby decided to sort out the kitchen first, so she set her large tote bag on the floor and pulled out a pair of yellow rubber gloves, a bottle of antibacterial spray and a black bin bag, then set to work. She put the pie and the burnt saucepan into the black bag, scrubbed the stove top, and pulled the bag out of the swing lid bin, then took all of the rubbish and recycling out to the big bins. Back inside, she blitzed the entire kitchen, thinking that there was no point doing half a job. She found a mop and bucket in the hall cupboard so she bleached the floor tiles too and opened the kitchen window to allow the tiles to dry, and to get some air into the flat.

While the kitchen floor was drying, she decided to look for an address book, so she pulled off her gloves and headed through to the lounge. The idea of going through Mr Mayer's things wasn't something she was comfortable with, and felt like a further invasion of his privacy, but she'd never forgive herself if there was a relative out there somewhere who needed to know what had happened. Seeing the two armchairs side by side, with only the small coffee table between them, brought a lump to her throat. It was probably exactly as it had been when Mr Mayer's wife was still alive, and Abby could picture him sitting there of an evening, wishing she was still with him. Abby knew from experience that grief was a physical pain – after all, she'd lost her mother and her baby, and after that, she'd lost Gavin too. What must it be like for a man of Mr Mayer's age, when he'd likely been married for most of his life?

She went over to the mahogany sideboard that had a light covering of dust, and gazed at the photographs lined up there. The first was a black and white wedding photograph that must have been taken in the 1950s or 60s, judging from the fashion and the style of photograph. A very young Mr Mayer stood next to a pretty young woman outside a church. He was wearing a dark suit with a carnation in the buttonhole, while she wore a dress that fell to mid-calf, with a round cowl neck, long sleeves and a cinched-in waist. Her pale court shoes were plain, and on her beehive hairstyle, sat a white headband with a lace bow. They looked so young and so happy, as if they'd found what they'd been looking for.

Abby continued to look over the other photographs, showing Mr Mayer and his wife through the years, until she found one that showed his wife holding a baby. She picked it up and peered closely at them. The baby was very young and the woman was gazing at him, her face full of love. Abby gulped, feeling the grief for her own child well up.

This must be the Mayers' baby. So was there a son out there somewhere?

Ernie had said something about someone called George. She wished she could ask him more about it now but he'd be in school. Perhaps Neil would know. She pulled her mobile from her pocket and fired off a quick text. She'd never seen a man visiting Mr Mayer, actually, she'd never seen anyone visiting him other than Neil and Ernie. Many families lost contact nowadays because of distance or time, as people dashed around in their busy lives, rarely finding the time to consider their own health and wellbeing, let alone that of family and friends. The modern world was such a chaotic one; it was a wonder anyone ever had visitors. Perhaps they were estranged. Lots of families rowed, cut relatives off and moved on with life. Just because people were related didn't mean that they'd automatically have a good relationship.

She put the photograph back then opened a drawer in the sideboard to look for an address book. She shivered as she found bills, bank statements, a variety of buttons and was tempted to stop then and there because this was making her so uneasy. But if she didn't do this, who would? There was a sock with a hole in the heel, that was presumably there to be darned (though who darned socks anymore, she didn't know) and a box of plasters. She closed the drawer and checked the next one, but all it held was wads of supermarket receipts and vouchers, some of which had expired a long time ago.

She crouched down and opened the cupboard doors of the sideboard. The aroma of old newspapers and peppermints rushed out, mixed with another scent, something floral. The cupboard held piles of old newspapers and a chocolate tin, the old-fashioned kind. She brought it out of the cupboard and carried it to the sofa. Perhaps she'd find something in here.

Abby placed the tin on the sofa next to her and pulled the lid off. There were lots of pieces of paper, most of them folded over, some of them yellowing with age. She lifted one of the smaller ones out and unfolded it, pressing it flat on her knees. It was dated a few months ago, and the scrawled handwriting made it difficult to decipher, but she read it through a few times and the words started to piece together into sentences. In the letter, Mr Mayer addressed a woman he referred to as *My Darling Julia*. Of course, his wife.

My Darling Julia,

I woke this morning thinking about a day we spent at The Cottage Garden Centre – your favourite place – a few years ago. We were going to have a browse and some lunch in the organic café there, but you spent over three hours looking at pots and plants, dragging me around again and again as you tried to make up your mind. The result, of course, was that you came away with enough plants to set up your own garden centre.

We did manage to have lunch but then, at the tills, you accused me of penny-pinching when I commented on the cost of your plants. As we argued, the poor cashier was staring at us in shock, and that made us both chuckle, our irritation soon forgotten.

I miss laughing with you, darling. I miss our trips

to the garden centre and if you were here right now,
I would give you all of my money to spend on plants.
Without you, money is worthless. Life is ... no, I
mustn't say that. I must try to make the most of the days
I have left. But I do miss you dreadfully.

I love you, Julia, and you are ALWAYS, ALWAYS
in my heart and in my thoughts.

Arthur X

Abby placed the letter to one side. She felt as though she was intruding on his most private musings. It looked like this tin was full of similar letters, expressions of love and grief that were never meant to be read. And yet ... if she didn't go through them, she might never find out if he had any surviving relatives. This tin could hold the clues to his life, so whether she wanted to or not, she'd have to go through it. Feeling uncomfortable but determined, Abby pulled out another letter and began to read.

Two hours later, Abby had gone through most of the papers in the tin and now she was a wreck. It was, as she had feared, full of love letters that documented Mr Mayer's – or Arthur as she now thought of him – life with Julia. Abby had stopped several times, questioning whether this was the right thing to do, but there was a chance she might find something in one of the letters, a clue to lead her to a family member or family friend. He had written about his memories, of good times and bad times, of their love and how it had evolved and deepened, over the years. Their passion had clearly burned brightly for a long time, and it had developed into a solid friendship, shared experiences, and to knowing each other inside out. It made Abby acutely aware of how special love could be, of how what she'd had with Gav had been lacking in substance, was one-sided and just plain wrong for them both. If she could find someone to love and who loved her the way that Arthur had, and still did, love Julia, then that would be wonderful indeed.

So far, she'd found no phone numbers or addresses, but she had a few pieces of paper left to go through. She started to leaf through them, glancing at them to confirm that they weren't what she needed, then she came across a neighbourhood watch newsletter. She wasn't aware of any such group, but then a quick look at the date showed that it was from 2002. She turned it back over and scanned the letter but its contents made her gasp as her heart raced unpleasantly. Arthur spoke about a boy named George, their only child, and how they'd lost him when he was just ten.

She stopped reading and closed her eyes, biting back the swell of her emotion. After George had died, Julia had held Arthur together through that time. Julia had been a strong woman, a fighter, and although she'd grieved dreadfully for her boy, she'd also refused to let Arthur give up. From the things he said in the letter, it seemed to Abby that Arthur had sunk into a deep depression, and that if Julia hadn't been strong enough for both of them, Arthur might have given up altogether. He'd cursed the cystic fibrosis that had stolen their child away and been their reason for not having another.

But Arthur had made it through and there had been happy times after that, they had survived, clinging to each other, loving each other, existing because of each other.

Then Arthur had lost Julia too.

Abby dropped the letter and buried her face in her hands, overcome by everything she had discovered. She sobbed for Arthur and for Julia, for George who had lost his life so young and for the family they had been. Arthur had had everything he ever wanted in his family then fate had ripped it to shreds before his eyes. No wonder he sometimes seemed grumpy, at odds with the world and the people he encountered. He had lost the people he cared for most in the world, and Abby knew exactly how that felt. Her tears slowed then started again when she thought of her own pain and loss, realising that she and Arthur had suffered in similar ways.

When she had dried her eyes, blown her nose and caught her breath again, Abby reached for the final few letters. She still felt bad about reading them but there seemed little point stopping now, as she already knew so much more about her neighbour. It had humanised him in her eyes, created a bridge between them, because life had been cruel to them both and it made her want to help him, however she could.

The final letters were about Julia's garden. Arthur wrote about her knowledge, her enthusiasm and her visceral need to be outside for as many hours a day as she could manage. It was as though her need to nurture, a need that had once been fulfilled by motherhood, had been channelled into the garden. Julia had planted seeds, tended seedlings, fed and watered plants, pruned them and treated them for bugs and diseases. She'd researched organic ways of doing things to avoid using pesticides and Arthur had said he could listen to her talk about what she'd learnt all day long.

Abby wondered how many people at Willow Court had benefited from what Julia had done and if, after she'd gone, any of them had bothered to check in on Arthur. Whether they had, at first, brought him flowers and cakes, meals for one, but as time wore on, they'd become caught up in their own busy lives, soon forgetting about Arthur and his empty flat. Perhaps they even *wanted* to forget because the elderly man represented what nobody ever wanted to become. By keeping busy, people were able to push their own fears and doubts aside, to avoid dealing with their deepest, darkest fears until the day when they too were claimed by a heart attack, by old age and loneliness, and by then it was too late to reach out because nobody cared.

What on earth was she thinking? Maybe being here, in this flat, had stirred up her own emotions and roused her fears. This was not productive at all. And yet, sometimes, she knew, she needed to face up to reality in order to be productive. Which was what she would be, what she needed to be. Abby would do everything in her power to ensure that Arthur found some happiness when he returned home. She felt a renewed energy in her mission to make the garden on Holly Street beautiful again. She would return it to its former glory and she would ensure that Julia's legacy lived on.

CHAPTER 23

Abby had spent the rest of the previous day cleaning and tidying Arthur's flat. After she'd read his letters, something that she was both ashamed of and intrigued by, she felt that she knew him so much better. She had a good understanding now of how the elderly man ticked. She'd worked at the care home with elderly people for years and often sat with them as they spoke to her about their lives and their families, their joys and their tragedies. Arthur had never done this, of course, but she hadn't exactly given him the chance. No one escaped life unscathed. And yet there was so much to enjoy in life, so much to savour ... as long as you weren't all alone. Some of the people at Greenfields Care Home had lots of visitors, some had none, but they all had the company of other residents and the staff. They were never far from human company. For people like Arthur, though, it was different. Unless they made contact with a neighbour or the council or a charity support network, they could become completely isolated. Yes, Arthur had Ernie and Neil, but that had only happened recently.

When Arthur's flat was spick and span – she hadn't ventured into his bedroom, as she felt that was definitely a step too far – and Abby felt happy that it would be clean and comfortable for Arthur to return to, she went back to her own flat and had a long soak in the bath. She'd then slept like a log, exhausted by her efforts and the distress of the previous few days, and she missed the reply from Neil that came through after eleven p.m.

She'd picked it up not long after waking, reading that Neil knew Arthur had once had a son but that he'd passed away back in the 70s. But Abby already knew that now. She replied with her thanks and asked if he was going to ring the hospital today. His reply pinged back within five minutes, letting her know that he'd already done it and they'd told him they couldn't give him information over the phone because he wasn't a relative. She'd been so caught up with Mr Mayer's letters and trying to make his flat clean and tidy that she hadn't thought to let Neil now about the hospital rules regarding patient information. Abby had flopped back on the bed, her stomach churning with uncertainty at the thought that Arthur could be in a worse condition, or a better one, but they wouldn't know either way. Unless they were relatives.

Abby used her mobile to check the visiting hours on the hospital website and saw that she could go in the late afternoon. So that was what she would do, although she suspected that they might well not let anyone other than relatives visit either. How she'd get around the fact that she wasn't a relative, she wasn't quite sure. Unless she pretended to be his daughter! She sent another text to Neil, telling him of her plans – he said he'd be around all day, as he'd taken the rest of the week off to be with Ernie.

After she'd eaten some toast, Abby pulled on her old jeans and a T-shirt, stuffed her feet into her pink glittery wellies and pulled her hair into a ponytail. The best thing she could do now was get outside and work on the garden. She'd done a lot but there was still a long way to go.

Abby stood back and admired her morning's efforts. The bright red begonias, white and pink geraniums and purple and white petunias gave the borders some cheerful colour. Jason had told her that they'd thrive in the summer weather once the risk of frost had passed and that they'd be a beautiful combination. He was right. Jason had slipped from her mind in the recent chaos, but being in the garden brought her thoughts back to him. He had used gardening as a way to deal with his bereavement and now, Abby could understand why.

She'd watered her fruit, veg and herb patches and pulled out any weeds she'd found sprouting up between the recently planted seedlings (she may have actually pulled out some of the seedlings by mistake but she was trying).

The garden looked good, but not good enough. She still needed to paint the shed, for instance. Jason had suggested it and it did seem like a good idea. The structure was sturdy enough, so it didn't need replacing, but it would look better if it was sanded down and freshened up. And now that she'd planted everything, she had to be patient and wait for it to grow. If Arthur came out of hospital next week, she'd have to describe it to him for him to understand what had been achieved, and she wanted him to be able to see the garden in its full glory, for him to feel that Julia would approve of what had been done here.

She checked her mobile and was surprised to see that it was after two. She needed to shower and grab some things for Arthur then head to the hospital. She'd tell them she was his daughter to ensure that she got in to see him, then she could at least leave him some things from home.

Abby pressed the buzzer at the door to the stroke unit and waited. She'd called ahead, this time claiming to be Arthur's daughter just in case they only let relatives visit, and she made up some excuse about having been away and only now finding out that he was at the hospital. She'd finally ventured into his bedroom, aware that she had to in order to get some of his things, then packed a small suitcase for him that she found on top of his wardrobe. She'd included essentials like pyjamas, tooth-brush, a spare pair of glasses – the paramedics had taken his others in the ambulance with them – and picked up some books, magazines and sweets at the gift shop in the hospital reception. She shifted now, from one foot to the other, worried that she'd be called out as an imposter, pretending to be one of Arthur's relatives. But it was a risk she was willing to take.

'Hello?' A face appeared at the glass, the dark eyes boring into Abby's.

'Hi ... uh ... I'm here to see my ... dad.'

'Name?'

'Mr Mayer. Arthur Mayer.'

The nurse buzzed Abby through the doors. After directing her to use the hand sanitiser, the nurse led her onto the ward.

Abby was surprised that she hadn't been asked more

questions or even expected to provide her ID. But then again, why would someone pretend to be a relative in order to visit a sick old man?

Abby followed the woman in her navy-blue scrubs and black crocs, the only sounds coming from the rustling of the carrier bag and their footsteps. The smells of antiseptic, cleaning fluid and (strangely) gravy filled the air, turning Abby's stomach. Her own experience of hospitals had been limited, but when she had been rushed in, it had turned into the worst time of her life. And, of course, there had been her mother's sudden decline that had ended in a hospital bed.

There were six rooms on the ward, each one with four beds in, and as they walked, Abby noted that most of the beds were occupied.

Outside one of the rooms, the nurse paused.

'Just to prepare you, Miss Mayer—'

'Abby, please.'

'Abby ... Just to prepare you, you'll find your father changed from when you last saw him. We're still conducting tests at the moment to discover the severity of the stroke and at this point in time, his care is described as acute. Some people recover very quickly from a stroke but most need long-term support in order to regain their independence. Rehabilitation depends on symptoms and severity, but we do encourage patients to be as active as possible as soon as their medical condition allows. Your father may require some aftercare at a clinic or outpatients and he might well need some assistance at home. I don't know if you live locally?' Her voice indicated that this was a question.

'I do, actually. Very close.'

'Right, well that's good. He's going to need support and encouragement and, please remember, a positive mindset is very important in these circumstances.'

'OK … thank you.'

'One more thing … Speech is usually affected in about thirty per cent of cases. Mr Mayer has spoken … briefly, and thankfully his speech doesn't seem to have been affected. He remembers who he is and some of what happened, but he's been sleeping a lot, so we're not sure of the extent to which the stroke has affected things like his long-term memory. Hopefully, seeing you will help.'

'Gosh! I hope not. I mean … it would be awful if he's lost his memory.'

'Hopefully he won't have, but time will tell.'

Abby wondered if medical staff had training in clichés to use when speaking to relatives. Sometimes, in these circumstances, they were the only words that could fill the silence.

And another thought made her armpits prickle. How would she explain it if Mr Mayer saw her and reacted badly? The nurses would be shocked and it would be terrible if he became agitated because of her. Perhaps she should just leave the stuff for him and go. She already felt responsible for the fact that he was in here in the first place.

'It's OK.' The nurse smiled kindly and touched Abby's arm. 'This won't be easy but you'll make his day.'

Abby didn't think so, but she couldn't turn around now.

She allowed the nurse to guide her into the room and towards a bed, where a man lay, his face as white as the covers pulled up to his chest. His eyes were closed, the white lashes fluttering on his cheeks. Without his glasses on, his bushy eyebrows seemed adrift on his forehead and the skin seemed tightly stretched over the dome of his head that rested against the pillow. She sat down in the plastic chair next to the bed and set the suitcase and carrier bag on the floor next to her.

'I'll leave you two for now but come and find me if you have any questions.'

The nurse's soft, assured voice reassured Abby. At least Mr Mayer – Arthur – was in the right place. At least here he'd have the care he needed.

She sat next to him, watching him sleep, wondering if he was dreaming about Julia. This close, Abby could smell the starch and bleach of the washing detergent, could smell the ketones on Mr Mayer's breath and see the thick white stubble on his chin. He seemed so fragile, as if he was hanging on to life by a gossamer thread. Or, in this case, by the drip that fed into a tube that was taped to his hand and by the medication that was likely thinning his blood.

She must have become lost in her thoughts, because when she looked at him again, he was staring straight at her.

'Ju … Julia?'

His words were so quiet, Abby wondered if she'd imagined them.

'You … J-Julia?'

'No!' She swallowed hard. 'No. Sorry. It's me, Mr Mayer.'

He frowned then shook his head and reached up to his face.

Of course. He didn't have his glasses on.

Abby retrieved them from the bedside cabinet and handed them to him. He fiddled with them for a while, trying to open out the arms, and Abby fought the urge to help him.

When he'd put his glasses on, he blinked at her from behind the familiar thick black frames.

'It's me, Abby, Mr Mayer. From Willow Court.' She thought it best to tell him in case he didn't remember her.

'Abby?'

'Yes. I live in the flat above Ernie.'

His eyes flickered. 'Ernie … Wh … Where?' His speech seemed slower, maybe because he had just woken up – or he could be suffering memory loss.

'Oh, he's not here. Neil and I didn't think he should visit yet but they both send their love and Neil said to tell you he's taking some time to work at home until we know how you …' She stopped speaking. There was no need to drown him with information right now. 'He said they're fine and they're looking forward to seeing you. When you're ready.'

'Ernie,' he said again, giving a gentle nod.

'I've brought you some things from home and some books and magazines from the shop. I wasn't sure what you'd like so I picked up a few thrillers and some magazines about planes and trains and … Well you can have a look when you want to. The bag is down there but I can put them into your cupboard for now. There are some toffees and barley sugars too.'

She became acutely aware that he was just staring at her as she spoke (or prattled on more like).

'Do you remember me?'

'Yes. I know you.'

'Good. Look ... I have to apologise for the other day. I didn't mean to ... to ...' Abby was certain this was harder than walking over hot coals. How on earth could she explain how bad she felt for making him so angry that he'd almost died?

'How did you get in here?' His tone sounded more curious than accusing.

'I told them I'm your daughter.' She cleared her throat. 'See ... They wouldn't tell Neil much on the phone because he said he wasn't a relative so I ... kind of ... fibbed a bit.' She cleared her throat again, wondering if he was about to erupt.

His eyes widened and the colour rose in his cheeks, contrasting now with the pillowcase and the blankets. Her gaze was drawn to a fingerprint on the left lens of his glasses.

The urge to jump up and run was overwhelming. She pushed her hands under her thighs and pressed her nails into the chair. It surprised her how this man still had the power to make her so uneasy, even when he was lying prone and vulnerable in a hospital bed. But this time, it was the fear that he'd out her as an imposter to the medical staff that made her heart beat faster and not anger and frustration at how stubborn and rude he was being.

Mr Mayer suddenly gave a gurgle that startled her and she leant forwards, worried that he was about to choke.

'Mr Mayer! Are you all right? Shall I get the nurse?'

He leant to one side, head bobbing as he closed his eyes. Then he gave another gurgle and Abby gasped.

'*Ha*!'

'Don't worry, I'll get the nurse.'

'No … No, s'all right.'

She met his eyes, open now, and saw tears escaping the sides of his glasses and trickling down his cheeks.

'I'm … OK. S'just … you. Ha! Ha!'

She lowered into the chair cautiously, ready to run for help if he started making the strange noise again.

'Me?'

'Yes. My daughter.' He gave a chuckle, and she realised that he hadn't been having an attack; he'd been laughing. 'So dry.' He smacked his lips. 'Can't … even … laugh properly.'

Abby poured him some water from the beaker on the cabinet then brought it to his lips. She'd been worried that she'd upset him but no, she'd made him laugh. It sent a pleasant warmth through her chest, slowing her heartbeat and relieving the tension in her shoulders

'Thank you.'

'Mr Mayer. I'm so sorry for everything. I hope you're OK.'

'Scared.' He nodded. 'It scared me a lot.'

'Me too! Dad!'

She felt her lips turning upwards in spite of how awful the situation was, and when she snorted too, she covered her mouth in horror. But soon, Mr Mayer joined in, both of them lost in a joint expulsion of laughter.

When they had calmed down, Abby helped Mr Mayer have another drink, then she sat with him for the rest of visiting time. They talked a bit about what had happened, about what would happen next and about Ernie. She didn't tell him about the letters she'd found, but did ask if there was anyone else he wanted her to contact. His reply was saddening; there really was no one. Then, when Abby ran out of things to say, she got a magazine from the bag and read to him until his eyelids dropped and he started to snore gently.

Before she left, she gently took his hand.

'Mr Mayer ...'

He opened his eyes and blinked a few times.

'Mr Mayer, I'm going now.'

'Arthur.' He gave a small nod. 'Call me Arthur.'

'Arthur. Gosh, it feels strange calling you that.' She smiled, feeling a bit shy now at this truce they seemed to have formed. 'Do you want me to visit again?'

He pressed his lips together then looked down at their hands.

'I can't ask you to come here again. You're young; you have a life of your own. I'm very grateful for today's visit and for what you've brought me. But no, don't come again. But send my love to Ernie and Neil.'

'Of course I will and I'm sure they'll want to visit you too.'

'Thank you, Abby. Your kindness is appreciated.'

The nurse from earlier entered the side room, a sign that visiting hours were over for today.

'I'll be back tomorrow,' Abby said as she walked towards the doorway.

'No ... don't worry now. No need.'

'I won't hear it. I'll see you tomorrow ... Dad!'

She winked at him then turned to leave, but not before she saw the beginnings of a smile play across his face.

CHAPTER 24

Arthur almost groaned when he woke up to find himself still in hospital. He'd been dreaming about dancing with Julia at a wedding. He'd been smartly dressed and young, she'd been as beautiful as ever, and they'd whirled around the dance floor with the ease and agility of their youth. He had felt so physically free, so capable of doing whatever he wanted and, more than anything, it had been incredible to hold his beloved Julia in his arms again.

Waking up in a hospital bed, to the sounds he was certain he'd never become accustomed to, or even tolerant of – people coughing and farting, calling for the nurse and the steady beeping of monitors and mumbling of old people – and he wished he could just jump out of bed, get dressed and head for home. He knew that wasn't an option yet though, and that if he did move too quickly, he could well cause himself some long-term damage. That was a joke! Wasn't ageing itself long-term damage? Besides which, he didn't know how far he'd even get. The doctor who'd spoken to him had run through a list of things that could happen if Arthur didn't take care of himself from now on, and had warned him that the risk of having another stroke was higher in the first year of recovery. He was classed as high risk anyway because of his age and the fact that they'd discovered he had high blood pressure. His reluctance to visit the GP recently had definitely not paid off. Julia would have made sure he got there, but without her nagging, Arthur hadn't bothered, preferring not to know if anything was wrong with him. And look what had happened ...

He closed his eyes again and tried to fall back to sleep. Then he might be able to recapture a fragment of the happiness he'd felt in the dream.

But no. He was awake now, dammit, and his body was demanding that he visit the bathroom. He sat up and automatically looked around for his stick, then remembered that he hadn't brought it with him. He'd have to call one of the nurses then, which he hated doing, but there was no way he was going to lie there and have an accident, especially seeing as he seemed to have developed some bladder weakness since the stroke and if he left it too long ...

When he was back in bed with a cup of tea, he thanked the nurse then watched as she walked away to see to another patient. It was so difficult being dependent on others; downright horrid in fact, and he hoped he'd be able to go home soon, because the idea of staying in the stroke unit for any length of time was abhorrent. It wasn't that the staff weren't kind, because they were – they were incredible and it made Arthur extremely grateful for the NHS – but he hated losing his independence.

He sipped his tea, enjoying the comfort of a good cuppa. When he'd been hit by that awful pain and everything had gone dark, he'd thought he was done for, that he was off to join Julia, and he hadn't been afraid of dying, only afraid of the pain. There was a sense of sadness that his time was up, but there was also a strange sense of relief and acceptance that he could be with his wife again. It could have been the hormones or natural painkillers, or whatever it was flooding his system, but it had helped him in that moment. It had all happened so quickly and that was probably the best way. He had vague memories of being roused afterwards by Ernie crying, by Abby and the paramedics, but mostly, it was a blur, as though he'd been watching it through a long cardboard tube or from a long distance.

He had to be thankful to Abby, really. The young woman had come to his aid, called by Ernie no doubt, but even so, if it hadn't been for her calling for an ambulance …

And then she'd come to visit him! Brought him his own pyjamas, slippers and other necessities, like his toothbrush and shaving equipment, as well as some reading material and sweets. Having his home comforts was wonderful and reminded him that he was lucky. Not everyone on the ward had someone to bring them things from home. Abby had also stayed with him for yesterday's afternoon visiting session, not rushed off as he'd thought she might do. They had talked, her mostly, because Arthur was quite tired, and then she'd read to him. He hadn't taken in a lot of what she had read, but he had been more grateful than he could explain for her presence. They'd not exactly had a good start as neighbours and Arthur felt heavily to blame for that, but having her sitting by his bed, giving up her time just to be with him … well that was something else. She'd said she'd be back today too. He wouldn't get his hopes up, but he'd seen the faces of others on the ward, he knew how lonely some of them were and how awful it was at visiting time when no one came. Arthur was counting his blessings.

The young woman had risen dramatically in his estimation and he had a deep sadness in his heart that he'd been so tough on the poor girl. Reacting as he had when they'd first met because he caught her with a cigarette in Julia's garden had been, he could see now, unfair. Abby hadn't known that the garden had once been Julia's space, neither had she known that Julia had died, leaving Arthur bereft. Also, when she'd dropped her shopping bag in the communal hallway and wine had leaked out onto the floor ... he'd overreacted then too. In fact, the more he thought about it, the more Arthur wondered if he'd actually been a bit envious of her youth and vitality. He'd assumed she was young and free, enjoying her carefree life while he was old and decrepit. It was a bit like he'd been with Ernie and Neil too, and he'd had no idea what they were struggling with. Abby, no doubt, had her own struggles too. Didn't everyone?

Life had taught him a lesson, opened his eyes, and he aimed to be a better person because of it. He'd lost those he loved, been lonely and grumpy and turned into the old man he'd never thought he would ever be. But the three wonderful people who had entered his life had changed that, three people who had been there for quite some time, essentially living under the same roof; three people Arthur had previously viewed with scorn.

It just went to prove that you were never too old to learn something new.

*

Abby's mobile buzzed with a text from Neil. She'd popped to see him yesterday on her return from the hospital and found him and Ernie both very worried (although Neil had been trying to hide his concerns from Ernie). She'd filled them in on Arthur's condition and upcoming tests, then told them she was going to visit him again the next day. Ernie had asked to go too, but she'd explained that it might be better if he waited a bit longer, just in case he was carrying any germs from school, because Arthur needed to recover his strength first. It was something she'd read in the stroke booklet the nurse had handed her as she'd left the ward, and she'd agreed with Neil that they'd use that as an excuse to keep Ernie away from the ward for now. Her main concerns were that it would upset Ernie seeing Arthur so weak and she wanted him to wait until Arthur was stronger. As long as everything went well, Arthur could make a quick recovery and come home, and then Ernie could visit him as much as he liked.

Ernie had asked her if she'd taken Arthur's stick to the hospital, and she promised to take it to him this afternoon. But for now, she intended to paint the shed. Jason said he might have some spare paint lying around, and even suggested that he'd help, but Abby didn't want to bother him about it. She was quite capable of purchasing paint then using it, so on her way back from the hospital yesterday, she'd stopped and picked some up.

Jason had sent her a text the day before yesterday asking how she was, that she hadn't replied to, she had been so caught up with Arthur's collapse and was too upset to think about anything other than Arthur. Then last night, her mobile had buzzed with another text from him, asking if she was OK and telling her he was a bit worried as he hadn't heard from her. She'd sent a brief summary of what had happened to Arthur and apologised for not replying sooner. He'd replied almost immediately, telling her to take care and let him know if she needed anything.

It had been a nice reply, friendly but not overly so, and she was glad of that, because she didn't have the headspace for much else right now. After their night out, when Jason had told her he had baggage, she felt sad that life had brought them together when things weren't at all simple for them. She knew what that baggage was, although she hadn't confessed as much. She also knew that she liked him … a lot … and that scared her. She wasn't in the right place to fall for someone, especially when she didn't know that much about him, other than that he was handsome, kind, good at gardening, enjoyed pub quizzes and had suffered a tragic loss in his past. And, of course, that he was very skilled with his hands, and those *arms* …

It had been a challenging few days and Abby knew that she was vulnerable. Combine that with how much she fancied Jason, and it could be a risky combination. The last thing she wanted to do was to wreck their budding friendship by flinging herself at him. So, to distract herself from thinking about Jason, and from worrying about Arthur, and from how tired she really felt right now, she'd head outside and freshen up that lovely old shed.

After sanding the wood, which felt like it took an age, Abby opened the tin of paint and picked up her paintbrush. She sang as she painted, loving how much better the shed was looking already. She'd chosen a forget-me-not blue and in the summer sunshine, surrounded by the rainbow colours of the bedding plants, it looked so pretty, as though it belonged in the newly planted garden.

She was on her second rendition of Bon Jovi's 'Never Say Goodbye' when she felt someone watching her. She stopped painting and turned slowly to find Jason standing there, his arms folded over his broad chest and a big grin on his handsome face. Heat flooded her neck, face and ears.

'Morning, Abby.'

She turned back to the shed for a moment to catch her breath. Bloody hell! Why was she reacting like a schoolgirl with a crush when she knew the score with this man; nothing could happen.

But her body betrayed her when she turned back to him and felt her nerve endings stir and tingle at his proximity.

'Hi, Jason.' She started at how flirtatious her voice sounded.

'Good job!' There was a smile in his voice, as if he was gently teasing her.

'Sorry?'

'The shed. Good job.' He nodded his approval.

They both stared at the shed.

'Thanks.'

'If you'd let me know you were doing it today, I'd have given you a hand.'

'Oh … I thought you'd have work. I know how busy you are. And besides which, it's only painting a shed. I thought I could probably manage.'

'Of course you can and I didn't mean it like that. I just would like to help. One of the advantages of my job is flexibility. My hours aren't set in stone, so I can sneak off for a bit if I need to. Besides, I wanted to make sure you were all right.'

'You did?'

He nodded. 'I know it's hard to work out someone's tone from a text message but after what happened with your neighbour ... I wanted to come and check ... if you needed anything.'

'Oh ...' He *wanted* to check she was OK! If she *needed* anything! How wonderful was this man? He was so self-assured but without being arrogant. How did someone develop that kind of confidence?

Come on, Abs, get a grip!

'Well I haven't done the back, so grab a roller or a brush and get stuck in.' She smiled at him, hoping he'd catch the playfulness in her tone, and he smiled back.

'Yes, ma'am.'

They made quick work of the rest of the shed, and Abby told Jason how Arthur was doing. He listened to her and asked questions, seeming genuinely interested in what she had to say. She couldn't help comparing him to Gavin – the man who never listened unless he heard his name. Abby watched Jason from the corner of her eye as he worked. He'd removed his checked shirt to reveal a fitted white T-shirt that clung to him like a second skin. As he moved, his biceps rippled and she could see the definition of the strong muscles in his back, the breadth of his chest and how he frowned when he was concentrating.

He was bloody gorgeous and quite a distraction. But a welcome one.

Again, she thought about Gav, who would never have got stuck in like this if there wasn't something in it for him. He'd have posed for at least five selfies, checked the footie scores, checked his appearance in his phone camera then sat down for a cuppa. Jason seemed oblivious to everything other than the task at hand. He was focused, clearly keen to get on and do a good job, and when he ended up with paint in his hair, on his forehead and his T-shirt, he didn't even seem to notice. He certainly didn't stop to take any selfies.

'How's that?' he asked, when he'd finished his side and came to help Abby with hers.

'That looks fabulous. Thank you so much.'

He shrugged. 'No problem. The garden's also looking good. You had any help yet?'

She dropped her gaze to her feet. 'A bit.' She hadn't exactly knocked on doors to let people know what she was doing; she was afraid of being seen as a nuisance and of being rejected by her neighbours. Some of it had to do with how Arthur had reacted to her and the rest was just social conditioning, a reluctance to ask others for help.

'From your neighbours?'

'Uh ... some of the children.'

'What, like Ernie?'

'Kind of.'

'You need more help, Abby. You can't do this all by yourself.'

'I know but I've been getting on really well on my own.'

'I forgot!' He put the roller on the tray. 'I have something for you. I was distracted by seeing you painting. Hold on ... I'll run back to the van and get it.'

Abby nodded and watched as he jogged off around the side of the building. When he appeared again, he was carrying a tall parcel wrapped in newspaper.

'Sorry about the wrapping but it was a rush job and I didn't have any proper paper at home. Anyway, this will recycle nicely,' he said with a grin.

He placed the parcel in front of her.

'You going to open it?'

She nodded and tore off the paper to reveal a beautiful wooden bird table. It was set on a triangular stand with a carved pole that led up to a wide rectangular table. Above this was a V-shaped roof that had leaves and flowers carved onto its surface. The table had low sides so food wouldn't fall off but the birds could hop in and out easily.

'It's beautiful, Jason.' Abby was gobsmacked. This beautiful man had brought her a beautiful gift. 'The carving on the roof and the stand are so … intricate. So exquisite. Where did you get it?'

Then Jason blushed and a shy smile crept onto his face. 'I made it.'

'You made this?' Her tone was filled with surprise.

He nodded.

'You are so talented. I have to give you something for it.' The lump in her throat was almost choking her now.

'No, Abby. It's a gift.'

'But it must have taken you ages to make it.'

'Not really and it's a hobby. Something I do to relax.'

'It's so beautiful.'

And as she gazed at it, to her horror, her eyes blurred and she started to cry. The tears ran down her cheeks, hot and silent, and she tried to wipe them away, but they just kept coming.

'Abby? I'm so sorry. I didn't mean to upset you.' His tone had changed to one of confusion.

'Not— you— but— the— last— few— days,' she squeaked.

And suddenly, Jason's strong arms were around her and she was pulled against his warm chest. She froze at first, a lifetime of holding back and hesitating was difficult to forget, then something in her gave way and she slid her arms around his waist and cried. It felt so good being there, being held. She felt safe, protected, that he would hold her up and support her, no matter what. So she surrendered to emotion, released the days, weeks and months of sadness, fear and frustration that had weighed her down. She cried until she was hoarse, until her eyes were sore and swollen and until Jason's T-shirt was drenched.

'How do you fancy going for some lunch?'

Abby peered up at Jason, aware that she must look dreadful after all that crying.

'Oh ... well, I'm, covered in paint and ... uh ... snot.' She covered her nose suddenly self-conscious.

'You can go and freshen up first if you want.' He smiled warmly and she realised that he wasn't judging her for breaking down, not at all.

'OK then. It won't take me long. Do you want to come and wash some of the paint off?'

She stepped back as he looked down at his wet T-shirt, already missing being in his arms. 'Or should I say tears? God, I'm sorry, Jason.'

'No need to be sorry.' He shook his head. 'But I could come up with you and change out of this. I can just wear my shirt.'

They tidied the painting things away then went up to

Abby's flat. She let Jason use the bathroom first, then jumped under the shower and washed away the morning's labours, the morning's emotions. She hadn't let go like that in years and it had felt really good to release it all, if a little embarrassing.

When she'd dressed in clean jeans and a black T-shirt, along with black pumps, she headed into the lounge. Jason was scrolling through his mobile, looking quite at home, almost as if he belonged there.

'All OK?' she asked.

'Yes, great.' He stood up and she couldn't help but notice how he seemed to fill her lounge. He was so tall and broad, so confident and so golden – from his hair to his tan. But it was his kindness that shone out of him, from his easy, friendly smile to his warm brown eyes. He barely knew her and yet he had let her cry her eyes out on his chest – and what a beautiful chest it had been – and he had sensed that she needed to do it, not letting go of her until she had finished releasing everything. In Abby's experience, men were rarely that understanding or that patient. He also didn't seem to feel awkward about it. Her resolve to remain friends with him, to hold back from anything else, was weakening by the minute. 'Shall we go?'

They walked along the pavement, enjoying the shade offered by the trees that had been planted long ago and now offered welcome shelter from the afternoon sun. Their foliage only allowed thin beams of light through, creating a dappled effect upon the pavement. The heavy stone planters installed by the council, as part of the City in Bloom project, were filled with colourful, sweet-scented flowers, and bees floated lazily from one flower to the next, drunk on pollen and the beauty of summertime.

Jason pointed out flowers that he thought would be good for Abby's garden and she listened, soaking up his knowledge, admiring his enthusiasm. Without the white T-shirt underneath his checked shirt, a V of his chest was exposed and with it a fine dusting of blond hairs against golden skin.

When they reached the park with the boating lake, Jason paused. 'What do you fancy then? Pub lunch or picnic in the park?'

'I really don't mind.'

Jason squinted up at the sky. 'It's such a lovely day, it would be a shame to head inside. Shall we grab some takeout from the café and go and sit on the grass in the park?'

'Sounds perfect.'

Lunch purchased, they followed the winding path around the boating lake then crossed the grass and sat down under the shade of a giant oak tree. Above them, a wood pigeon cooed in the tree, the sound soothing, comforting. Out on the boating lake, ducks, swans and geese sailed, ducked and dived, before climbing out onto the concrete bank to dry in the sun or take flight and disappear into the blue, cloudless sky. A couple rowed a small boat across the water, their laughter drifting on the warm breeze. It was a perfect afternoon and Abby felt that she could easily lie down on the grass and snooze. The grass had been recently cut and the sweet, fresh aroma reminded Abby of childhood and carefree summers spent with her mum, endless weeks when nothing mattered other than enjoying the fresh air, eating ice cream and staying up late. She'd had a good childhood – she'd felt secure and loved, and the memories of those days were happy. Not all children were so lucky, take Ernie for instance. She hoped that he was all right and that even though his mum wasn't around, he'd have happy memories too.

'You look thoughtful,' Jason said as he set a bottle of ice-cold water in front of her then a packet of cheese salad sandwiches.

'I was just thinking about how childhood can be such a brilliant time. Not for everyone, I know, but I had a wonderful mum and a happy home. It's just as I got older that things kind of ... deteriorated. Sometimes I miss the simplicity of being a child, when I thought my mum would be there for ever and I believed anything was possible. I actually thought for a while that I would grow up to be a mermaid ...' Abby swallowed down the sudden swell of emotion.

He nodded. 'I know what you mean. I had a good childhood too. We didn't have much money but we had a lot of fun. And I was convinced I'd be an astronaut and when that seemed unlikely, I decided I'd become Action Man.'

Abby unscrewed the cap of her water and took a sip. It was cold and refreshing.

'I didn't grow up in Manchester,' Jason said as he opened his sandwiches.

Abby didn't want to let on that she'd researched his background, not right now anyway, so she made quite an unconvincing non-committal sound ...

'I grew up in Sevenoaks in Kent. I have a brother – John – who's three years older than me and is a lawyer, and my mother was a stay-at-home mum while my dad was an accountant. We lived in a three-bed semi in a nice cul-de-sac, holidayed every year in Cornwall and life was pretty easy-going.' His tone was warm as he spoke about his childhood.

Abby bit into a sandwich and chewed thoughtfully, wondering if he'd stop there or tell her more.

'I went to uni – the University of Kent, so I didn't go far ... I didn't want to at that point to be honest.' He laughed self-deprecatingly. 'I read for a BSc Hons in biology, then realised I'd probably need to take another qualification to get a job, so I did a PGCE in further education. That led to me lecturing at the local FE college full-time.'

'Did you enjoy it?'

He nodded.

'It was a good job. I still do some teaching here in Manchester ... but not as many hours as I used to do.' His voice was softer now.

'Why did you ...' Abby paused. Not sure if asking him to elaborate further was a good idea.

'Why did I move to Manchester?'

'Yes. You don't have to tell me. It's none of my business, really.' She shook her head, afraid of hearing him tell her what she already knew about his past. She was worried that he'd get upset or even angry – grief provoked an array of emotions in people.

'It's OK ...' He wiped his hands on a napkin then drank some water. 'At the college, in my very first year there, I met someone.' A muscle in his jaw twitched, as if saying the words physically hurt him.

Abby held her breath. She wanted to hear more but also knew what was coming – she didn't know if she could stand to hear how painful it had been for Jason to lose the woman he had loved.

'Emma was a maths lecturer and such an intelligent woman. She was sharp, funny, warm ... reminded me a lot of Rachel Riley.'

'She sounds amazing.'

He met her eyes. 'She was.'

'Was?' Abby gently probed, giving him the chance to talk about his wife but a way to back out if he preferred. Guilt brought colour to her cheeks and she drank some water to try to cool down. She wished she didn't know what had happened or that she was now pretending that she was oblivious to Jason's loss, but telling him now would make this incredibly awkward and perhaps Jason needed to talk about it.

'We married a year after our first date. There didn't seem any sense in waiting longer and we were happy. Really happy. Then ... after a few years, we decided to start a family and Emma got pregnant straight away. We were shocked but delighted.' He smiled and his eyes took on a faraway look, as if he was actually gazing back into his past.

A silence fell between them and Abby leant back against the tree. This wasn't easy for Jason but there was no rush; they had all afternoon if he needed it – at least until she had to get to the hospital to make visiting hours. She had unburdened on him and wanted him to feel able to do the same. Sometimes, it was good to cry and talk about difficult things.

'It's not a happy story, Abby,' Jason said, breaking the silence.

'If you want to tell it, I want to listen.' She turned her body towards him, to show he had her full attention.

He drained his water.

'OK ... well ... Emma had gone on a teaching course in a London hotel. She took the car to the station because it was a Wednesday. I had an evening class so couldn't have picked her up. I remember gazing out of the window during my class and looking forward to cuddling up on the sofa later at home. The sky was black, the rain running down the window and I knew it would be bad on the roads. When my mobile rang on my desk ... I wasn't going to pick it up ... but it was her number. I answered, excusing myself to my students, and expected to hear her voice but it wasn't. It was the police. She'd stored my number as her ICE contact.'

He swallowed hard and his Adam's apple bobbed several times. This was incredibly difficult for him. Abby reached out and squeezed his hand, not sure if it was the right thing to do but sometimes human contact helped. She knew how much his hug had helped her when she needed comfort earlier. He had helped her and she wanted to help him.

'A HGV had skidded in the rain, the driver lost control and it toppled sideways, crushing Emma's little car. I always told her to get something bigger but she wouldn't, said she liked how easy it was to park. The ... the traffic police who attended the scene said she was likely ... kil— *gone* instantly. The baby too.'

He shifted his position and hugged his knees to his chest.

'I suspect it doesn't feel real, does it? Even now,' Abby said quietly.

Jason shook his head. 'It's like it happened to someone else. It was over three years ago, but sometimes it feels like it was yesterday that I kissed her goodbye and watched her climb into her car. I mean ... Emma was beautiful, smart and so full of life. She was carrying our child and had a lovely little bump. She didn't deserve to die like that. But one minute she was there, the next she was gone.'

'Life can be so cruel.'

'You're telling me.' His voice sounded choked and he took a few deep breaths then cleared his throat. 'I couldn't stand to be in the college where we'd worked together so I quit my job. I kept expecting to see her walking the hallways, making a coffee in the staff kitchen, lecturing in her classroom. It was unbearable. Then I sold our home too. It was just too painful being there alone. Moving was the next step for me. Running away my mum called it, but she also said she understood, while warning me that it would catch up with me at some point.'

Abby placed a hand on his shoulder.

'Are you still running?' Abby's voice came out small, vulnerable, filled with her sorrow for what Jason had suffered.

He pressed his lips together then looked up. His eyes were black now, the soft brown swallowed up by his pupils. He ran his gaze over her face, her lips, her shoulders then leant back against the tree.

'To be honest ... I don't know. I tried counselling ... bereavement groups ... and they helped in the early days but then I felt that I needed to move on. Exercise and being outside help me, keeping busy, helping other people with projects. If I didn't, I'd just be giving up. Emma wouldn't have wanted that.'

'I understand. I haven't been through what you have … I mean … losing your wife and unborn child like that is absolutely horrendous … but I did lose my mum and … and my baby.' Her voice thickened with her own grief.

'You lost your baby?'

'I had a miscarriage.'

'I'm so sorry.'

They sat in silence for a moment, each lost in their own pain as well as in a sense of mutual understanding.

'Look at us, eh?' He gave a rueful smile.

'We're surviving.'

He nodded. 'We're living and making the best of what we have.'

'That's right.'

Abby tentatively slid her hand along his shoulder and he met her gaze then opened his arms to her.

'Fancy another hug?'

She leant into him, her arms around his neck as he slid his own around her waist and they stayed that way for some time. It was warming, comforting, to be held by another human being, someone who understood the sharp pain of loss, someone else who had survived. Jason had been wounded, but he was healing. Abby had been hurt, but she was healing too. They both had a long way to go, but each day was a step in the right direction.

They were survivors.

CHAPTER 25

Ernie flopped onto the sofa and released a long sigh. It had been almost three weeks since Arthur had been taken to hospital and Ernie was missing him dreadfully. It was making his tummy all fluttery like when he thought about his mum, and not even cartoons could help him forget about it. He was very worried about Arthur and frustrated by the fact that he wasn't allowed to visit him. His dad said it was because Ernie might have picked up germs at school that he could then accidentally take to Arthur. Ernie understood that children carried lots of germs, and right now there *was* a nasty tummy bug in his school, but he also didn't think he had that many germs and he was certain that the funny feeling in his tummy was caused by worrying. He didn't get ill very often and his dad had always said that he had a strong constitution. Ernie had asked what constitution was, which made his dad laugh and ruffle his hair, then tell him it meant that he fought off bugs like a superhero.

He wished he was a superhero – then he could make Arthur better so he could come home. Ernie missed seeing Arthur in the mornings, he missed seeing him after school, he missed their dinners and their games of dominoes. The only good thing was that Dad had been home more because he said he needed to be there for Ernie.

Abby had stopped by last night after visiting Arthur and said that the doctors thought he had made good progress and might be able to come home in a few weeks. Ernie really hoped so, he didn't know how much longer he could wait to see him.

He sighed again. Sometimes, it was very difficult being a child.

'What's up with you, Ernie?' Jax said as she entered the lounge.

'Nothing.'

'That was a big sigh for nothing.'

He stood up and pushed his hair out of his eyes. He needed a haircut; it always grew so quickly.

He didn't want to talk about it with Jax. She didn't really understand why he was so sad for Arthur. She'd said he was a grumpy old man and that if he hadn't been such a stress-head then he probably wouldn't have made himself ill. That had upset Ernie, but Dad had told him not to take any notice. He'd said Jax was a teenager and teenagers often said hurtful things that they didn't mean.

Jax stood in the doorway staring at him with an expression on her face that Ernie couldn't read. He felt as if she wanted to tell him something.

'Ernie ...' She sniffed. 'You haven't been yourself these last few weeks. I'm worried about you. You don't want to get up in the mornings, you don't eat as well as you used to and you don't laugh at cartoons anymore. Look ... how about we have hot chocolates with marshmallows on the top and watch a film?'

'I have to do my homework.'

'You can do that later ... or tomorrow, or even at the weekend.' Jax held out her hands, palms up, smiling at him.

'I don't know. I have lots to do.'

'Look, I'll give you a hand with it or your dad will.'

Ernie chewed his bottom lip. It was tempting.

'Go on, Ernie. Let's have a relax.' Jax was grinning now. 'I bought choccie biscuits.'

Ernie softened.

'Well, OK, but I need to change out of my uniform first.'

'You do that and I'll put the kettle on.'

'OK.' He heaved himself off the sofa and started trudging towards his room.

'Ernie?'

'Yes.'

'It'll be all right, you know.'

'I hope so.'

'Mr Mayer ... He might be grumpy but he seems like a fighter, and I don't think he's going to give up easily. He'll be home before you know it.'

Ernie nodded as he left the room. He really hoped Jax was right.

'Was that the door?' Jax asked, peering up from her phone.

The lights on the TV flashed, sending shadows across the lounge walls. It was light outside but Jax had pulled the curtains so they could watch the film. Jax said it would be like going to the cinema.

Another knock at the door made Jax pause the film.

'I'll get it.'

Ernie jumped up and went to the front door, opening it to find Abby smiling down at him.

'Hi, Abby.'

'Hi, Ernie.'

Abby was wearing shorts and a T-shirt with her hair in a ponytail. She had freckles on her nose and her eyes were shining. She looked so pretty and Ernie suddenly felt shy.

'It's a lovely afternoon and I thought you might fancy helping me in the garden.'

'We were watching a film.' He gestured at the room behind him.

'Oh … OK … well you could always come and help in the garden now if you liked, then watch the rest of your film later, perhaps? I'm going to visit Arthur this evening instead of this afternoon, so I have plenty of time. I wanted to take him something from the garden.'

Ernie glanced behind him to see Jax standing in the lounge doorway. Her mobile was in her hand and she was looking from the screen to Ernie and Abby and back again.

'Um …' Ernie did quite want to go outside but he didn't want to be mean to Jax who probably wanted to watch the rest of the film with him. He'd seen more of her since Arthur had gone into hospital but he also knew she would prefer to be with her boyfriend. The boyfriend she claimed she didn't have but Ernie had seen one of her messages to him and it had been about kissing. He thought Jax was probably in love like the people in films often were. They pretended not to be but he could always tell because of the way they gazed at one another and the way they pretended not to like one another.

'It's fine, Ernie,' Jax said as she finally tucked her

mobile into her pocket. 'Your dad will be back in an hour so I could ... go now ... uh ... if Abby doesn't mind watching you.' She peered up at Abby from under her very long eyelashes, the ones Ernie thought looked like curved spider's legs. He'd seen her sticking them on with glue one day when she'd brought him home from school and he'd asked what she was doing. She'd told him she was going out that evening, so wanted to look her best. Ernie wasn't certain that putting white glue along her eyes then sticking the spider's legs to them was looking her best, but then she was a girl and he didn't understand girls at all.

'Yes, of course I will.' Abby smiled. 'As long as Ernie's happy to help me in the garden. I know you've been busy with your dad and school these past few weeks, and I haven't been in the garden much because of all that rain last week, but it's lovely today.'

'I'd like to help.' Ernie smiled at Abby. 'Just need to put my trainers on.'

As he ran to the cupboard in the hallway, he smiled to himself. He'd been finding it hard to focus on the TV and some time outside would be nice. He might even be able to ask more about Arthur and try to persuade Abby to let him go to the hospital too.

Outside in the garden, there was a lovely smell that Ernie guessed was coming from the colourful flowers that had been planted there. There was a man Ernie didn't recognise helping too, a tall man wearing a green T-shirt and shorts. He had blond curly hair that was sticking up, and a streak of mud across his forehead.

'Hello,' the man said. 'You must be Ernie.'

'Yes.' Ernie looked down at his shoes, feeling shy.

'This is Jason,' Abby said. 'Jason, meet my neighbour, Ernie.'

Jason held out his hand and Ernie stared at it.

'Shake hands,' Abby whispered, so Ernie did. He wasn't used to shaking hands with people and it felt a bit strange, but he knew it was what grown-ups did when they met for the first time. Grown-ups could be so silly sometimes.

Ernie wiped his hand on his T-shirt just in case there was mud on it from shaking hands with Jason. When he looked up, Abby was smiling at him and her cheeks had gone bright pink.

'We have something special out here, Ernie, that we thought you might like to help with. It's in the shed. Jason brought it over as a gift but I haven't had a chance to set it up properly yet.'

Ernie looked from Abby to Jason, wondering what the gift could be. Did she have a lawn mower that they could sit on and ride around the garden, or a football net so they could have a tournament?

Abby opened the shed and went inside. When she came back out she was carrying a large wooden stand.

'What do you think?' she asked as she set it proudly in front of Ernie.

'What is it?' he asked, worried that he'd seem silly. He stepped closer to it and touched the roof then peered underneath it.

'For the birds!' she announced. 'Jason made it.'

'Oh, I see! So you put food on the table,' Ernie said, as he looked at the small platform underneath the roof. 'Then the birds can eat there and not get wet even if it's raining.'

'Exactly!' Abby giggled. It was a light, excited sound and it made Ernie smile too. 'Where shall we put it, Ernie?' Abby asked.

He looked around the garden, thinking where the best place for a bird table would be, then pointed at the far corner where there was a space. 'Over there, so they won't poo on your fruit or veg and so no cats can jump at them from the wall.'

'Good idea. I knew you'd be the perfect person to help with this.' Abby winked at him, making him feel all warm inside. She always made him feel happy which was one of the reasons why he was glad she was his friend. In school, he rarely felt happy, so he liked spending time with Abby.

Once they'd put the bird table in place and Jason had secured the base with some bricks, Abby said, 'There's some birdseed in the shed, Ernie, if you want to get it.'

He nodded then ran to the shed and went inside. It had been painted a nice blue colour and Ernie could smell the paint they'd used. He wished they'd asked him to help with the painting because he'd have liked that, but then he hadn't felt like doing much the past few weeks. He'd felt very tired and sad and had been glad to sit on the sofa and stare at the TV. Not even chip shop chips and gravy had helped ease his tummy butterflies.

The inside of the shed was quite dark, and Ernie wondered if there were spiders and other creepy-crawlies in there. On a workbench against the one wall, he saw a bag with plants and birds on the front, so he picked it up. He tried to read the letters on the front but the familiar sensation of confusion crawled up his neck and made his face hot. This must be the bird seed because it had some birds on it, so he took it outside.

Out in the light again, he blinked hard, his eyes watering a bit because it was so bright. Over by the bird table, Abby and Jason were talking and Abby had a funny smile on her face. She was looking up at Jason and he was gazing down at her. Abby was swaying slightly, as though a gentle breeze was pushing her from side to side, and Jason said something that made Abby laugh and touch his arm. His mouth dropped open. He'd seen this before on TV. Abby and Jason fancied each other!

He carried the bag over to them then coughed, as if clearing his throat, in the way he'd seen people in films do when they wanted other people to know they were there.

It was nice to see Abby smiling so much. That other man, Gavin, who had been with Abby when Arthur got sick had made her sad and angry, and Ernie wasn't sure if he liked him. But this man, Jason, had a big smile and kind eyes, and Abby clearly enjoyed being with him. He wondered then, if they got married, whether they'd live here. Ernie would miss Abby if she moved away.

'Here's the bird seed.' Ernie handed Abby the bag.

'Fabulous!' Abby took the bag from Ernie then frowned. 'This isn't bird seed it's—'

She looked at Ernie. Then at Jason.

'It's ... for ... encouraging birds to visit the garden. Yes. That's what this is for.' Her cheeks went very red. 'Hold on a minute, I'll check the shed and see if I can find the other bag.'

She hurried over to the shed and emerged quickly, carrying a different bag. When Abby reached them, she tore the corner off the bag. 'Let's put some of this on the table and see if the birds come, shall we?'

Ernie held out his hand and Abby sprinkled the seed into his palm. It felt funny, hard and lumpy. He ran his thumb over the seeds. 'Do the birds like these?'

'They love it, that's wild bird food,' Jason explained. 'They like all the different seeds and they're good for them, too.'

Ernie nodded.

When they'd sprinkled a generous amount on the table, they took the bag back to the shed.

'Right then, Ernie. How are your weeding skills?' Jason asked.

Ernie thought about it for a moment. 'Pretty good.'

'How do you fancy tackling that patch of earth and pulling out anything that shouldn't be there?'

Ernie stared at the patch Jason had pointed out. There were some herbs there that Abby had planted a while ago and they'd grown quite bushy, probably because of the rain, but in between them, he could see other green leaves.

'I can do that.'

Jason handed him a small white plastic tub. 'Put anything you pull out in here.'

'OK.' Ernie nodded, feeling very grown-up at being trusted to do such an important job.

'If you're not sure if something is a weed, just give me a shout and I'll check for you.'

'And take these.' Abby gave him some gardening gloves. 'You need them to protect your fingers. They're adult ones, but small, so they should be OK, if a bit loose.'

Soon, Ernie's face was damp with sweat and his hands were hot in the baggy gloves, but he was determined to get every last weed. He gently lifted the plants, peering under them for stray weeds and making sure that he pulled them out carefully and got the roots too, as Abby had shown him before when he'd helped in the garden. It was hard work but he liked it too because it helped calm his tummy butterflies.

'How are you getting on, Ernie?' Abby asked as she looked into his tub.

'Good, I think.' He peered up at her.

'You really are. Well done!' She held out a hand and Ernie stared at it. Did she want to shake hands? 'High five, Ernie!'

'Oh! High five!'

They tapped hands and smiled at each other.

'Who fancies a drink?' Jason asked. 'I have some cans of lemonade in my cooler.'

'Me, please.' Ernie watched as Jason pulled the blue plastic box out from under the bench, opened the lid and brought out three cans. He handed one to Abby and one to Ernie, then they sat on the bench, Abby between them, and opened their drinks.

'What do you think of the garden now, Ernie?' Abby asked.

'It looks really good.'

Ernie was amazed at how much work Abby had done. She'd cleared out all the rubbish and made it look like a proper garden.

Ernie sipped his drink and bubbles went up his nose, making him sneeze. ''Scuse me!' He rubbed his nose with his palm. 'It's not a cold ... it was the bubbles from the lemonade. I … I could go to see Arthur, Abby, because I don't have a cold, I promise.'

'Hey, it's OK.' Abby squeezed his shoulder. 'Arthur is getting stronger and will hopefully be home soon. The whole germs thing is about the other patients as much as it is about Arthur. Some of the patients on the ward are very poorly.'

Ernie nodded. 'I just want to see him.'

'And he wants to see you too. It won't be long.' Abby gently squeezed his hand. 'Do you think Arthur will like the garden?'

'I think he will. He can sit out here and relax. He needs to relax more.'

'He really does.' She nodded.

'Well let's make sure that the garden is perfect for when he gets home, shall we?' Jason asked, leaning forwards to smile at Ernie.

'Are you moving in then?' Ernie asked, suddenly.

'Moving in?' Jason raised an eyebrow.

'Well, yes. I thought you might be Abby's new boy-friend.'

'Oh!' Jason's eyebrows shot up his forehead now.

'No, no, Ernie. Jason is my friend, not my boyfriend.' Abby gave a funny laugh that sounded as if she'd forced it out, like Jax did when she was speaking to her friends on her mobile.

Abby and Jason were both turning red and staring off in different directions as if they couldn't look at Ernie or each other.

'OK,' Ernie said, then he finished his can and stood up. 'We'd better get to work for Arthur then.' He would never understand grown-ups. If they liked each other, why not just be honest?

'Yes, indeed,' Jason said as he took the empty cans over to the recycling bins.

Ernie turned back to Abby, to ask where he should start, but she was watching Jason with a funny expression on her face. Whatever they said, Ernie could see that they fancied each other. It was – as they said in the films – written all over their faces.

'Jason seems nice …' Ernie said, another thing he'd heard people in films say when they wanted more information.

'Yes … yes he is.' Abby nodded as she quickly looked away, and even though she tried to seem like she wasn't thinking about Jason, Ernie could tell that she was. Her cheeks were red, her neck was blotchy and she was chewing at her bottom lip.

He couldn't wait to tell Arthur!

Abby stretched out her aching legs on the sofa and set her laptop on her thighs. It felt so good to sit down. She'd had a busy Monday between a supermarket trip, working on the garden with Jason and Ernie and visiting Arthur. He was quite a bit better now, getting stronger every day and responding well to treatment and rehabilitation, and it was hoped that he'd be well enough to come home within the next few weeks.

She smiled as she remembered the time in the garden earlier. She'd seen Jason a few times a week since their deep discussion in the park. They had a connection, an understanding of each other. They'd talked more about their losses and Abby admired how Jason dealt with his feelings, how he'd lost so much and yet he still smiled, still joked, kept moving forwards. He'd never forget his wife and child and he was still grieving for them, that much was clear – he probably always would – but he also had a determination to keep living, to do what he could to improve the lives of others, something which Abby found quite inspirational. She felt that she could talk to him, be herself around him, and that he never judged her. It felt unusual to her because she'd felt judged by Gav for so long, as if she had to walk on eggshells in case she said something he disagreed with or something that would give him fuel to mock her. Jason listened to her, really listened, his brown eyes warm and attentive, his replies considerate and encouraging.

She blew out a deep breath. She knew this was a bad idea, that she couldn't fall for Jason; it wasn't the right time for either of them, but it was difficult not to feel drawn to him. Powerfully drawn to him. For so many reasons. And today ... it had been embarrassing when Ernie had assumed that Jason was her boyfriend, but quite nice, too. He'd seemed so certain that Abby and Jason were a couple. She hadn't been sure what Jason's reaction suggested about his feelings for her as he'd blushed and seemed surprised, but she did know that Jason's situation was complicated and he wasn't in the right place to get involved with someone right now. And yet ...

She needed to have a chat with Lisa about it but part of her was reluctant to tell her. Lisa might become too excited, and that could lead to her putting pressure on Abby and in turn on her relationship with Jason.

She logged onto her blog. Her daily posts, even the short ones, were gaining lots of views and visits and comments like they used to when she posted there regularly. She had new followers but her old followers, who'd responded to her posts about her mum and her grief and her miscarriage, were also interested in her gardening project. She'd blogged about the garden, about the work that had been done there and about the progress of the things she'd planted. It was still anonymous, which she liked, because it offered a sense of privacy for her and those who visited. Of course, the anonymity had been more important when she'd blogged about things in her personal life like her mother and the baby, but she still found it comforting even now she was blogging about the garden and plants and garden pests.

Perhaps it was time for a post about her life and how it had changed recently ...

She started to type and found herself writing about the breakdown of her long-term relationship, moving into a new flat, meeting new people, meeting someone new who was a friend – but who made her feel more positive than she had done in ages – and about how she was letting go of the past and her ex, that she could now see clearly how bad he had been for her.

When she'd finished, she was surprised to find that the room was in darkness, the only light coming from her laptop and from the streetlights that now glowed outside. She read back through what she'd written and the positivity in the message made her smile.

Abby felt strong, something she hadn't always given herself enough credit for. She was a survivor and she had a lot to be proud of. When she thought back to finding that text on Gav's phone and to that awful day in her employer's office at Greenfields Care Home, it could have been years ago. It was as though Abby was a different person now, as if she had evolved with each blow to her heart and her confidence. Life had shaped her and would continue to do so. But that was good, that was OK, because Abby was prepared to embrace whatever came her way. In fact, she intended to run headlong into life rather than waiting for it to come to her.

CHAPTER 26

'Are you sure that we invited everyone?' Abby asked Ernie as they descended the stairs to the communal entranceway.

'Yes, Abby, we posted an invite to everyone at Willow Court.' Ernie stopped by the front door and smiled at her. 'You worry too much.'

As he shook his head, Abby felt her lips twitch. Sometimes, Ernie was more like an old man than a young boy. Perhaps it was because he'd spent so much time with Arthur, perhaps it was because he had an old head on young shoulders. Either way, it was very cute.

When she had still been reticent to invite her neighbours to help with the garden, Jason had suggested holding a barbecue that Saturday as a way of getting to know people and showing them what she'd been doing. Abby had to admit that inviting people to a barbecue sounded preferable to inviting them to work on the garden. People couldn't get annoyed with you if you fed and watered them, but they could turn their noses up at an invitation to work for free. She'd created invitations on her computer with Ernie, stating that there would be the first ever Willow Court Garden barbecue, starting at 6.30 p.m. that Saturday, and that everyone was welcome.

That morning, Abby and Jason had gone shopping and bought a load of food, along with wine, beer and soft drinks. Abby had also loaded crisps, breadsticks, condiments and plenty of freshly baked rolls into the trolley. It hadn't been cheap, but she'd hoped it would be worth it. If not, she'd be eating burgers and buns for weeks. Jason had offered to pay for half the shopping but she'd refused, stating that this was her barbecue, and that he could pay if he held one at his home.

As they reached the bottom of the stairs, Ernie opened the security door and held it so Abby could carry the box of food out. They went around to the garden where Jason was already setting up. He'd brought two trestle tables over that he sometimes used for events with his gardening organisation, and had draped them with paper tablecloths held in place with corner clips. The paper plates and cups were already laid out along with the condiments, napkins and bottles of Coke and lemonade, beer and wine. Abby set about arranging the crisps and other nibbles then made two piles of bread rolls that she covered with the net protectors she'd bought in the pound shop to keep the bugs off the food.

'I'm going to get Dad now,' Ernie said. 'Or he'll forget the time and sit in front of the sport all night.'

'OK, Ernie!' She waved him off then walked over to Jason. 'Something smells good.'

He'd set the barbecue up away from the trees and flowers with a small table next to it for the meat and vegetarian options.

'Food always smells better when it's cooked in the open air.'

'Fancy a beer?' Abby said.

'Please.'

Abby opened two bottles then handed one to Jason and he clinked it against hers.

As she sipped her beer, she thought about how someone looking out of their window at them might think they were a couple. They'd been spending time together, a lot of it in the garden, and it could easily look as though they were together. The thought made her warm inside.

'What if no one turns up?' Abby chewed her lip nervously.

Jason shook his head, smiling his easy smile. 'Of course they will. How could they decline the offer of our delightful company?'

'I hope you're right.'

She sipped her beer again. It was cool and slightly tart, refreshing and thirst-quenching. The last party she'd held at Willow Court had been her flat-warming and it had gone well. She'd felt proud of herself for hosting a party after so many years of Gav being Mr Antisocial – at least when it came to her friends. She was so glad of Jason's support this evening. Having him at her side made her feel more confident about meeting her neighbours, as if she had a wingman. If no one turned up, then Jason would be there. If people did turn up, Jason would help her get to know them and ensure that they were well fed. She could have done it without his help, but it wouldn't have been as much fun.

'Trust me.'

He flipped the burgers that were sizzling over the hot coals.

'I do,' she replied, her words holding more significance

than she'd intended, at odds with the lightness of the afternoon.

Jason held her gaze and her heart pounded. She suddenly felt hot all over and was glad she'd settled on her outfit of a cool, floaty white cotton dress with thin straps and gold gladiator sandals.

'Abby, I—'

'Hello, you two!'

Abby jumped as Lisa's voice cut through the moment like a blade.

'Lisa! Fiona!' Abby squeaked, before setting her beer down, hurrying over to her friends and hugging them both.

'Sorry, love, did we interrupt something?' Lisa muttered as she handed Abby a bottle of wine.

'No, of course not.' Abby turned the wine bottle in her hands and pretended to read the label.

'You sure? It looked like you were about to snog.' Abby met Lisa's teasing eyes and Lisa waggled her eyebrows at her.

'No ... no we were just talking.'

'Just talking,' Fiona said to Lisa and they winked at each other, making Abby cringe. Was she being that obvious?

'What's in the boxes?' Abby asked as Fiona set them on the trestle table, to change topic more than anything else.

'Dessert options. Thought you might have forgotten to get something.'

'Oh God, I did!' Abby smacked her forehead. 'Plenty of savoury but nothing sweet.'

'Good job we came then.' Lisa picked up a beer. 'He does look rather delicious, mind, Abs.'

'I agree.' Fiona nodded. 'From an objective perspective, of course. Men not being our thing and all that.'

'Of course,' Lisa agreed.

Abby looked over at Jason where he was oblivious to anything other than the task at hand. In khaki shorts and slightly paler T-shirt, with a pair of grey boat shoes, he looked as good as he always did. He'd had his blond curls trimmed that week so his hair was now shorter at the back and sides and slightly longer on top. As she watched, he pushed it back from his tanned forehead, the movement showing his muscled arms. His legs were tanned too, his calves toned and strong. And he had no idea how attractive he was. He'd probably grabbed that T-shirt and shorts off the rail in the shop without much thought, the same with the shoes. Jason was no fashionista, no narcissist, even though he had every right to be with his Hollywood good looks and that firm body. But for all that he was attractive, it was the man behind the good looks that Abby was more and more drawn to. He was such a kind and supportive person, so easy-going and sweet. In spite of what he'd lost, he still had a ready smile and was keen to make the most of each day. She couldn't imagine Jason cheating on a partner, couldn't ever picture him betraying a friend let alone a lover. Jason Armstrong was, in Abby's eyes, perfect.

'You like him.' Lisa nudged her, dragging Abby from her thoughts and bringing heat to her cheeks.

Abby turned to meet Lisa's gaze. She could deny it, but what was the point? She knew it was written all over her face, as surely as it was written all over her heart.

The main thing Abby would remember about the evening was the laughter. All around her, people were smiling and talking and having a great time. She'd seen these people in the car park, on the street, in the local supermarket, sometimes even in the garden, but this evening, they had come together in the garden on Holly Street. She couldn't yet remember all the new names, but something told her that that with time, she'd know each and every one.

Lisa and Fiona had been amazing, proving yet again what good friends they were. They'd helped with the food and drink and had her back when she'd run out of rolls by rushing to the local shop to top up their supplies. Fiona hadn't even murmured when a little boy had picked up a tomato sauce bottle and squeezed it a bit too vigorously, causing the sauce to fly over his hotdog but also over Fiona's denim shorts. She'd simply grabbed a napkin and wiped at her shorts, ignoring the red stain that covered most of her left thigh.

Ernie had been like some kind of tiny efficient butler, filling plastic glasses, taking empty plates away and dividing materials into recycling piles. For such a young boy, he was so thoughtful and sensible, and he took his role in the evening very seriously. Neil had been Jason's assistant at the barbecue, taking cooked meats and vegetarian burgers and sausages to the tables and passing Jason new ones to cook. They'd made a good team and again, she had marvelled at how Jason seemed able to get along with anyone. Perhaps he made everyone feel the same way he made her feel; that he was truly interested in what they had to say, that he wasn't judging them at all.

As for Abby, she'd introduced herself to her neighbours and explained what she'd done to the garden and hoped to do in the future. She also explained – to those who had asked – about Arthur and had agreed to pass on their best wishes. Of course, she was realistic, she knew that some of them had come for the free food and drink, like Josh and Floyd, the two young men who rented a flat overlooking the garden. They'd arrived, had a few drinks, eaten their fill then headed into town for the evening. Abby doubted they'd be helping out anytime soon, but at least they'd shown their faces. That was almost as important.

More positive about the garden had been a lovely lady, called Bonnie, and her husband Ned – both in their sixties. They had bought their flat last year after their son emigrated to Sydney to be with his Australian bride. Bonnie was bubbly and friendly, while her husband was quiet and seemingly happy to let his wife do the socialising.

Then there was Aisha, a beautiful young woman with incredible long, dark shiny hair, and her boyfriend, Oliver, a sports physiotherapist employed by a local football team. The young couple were clearly very much in love, if their hand-holding and frequent glances at each other were anything to go by. They both said that they'd love to get involved in the gardening.

When Abby had gone to replenish drinks, Lisa had come to her side.

'Having fun, Lisa?'

'It's turned into a fabulous evening!' Lisa swayed, the wine she'd enjoyed clearly affecting her balance. 'However ... look over there. I think you might have competition for the handsome gardener.'

Abby had followed Lisa's finger to the barbecue where Neil was flipping burgers and Jason was talking to a woman. She had white-blonde hair and an hourglass figure, every inch of which was shown off dramatically in a neon pink mini-dress. As Jason talked, the woman laid a hand on his upper arm and threw back her head, causing her hair to swish over her shoulders and her pneumatic bosom to rise even higher.

'Oh …' Abby's stomach churned, a familiar and horrid feeling like bile rising in her throat. 'Who's that?'

'One of your neighbours, I guess. Go and introduce yourself.'

'No … she's busy talking to Jason.'

'And so should you be.'

Abby had shaken her head vigorously. They were good friends, had been supportive of each other, but at the end of the day, what he did was up to him. If he was attracted to that woman (who was very beautiful, if in quite an obvious way) then she had no right to interfere, even if she did want to grab a sausage and throw it at the woman.

Instead, she had pushed her shoulders back, turned to find a clean glass then poured wine into it before taking a swig. Then another one. Then she'd drained the glass before refilling it.

'Abby … I'm not going to push you here but are you sure you don't want to … butt in?' Lisa squeezed Abby's shoulders, holding her gaze. 'I know you like this guy.'

'I do. But … even if we were … seeing each other … he'd still be entitled to speak to people.'

'Of course he would. It's just that it looks like that woman is making a play for him.'

'And it's up to him to decide what to do.'

The evening had gone really well and she'd had such a lovely time, but seeing that happen right in front of her was making her wobbly. It was because of her past, she knew that, but not everyone was like Gav.

She had drunk some more wine then plastered on her best smile. She had neighbours to talk to, people to involve in the garden project. She wanted to create a real community here. Granted, losing the man she liked to one of her neighbours wasn't the community sharing she'd had in mind, but then life didn't always go the way she thought it would. Perhaps she'd just imagined that the connection between them was something more; perhaps the attraction had been on her side alone.

So she'd circulated, trying hard not to watch Jason and the woman from the corner of her eye, trying not to care.

But try as she might, she did care. Sometimes the heart had a mind of its own.

As the evening wore on, people eventually returned to their homes and Abby and her friends were left clearing up. Ernie was yawning madly, and it was clear that he needed to go to sleep.

'Neil, don't worry about this. Why don't you take Ernie home? He's exhausted.'

She pointed at the bench where Ernie was curled up on his side, fast asleep.

Neil nodded.

'All right then.' He went over to Ernie and gently roused him. 'Come on, Ernie.'

The little boy opened his eyes. 'I'm not tired, Dad.'

'Yes you are. Come on.' Neil held out a hand.

'Okaaaaaay.' Ernie got to his feet and Neil protectively wrapped an arm around his shoulder. Seeing them like that made Abby experience a familiar pang of longing for what she'd lost. She glanced at Jason, wondering if he felt it too. But Jason was smiling at the pair and he gave them a wave before carrying on with cleaning the barbecue.

'I thought we could pop this in the shed once it's cooled down. Although …' He looked up at the dark sky. 'It's not going to rain tonight, so it'll probably be fine out here.'

'I can put it in the shed tomorrow,' Abby said as she took the tongs and spatula from him. 'I'll put these in the dishwasher when I go up.'

'Good plan.' Jason smiled.

'Righty-oh, Abs, if you don't need us any longer, Fi and I will head home.' Lisa squeezed her shoulder.

'You don't have to go,' Abby said as she accepted their hugs. 'You can always stay at mine.'

'It's fine,' Fiona said. 'I'm driving anyway, I haven't touched a drop this evening. Unlike my darling fiancée.'

'Well if you're sure.' Abby smiled. 'Let me know if you fancy brunch soon.'

'Will do. Perhaps tomorrow? Or … well, let's see how tired we are in the morning, but if not, we can do it next weekend. You might, uh … be tired yourself anyway.' Lisa winked at her then peered around her at Jason.

'Behave yourself,' Abby muttered, giving Lisa a hard stare.

'Always!' Lisa hiccupped and Fiona rolled her eyes at Abby.

When the garden was finally tidy again, Abby stretched her arms above her head and yawned.

'That was busy.'

'And a roaring success.' Jason held up his hand for a high five.

'It did go well, didn't it?'

'You've got some people keen to help out of it, anyway.'

'I know. Bonnie, Aisha and Oliver said they'll help however they can.'

'Abby …' Jason stepped closer to her. 'I was thinking …'

'Hey, you two! Ooh, where did everyone go?'

Abby sighed inwardly as the blonde in pink tottered around the corner towards them.

'I just went inside to phone the twins and—' She looked at Abby. 'I have twin daughters.'

'Abby, this is Nadine. She lives at Willow Court too.'

Abby looked from Jason to Nadine and back again. Was she in the way here? Or was she being too sensitive?

'Perhaps I'd better head inside,' she said quietly.

'No!' Jason placed a hand on her arm. 'Please, stay,' he muttered.

Nadine had reached them now and was standing very close to Jason, who was also standing close to Abby which made for an uncomfortable triangle.

'How about a nightcap, Jason? I have a delicious vodka or, if you prefer, I have sparkling wine in my fridge,' Nadine said as she reached out and placed a hand on his arm. Her pupils were huge and it was clear that she'd had a fair bit to drink.

Jason snatched his arm back and slid it around Abby's waist and pulled her closer. He did it so quickly and so powerfully that she gave a small sigh of surprise. He pressed a kiss to the top of her head, and Nadine's thin drawn-on eyebrows rose up her forehead.

'Oh! You two are ... Oh! You didn't say anything earlier.'

'That we're together?' Jason gave a low laugh that Abby felt rumble through his chest. 'I thought it was obvious. We've only got eyes for each other.'

Abby snuggled closer to him, playing along and enjoying it probably more than she should have done.

'Shall we head inside, darling?' she asked.

'Yes, I think so.'

'I ... uh ... it was lovely to meet you both.' Nadine grinned at them, revealing perfect porcelain veneers. 'Thanks for everything you've done to the garden, by the way. My girls are staying at their father's tonight ...' She wrinkled her nose. 'But they love to read and it'll be lovely for them to have a place to sit with their books.'

'It's *our* pleasure.' Abby smiled at Nadine, wondering now if there was more to this woman than the shiny front she seemed to paint on. She was very pretty under the layers of fake tan, lipstick and make-up that actually covered her natural beauty. Abby imagined that without the tan and mascara, Nadine probably looked years younger than she did with it on. She also seemed OK with the fact that Jason was with Abby, even though her initial reaction had suggested that she'd been keen to see out the night in Jason's company.

'Night then.' Nadine smiled then tottered off around the building.

'Thanks for that,' Jason said, his arm still tight around her waist.

'You're welcome. To be honest, I thought you might like her.'

He gently released Abby and met her gaze.

'She seems like a nice person but she's not my type at all.'

'You have a type?'

He laughed. 'Not that I know of, but she's a bit ... scary if I'm honest.' He shivered and Abby giggled.

'I can't get over you, Jason. You're so unlike any other man I know.'

'Is that a good thing?' he asked.

'It really is.'

'Look ... I've been trying to ask if you fancied sitting out here for a bit in the quiet. I have something in the cooler that I put in the shed earlier. But it's just for us.'

'OK ...' Abby's stomach fluttered. Jason had something just for them?

While Jason went to the shed, Abby sat on the bench and stretched out her legs. It was good to sit down after an evening on her feet. The sky was dark except for the silvery glow of the moon and stars twinkling like jewels. A few clouds drifted slowly along, like wisps of smoke carried by the gentle breeze. It had been a glorious summer day and although it was cooler now, the air was fragrant with sweet flowers, cut grass and barbecues. In that moment, Abby believed it was the most wonderful scent she had ever encountered.

When Jason returned, he sat next to her and handed her two plastic glasses, then he produced a bottle of champagne.

'Are we celebrating?' she asked as warmth flooded through her. She'd only ever drunk champagne at

Christmases and birthdays. It was a drink that seemed extravagant, luxurious and special. Gav had claimed that he didn't like it, but Abby had thought he was just too mean to buy it – and they rarely had anything to celebrate.

'We are.' Jason popped the cork and it shot off into the shadows of Willow Court. Some windows were as dark as the sky, while others were lit from within. Until this evening, they'd been the homes of strangers; now they belonged to people she knew. They glowed warmly, hinting at the lives that went on behind them. Abby had sat here before, wondering who was inside, but now she'd met quite a few of her neighbours and it made her feel even more connected to this place.

'What are we celebrating?' she asked as he poured the bubbly into their glasses.

'Life. Including Arthur's recovery.'

'He's still not fully recovered, but the medical staff said he is on the mend and the signs are good.'

He tapped his glass against hers then they drank, holding each other's gaze as they did so. The bubbles from the champagne went up Abby's nose and she laughed at the sensation.

'What is it?' Jason asked.

'Bubbles.'

'You're so pretty when you laugh, Abby.'

Something passed over his face that sent a wave of concern hurtling through Abby.

'What's wrong?'

He shook his head.

'Jason, please ... we've been honest with each other up until now and I don't want that to change.'

'I know. I don't either. I just … sometimes I feel guilty.' He cleared his throat.

'What? But why?'

'Because I never thought I'd ever like someone again, but … I like you, Abby.'

'Does that feel wrong then?' She shifted on the bench, fear rising in her throat.

'When I think about …'

'Emma?'

'Yes.' His reply was soft, the emotion behind it evident. Abby put a hand over his.

'That's understandable.'

He stared into his glass. 'It is?'

'Of course. You're still alive, you still love her, so it feels like a betrayal.' She squeezed his hand. 'But it's not, you know?' Her voice rose slightly on the question.

'See and now you're being so understanding that I feel worse.'

'I can't win, can I?' She leant her head on his shoulder, gritting her teeth to hold her emotion back.

They were quiet for a while, then Jason said, 'I feel like I lost so much, and now I've won again.'

'How so?'

'I loved Emma, we were happy, but then … she was gone. And now … I've met you and you're just amazing.' His voice wavered and Abby's heart leapt.

She smiled into the darkness. Jason thought she was amazing. She was making him as happy as he made her.

'I think you're amazing too.'

They sat there until they'd drained the champagne bottle, as the lights in Willow Court went off, as out on the street the footsteps of people heading out and those making their way home echoed through the air, and as somewhere, off in the distance, a cat meowed to be let inside.

It was the perfect end to a perfect day, and Jason was right; it felt like they really were celebrating life.

CHAPTER 27

Abby unlocked Arthur's front door then pushed it open and Arthur stepped inside. He released a sigh that he felt he'd been holding in for weeks. He was home. At last!

It had been seven weeks since he'd collapsed on his lounge floor, seven weeks since he'd experienced that blinding pain in his head, since he'd had any peace and quiet. And he had missed that, as well as having some time to himself. In some ways, being in hospital had been almost pleasant because he had had a constant stream of company, but there had been times when he'd longed for his own armchair, his own bed and his own space. It was all well and good having nurses, doctors and other medical staff looking out for you, seeing to your every need, but a grown man needed some time to himself now and then, and being home meant that he could have that time.

His flat smelt ... different. He'd expected it to smell stale, of old food and unopened windows, but it didn't; it was fresh and ... floral. As he entered the kitchen he saw why. On the table, in one of Julia's cut-glass vases, was a large colourful bouquet of summer flowers. Their fragrance filled the room, as sweet and uplifting as a summer's day. He set his bag of medication on the table next to the vase then shuffled through into the lounge. There was another vase on the sideboard, filled with the long green stems of lilies and the thinner, almost spiky, stems of gypsophila. The room was cool and fresh, as though the windows had only been recently closed, and there wasn't a speck of dust to be seen, which explained the aroma of furniture polish.

'What's it like being home?' Abby asked him.

He turned to her, his throat constricting. She'd been so kind to him, so patient and accommodating, and he was feeling far more emotional than he usually did. Abby had picked him up from the hospital and brought him home. He'd told her he would get a taxi but she'd insisted on collecting him. She'd said that Ernie and Neil would've been there too, given half a chance, but Ernie had school and Neil had a meeting to get to. They'd be round later on to see him, though, so he would have a chance to settle in first.

'It's ... wonderful, Abby, just wonderful.' He offered a wobbly smile.

Arthur was really looking forward to seeing Ernie. It was such a change from how he used to feel about the lad. It was almost laughable how annoying he'd found the small boy with his energy and noise levels, but now, Ernie was an important part of his world. He'd missed Ernie badly, but understood that it was better to keep him away from the stroke unit because he didn't want Ernie seeing him like that, surrounded by others who'd suffered all manner of complications caused by strokes. Ernie was still very young and there was no need to subject him to what would undoubtedly be an upsetting experience, especially when Arthur had been told he would be able to return home when the medical team had worked out the right medication for him and were certain that he was out of danger.

'I've set your bag on the bed for you, Arthur. I can unpack it too if you'd like.' Abby stood in the lounge doorway, her hands clasped in front of her as though she was nervous.

'No, that's fine, thanks, Abby. I can unpack and put my washing on.'

He lowered into his armchair and smiled at its familiar comfort, at how it cushioned him perfectly as it had always done.

'Are you sure? It's no trouble at all.'

'No, don't worry yourself.'

'But, Arthur … with the … uh …' She blushed and lowered her eyes.

'You mean the muscle weakness in my left arm?'

'Yes,' she whispered. 'So it might make sense if I help you a bit … just while you settle in.'

He nodded, wanting to refuse but knowing that what she said did make sense.

'Well, this time then, but I will need to try to start doing things again.'

Abby smiled, relief etched on her features. 'You will, but in time.'

'All right then, lass.'

'How about a cuppa?'

'I don't have any milk in,' he said, shaking his head.

'Yes you do. I went to the supermarket last night and got you the essentials. If you make a list of what else you need, I can get those for you later.'

'Abby ... there's really no need. I'm quite capable of going to the shops.' He said the words but a heaviness settled in his heart. The thought of going out alone, unaided, made him break into a cold sweat. What if he didn't fully recover and ended up having to rely on others for the rest of his days? He hated the thought that he might lose his independence completely.

'Arthur ...' Abby looked at the sofa. 'Is it OK if I sit down a moment?'

'Of course it is. You don't need to ask after everything you've done for me. You go ahead and make yourself at home.' His lips twitched slightly, in spite of the gravity of the situation, because two months ago, he'd never have said those words to his female neighbour.

'Thanks ... well ... look ... This is hard for me to say but ... You might not be ready for that yet. The doctor at the hospital said that you could come home as long as you take it easy and follow the discharge plan.'

'I know.' He set his stick against the small coffee table and slowly stretched out his hands on his knees. 'It's hard to give up my independence though.'

'It doesn't have to be permanent, Arthur. Just until you're stronger. You've made what they described as a positive recovery, so you'll be back to ... full strength ...or thereabouts, soon.'

'I wish ...' He gave a rueful chuckle. 'That would take me back to about ... 1985, I think. Oh to be young and strong again and in peak physical condition.' He shook his head sadly. Youth disappeared like sand through an egg timer, and once it was gone, you couldn't get it back.

Abby shifted on the sofa and he noticed that she was worrying her bottom lip.

'What is it?' he asked, watching her carefully.

She glanced around the room before meeting his gaze. 'It just feels a bit … strange being in here like this.'

'Because I've always been such a miserable old grump?'

Her eyes widened and she smiled. 'Yes … kind of.'

'Don't worry, Abby, I'm teasing you. I don't think you have any idea how grateful I am to you, do you? You saved my life. Now, it might not be much of a life but it's the only one I've got. You saved me and you've visited me every day since I went into hospital. Abby … there are people out there with family who don't do that for them. You have a heart of gold, lass, and I am forever in your debt.'

She was shaking her head now. 'No, Arthur. You're not in my debt at all. I was … I *am* glad to help. Everyone should have people around them who care.' She wiped at her eyes with the back of her hand and sniffed. 'Now … how about that cup of tea?'

'That would be lovely, thank you.'

Abby left the room and Arthur looked around. It was the same room as before and yet it was somehow different, as if he was seeing it through fresh eyes. Perhaps that was what a near-death experience did for you … Helped you to see things anew. Arthur had lost so much over the years and, at times, he had wished he could leave the world too. But he'd had a wake-up call and a brutal one at that. He had a second chance here, probably the last chance he'd get. He intended to make the most of it, to live and live well, whether his second chance lasted days, weeks, months, or maybe even years. Abby and others had shown him enormous kindness and compassion;

they had opened his eyes to the goodness that still existed in the world.

He had been alone – but he wasn't any longer.

Abby set the two mugs on a tray then added a plate of custard creams and a straw for Arthur – just in case, although he had been drinking without one the past few days – and carried it through to the lounge. She set it down on the small table next to Arthur then picked up one mug and went to the sofa. There was a chair right next to his, separated only by the small coffee table, but she couldn't bring herself to sit there as she suspected it had been Julia's.

On the journey home from the hospital, Arthur had been quiet, pensive even, and she hadn't wanted to ask how he was feeling in case he didn't want to tell her. Besides which, he'd probably had enough of people asking him that question recently. He was better but he also seemed tired and she knew that if she was in his position, she'd be glad to get back to her own space and to some peace and quiet. The stroke unit was a wonderful place, a ward where miracles happened on a daily basis, where the NHS staff were incredibly dedicated and caring, attentive and professional, but the ward was always noisy, between the monitors, telephones, the busy staff, the patients and their visitors. Plus, there was virtually no privacy there, and she knew that Arthur was a man who valued his.

Before he was dismissed from the ward, Arthur had been given one final assessment, a variety of medication, and a discharge plan. He'd receive visits from a district nurse and from council-led services like meals on wheels, as well as a cleaner who would visit twice a week. He'd also have continued physiotherapy as an outpatient for the next few months. Arthur had tried to insist that he didn't need further care, but Abby could see that he knew he did.

She wrapped her hands around her mug and watched the steam rising.

'Would you like the TV on?' she asked.

Arthur shook his head. 'I'm just enjoying the quiet, lass, thank you. Lovely it is.'

'Would you like me to go then? I don't want to outstay my welcome. I've added my number to your mobile so you can call me if you need anything.' She didn't really want to leave him yet. She was worried that something could happen to him if he was left alone so soon after returning home.

'Abby … If you'd just stay for a while longer … I'd be very grateful.' He spoke softly, and Abby knew that he was embarrassed having to ask, but it was understandable that he'd be afraid.

'Of course.' She didn't have to rush anywhere today. She'd thought she'd get out into the garden later to get it ready to show Arthur, but apart from that, she had set today aside to be there for her neighbour. She still wasn't sure whether it was a good idea to raise the subject of his letters to Julia, to let him know that she'd found them and read them, but she felt as though that was a deceit between them, one that she should confess. She had been looking for his address book, though, and hadn't set out to invade his privacy, but she didn't know if he'd accept that explanation.

'Arthur?'

'Yes.' He pushed his glasses up his nose and met her eyes.

'I need to tell you something and I hope it's not going to upset you.'

He straightened in his chair. 'What is it? Is Ernie all right?'

She nodded. 'Yes, yes, Ernie's fine. It's not about him … it's about me. And you. And something I did.'

'OK …' He frowned, clearly puzzled.

'When you were taken away in the ambulance, I didn't know what to do. I tidied up a bit then came back the next day to see if I could find anyone to contact to let them know what had happened to you.'

'Right.' He wasn't smiling or frowning now, but his eyes were fixed on her.

"And I … I had to looked around to try to find an address book.'

'And?'

'I went in that cupboard because it seemed the most obvious place to look and I found … a tin full of paper.'

Arthur's eyes widened and his mouth dropped open.

'Ah …' He pressed his lips together now and used his right hand to shift his left one on his lap.

'I'm so sorry … but I read through the … uh … the letters because I thought I might find something in there like a phone number or an address. Anything really.'

'But you didn't.' It wasn't a question.

'No I didn't,'

'But you read my letters to Julia?'

Abby couldn't read his tone and his face was expressionless. She tried to imagine how she'd feel in his situation, how it would feel to know that someone had read your private thoughts. It would be like someone reading the things she and Lisa wrote to each other on Facebook messenger when they weren't able to chat, or like someone entering her head and seeing exactly how she felt about Jason. It would be embarrassing, probably, to have someone hear your most private thoughts.

'I'm so, so sorry. Please don't be angry with me. I was only trying to help.'

Arthur lifted his right hand and slid his fingers under his glasses to rub his eyes. When he met her eyes again, he smiled.

'Abby … those letters were written because I couldn't speak to my wife, because I needed an outlet when my grief felt unbearable. I …' He paused and took a deep breath. 'I have missed her so much.' He dropped his gaze and Abby felt as though her heart would break for him. She got up and went to him, sitting in the chair next to his now and taking his hand.

'It's OK, Arthur. Let it out. I'm here.'

She pulled a tissue from the box on the table and handed it to him and he dabbed at his eyes. Abby had an urge to wrap him in a big hug but she had no idea how he'd feel about that and the last thing she wanted to do was to make things awkward again, so instead, she held his hand while he composed himself.

'It's OK to grieve, Arthur. You lost the person you loved more than anyone in the world. Of course you miss her. Of course you do.'

He nodded. 'Julia was my world and I always thought I'd go first. That's how it's meant to be, right? The husband goes first as women are meant to be better at coping.'

Abby gave a rueful smile. 'Apparently. I think we just tend to be better at releasing emotion.' She thought about what she'd just said. 'Sometimes, anyway. Your letters are beautiful, Arthur. Julia was a lucky woman to have you love her so much.'

Arthur sniffed then looked up. 'I was the lucky one.'

They sat in silence for a while, listening to the tick of the clock and the birdsong from outside. Their tea turned cold and Abby realised that Arthur might need a drink as he had to stay hydrated.

'Shall I make us a fresh cuppa?'

'Yes please.'

When she returned from the kitchen, she set Arthur's next to him then picked up her bag and pulled out the paperback she'd purchased in the hospital shop. A thought occurred to her.

'Would you like me to read to you?' she asked tentatively and held the book out for Arthur to see the cover.

'What's it about?'

'It's called up lit, which means it's an uplifting read. It's a story about … well, basically about a woman who had a tough life but … things are improving for her.'

Arthur laughed. 'How has her life been tough?'

'Why don't I read it to you and you can find out?'

'That would be lovely, Abby.'

'OK then …'

As she read to him, Arthur nodded and smiled, but after about twenty minutes, his chin dropped to his chest and he began to snore gently. She reached for the crocheted blanket on the back of chair then draped it gently over his knees. The poor man was clearly exhausted, drifting off like that. She'd stay and watch over him, be here when he woke up. He had a journey ahead of him and although he'd done well to recover as much as he had, there was no telling how the stroke would affect him long term. Abby wanted to help him along that journey, because everyone deserved a helping hand.

Ernie had been so excited all day about getting home to see Arthur and now something awful had happened. He couldn't believe it; he'd never been in a fight before in his whole life. Now the headteacher had said Ernie had to wait in the classroom until his dad came to collect him, but first she wanted a meeting with him. Ernie kept biting his lip to keep himself from crying but some tears had escaped anyway, rolling down his cheeks and making the graze on his chin sting along with the swelling around his eye.

Last night, when Dad had told him Arthur would definitely be home today, he'd run around the flat cheering. He'd been looking forward to seeing Arthur, and he was as excited as he got at Christmas. He hadn't seen Arthur for weeks and he couldn't wait, even though Dad said Ernie would need to be quiet and calm around Arthur.

But somehow, Ernie's excitement had been too much to contain and he'd found it harder to concentrate than usual. The supply teacher who'd turned up at the school was one he hadn't seen before (they changed a lot) and she'd told them that she'd been given a list of things to do with the class that day. First on the list had been the mid-week spelling test and Ernie had felt his joy at the thought of seeing Arthur trickle away as the test had begun. He'd tried to do the usual thing and copy from someone on his table, but today the other children had covered their work so he couldn't see a word. Of course, Ernie still got some words wrong when he copied them down, but at least it meant he'd get some right. Today, however, he'd got zero.

A big fat zero.

The worst thing about it was that the supply teacher had insisted they swap their books to mark one another's work. Ernie had got up and gone to her desk and asked her to mark his, whispered please and thank you, but she'd refused and told him to go back to his table. So then he'd tried to mark his own work but one of the girls had told on him and the teacher had made him give his notebook to Jamie Jones.

Ernie had been unable to tell if Jamie's spellings were right as the teacher had read them out so quickly that he couldn't follow. He'd started to feel sick and his hands had slipped as he'd tried to hold his pen. Then, when the teacher had finished reading the words out, Jamie had stood up and laughed loudly before shouting, 'Ernie got ZERO!' so that everyone heard. All the children in the class had laughed and the teacher had shouted at them to be quiet, but it was too late. Ernie had reached for his book to take it from Jamie but Jamie had kept holding it away from him, teasing him. Then, Jamie had muttered that Ernie's mum had probably left because he was so stupid – so Ernie had reacted.

He knew it was wrong to hit people but he'd been so embarrassed and angry and hurt and the teacher wasn't helping, so he'd punched Jamie in the tummy. He hadn't hit him hard but it made Jamie get up and grab Ernie by the throat then punch him in the eye. That had hurt. A lot. And as he'd fallen over, he'd bumped his chin on the desk too.

Now he was in trouble because the teacher had seen that Ernie started it all by hitting Jamie first. But she didn't see Jamie making fun of him and winding him up. She didn't hear what Jamie said about his mum. What would Dad say? What would Arthur think? Not only was he stupid to get all of his spellings wrong but now he was also a bully. Everyone was going to be so disappointed with him.

He sniffed hard then buried his head in his hands.

Ernie sat in the passenger seat of the car and waited for his dad to get in. When his dad had come to get him from school, he'd had a long talk with the head teacher and Ernie had had to wait outside the head teacher's office. He'd been so tired by then and felt like lying down across the seats and going to sleep. But he knew that if he did that, he'd be in even more trouble, so he stayed sitting up, and tried to go through his times tables in his head instead.

Then Ernie had had to go into the office and he'd had another telling-off, this time by Dad too. He'd wanted to explain why he'd hit Jamie Jones but the words wouldn't come out, so he kept quiet instead, and the headteacher said she could see that he was upset, so perhaps he needed some time at home to calm down. She'd told Ernie's dad to ring her the next day so they could speak further and try to find a way forward.

So now, Ernie had to go home with Dad and he was worried about how much he'd let his dad down. What if Dad decided he'd had enough too and left like Mum did? The thought brought fresh tears and he let them roll down his cheeks and plop onto his shirt.

'OK, son, what's all this about?' Dad asked as he sat in the driver's seat and turned to look at Ernie. 'I know there's more to it and I also know that you're not a bully, you don't usually go around hitting other people, so I'd like to know why you did that today.'

'Jamie was ... picking on me.'

'In what way?' His dad sounded so sad that Ernie felt even worse.

'He ... made fun of me because I did badly in the ... spelling test.'

'Hey ...' His dad took his hand. 'Everyone has off days. But you can't punch everyone who makes fun of you. I agree that it's not acceptable to make fun of others over things ... especially when they don't do well in a test, but physical violence is not the way to go, Ernie.'

Ernie nodded. 'I know and I'm sorry, Dad.'

'You've been worried about Arthur and excited about seeing him, so I understand that you've been a bit more emotional than usual, but even so ...'

'He said ... he said something about Mum.'

His dad's eyes widened and the deep lines on his forehead appeared.

'What did he say?'

Ernie didn't want to tell dad in case it upset him even more, but he was also afraid that it was true.

'He said that Mum ... that she left because I'm stupid.'

'Bloody hell!' His dad closed his eyes for a moment and took some quick breaths.

Ernie watched his dad closely, worried that what Jamie

had said might be true and hoping that his dad would forgive him.

'Ernie, you're not stupid. Not at all and that was a terrible thing to say. Mum didn't leave because of you. She wasn't happy in herself and wasn't happy being with me anymore.'

'No, Dad ... that's not true.'

'It is, son. Your mum loves you very much but she was sad and not very well. Sometimes that happens to grown-ups and they need to have some time alone. Away from everything.' His dad said the words softly, as if he was afraid of what they meant, but Ernie was glad to hear them.

'If Mum wasn't well ... then she might get better and she might come home?' His tone rose hopefully.

His dad sighed. 'I don't know, Ernie. I wish I could tell you that she will come home. I wish I could promise you that she'll get in contact, but I can't. Even grown-ups can't control everything. All I can tell you is that she did – and does – love you and that, yes, one day, she might come back. But we can't keep our lives on hold ... by that I mean that we can't stop living in order to wait just in case she does come home.'

Ernie thought he understood what his dad meant and he could tell that it wasn't easy for his dad to talk about. But at least he was talking about Mum now. It helped Ernie to be able to talk about her because when he held it all inside, it hurt more.

'I do miss Mum, but I'm so glad I have you, Dad.'

His dad's eyes shone and he ruffled his hair then nodded.

'I'm so glad I have you, Ernie.' He gazed out of the

window for a few moments then cleared his throat. 'So this spelling test. How bad was it?'

'Bad,' Ernie whispered.

'Is there anything else you need to tell me?' His dad sighed. 'I love you, Ernie and I'm always going to be here for you. Nothing you tell me will make me angry or upset with you. I promise. I just want you to be happy.' His dad turned his head and gazed out of the driver's side window and Ernie swallowed hard. His throat was aching and his eyes were stinging from crying.

'I am happy, Dad.'

His dad's shoulders were shaking and Ernie realised with horror that his dad was crying.

'Don't cry, Dad. I'm fine, honestly, I'm fine.'

When his dad turned back to him, his eyes and nose were red.

'I'm happy, Dad, I promise you, but I am ... I find reading and spelling hard.' There. He'd said it out loud. Would his dad now think he was stupid?

'I had a feeling that something like this was going on. When your headteacher rings me tomorrow, I'll speak to her about it. I don't know much about school, but perhaps there's something they can do to help.' He wiped his eyes with the back of his hand. 'We'll find a way to sort this, Ernie. Don't you worry.'

'OK, Dad.' Ernie nodded, trying to be brave. 'Thank you.'

'I'm your dad. It's my job.'

When his dad smiled at him then, Ernie's heart lifted. If Dad said it was going to be OK, then it would be. Wouldn't it?

*

Abby had just finished washing the plates from lunch when there was a knock at Arthur's door. She wiped her hands on the towel then went to answer it.

'Hello!' She smiled at Neil and Ernie, then frowned when she saw the expressions on their faces. 'Is everything all right?'

Ernie was staring at his shoes and didn't meet her eyes.

'Ernie had a bit of trouble at school so I had to pick him up early.'

'Oh dear ...' Abby stepped back. 'Are you coming in to see Arthur?'

'We'd like to if he's up to visitors.' Neil nodded.

'Of course. Come on in. We've just had a sandwich. Would either of you like one?'

'I'm fine, thanks, but Ernie might be hungry.' Neil laid a hand on his son's shoulder and Ernie looked up, making Abby gasp.

'What happened, Ernie?'

'I was in a fight ... Please don't tell Arthur.' He spoke urgently, his eyes shining.

'I don't think you'll be able to keep that secret. You have a black eye and a big scrape on your chin.' Abby was filled with concern.

Ernie's bottom lip wobbled.

'Tell you what, come in the kitchen with me and let's get some ice on it before you go to see Arthur.'

Neil went through to the lounge while Abby and Ernie went into the kitchen. He sat on a chair and Abby filled a sandwich bag with some ice then wrapped a clean towel around it.

'Here, hold this against the bruises.'

Ernie nodded. 'I really want to see Arthur.'

'He really wants to see you too.'

'I didn't want to see him like this, though.' A tear rolled down his cheek and plopped onto the floor.

'Do you want to talk about what happened?'

Ernie's face scrunched right up, and Abby couldn't help herself, she crouched down in front of him and wrapped her arms around his small frame. For a moment, he was still, then he flung his arms around her neck and sobbed. She held him tightly, rocking him gently as she imagined a mother would, and they stayed that way until he calmed down.

'Ernie?' It was Neil. He'd come into the kitchen and was looking at his son with an expression of weariness and concern. It must be so difficult sometimes being a single parent, having to deal with everything alone. Abby knew Neil worked long hours and relied on others to help with Ernie. But it meant that there was one income coming in, one person to be both mum and dad to Ernie, one person to tend to him when he was sick, to ensure that he did his homework, to wash and iron his clothes, cut his nails ... the list went on and on. Something was wrong with Ernie, he hadn't ended up with a black eye and a bruised chin for no reason at all.

'I'm sorry, Dad.'

'I know you are and it's OK, like I said to you in the car.' Neil smiled sadly at his son. 'Let's go and see Arthur. Perhaps then we can talk a bit more about what happened?'

Ernie nodded and headed into the lounge.

'Shall I make you a sandwich now?'

'Uh ... Abby ... I'd be really grateful if you'd come with us for a moment.' Neil's cheeks coloured. 'I'm not sure how to … to deal with this and I hoped you might have some ideas. Ernie can eat in a while.'

'OK.' Abby nodded. 'I'll help if I can.' She was getting really worried now.

Neil turned to her.

'Ernie trusts you, Abby. He speaks about you a lot and he respects you. I'm worried that, in spite of my best efforts, I'm getting this parenting thing wrong. At least … something's wrong and I'm not sure what. Ernie misses his mum, I know he does, and I'm trying to sort that out, but there's something else going on. He mentioned being bullied because of problems with his reading and spelling. If we all talk to him, we might be able to get to the bottom of it.'

'Of course.' She placed a hand on Neil's arm. 'Let's see what we can do.'

'Ernie, lad!' Arthur smiled as Ernie slowly entered the room. 'It's wonderful to see you! I have missed our time together so much! So what are you doing here at this time? Your dad said you had an early finish from school.'

Ernie kept his eyes on the floor, his head down. Arthur would have got up if he thought he could do it without wobbling, but even after a snooze he was more tired than he'd thought he'd be.

'Ernie? What is it?' He'd never seen Ernie like this before, not even in the days before they became friends. Ernie was always so full of life and mischief.

The boy stood in front of the sofa.

'I did a bad thing.'

Arthur shifted forwards on his chair.

'Come here, lad.' Arthur waved his hand to gesture to

Ernie that he should come to him. 'Come and give me a hug.'

Ernie approached him like a nervous animal.

'Look at me.' Arthur reached out his right hand. 'I can't ... can't hug you properly as my darned left arm isn't quite right yet.'

Ernie looked up at that, worry crossing his features.

Arthur gasped. 'Whatever happened to you?'

'I was in ... a fight.'

'You? Not you, Ernie?' Arthur heard the disbelief in his own tone.

'Yes.'

'But why?'

Neil entered the room, closely followed by Abby. 'Ernie didn't say a lot at school, I mainly heard the other boy's version of events from the headteacher, but then in the car, we spoke about why it happened. The other boy was picking on Ernie because he didn't do very well in a spelling test.'

Abby and Neil went to the sofa and sat down, both as stiff and formal as if they were there for an interview.

'I'm sorry.' Ernie dropped his gaze to his feet again. 'So sorry.'

'Sit down, Ernie. Tell us what happened.'

Ernie looked around but the sofa was occupied.

'Take the chair. It's OK.' Ernie bit his lip. He did sit there when it was just him and Arthur, but now he was clearly struggling with it. Was it because he thought he'd been naughty and he didn't know if Arthur would be annoyed with him?

'Ernie, it's fine. Please sit down. I've missed our chats and I want to help you if I can.'

Ernie sat down slowly in Julia's chair. He had sat there before but Arthur knew the lad was always a bit nervous about it, that he felt it was Julia's chair and should be reserved for her. 'Julia wouldn't mind, I promise.' And Arthur meant it. All he wanted in that moment was for Ernie to be OK.

'Tell us how you got into a fight, Ernie,' Neil said, lacing his fingers together. 'If we begin at the beginning, so to speak, for Arthur and Abby, then perhaps we can get this all cleared up and I can explain it in full to the headteacher.'

'OK ...' Ernie cleared his throat and Arthur's heart went out to him. He was a good boy, had a lovely nature and was so thoughtful. Arthur couldn't imagine what would drive him to violence of any kind.

The explanation came slowly at first, then the words tumbled out, laced with sobs and sniffs. Neil got up and perched on the arm of the chair then hugged Ernie to him. Finally, Ernie fell silent again. Arthur looked at Neil and Abby and saw that their expressions were as serious as he imagined his own was.

'How long has this been going on, Ernie? The trouble with reading and spelling?' Neil asked before rubbing his hands over his head.

'Ages, Dad. I think I'm stupid.' Ernie sniffed loudly and Arthur's heart fluttered with sadness. He couldn't bear to see the lad so distressed.

'Oh, Ernie!' Abby shook her head. 'That doesn't make you stupid at all.'

'No it doesn't,' Neil added. 'I'm just ... since you told me in the car, I'm just relieved that it wasn't something else. I'm sure this is fixable. I knew you wouldn't hit

329

someone without a good reason.' He frowned. 'Not that there's ever a good reason to hit someone, but what I mean is ... I'm just glad this is something we can sort out.'

'But that's what the children in my class say. And ... when Jamie said ...' Ernie glanced at Neil and he nodded. 'Jamie said my mum left because I'm stupid ... I didn't mean to hit him but I wanted him to stop saying it and to stop showing people my ... my zero.' His voice wavered and his little hands were clenched into fists as he remembered his anger and embarrassment.

'Ernie, have you told your teacher that you're having trouble?' Abby asked gently.

'No. But my teachers change all the time.'

Neil nodded. 'The main teacher has been off for a while and they've had a string of supply teachers going through the school.'

'So there's been no continuity and no one has noticed that Ernie's had some ... difficulties.' Abby met Arthur's eyes. 'This can be sorted.'

'It can?' Ernie asked hopefully. 'Dad said it could be but how?'

'You could have some help with your spelling and reading, something that will give you ways to cope.'

Ernie frowned and Arthur reached over the table and squeezed his hand.

'But I don't want to be different.'

'We're all different, Ernie. All of us.' Abby smiled. 'It's nothing to be afraid of. See ... there's something called dyslexia, my friend Lisa has it. She wasn't diagnosed until she was a lot older than you and she spent a lot of time thinking she wasn't very clever. But she is and she's now very successful, a talented designer. If it is dyslexia ... it doesn't need to hold you back at all.'

'I'm really good at maths.' Ernie straightened in his chair.

'I know you are. You worked out all the measurements for the flowerbeds and for the plant food ...' Abby froze and her eyes widened as she looked at Arthur but he smiled at her and she visibly relaxed. He wasn't quite sure what was going on with the garden but it didn't matter right now. 'Ernie is really good at working out measurements.'

'So it could be dyslexia?' Neil asked.

'Could be. I think it would be best if you have a conversation with Ernie's headteacher and ask them to test him for it.'

'Will do.' Neil nodded. 'I'll speak to her first thing tomorrow.' Neil sounded determined and positive and Arthur felt as proud of him as he would have had he been his own son.

'Good, that's settled then.'

'I have some news too.' Neil smiled shyly.

'What is it, Dad?'

'I've ... um ... accepted redundancy from my firm.'

'What's redundancy?' Ernie asked.

'It means they've got to let some people go, so they asked if anyone would be prepared to give up their jobs.'

'You won't have a job?' The fear in Ernie's voice made Arthur's heart flutter.

'Well I will because I've already accepted another one. I start in two weeks.'

'What is it?' Ernie looked up at his dad.

'Delivery driver for one of the big online firms.' Neil

sat up straighter on the sofa. 'It offers more flexibility in terms of hours, and means I can be here for the school run and make time up at weekends if need be. I can be here to help you too, Arthur.'

Arthur coughed, suddenly embarrassed. He wasn't keen on this needing help thing at all.

'If you need help, that is,' Neil added. 'We all know how independent you are.'

And in spite of the serious conversation they'd just had about Ernie, Arthur smiled inwardly, at the fact that he was a stubborn old man and that these people in his lounge knew it; at the fact that he'd been such a grump and not made an effort to get to know his neighbours sooner; and because he was happy. His lounge had people in it after all these years. And they were very special people indeed.

'Yes, well, I'm happy to help you out too. We all need a hand now and then,' Arthur said sagely.

'Indeed we do,' Neil agreed. 'And you've helped me many times by having Ernie round.'

'This is what you call teamwork.' Ernie leant against his dad as if he needed him to hold him up physically as well as emotionally.

'Yes, indeed,' Arthur replied. 'We are now a team.'

He liked the sound of that very much indeed.

CHAPTER 28

Abby closed the security door behind her and stepped out into the early morning air. It had been three days since Arthur had come home from hospital. She was able to anticipate Arthur's needs both in terms of when he wanted help and when he didn't thanks to her time at the care home. He had some external help, but Abby and Neil had also agreed on a plan so that Arthur always had help or company should he need it. Of course, their elderly neighbour was still fiercely independent, and there was a fine balance between helping him and getting on his nerves, so they knew they had to tread carefully.

In the past, Abby might have thought this sense of responsibility towards her neighbour could have been a weight on her mind, an irritation even, but it wasn't at all. She wanted to help and hated the thought of Arthur being lonely. If he'd had that attack and not been discovered by Ernie, who knew what could have happened? It didn't even bear thinking about.

Jason texted last night to ask if she fancied doing something today and she'd said yes, as long as Neil could be around for Arthur. He'd said he was doing Arthur's grocery shopping then he and Ernie would have lunch with Arthur and probably a dominoes tournament, so Abby didn't need to rush back.

Things were looking up. She hadn't heard from Gav for a while, the garden was looking good and would be in full bloom when Arthur was ready to see it – she had suggested a short walk in the garden yesterday, but Arthur had told her that he wasn't quite up to going out of the flat just yet – and Abby had decided to take the pressure off herself and just enjoy the summer. Life and her career options would still be there when the autumn arrived.

Jason pulled into the car park at Willow Court and waved, making her stomach flip. The idea of going out somewhere together made her pulse race and she hadn't been able to stop smiling since he'd invited her. The more time she spent with him, the more she liked him. They were both busy; he had his gardening work and his lecturing, and she had the garden and now Arthur. It was good to be busy, good to feel needed. And time spent with Jason was the icing on the cake.

She approached the car and he opened the passenger door for her.

'Morning.' She got in and smiled at him, admiring how handsome he was. The car smelt of his aftershave, fresh and woody, and he looked ready for summer in his black cargo shorts and grey T-shirt.

'Hi, Abby.' His smile lit up his face.

'Are you sure I didn't need to bring anything?' she asked. 'Not even some drinks or sandwiches?'

He shook his head. 'Nope. I've taken care of everything.'

'Where are we going?'

'On a mystery tour. I thought it would be nice to get away from Didsbury for a few hours.'

'Oooh! Sounds intriguing. I'm looking forward to it.' She buckled her seatbelt and tried to stop smiling so broadly, worried she might look a bit ridiculous.

As Jason drove, Abby's stomach fluttered as she tried to guess where he was taking her. No one had taken her out like this in years. Gav hadn't bothered trying to surprise her for ages, at least not with good surprises – finding a sext on his mobile from another woman didn't count.

'How far are we going?' she asked.

'It'll take just over an hour.' He glanced at her and smiled. 'Are you excited, Abby?'

'I am!' She giggled. 'It's been a long time since I was taken on a mystery trip.'

He reached over and briefly squeezed her hand. 'That's sad to hear. You deserve to have nice surprises.'

During the journey, they talked about everything and nothing, and a variety of songs played on the radio. They hadn't met up since the previous weekend because they'd both been so busy, but Abby thought time and space was good for them both as it gave them a chance to think about what they both wanted from their time together.

'Almost there,' Jason said after they'd crossed over about four roundabouts. Abby, not having the best sense of direction, knew they were in Liverpool but wasn't sure where. Jason pulled into an open-air car park and cut the engine.

She looked around.

'Do you know where we are now?'

He lowered the windows.

She shook her head, but she was sure the air had changed, that it had a briny tang to it.

'We've come to Formby. There's a beautiful beach

here and seeing as how it's such a lovely day, I thought we could have a walk then have a picnic, possibly even a paddle.'

'I haven't been to the beach in such a long time,' Abby said, excitement fizzing inside her. 'Thank you.'

'You don't need to thank me but I do think we need to make sure that you get out more.' He wiggled his eyebrows at her.

Abby laughed and tapped his arm. 'I'm not a recluse.'

'I know that.' His gaze softened and Abby's chest tightened in that funny way it did whenever he looked at her like that.

'Do you come here often?' Her voice squeaked out and she coughed, embarrassed. Did Jason have any idea what an effect he had upon her?

'Not really. It's not quite the same going to the beach on your own. I mean ... I have come here and gone to other beaches to walk and think and that ... but it's always better with company.' He peered at her from under his thick lashes, small pink spots appearing on his cheeks. Jason wasn't actually saying it out loud, but he was letting her know that he got lonely too, that he appreciated having her along for the ride.

They got out of the car and Jason went to the boot, bringing out a large rucksack and a rolled-up picnic blanket, then slipping off his trainers and putting on flip-flops.

'Are you OK in those?' He nodded at her white plimsolls.

Abby shrugged. 'They'll get sandy but I can throw them in the washer when I get home.'

'No need.' He reached into the boot and handed her a

carrier bag. 'I picked these up just in case. You're about a size five, right?'

'Spot on.' Abby raised her eyebrows as she accepted the bag and looked inside. 'You bought me flip-flops?'

Jason shrugged. 'I didn't know if you had any and I didn't want to ask in case you guessed where I was taking you.'

'Thank you! They're lovely.' She stared at the flip-flops, admiring them, and her vision blurred. Jason's thoughtfulness never ceased to surprise her. She blinked hard to clear the tears from her eyes and pulled the flip-flops out of the bag.

Abby removed her plimsolls and dropped them into the boot then slid her feet into the light blue flip-flops. They were soft and comfortable; the bit that went between her toes was material rather than hard plastic.

'These can't have been cheap,' she said as she eyed the surf brand label. 'I'll have to pay you for them.'

'No, you won't. They're a gift.'

'Well in that case, thank you again.' Her voice sounded soft to her own ears, the voice of a woman falling for someone.

She admired her feet in her new flip-flops while Jason locked the car up, then they headed towards a sandy path. Abby walked alongside Jason, breathing in the warm air that was fragranced with the promising tang of the sea and earthy pine aromas from the nearby woodland. Around them, the dunes rose, sand-covered grassy mounds. Their feet left imprints in the soft sand on the path as they walked, and Abby felt the wonderful childhood excitement of a trip to the beach.

Soon, they had passed through the dunes and before

them lay the beach, a blanket of sand stretching as far as she could see. To their left and right, then straight ahead was the sparkling blue expanse of the sea. People were dotted around the beach, setting up wind breakers and deckchairs, and some were in the sea, heads and shoulders bobbing up and down in the water.

Abby stopped and gazed at the beauty around her, experiencing a wave of memories that were clamouring to rise to the surface invoked by sights, smells and sounds. Her mum digging in the sand with a plastic spade then filling a small bucket before flipping it over and patting the bottom. Abby then carefully lifting the bucket to reveal a perfect sandcastle. Another memory rushed in, of paddling in the shallows with her mum, their trousers rolled up and the pair of them squealing as the cold water rushed over their feet and legs. Such sweet memories.

Gulls cried overhead, bringing Abby back to the present, the engine of a small boat out at sea whined as it cut through the water and children screeched and laughed as they ran into the waves. Abby felt at once free and yet weighed down; free because of the beach and the feelings it always conjured, but weighed down because of the past and the grief for her mum, her baby and for her own childhood that was long gone.

'Abby?' Jason touched her arm. 'You OK?'

'Yes ...' She nodded and smiled. 'I was just a bit overwhelmed.'

'I understand. It's because it's so beautiful here. Come on, let's go and find a good spot to set up the blanket.'

He took her hand and she was glad of the support, of his reassuring presence as they walked along the sand. The breeze toyed with her hair, lifting it and tickling her cheeks, her throat, her lips. She tucked it behind her ears, angling her chin so it would blow backwards and not into her face.

'How about here?' Jason asked as he pointed at a quiet spot with a dune behind it and an open patch of sand in front.

'Perfect.'

They spread the blanket out then weighted it down at the corners with their flip-flops.

'Are you hungry?' Jason asked.

'Not really. Not yet.' Abby shook her head. She'd been too excited to each much breakfast but she still didn't have much of an appetite and it was only just after ten.

'Fancy a paddle then?'

'I only have these with me so I can't go in for a swim.' She gestured at her cropped jeans and white vest top. 'I left my cardigan in the car because it's so warm.'

'I have a spare T-shirt if you need it ... just in case you do get wet.'

'Is there anything you're not prepared for?' She laughed to show she was teasing him.

Jason stood up. 'I think we should go in ... just for a paddle.' He raised his eyebrows in challenge.

'Oh, Jason, I don't know. Uh ...' It did sound like fun but what if her clothes got wet?

'Abby ... come on! The water looks amazing!' He was so enthusiastic and so keen to get the most out of the moment that Abby knew she couldn't possibly refuse.

'Race you!' he yelled, then he ran towards the water.

Abby followed, laughing as she ran. When was the last time she'd run like this? Jason splashed into the sea sending droplets into the air and as they landed on Abby's warm skin, she shivered and laughed. Jason plunged into the water head first making Abby gasp. He was fully clothed!

When his head rose above the water, she shook her head. 'Your clothes are soaking.'

'It's fine. I brought spares. I just couldn't resist the water!'

'You should've brought your swimming gear.'

He swam back towards her. 'I didn't know for certain that I was going to dive in. It was spur of the moment. Come here.' His eyes were filled with mischief.

'No.' She stepped backwards, her heart pounding. 'I can't get my clothes wet.'

'I have something you can borrow, remember?'

'Jason, I'm thirty-six not six. I can't go to the beach and jump into the water fully clothed.'

'Why not?'

'Because.'

'Because what?'

'I'm an adult. I have to be ... responsible.' He had reached her now and as he stood up, water poured from him like a waterfall, gushing from his T-shirt and from the legs of his shorts. Something sparkled in his eyes and Abby's chest filled with delightful panic. He was going to misbehave.

She turned and tried to run but he caught her and lifted her off her feet, turned towards the depths and waded quickly into them. Abby squealed as cold water rushed over her and she squirmed but Jason kept hold of her until she stopped wriggling. She held on tight to him, her arms around his neck and her cheek touching his. They laughed together, oblivious to the cold water on their sun-warmed skin, to the other people on the beach and to their clothes, heavy with salt water.

'How does it feel?' Jason asked, his breath tickling her ear.

She paused for a moment, focusing on different areas of her body, from her legs where the water caressed her skin, to the pounding of her heart against her ribs and the strength of Jason's arms, to the feel of him against her, his clean-shaven cheek pressing against her skin, slippery with sun cream.

'It feels … incredible,' she said as she turned her head and met his eyes. They were so dark, his gaze so intense that the world around her faded away and there was nothing except Jason.

The kiss that followed stole her breath away and turned her world upside down.

CHAPTER 29

Ernie was in Arthur's kitchen drying the lunch dishes after his dad had washed them. They'd gone out early that morning to get Arthur's shopping and were going to spend the afternoon playing dominoes until Arthur needed a nap.

It had been quite a difficult week for him, but he also felt better that his worries were out in the open now. Abby had said that to him yesterday, when he'd seen her in the garden after school. She'd said that getting things out in the open often helped because secrets could be damaging and make things seem worse than they were.

'All done, Ernie.' Neil dried his hands then filled the kettle and switched it on to boil. 'I'm just going to pop upstairs to grab that cake.' He winked at Ernie. They'd bought it for after lunch as a surprise for Arthur.

'OK, Dad.'

Ernie folded the tea towel and set it on the draining board then went into the lounge. Arthur was sitting in his chair watching the lunchtime news.

'Everything done, lad?'

'Yes, all tidy.'

Ernie sat on the sofa but Arthur shook his head. 'Sit here.' He gestured at Julia's chair.

'Are you sure?'

'Stop asking me if I'm sure.' He shook his head again but couldn't help smiling. 'It's good to have someone using it.'

Ernie nodded then went to Julia's chair and sat down. He turned so he could look at Arthur.

'Are you feeling OK?' he asked.

Arthur chuckled. 'How many times are you going to ask me that?'

'I'm sorry. I just worry that you might feel ill and not tell me and I want to … be ready in case you fall again.'

'I'm fine, Ernie. I'm doing everything the doctors and nurses told me to do. I don't like *taking it easy* as they call it, but with my hip and this funny old left arm that doesn't always do what I want it to, sometimes sitting down a bit more does help.'

'Is your hip sore today?'

'A little bit. But the sunlight coming through the window is helping.'

'How?'

'It's nice and warm and when it's warm, my joints don't ache so much.'

Ernie nodded. 'Good.'

'How are you feeling about everything at school now?'

Ernie thought about what had happened since, how Dad had spoken to the head teacher twice and how they'd gone in yesterday and had a big talk with the headteacher, a meeting with Jamie Jones and his mum, how they'd had to say sorry and shake hands. It had been hard at first but he did feel better about it all now.

'Yeah, I'm OK. I'm not looking forward to the tests that the reading teacher will do next week but she said they're not bad tests, just to see how they can help me.'

'That sounds positive, lad.'

Ernie nodded. 'She helps kids with spelling and reading and lots of other stuff.'

'She's called an ALNCO.' Neil said as he entered the room. 'It means additional learning needs coordinator,'

'Quite a mouthful!' Arthur laughed. 'I guess that's why it's abbreviated.'

'What does abbreefated mean?' Ernie frowned.

'It means shortened, Ernie,' Arthur explained. 'ALNCO is an acronym.'

Ernie nodded but he had no idea what that was either.

'An acronym is when a new word is formed using the first letter of each word in a title.'

'Oh right ... Shall we play dominoes now, then?' Ernie reached for the box on the small side table.

'Yes, let's. Anything to get off this topic, eh?' Arthur gently nudged him.

'You know me so well, BFF.'

Arthur turned to Ernie's dad and frowned and Neil shrugged.

'Best friends forever,' Ernie said, trying to wink at Arthur, but he couldn't quite get the one eye to close without the other one, so it became more of a blink.

'I couldn't agree more,' Arthur said.

Then they tipped the dominoes out onto the table and the game began.

Abby lay back on the picnic blanket and luxuriated in the afternoon sunshine.

'Lunch was delicious,' she said as she peered at Jason from under her sunglasses.

'I hoped you'd like it.'

They had eaten the picnic after their impromptu dip in the sea and a quick change behind the sand dunes. It had been stored in a small cooler bag that he'd stuffed in the bottom of his enormous rucksack. And it had been wonderful. He'd popped to a deli before picking Abby up, and selected mini asparagus and goats cheese tartlets, fat juicy sundried tomatoes in rich virgin olive oil, fresh crusty rolls with French brie, and big, red English strawberries for dessert. They'd washed lunch down with bottles of cloudy lemonade then finished with a flask of fruity, fragrant black coffee.

Abby had thoroughly enjoyed everything about today, from the drive there, to the surprise swim in the sea. But her favourite part had to be the kiss they had shared in the water, their arms wrapped around each other, their bodies so close and their mouths meeting with such passion yet such tenderness. Abby felt as though she had been kissed properly for the first time in her life. Why had she wasted so much time with a man who clearly didn't love her and who clearly felt no such desire for her?

Jason was everything Gavin was not.

'I guess we should head back.' Jason was lying next to her, his head propped up on his arm.

'Do we have to?' She fluttered her eyelashes.

'Well, we could stay here but I think the car might get clamped if it's in the car park overnight and if we don't leave soon, the traffic will be bad.'

Abby sat up and pushed her glasses up her nose.

'All right then.'

'We can come here again though ... if you like.'

She stroked his forehead, brushing aside a few blonde hairs that had fallen over the smooth golden skin.

'I would love to do this again.'

He sat up, taking her hand to kiss it, then they packed up their things, rolled up the picnic blanket and made their way to the car.

Back in the passenger seat, as Jason drove them home, Abby's heart brimmed with happiness. She had sand just about everywhere, especially in her hair and between her toes, her lips tasted salty and she could feel the salt tightening her skin, but her overriding sensation was of being alive. Her nerves tingled, her mind buzzed and she was filled with longing. It was longing to be with Jason again like this, longing to return to the beach with him soon, longing to fill her life with good times like these.

If she hadn't decided to start blogging again, to improve the garden on Holly Street, she might never have met this wonderful man. Abby didn't need anyone to complete her, but a man like Jason ... no, *actually* Jason, could make life a whole lot more interesting, a lot more exciting.

An hour and a half later, they pulled into the car park at Willow Court and Jason cut the engine.

'Thank you so much for a fabulous day. I had so much fun.' She reached out and took his hand.

'Me too.' He laced his fingers through hers so their palms met and he rubbed his thumb over her skin. 'You can keep those if you like.'

Jason nodded at the T-shirt and shorts Abby was wearing. He'd packed them as spares and both hung on Abby's frame, but they smelt of his fabric softener and were smooth against her skin.

'I might just keep them, you know! They do fit me *so* well.'

They sat there smiling at each other, now slightly shy because they were back in reality, neither of them wanting to say goodbye.

'Do you have plans this evening?' Abby asked.

Jason shook his head.

'Me neither. I mean ... I'll pop in on Arthur, but apart from that ... I was thinking I might order a pizza.'

'What kind of pizza?' Jason raised an eyebrow.

'Chicken tikka perhaps. Or mozzarella and roasted vegetables.'

'My favourite.' His lips twitched.

'Which one?'

'Both. Either.' He shrugged.

'Jason ... would you like to order pizza with me?'

'I'd love to. I really don't want to go home now.' He raised her hand and kissed each of her fingers in turn. It made her heart pound and desire curl inside her.

'I really don't want you to go, either.' Her voice was thick with longing.

He leant over and cupped her face with his hands. They were big, warm and strong. As he stroked her cheeks, the tiny calluses on them tickled her skin and a tiny moan escaped her lips.

'Let's go inside,' she whispered.

'Yes.'

They got out of the car and grabbed Abby's things from the boot then went into Willow Court, all worries and hesitation forgotten in their need to be alone together.

*

They hurried up the stairs, giggling and breathless, and Abby was filled with excitement and nerves about what would happen next. But it was such a wonderful feeling; the unknown was no longer scary.

They reached the second floor and paused for one more kiss, then Abby opened her bag to look for her key.

'Umm ... Hello, Abs.'

She looked up and the smile dropped from her face.

'Been out for the day have you?'

'Gav ...' She shook her head, her joy seeping away. 'What are you ... Why are you ...'

'I need to speak to you, Abby. Please.' There was desperation in his tone.

He held out his hands, silently pleading with her, and it was as though someone had thrown a bucket of ice-cold water over her.

She turned to Jason, not knowing what to say.

'I'll go,' he said, his hands in his pockets, his eyes flicking between her and Gavin.

'You don't have to.'

'I think I do. I'll text you later.' A muscle in his jaw was twitching and there was hurt in his eyes.

'But ... what about pizza?'

He shrugged. 'Another time, eh?' His tone had changed, hardened, and Abby wanted to cry at the unfairness of the situation.

As he turned and headed down the stairs, Abby could have screamed. They'd had such a wonderful day and now Gav was here to ruin it all. Again. When would he ever leave her life for good?

*

'So what is it this time, Gav?' Abby asked coldly.

She scowled at him across the kitchen table. She'd decided not to invite him into the lounge in case he tried to get close to her again. Having the table between them would be a good way to maintain a physical distance. She hadn't even offered him a drink. She was so mad with him for ruining the day, for ruining her time with Jason.

'I had to come and see you.' He was resting his elbows on the table and he buried his face in his hands.

Abby felt a flicker of compassion for him. She hated to see him upset, but she also hated the way he'd imposed himself upon her afternoon.

'Abby … the baby … my baby …' He looked up and his bottom lip wobbled. 'I got everything ready at the house. I bought things for the baby and for Belinda. I was actually getting excited about it. And then …' His voice had risen and he was staring at the table as if he could see through it. 'Then … she … told me it's not mine.'

'What?' Abby gasped. 'Not yours? But how?'

Gavin met her eyes and shook his head. 'The scan showed that the pregnancy was further along than she thought. She didn't let me go and I wondered why, then she didn't say anything immediately. But this morning I was talking to her about possible names and she burst into tears. She said that she'd been trying to tell me but was worried about hurting me after everything I'd done for her.' He raked a hand through his hair and in the kitchen light, Abby could see that he had grey at his temples that hadn't been there before.

'Whose is it then?'

'Her ex-boyfriend's. She said there was no way it could be mine as we hadn't slept together at that point.'

Abby felt like a deflated balloon and she slumped in her chair. What a mess!

'So what are you going to do?'

'Belinda is quite traditional and she said she couldn't possibly stay with me now. She said she needed some time out and that she might even go back to her ex ... if he'll have her. Apparently, he always wanted children.'

'Oh.' Abby didn't know what else to say. Gav had cheated on her with Belinda, set her up in their home then had been playing house so well that he'd come to want the baby and was looking forward to becoming a father.

'I can't be alone, Abby.' He reached over the kitchen table. 'Please come back to me.'

'What?' Abby pushed her chair back so hard that it screeched on the kitchen floor. 'Come back to you? Gav, have you learnt nothing at all?'

'I'm sorry. Really, really sorry. I've been a total idiot and I should have realised how wonderful you were before. I messed up but I could be better.'

He looked so pitiful in his crumpled T-shirt with his stubbly face and messy hair, that in spite of her shock, she felt pity wrestling with her anger.

She sank back onto her chair. 'Gav, it's not going to happen.'

She held out her hand and he took it.

'I care about you but not in a romantic way. I'm sorry Belinda hurt you but you'll get over it. In time.' She spoke gently, hoping he would see sense.

'You won't come home?' he asked tentatively.

'It's not my home anymore.'

He nodded. 'I guess I knew that before I came here. I didn't know what else to do.'

'I know. Your timing could have been better but … It doesn't matter. Do you want a cup of tea?'

'Yes, please.'

She squeezed his hand then stood up and went to the kettle. She'd be here for Gavin as a friend, listen if he needed to talk, but any other feelings she had for him were long gone. He'd be all right now. It was sad because he'd lost another baby, even if this one wasn't really his, but it was a good thing that Belinda had come clean. A life based on lies wouldn't have been good for anyone, especially not the baby.

Epilogue

September had come, bringing with it the glorious shades of autumn as the leaves on the trees surrounding Willow Court turned red, gold and orange, and the garden showed off its autumnal range of plants.

The garden was maturing beautifully. In the borders, the vibrant pink, white and purple petals of the hardy heather gave enduring colour. Purple and bronze dahlias filled the variety of pots dotted around the garden, interspersed with yellow and orange torch lilies. The herb beds were filled with luscious and well-tended herbs that had served Abby and her helpers well through late summer and into autumn. In the patch of earth next to the shed, they'd planted blackberry bushes that now bore fruit ripe for the picking, and Abby was hoping to make some of them into jams and pies. The fruit trees still had a way to go in terms of growth, but they'd also had salad leaves and tomatoes from the raised beds and portable plastic greenhouse, and would eventually have potatoes from the bags Jason had brought.

Arthur had experienced a bit of a setback two weeks after he'd come home, and he had taken to his bed for a while, thinking he was on his way out. But with time and care from Abby, Neil and Ernie, he had rebuilt his strength and been persuaded to get up and carry on. Some depression and anxiety was, the doctor had told Abby, perfectly normal after a stroke. She had told Abby and Neil to give Arthur time and to do what they could to make him feel more positive.

Arthur had finally ventured outside a month after he'd returned home from hospital and his reaction to the garden had surprised Abby.

He sat on the bench, gazed around him and started to cry, so Abby had sat next to him, held his hand and been there for him. After that, they had sat outside every day when it was warm enough and it cheered Arthur enormously. He was feeling a lot better now. He still got tired, but on the days when he'd had some fresh air, he felt stronger, more alive.

'Julia would have loved what you've done,' he said to Abby now, not for the first time.

'I'm glad, Arthur. Really glad that you like it and that Julia would have done too.'

They were sitting side by side on the bench. Arthur had a lightweight blanket over his knees to protect him from the breeze, and they were drinking tea from a flask.

Next to them, on a picnic rug that had been set on the patio area, were Jax and Ernie. They were going through a book that Ernie's reading teacher had given him, to help him develop his literacy skills. It wasn't something Ernie enjoyed doing, but Arthur had promised him that if he did this now, then they'd have chip shop chips for lunch. Ernie would do anything for chip shop chips!

'Arthur, is there anything you'd like me to do to the garden? Any plants you'd like to see? Anything you think Julia would have liked?'

'Actually, I've got something for you,' Arthur said as he picked up the parcel he'd smuggled outside under the blanket.

'For me?' Abby frowned. 'What is it?'

'They're not new,' he warned as he handed her the parcel. 'They were Julia's. But they might come in handy.'

Abby tore off the paper and gasped.

'I can't take these, Arthur.'

He nodded. 'Yes, you can. Julia would have been glad to see them go to a good home.'

Abby placed the books on the bench next to her and flung her arms around Arthur, hugging him tight. He seemed a bit embarrassed by her display of affection at first, then he hugged her back with his one arm and patted her.

'Thank you so much,' she said when she finally released him.

'It's my pleasure,' he said gruffly.

Abby opened the top gardening book and ran her fingers over the yellow Post-it note.

'This is Julia's writing?' She gazed at the beautiful loops and curls of the handwriting.

'Yes. I left her notes in because they might be useful too.'

'But aren't they … too precious to you?'

Arthur patted Abby's hand where it rested on top of the books.

'And so are you. Plus I know you'll look after them.' He nodded sagely but his cheeks were flushed with pleasure.

Abby met his gaze, her eyes shining.

'Thank you, Arthur. Not just for this but for being my friend.'

'What are friends for?' he said, a smile playing on his lips.

Abby gazed at the books on her lap. She wanted to flip through them, to read Julia's notes and look at the beautiful photographs but she didn't want to do it right there in case Arthur found it difficult. He'd made such a good recovery but she was always conscious of the fact that he shouldn't get worked up, that he was, in some ways, still fragile. And precious to her, to Neil and to Ernie.

Little Ernie. She looked at him sitting on the rug with Jax practising his reading, his forehead wrinkled with concentration and his tongue poking out of the corner of his mouth.

Arthur had come a long way over recent months and so had Ernie. Before school had finished for the summer, Lisa had gone in to deliver a talk about dyslexia and how it had affected her life when she was younger, before her diagnosis, but how she hadn't let it beat her and now she had a successful career in fashion. The children had apparently been in awe of the fashion designer and the headteacher had asked if Lisa would go in again to speak to the children and to possibly do some workshops with them. Lisa had agreed, of course, and had also managed to get some equally successful dyslexic friends who worked in a wide variety of jobs to do the same.

Neil had hired a specialist tutor during the summer holidays and it had made a big difference to Ernie's confidence. They had all done their best to build Ernie up, to let him know that everyone was different, everyone had difficulties and that that was OK. She was also impressed with Jax and her dedication to her cousin. She'd been around a lot to work with Ernie since he told them what had been happening and her love for the little boy was clear.

The garden had been well used over the summer and many of her neighbours had come out here to cook on the barbecue, to hold birthday parties and to help out. All of Abby's hopes for the garden had been surpassed as people added large planters, raised wooden beds and hanging baskets that they had hung from hooks on the building and from the sides of the shed. There were now three bird tables dotted around the garden and a pretty stone birdbath that Nadine had picked up in a school jumble sale. Nadine had turned out to be very sweet and self-deprecating, and her world revolved around her twin daughters. Abby had shared a bottle of wine with her on more than one occasion and they were becoming good friends.

And then there was Jason. After they'd been to the beach that day and returned home to find Gav waiting, they'd discussed their feelings at length and decided to take things slowly. They liked each other very much and their strong mutual attraction was clear, but they were aware that they were both still vulnerable. So they were dating and enjoying each other's company with trips to the beach, meals out and plenty of visits to garden centres. One of their favourites, with the arrival of autumn, was the local arboretum and nature reserve, where they'd spend hours strolling along the paths, admiring the changing colours of the leaves and where Abby would test Jason's knowledge of the names of the trees. It was a wonderful place to go, to appreciate nature's incredible variety and she felt grounded there, a part of the world around her. And when Jason did things like taking her hand, brushing stray leaves from her hair and holding her in his arms when they kissed tenderly, Abby felt so warm and treasured.

Abby was happy, she felt fulfilled, renewed. Life had been difficult in the past and she would always bear the scars, but that's all they were now – scars – and Abby felt that she had come a long way in the healing process. She had friends who were as good as any family, she was part of a community, and it had all started with her decision to transform the garden on Holly Street.